BLOOD DESCENSION

THE BLOOD SAGA:

BOOK 3

By

MAQUEL A. JACOB

MAJart Works ©2020

MAJart Works

2001 NW Aloclek Dr #211

Hillsboro, OR 7124

www.majartworks.com

Cover Design by Dar Albert

www.wickeddesigns.com

Illustration by Nelli Valova

https://www.dreamstime.com/blackmoon979_info

Blood Descension/ Maquel A. Jacob -1st ed.

ISBN 978-1-950438-21-1

CHAPTER ONE

New Trade Deals

Darkness enveloped Pridric as he made his descent through the narrow staircase towards the bowels of his castle. His blond hair, slicked back in its usual austere ponytail, and pale skin disappeared in the gloom.

Wearing a black suit with a deep purple shirt and black tie, he blended in seamlessly. Black stone deepened the feeling of walking inside a cavernous pit with no way to escape.

He used his hands to feel along the walls as a guide, letting his fingers run across the damp stone collecting condensation as he breathed in the scent of stale moisture. His black nails grew sharp, scraping across the surface.

The stairs became visible as his eyes glowed red, adjusting to the dark. Anyone with foresight would have brought a flashlight or a torch. He had thought about putting a string of lights down the steep stairwell along the top, but that would ruin the aesthetic.

The dark was an old friend. Nothing to fear.

Every tiny click of his heels hitting the steps made him wince. He softened his footing to ease the sound of his perfectly shined black boots as they struck the cold, hard stairs. He found it silly to think he would awaken anyone so far away from the central part of the castle.

No one even knew he had come this way. He made a point of sneaking out of bed, making sure not to stir his wife. Then, bypassed the guards, who rarely paid attention to his movements unless he commanded them. The quiet early afternoon found most of the castle asleep.

Only a few servants milled around doing chores.

Soft, tiny threads grazed across his face, forcing him to halt, almost losing his balance. He waved one hand to push the invisible cobwebs away while planting the other firmly against the wall to stop his fall as he spat out any web that may have gotten in his mouth.

He always forgot to keep his lips pursed thin when going down. One day, he would find the spider responsible for the giant webs that spanned the entire width of the corridor. Every month, a new one appeared. He felt the creature mocked him.

Regaining his balance, he proceeded towards the bottom. The landing made a sharp turn to the left. He followed the short distance halfway in to a set of double doors. Taking a sharp breath, he tasted ancient wood mingled with wet air. The eight feet wide doors ornate dark metal bars were accented by fleur-de-lis carved on the ends.

He placed one hand on the right side and let it slide along the latch.

Why have I come down here?

He pressed his cheek to the wood. Hearing a faint noise, he listened. The soft suction of pumps working in slow succession became audible. Pridric lifted his head from the door and undid the latch. He pushed the door open and stepped inside the equally dark crypt.

Motion lights embedded in the ceiling flickered on one by one throughout the room, illuminating the well-oiled machines along the walls. Their black lacquered metal resembled snakes running down to the floor and underneath.

Giant plaques engraved with his family crest covered the floor. They were four feet apart to make way for the cables running through. Thin layers of dust formed on the surface from his last visit.

He checked the main console on the wall to his left and watched the output levels for each unit. It's too much! At the current rate, his supply would dwindle within the next four years. The culprit for the drain was the reason he had come, but not only that. He wanted to see for himself if the flow had sped up naturally or something else caused it.

The crypt spanned about two thousand square feet. He had to walk a bit to reach the plaque three quarters of the way, avoiding the cables wiggling back and forth from liquid pumping through them into the floor. He stopped at the plaque and knelt by its edge, hesitating to press the release mechanism under his hand.

What do I expect to find, really?

Pridric had long suspected his race held many secrets. He snorted, getting a whiff of the massive amounts of blood in the chamber. *Let's see what's inside, hmm?* He pressed the panel, and the plaque rose, venting as it cleared the floor. The cables remained intact since he didn't dare press the other panel to disconnect them.

After five minutes of waiting, he finally got to see the large coffin settle as the holding beams below it snapped into place. There it sat, three feet off the ground, positioned at his waist. Pridric ran his hands along the crest, then slid them under the edge to break the seal.

The hydraulic hinges slowly opened the coffin lid. The first bit of light that entered showed only a dark silhouette, then revealed the body inside.

He stared at the flawless features of Tavelo, known on Earth as Count Valentin Durante, lying in a deep slumber. Hair black as pitch against creamy smooth, tanned skin accented by slightly pink full lips. The arms lay crossed below his chest. He wore a blue silk kimono with silver designs along the trim. Pridric narrowed his eyes at the attire.

No doubt, one of his coven servants had come and dressed him years ago.

The color of his skin suggested Tavelo neared awakening. Not yet. Pridric had many plans in the works and did not want interference. He moved a few strands of hair from Tavelo's face. A sense of overprotectiveness crept in, even though they were only a few years apart in age.

Leaning into the coffin, Pridric's waist length ponytail slithered forward and landed on Tavelo's arms. He listened to the steady heartbeat. Strong, healthy, undamaged.

Footsteps echoed outside the door, causing Pridric to raise his head too fast, bumping it against the inside of the coffin's lid. He cursed softly and stood straight, turning towards the entrance.

One of his guards came into view, filling the doorframe. A black cape attached at the shoulders covered his slightly dirty silver armor. His longsword hung loose at his waist in a sheath branded with the family crest. He held a smart phone in his hand that he glanced at briefly before walking in.

"Count Ambrook." The guard greeted him.

He cringed at the name he had taken when he assumed rulership of the vampire coven over two hundred years ago. They all had. At the beginning, crash-landing on Earth seemed a blessing in disguise. Yet, after dealing with humans, vampires, and werewolves for so long, his kind were having second thoughts.

"What is it?" He wanted to ask how the guard knew he had come down into the crypt. "Be brief."

"Of course, my lord." He bowed low, then stood. "Countess Ambrook demands." he cleared his throat. "That you accompany her for a late afternoon chat." He gave Pridric a sorrowful look. "At once."

Pridric sighed, slumping his shoulders.

So, I hadn't snuck off undetected after all.

"Very well. Tell her I will be there shortly."

The guard bowed again, then left the room. Pridric glanced back at Tavelo. He stared, waiting to see a finger twitch to prove his theory correct. When nothing happened, he slammed the lid shut and pushed the release panel on the floor with one foot. He waited until the coffin went flat among the base boards before leaving.

I need you to stay in there a little longer.

London's near empty streets sat quietly. Many of the shops had few patrons. Fear permeated the air. Pridric walked down the main fairway with Chancellor Rayne beside him and two guards close behind. He wore a simple dark suit with a white shirt and blue tie with a matching handkerchief tucked inside the breast pocket. Chancellor Rayne and the guards matched.

The city still struggled to get its legs back after the horrors of the emperor followed by the covens going on a hunting spree out of frustration with humans. He recognized the bad judgement call on his part and secretly chastised the others for going along with it.

They should have stopped me!

Up ahead, he could see the docks bustling with activity. Commerce and trade were back in full swing. To ease the afternoon heat, some of the dock workers stripped down to wearing just pants and tank tops, while others opted for shirtless.

Two more hours until sunset and the heat showed no signs of letting up. Pridric looked at the sky. Streaks of orange and purple crept over the horizon.

Beautiful.

"Are you sure about this, my lord?"

Chancellor Rayne asked dubiously.

"We all agreed to combine our resources and make trade more profitable."

"Yes. But what you are about to do would be frowned upon."

"Hmm. Who's to stop me? Tavelo?" Pridric smirked. "He's asleep."

He could sense Chancellor Rayne's body cringe at the retort. His man would tell no one of his plan but it may put a strain on their relationship.

So be it. The Marchand coven would agree with me. I hope.

A twenty-foot stack of crates with the Durante crest burned into the wood sat on the lower dock. The pier master came up to him, tablet in hand.

"Is there a problem, sir?" The man adjusted his skullcap over bushy grey eyebrows. Light dust covered his thick jacket. He pointed at the cargo. "This one needs a signature."

"I know." Pridric smiled politely.

"There's been no one from the Durante Holdings all week."

"I will sign for it in their place."

The pier master balked. "I can't let you do that," he stuttered.

Pridric turned to the man, and their eyes met as his glowed red with anger.

"You will." He seethed.

The man held out the tablet, his hands shaking. Pridric nodded to Chancellor Rayne, who took it and pulled up the cargo's manifest. He turned it around with the signature screen up. Pridric scrawled his name with a fingertip.

"Now, split it in thirds. I want one shipped to Germany, one stays here, and the other to its original destination in Asia."

The man took back his tablet and tucked it under his arm.

"This is illegal, just so you know."

"I don't care," Pridric snapped. "Do as I ask."

He turned and headed to the other shipments on the docks. Chancellor Rayne chatted up the goods inspector while he searched for more Durante Holding crates.

As he rounded a corner through a maze of metal containers, he nearly ran into a worker staring down at his tablet while walking. The two men stopped short of ramming into each other. Pridric saw the De Luce logo on the man's shirt pocket.

"My apologies, Count Ambrook. I wasn't paying attention." The young man smiled.

Under a baseball cap with the same logo, Pridric made out neatly tucked short blond hair. His blue eyes beamed with pride.

What are you so proud of?

Pridric gave him a chastising stare.

"Yes, that was obvious. What are you in such a hurry for?"

"Oh!" The young man grinned. "Queen Erena made me proxy for the Durante Holdings since the workforce suddenly collapsed. I'm checking on the cargo."

Shit! Damn it, Eterenia!

"Is that right?" No need to hide it. What's done is done. "I already signed for one of them with my executive order. I wish she would have told me sooner."

The way the young man's eyes appeared to darken, like a deep ocean, made Pridric seethe.

"I'm not sure that's acceptable, Count Ambrook. My Queen will be most displeased."

"It's only the one. Rest assured; the same revenue will be generated."

"That's not the point, though," the young man stepped back. "Is it?"

Should I kill him?

Pridric frowned at the thought. It would cause more strife if he did. From the young man's demeanor, it may come to that.

Chancellor Rayne arrived behind him.

"What's going on here?"

"Count Ambrook was telling me how he illegally signed for and confiscated a Durante Holdings cargo."

"Who is this?" Chancellor Rayne asked, pointing to the man.

"The Durante proxy Queen Erena appointed." Pridric's lips pressed thin.

"Oh my." Chancellor Rayne walked up to the proxy. "Now, you should know there's nothing sinister about this. Your Queen should have informed us. Count Ambrook used his executive order according to the covens' agreement."

"Hmm?" The proxy cocked his head to one side. "I will have to report this to my Queen." He brought his head up and walked past the two men. "After I secure the rest of Count Durante's property."

Pridric stood with clenched fists at his sides. Chancellor Rayne turned to him.

"Well, isn't he a little snot? I warned you, my lord."

"I'm not doing anything wrong!"

The two men headed back towards the main docks to check on the Ambrook cargo.

❀ ❀ ❀

"What you did was wrong!" Yutel's, known as Grieger, voice exploded into the room. "If you had done that with my goods, I'd have strung you up by your damned entrails!"

Eterenia's sitting room went silent. The coven leaders sat uncomfortably in the otherwise plush chairs, forming a circle around the drink cart. A three-tiered platter with tiny desserts sat atop it. Muted sunlight cast shadows across the floor.

Pridric, who stood indignant in front of his seat, slammed down in his chair at the verbal assault. Eterenia gave him an icy stare. She seemed none too pleased, indeed.

Crumbs fell from the flaky crust of her pastry, held in limbo at her lips. They freckled in her lap on the dark blue pencil dress with a thin belt at the waist. Sighing, she shoved it in her mouth and chewed quickly, not savoring the sweetness.

"Tell me, Pridric." She swallowed, while using a finger to wipe away any excess crumbs. "Have you lost your mind, or have you decided our partnership is no longer of interest?"

"I think no such thing!" Pridric rose back up. "Is collective profit not our goal?" He returned her stare. "Are you not doing the same by appointing someone from your coven to handle his affairs?"

"Oh, ho!" Darean, head of the Sapienti coven, called out. "That is completely different. Tavelo had given her access long before all this and she has a vested interest."

"Give it back." Eterenia demanded softly.

Pridric smirked and slumped into his seat. "No." The other's gasped at his boldness. "Besides," he shrugged. "I already split up the goods." He picked his glass of whiskey off the nearby side table and took a sip, crossing his legs.

Quiet until now, Holnar, the Marchard coven leader, spoke.

"Yes, the goal is as you say. But there are correct procedures to go through. Eterenia did what was necessary. You." Holnar's eyes glowed silver. "Did not." He too took a sip of his drink, an expensive bourbon. "No one here will save you when Tavelo awakens."

"I may just hold you down for him." Eterenia smiled.

"Oooh!" Chalayl, whose coven called her Queen Celeste, squealed. "You should battle in that underground arena of yours." She reached for the desserts and picked a macaroon. "That way, you'll already be at home to recuperate."

Pridric flashed towards her.

Yutel's massive frame, towering over him with glaring red eyes, thwarted the move. Eterenia stood a nanosecond too late. Pridric didn't move from his position, mere millimeters from Yutel's chest.

"Sit down, Pridric." Yutel's deep voice resonated in the air.

Eterenia watched Pridric slowly step back to the front of his seat, then plopped down. Behind Yutel, Chalayl posed in defense mode, had both hands on the edge of her chair, ready to pounce.

"We are not heathens! Control yourselves."

Darean slapped his napkin on his thigh in exasperation.

Eterenia eased into her chair. *That's debatable.* The crumbs flittered to the carpet. *Earth has changed us. And not for the better.* She placed a hand on the side of her head and leaned into it, bracing her elbow on the chair's armrest.

"You will not do this again." Holnar softened his tone to ease the tension. "The proxy Eterenia has appointed will take over. If you must keep your fingers in this, you can oversee the shipments."

"Fine." Pridric brooded in his seat. "I will."

"Just so you know," Chalayl said, smacking on a mini cake. "We weren't joking when we said none of us will defend you from Tavelo."

Her devious smile made Eterenia cringe.

Why do those two not get along?

She eyed Holnar who shook his head. But the fact remained; Tavelo would not be amused. And given his new, awakened form, Pridric would be in a world of hurt.

Howls echoed in the night across the Durante castle grounds as a pack of werewolves ran under the bright moonlight. A sentry of vampires guarded each perimeter to make sure they didn't stray too far into the town. The wet blades of grass brushing against their fur flecked misty droplets back into the air. Rain had left a layer of moisture on the warm landscape. It had been hot earlier, causing most of it to evaporate on contact.

Tesul's nostrils flared as he breathed in the scent of damp earth and crushed greenery. His speed created a slight wind that bristled the hairs on his back, cooling him down. In the dark, his glowing yellow eyes were like beacons. Patches of wet dirt flew back from his paws, digging deep and releasing their grip.

Mingled in the air was the smell of prey ahead. A four-point deer losing its advantage of distance trying to flee its pursuers. There would be no escape. From ahead, two other wolves crossed its path. It skidded, swinging its body around to head in the opposite direction.

Tesul leaped forward, and the two crashed. He took down the deer, clamping his massive jaws into its neck. The sound of flesh ripping enticed the others. He tore out a chunk, getting first rights, then let the others take part.

He led his pack on a night long hunt. Even in his primitive animal state, he felt a sense of dissatisfaction with the short-lived escapade. The werewolves were only allowed to indulge in their nature once a month. The vampires had the same rules, yet they broke them at every turn. The sky turned a dark blue, the stars fading, signaling the pack to return.

Approaching the castle, Tesul morphed back into human form, his naked body covered in blood from multiple kills. The other four in his pack did the same, not bothering to wipe themselves off. The two vampires at the dungeon entrance held the doors open for them.

They made their way to the communal showers down the dark stone corridor.

His master installed the proper drain system long ago with filters to handle the blood and debris that washed off every time they came back. He was thankful for Count Durante's generosity over the decades.

Unlike the other coven leaders, the Count had formed an alliance with the werewolves. The former leader of his pack, his father, was a hybrid resulting from Count Durante biting him.

The group entered the enclosed stone chamber with three shower heads on each side embedded in the walls. Tesul turned the brushed nickel dial at the entrance and all six sprayed powerful jets of hot water. Steam rose, filling the room. They all stepped in to be pummeled clean. The diluted blood swirled down the drain in the center.

Tesul ran his fingers through his thick brown hair, making sure the water got every section. The last thing he needed was to go to his personal quarters and have Adelia smell any trace of blood on him. A small smile crept onto his lips.

My princess.

With his master in a deep slumber, leaving the coven without a leader, Queen Erena insisted on her daughter taking temporary reign with him by her side.

Nothing of dire consequence since the coup years ago had occurred as of late. He heard about Count Ambrook's little stunt, and Adelia was not happy about it, either.

From what he had gleaned from the conversations between the leaders, even on their home world, his master's family was taken advantage of when it benefitted the others.

The water ran clear.

Tesul turned it off and walked out to the other room where towels were laid out. A clean set of clothes sat in four neat piles next to them on the benches.

"Do you think we should keep a better eye on the vampires?" One of the men in his pack asked.

"What are you thinking?" Tesul stopped drying himself and looked over at him.

"Someone here must be feeding Count Ambrook information. That shipment was important."

Tesul frowned as he resumed drying off.

The female in his pack used her towel to rub the excess water from her hair then spoke.

"I hate to think that. Most of the Durante family are not a bunch of backstabbers like the others."

"True," the second male of the pack said. "Which means it may be a plain old vampire who works the docks."

That made Tesul perk up. It had never crossed his mind that may be the case. Endagas were tight, loyal, and fiercely protective of his master. He smirked. Count Durante hated being called master. Tesul chose not to call him by his true name. He felt it would only cause confusion.

"We contact the other pack in the morning and have them sniff out any clues." Tesul tossed the damp towel on the floor and sat on the bench to get dressed. "Until our master awakens, we have to protect the castle and everyone in it."

"Agreed." The female replied.

They all tossed their towels in a pile along with Tesul's and donned their clothes. Two of them went to relieve the two guards outside the dungeon door, while the other two went up the stairs into the main level of the castle to switch with the entrance guards. Tesul followed them up, then turned into the hallway on his left.

Along the way, he bowed to the noble class that walked by. The vampires gave him dirty stares and moved from his path, not greeting him. Which made the allegations from his pack even more real. The smell of blood permeated the halls. The vampires hurried to their chambers to sleep for the rest of the day. Daybreak barely creeped through the windows.

Tesul arrived at his quarters and flung the door open. He stood still, waiting for an attack. None came. He made his way into the room. On the massive bed lay Adelia, sound asleep, with their little one snuggling against her bosom.

He cocked his head, staring at them lovingly. With the stealth of a ninja, he crept onto the bed and laid beside them.

Their son's dark hair had grown into a thick mop that slightly curved at the ends. Full lips like his mother were partly open, a small bubble of saliva vibrating as he breathed. He used a finger to move a strand of hair from his tiny face.

"Did you have a good hunt?" Adelia's voice barely a whisper, cracked from sleep.

"It was acceptable." He looked up from their son and met her stare. "Did you sleep well?"

"Not really." She sat up, careful not to jostle the boy. "He's a menace."

Tesul stifled a laugh. He understood. Their son was a ball of energy with no off switch until it all ran dry and he fell asleep.

"Has he been out long?"

"About three hours." She wiped her eyes with balled fists. "Your turn."

"I can't. There is an issue that needs handling."

Adelia pouted, making her resemble a spoiled schoolgirl. At nearly a century old, she should have outgrown such a thing.

Tesul ran a hand down her face.

"We think there may be a vampire spy for Ambrook in the castle."

Her pout turned into a hateful expression.

"The shipment." She sat up.

The thin nightgown shifted and one of the spaghetti straps fell off her shoulder. Her waist length blonde curls were in disarray. A tangled mess. He sighed and eased off the bed.

"I'll get the nanny. You have a full plate today."

"Ugh!"

She flopped back down on the bed in a heap.

He went to the closet and perused the wardrobe inside. One of the perks of being the mate of a princess was choosing her attire. Let's see. His gaze moved down the rows of business dresses.

What trait shall you portray today?

The Awakening

The smell of blood filled Tavelo's nostrils. In the blanket of pitch black, he felt his body confined to the limited space. A coffin. He was certain of it. With each slight movement, the tubes connected to his flesh pulled taut. Whirring accompanied the gentle sway of the coffin rising.

Only one coven had such a setup.

It didn't surprise him that Pridric would have taken possession of his body to the underground catacombs within the Ambrook castle. He wondered how long his slumber had lasted.

And who decided to bring him back to the living?

He let his breathing slow to a crawl as he centered himself. The blood made his heart race, enticing an intense hunger.

Memories flooded his mind. He barely made out the images of a gigantic form seen from his own eyes. That's me! The words of the emperor stating he had been searching for him all along. An ancient bloodline.

A Volshin.

The coffin stopped moving. Its lid creaked open, letting beams of muted light in. He could see a hazy reflection in the high polished edges and the deep red of his own eyes. With the lid fully open, he glanced up to see who stood over him.

Baltise, Chase Ambrook's guardian and also a Volshin, stared into the coffin. His soft features brought delusions of innocence when he was nothing of the sort. The room grew silent as a tomb with no one else present. *Hmm?*

Tavelo slipped his hands apart from where they rested on his chest and braced himself against the coffin's inner walls. He rose to a sitting position. His dark hair splayed around him. He noticed how long it had grown.

"Hungry." He heard his own scratchy voice whisper. The tubes detached, slithering back into their housing below. He looked at Baltise. "Why?"

"Count Ambrook diluted and slowed down your platform's feed. He wanted you to sleep longer."

That soft tone, part of Baltise's charm, sounded almost demure.

"Is that so?" The top of the coffin tilted up at an eighty-degree angle. "And now he wants me awake?"

"No." Baltise stepped back as Tavelo came forth. "He does not know I have done this."

"And why have you?"

Tavelo towered over the little thing, his red eyes locking with Baltise's.

"I don't trust him. He has a bad agenda for the covens, and also the Volshins and Katalings."

"Of course he does." Baltise handed him a bag of blood with a drinking tube attached. He took it and sucked the whole thing dry within moments. He let out a sigh. "That's a little better."

Hard boots on stone echoed from the corridor, and a group of soldiers clamored through the entrance. They moved to the sides of the door frame, allowing Pridric and his Chancellor to enter.

Pridric's eyes glowed silver with rage as he stomped towards them, pushing the two soldiers closest to him out of the way. Chancellor Rayne stayed near the entrance with his lips pursed thin.

"What are you doing?" Pridric yelled at Baltise.

The young Volshin flinched, shrinking back.

"This is unacceptable. How dare you decide for yourself to hinder my orders!"

Tavelo glared at Pridric. Bloody wings sprouted from his back, spanning six feet on each side. The soldiers went pale and Pridric stopped in his tracks. Tavelo's fangs grew long, protruding down to his chin. He tilted his head to one side and his wings flexed, causing a minor wind that blew everyone's hair back. Baltise hid behind him, his small fingers clutching Tavelo's inner thigh.

"Hungry," he said again, slurring because of his excessively long fangs.

Pridric's eyes went wide with fear.

"Get out!" He waved a hand behind him to the soldiers. "Now!" They scrambled back out into the corridor. Chancellor Rayne stood his ground. Pridric turned to Tavelo. "You need to restrain yourself! I won't let you go on a hunting spree in my coven." He straightened his posture. "You are under my care and jurisdiction."

Tavelo took hold of him by the neck in a flash. They went flying into the far wall, Pridric's body embedded in the stone. Tavelo's taloned hands were around his neck, holding him there.

Chancellor Rayne loudly cleared his throat to get their attention.

"If the two of you are done saying hello," he stepped down onto the first step. "We have much to discuss." He gave Pridric a pitiful look. "I hope you are prepared to face the consequences, my lord."

Tavelo released Pridric, retracting his fangs and wings. He glanced behind him at the ruined fabric of his favorite kimono and frowned. Pridric shook crumbled debris from his suit and sidestepped away from him to Chancellor Rayne. He addressed Baltise.

"I will deal with your insubordination later." Pridric gestured with one hand at the entrance as he eyed Tavelo. "Coming?"

Tavelo followed him and Chancellor Rayne out with Baltise not far behind. A few soldiers remained in the corridor, not willing to abandon their master in a crisis. He smirked at them as he passed. Heading up the dark staircase, he sent a telepathic message to Eterenia.

I'm coming back to you.

Eterenia shot up from her throne, eyes wide. She had an iron grip on the sides, her knuckles turning white. The folds of her navy-blue satin gown slid from behind lazily off the seat and the hem touched the floor. Her Valkyrie placed a hand on her sword, scanning the room for hostiles.

"What is it, my Queen?" The Valkyrie stepped forward, peering towards the corridor outside the throne room. "Are we being attacked?"

Realizing she probably looked deranged, Eterenia changed her demeanor, easing back onto her throne.

"No. I'm sorry. There is no threat." The Valkyrie seemed dubious. She waited until the warrior unhanded her sword and rejoined her side. "I got a message from someone I cherish."

The Valkyrie leaned close, whispering.

"You don't mean…"

Eterenia nodded. She half listened to the reports of the day, her mind now occupied with Tavelo.

I'll be waiting. She replied with a smile.

Two guards escorted Baltise back to Chase's and his chamber. They opened the door and pushed him inside. The moment they left, Chase came rushing in, his face flushed with anger.

"What the hell were you thinking?" He came up to Baltise. "My father could have killed you for this!"

"No, he couldn't," Baltise replied softly. He stared at Chase, who then flinched. "Besides." Baltise turned away from him. "What he's doing is wrong."

"I know that!"

Chase sat on the bed, placing both hands on his head. The entire castle had suspicions about their coven leader's actions. Baltise understood Chase's precarious position. He had heard from spies about the Durante coven and felt they needed their leader back. The other coven successors were being cut out of the business dealings.

That wasn't fair either.

"Your father is making enemies of the others. You all have to do something. Force your way into the conversations."

Chase looked up and stared at Baltise in awe. He had never heard him talk so much. Or to anyone else. Baltise never wanted to express himself for fear of retaliation. Being a lowly servant in the dungeons meant he had no say in his life. Until now. As Chase's mate and mother to his children, they treated Baltise better. Not by much. And Chase constantly fought his father's guards over their rough handling of him.

They never did that in front of the Queen. Chase's mother would have all their heads. She chose to not be privy to the coven's business dealings. Baltise had broached the subject with her once, and she shrugged it off. Let them feel powerful, she had said.

That got harder to do.

"Why now?" Chase stood. "What could be so dire that you poke my father's wrath?"

"You'll see. When Tavelo returns to his coven."

"Did you just call Count Durante by his real name?" Chase curiously stared at him. "When did that happen?"

"It's not much of a secret."

A high-pitched squeal erupted from the halls and their youngest daughter came barreling in. Blonde curls bounced around her head as she ran breathless on bare feet towards her father. Her big blue eyes were wide with fervor while she panted.

The yellow nightgown wrinkled as she clung to his legs.

"Run from me? You silly girl." Queen Ambrook walked into the room. Her lips thinned as her head tilted slightly, a playful gleam in her eyes. "You will take a bath today."

"No!" Their daughter squeezed him tighter. She buried her face in his thigh. "Don't wanna'."

Trying to get her into a vat of soap and water became a weekly event. On occasion, Baltise commissioned help from the Queen who managed to corral the little one. Then there were times like now when she got away and came looking to her father for rescue.

She should know better by now.

"Sweetheart," Chase knelt before her. "We've talked about this. You can't go around being filthy. It makes your mother and I look bad. And your grandmother."

"This is what happens when you let her roam the grounds untethered," his mother chastised him.

Chase sighed.

Picking up his daughter, he grabbed her chin.

"You will obey your grandmother." She pouted, flopping her head on his shoulder.

The Queen's personal maid, waiting in the doorway, raised her arms out to the girl. She wiggled out of his grasp and ran to her. Baltise shook his head, feeling defeated as they all were.

Their oldest daughter stayed out of the way most days, reading in the library even at school. The little one had a twin brother just as rambunctious, though not necessarily disobedient.

As the maid left with their daughter in her arms, the Queen turned to them, addressing Baltise.

"That was a foolish thing you've done."

"I was right."

"That doesn't make it the correct action."

"If you knew." Baltise clenched his fists.

"I know plenty," the Queen seethed, stepping close to him. "Your timing is bad."

Chase looked back and forth between them, then grew angry.

"What is going on?" His eyes turned red. "I'm tired of being in the dark."

His mother balked at him.

"You have put blinders on about your father for decades. Now you want to see what kind of monster he is underneath that immaculate façade?"

Chase reared back at her verbal assault. Even Baltise knew that hurt. His mother's face softened. She went to him and placed a hand on his cheek.

"I know he's not perfect." Chase leaned his face into her hand. "I wanted to see him change."

"Oh, my poor child. It would take a lot for that to happen." She removed her hand. "If you are not allowed at the table, make your own."

She left the room, giving Baltise one last warning look as she entered the hallway.

"Well, that's easier said than done." Chase sat back on the bed. "Adelia is leading the Durante coven. Olette and Olivier have gone missing. Falson hasn't left the Sapienti coven in years and no one seems to know anything. The rest checked out of the game."

"I think they are biding their time and awaiting a signal from you."

"Is that what your spies tell you?" Chase smirked, turning to him. His smile faded.

"Yes." Baltise met his gaze.

A new expression, one of conviction, crossed Chase's face and Baltise breathed a little easier. He didn't want to force his mate into the fray. Instead, he would nudge him onto the right path.

While Tavelo still slept, Baltise had tapped into his mind, searching his memories of their home world. He learned a lot. Enough to know the last person the covens needed as a leader was a Strana.

Tesul arrived at the front gates of the Ambrook coven not long after sunset. He sat in the back seat of the luxury SUV, driven by a vampire servant. The driver pushed the call button on the panel outside the gate. A buzz rattled before the gates swung open. The driver maneuvered the vehicle through and headed down the curved driveway lined with tall green immaculately trimmed bushes.

The artificial new car scent made his nose twitch. Having the car smell that way came from old caveat from a previous decade. He pushed the control on the door panel to roll the window down a quarter. The air, filled with the smell of greenery, decayed stone, and stale destruction, filled his lungs as he took a deep breath.

His muscular frame took up an entire side. The impeccably tailored black suit let him move comfortably. His hair, swept back in a ponytail, accentuated his chiseled face. Adelia hated his hair like that. She preferred it untamed.

He reached into the pocket behind the front passenger seat, pulled out a thin six-inch box, and set it on his lap.

On the way, he contemplated if he should warn his master about the things going on at the docks with the company shipments. Many in the coven were angered by the unfoolding events. The thought of his master in the hands of a potential enemy pissed him off.

As Count Durante's personal guardian, he felt more than peeved when Ambrook suggested he abandon his master for an entire decade.

He didn't trust Count Ambrook to not do anything unsavory to his master's body while it remained in stasis. Tesul only agreed because Queen Erena begged him to stand down. That she would ensure his safety. *But now he is awake!*

And he knew his master had woken angry. Not knowing what happened at first, then realizing the emperor had escaped.

The driver shut off the engine and glanced back at him. The head Proxy, Armon, dressed similar to Tesul, got out from the passenger seat, buttoned his jacket, and closed the door.

Chestnut waves combed back from his face barely brushed the top of his shoulders. His brown eyes had an amber tone, making them seem golden in sunlight, tinged with cinnamon at night.

Tall and slender, he exuded class. Like a young millionaire with street smarts.

A high-priced thug.

Tesul flung open his door and stepped out as well onto Ambrook property. He tucked the box under one arm. Together, they walked to the front door.

To their surprise, Chancellor Rayne greeted them. He stood in the entrance with that stern expression everyone always saw.

"Tesul. How good to see you again." Chancellor Rayne gave a small bow of his head.

"We've come for our master." Armon sneered.

Chancellor Rayne frowned. Tesul almost thought about apologizing. The remark did border on rude.

"Of course. Please." He gestured them inside. "Let's fetch him."

Tesul changed his mind.

"We thank you for keeping him safe all these years. You have our gratitude."

Chancellor Rayne's demeanor softened.

"It was the least we could do."

The group walked up the winding staircase to the third level, then down to the fourth door on the right. Chancellor Rayne opened it, stepping aside for the two guardians to enter.

At the bay window, wearing a kimono tattered in the back from when his wings must have sprouted, Tavelo stared out in the distance, not moving. His hair had grown twice as long, touching the back of his ankles. Long black talons replaced the formerly well-manicured nails.

When he finally turned around, Tesul nearly flinched at the blood red irises.

He's half in transition!

"Tesul. Armon." His master seemed to breathe their names. "So glad you've come."

"You belong at home." Armon clasped his hands in front of him. "Of course we would come for you."

Tesul pulled the box from under his arm and handed it to Tavelo.

"I thought you may want this for better comfort."

His master's body appeared to float towards him. Tavelo took the box and opened it.

"Ahh." He took hold of the fabric within, letting the box drop to the floor. The silky, dark gray cover shimmered in the light. "It is glorious. Thank you." He removed the tattered blue one, tossing it to Armon, who caught it with one hand, then donned the new one. "That's better."

"Shall we?"

Armon lifted an arm towards the door.

"Leaving so soon?" Chancellor Rayne asked. "Did you not want to meet with Count Ambrook and tell him how grateful you are?"

Tesul's eyes turned yellow. "No."

Armon walked past, followed by their master. Tesul took up the rear. Not one of them addressed Chancellor Rayne as they left. And he didn't bother to follow either.

Outside, the driver waited beside the vehicle. A cigarette hung from the corner of his mouth. His eyes went wide briefly before he regained his composure. Tesul commended him on his restraint. To say their master's appearance left them in awe would be an understatement.

"Good to see you, Count Durante." He opened the passenger door. "Let's go home."

As he got into the vehicle, the ends of his hair got tangled around his legs. In frustration, he pulled free and situated himself in the seat.

Tesul went around to the other side and got in. Armon returned to the front passenger seat.

The driver slid in. He pushed the start button and let the quiet engine purr. He headed back the way he came, the gate already opening as the vehicle approached. Once clear of the Ambrook property, he sped up.

They rode the first two hours of the trip in silence.

"Master Durante," Armon began.

"Don't call me that." The vehement tone from their master jarred them. As if sensing it, he sighed, letting his hands flop lazily in his lap. "I am not your master. And you know my true name."

"Yes, but the other vampires in the coven don't know that." Tesul stated.

"Fine. When we are in confidence, refer to me as Tavelo. Or Endaga if you must."

"We could occasionally slip. That is why we still call you by Durante even in private."

"And also, the businesses are under the Durante name," Armon added.

"Unh." Tavelo responded in disgust. "How goes the business? I assume you all have been keeping it afloat in my absence."

Tesul shifted uneasily in his seat. Armon looked away so his master couldn't see his face.

"I think it best if we wait until we get home, and you have time to get reacquainted with the coven," Tesul said tentatively. "It's been so long and much has changed."

Tavelo's eyes narrowed.

"What's happened?" He turned to Tesul. "Tell me."

"I really insist that you wait. I'm sorry."

No one spoke the rest of the way. Tension grew thick in the air.

❀ ❀ ❀

Durante's castle loomed ahead.

Tavelo immediately hissed at the scene. The front of the property had a secondary wall with guards all along its edges. Vampires were patrolling the grounds. Most of the windows had small lights shining, even though he was certain no one occupied them. The hostile environment appeared on the verge of a fight starting.

With who? He glanced over at Tesul and saw the werewolf's brow furrowed.

A guard carrying an assault rifle slung across his shoulder came to the center of the road and raised a hand for the vehicle to halt. Tavelo stifled a growl. The vampire stepped closer, peering into the windshield. Recognizing the driver, he waved them on.

The vehicle parked at the entrance, and all got out except Tavelo. He tried to curb a fit of rage stirring. A vampire came charging out and accosted Armon. Tavelo recognized him as one of the elite members within the coven.

A sniveling, greedy creature from the lower families who married into his, thus elevating his status.

"Who gave you permission to take one of the cars, and a werewolf off the property? We have rules for a reason!"

"It was an urgent matter," Tesul answered.

"No one asked you, mutt. Just because you knocked up that whore and the master's favorite pet doesn't mean you get to address me."

He emphasized 'me' with a vicious tone.

Tavelo had enough.

Conscious of his new robe, he removed it, placing it neatly on the seat. He exited the vehicle. In a flash his hand wrapped around the vampire's neck, lifting him off the ground. The other guards turned towards them, weapons poised. Tavelo's wings expanded as his fangs grew.

"Give me one reason not to tear you apart."

The vampire's eyes widened with terror.

"Count Durante!" He struggled in Tavelo's grasp. "I…"

The other guards looked around in confusion, not sure what to do. Armon addressed them.

"Are you so daft that you would attack the leader of this coven?" He yelled. Turning to Tavelo, he said, "Give us your word, and we will purge them all without prejudice.

"Wait," the vampire elite gasped. Tavelo lessened his grip. "My apologies. If they had told me they were retrieving you, I would have sent an entourage."

"That still doesn't explain the disrespect you showed my personal guards who I deem precious to me." He squeezed his neck. "Do you treat Princess Adelia in the same manner? My stepdaughter?"

The vampire didn't answer. Tavelo almost snapped the vampire's neck when a woman ran out and forced herself between them. His cousin the vampire had married.

"My lord! I beg you!" His cousin held her arms outstretch. "He will make amends, I promise you. Do not kill him. Please!"

Tavelo's lips thinned as he went deep in thought, not weakening his grip. He knew killing him would put a damper on his homecoming. And he didn't want to return like this. Murderous intent added to the tension he felt.

A quick psychic scan found vampires not of his coven among the others.

He let go, dropping the vampire at his feet.

While the man held his neck, gasping for air as he tried to breathe normally with his wife consoling him, Tavelo stepped over the threshold of his castle. Stark black and red replaced the majestic blue with silver that usually greeted him. Signature vampire colors from the old country.

The grand foyer, once full of life, now lay barren, with a guard blocking most of it from the corridor traffic.

A group of guards marched to the entrance, their intent to harm heightened. They got within fifty feet, their swords raised high, and stopped in their tracks. The leader's expression turned to horror.

"Count Durante?"

He whispered, lowering his sword.

Before he could signal his men to drop their weapons, two of them charged at Tavelo.

"Abomination!" the first ran forward, screaming.

The leader went pale as he watched the two reach Tavelo's range of attack. His wings swung up, its spikes vertically slicing them open. The other guards sheathed their swords and bowed to one knee.

"So good to have you back, Lord Durante." The leader raised his head. "Welcome home."

Tavelo and Tesul continued into the castle and headed to the staircase. Armon snapped a finger at two guards standing outside on the steps. He pointed to the fallen bleeding on the floor.

"Clean this mess."

The first guard scoffed.

"We're not servants," he spat. "Get one of those house mutts to do it."

Armon moved on him and set his talons under the man's chin. They grew, piercing the skin.

"You are a servant of House Durante." Armon seethed. His eyes glowed red. "Disobedience is cured by death. Do you understand?"

"Yeah," the man gasped, his eyes narrowed.

Armon withdrew his talons and stepped back.

"Then get to it." He pivoted towards the main corridor and walked up to the guard leader. "Make sure it gets done."

"Does this mean we can kick those infiltrators and freeloaders out?" The leader asked.

"Oh, I am sure Lord Durante will clean house once he is acclimated."

"Thank the heavens." The leader went to the unruly guards and began instructing them on how he wanted the mess removed, including the two vampires that were struck down. "And, hurry up, too."

With that task taken care of, Armon headed to Tavelo's private chamber. He removed his suit jacket and draped it over his arm as he entered. Tesul stood on one side of the room while Tavelo angrily stripped off his bloodied clothes.

Fully naked, he turned to them with silver eyes.

"You will tell me what is going on in my castle!"

Tesul held out the dark blue silk robe in his hand and Tavelo snatched it from him. He put it on, fastening it shut, then looked down in disgust, realizing blood still covered him. He whipped it off and marched to the bathroom.

"Do not move from this room until I return."

Tesul picked up the stained robe and frowned. Armon tossed his jacket on a nearby chair and went to the wardrobe. He opened it wide and took out the first robe that caught his eye. All of them were floor length in various colors of silk and satin. He grabbed one of deep fuchsia.

"Better get this to him before he storms out butt naked." He threw it to Tesul. "And then we have to deal with his rage after updating him on the situation."

Tesul nodded and headed into the bathroom. Steam billowed out into the room. He disappeared into it, coming out seconds later. He went right to the chair by the bed where he sat in silence. Armon repositioned his jacket on the back of the other one and did the same.

Twenty minutes went by before the door opened. Tavelo came out, looking as he did decades ago. His wet hair laying at the small of his back. Tesul raised an eyebrow and peeked around him at the bathroom floor. A sea of jet-black strands covered the tile. The short blade he kept in the cabinet lay on the side of the sink.

"Are you calmed down?" Tesul asked.

Tavelo climbed onto the center of the bed.

The robe flowed around him like liquid when he crossed his legs.

"Tell me."

Armon shifted in his chair and leaned forward.

"The other coven leaders went on a hunting spree for weeks until they felt satisfied humans were terrified enough to not test them. We asked Ambrook to transfer you to the castle. He refused, stating his coven was the only one equipped to handle..."

"Imprison," Tesul interjected.

"A Volshin of such strength and magnitude." Armon continued. "Queen Erena was pissed. With you in stasis, that left the Durante coven without a leader. Ambrook tried to persuade the other covens to let him take over, but Queen Erena sent Princess Adelia."

"He didn't want to be outdone just yet." Tesul turned to Tavelo. "Two years ago, Queen Erena appointed Armon to assign you a proxy for the Durante Holding Company."

"Before he could check on another major shipment, Ambrook had already used his privileges to redirect the goods." Armon took a deep breath. "The rest of the covens were not happy."

"I'm not happy!" Tavelo's eyes turned red. "What does any of that have to do with vampires not of this coven ordering my family to do their bidding?"

"Things got dicey in your absenceso the other covens sent guardians to keep the peace." Armon frowned. "None of the coven leaders have been to the castle since. They don't know what transpired here."

"Princess Adelia has kept her mother at bay for now. If she knew..."

"These walls would weep with blood," Tavelo stated, bluntly.

His eyes fluttered as his body seemed to tilt. He jerked upright, angered by his own weakness.

"You need to rest." Tesul stood.

"I've been resting for over a decade!"

"Properly." Tesul pushed him lightly, forcing him to fall sideways onto the bed. "Sleep. We will discuss the issue in the morning. Away from prying eyes."

Tavelo instantly fell asleep.

Armon got up and pulled the blanket over him. He gave Tesul a knowing stare. Things were going to get a hell of a lot messy when their lord woke.

Inside Rivalry

Sunlight pierced the thin fabric covering Tavelo's windows, startling him awake. He sat up, his hair splaying around him, and stared at the grandfather clock directly across the room. Ten in the morning. The blanket slid off and he took stock of his body's condition.

I feel drained.

A stale, cottony metal taste permeated his mouth. He tried to create moisture by rolling around his tongue that merely stuck to the insides. His stomach gurgled, not eating since Baltise brought him out.

His chamber door opened. Tesul came pushing a serving cart of various foods in and stopped at the side of the bed. He knows me well. Tavelo's mouth finally began salivating.

"There's fresh, raw meat, melons, cheese, some soda bread, and wine." He sat in the chair. "I suggest the meat first."

Tavelo stared at the large spread with nearly two pounds of sliced meat displayed prominently in the middle of it all. He took the long-pronged fork and speared one of the thick pieces, greedily shoving it in his mouth. The taste rushed through his whole being as the blood coursed in his veins. With eyes closed, he threw his head back in euphoria, savoring the freshness. He let out a long sigh of ecstasy.

"Better?"

"Umm." Tavelo finished chewing and speared another piece of meat. "So good."

Tesul watched him eat, not saying a word until all the meat along with the bread and cheese were gone.

"What would you like to do today?"

Tavelo picked up the glass of red wine and drank a third of it.

"Besides hang Pridric by his entrails?"

"Yes, my lord, besides that."

Tesul glanced over at him.

Rolling his eyes, Tavelo set the glass down.

"I want those other coven members out of my castle." He locked into a staring match with Tesul. "And a meeting with the others."

A loud ruckus from the hallway made him look up. Before he could ask what was going on, a little boy dressed in a blue onesie ran into the room and leap, crashing into him.

"Grampa Tavo!"

The boy's weight pushed Tavelo backwards into an awkward position as he tried to hold the child at bay. Tavelo managed to get his legs straight and looked at the boy. Cute. Then it struck him. This child of Tesul and Adelia, being only a few years old, he did not know. He turned to Tesul.

"Want to explain this?"

"Well, what did you expect?" That haughty tone, dripping with disgust replied. "Were we supposed to not be carnal while you slept?"

Princess Adelia entered the room followed by a tall boy with thick brown hair wearing a tee shirt and leggings. *That's the one I remember as a baby.* He had a bored expression until he saw Tavelo. The boy stepped up to the bed and attempted to wrench his little brother off.

"He's still recovering. Get off."

"No! Mine!"

The older boy's face softened.

He looked down on Tavelo.

"Guess you don't really recognize me. I was still a baby when you last saw me."

"Oh," Tavelo sat, the little one still attached like Velcro. "I do. You're Sully" Then he tilted his head in confusion. "How does he know who I am?"

"We talk about you a lot. Mom doesn't want to show it, but she missed you."

"I did no such thing!" She pushed her unruly blonde hair from her face. "He could have stayed asleep for all I care."

She looks exhausted.

The black tight knit shirt with a black maxi skirt of the same material didn't hide the extra flesh she had gained. Tavelo became angry at the beaten down woman before him. Adelia may have been a spoiled brat but stronger than most and fierce.

As if reading his mind, Tesul stood to go over to her. She frowned, stepping back, anticipating the loving gesture. Tesul got his arms around her and squeezed.

"Good to see you're up." Tesul whispered softly in her ear.

Adelia's body sagged into him. She reluctantly returned the hug. The little one turned to them, a sadness creeping over his face. Tavelo pulled him tight and the boy cuddle into him.

"I hope you're up for a purge, Princess."

He saw her demure expression turn to rage. She pushed away from Tesul.

"It would be my pleasure to scrub this castle of vermin." She pulled down her shirt to straighten it. "I was tiring of being disrespected by those lowly invaders."

"Is there a meeting scheduled any time soon?" He asked.

"Next week." Tesul answered. "She's not allowed to attend. A decree from her mother."

"She wanted to keep me away from the politics

and nastiness."

"Well, that didn't work, did it?" Tavelo snapped, raising his brow.

"So, what do we do first?" Adelia's eyes gleamed.

"The punishment shouldn't be too severe. You've already shed blood on arrival." Armon said.

"I heard about that." Adelia snorted. "Wish I was awake to see it."

Tavelo stared up at the ceiling, deep in thought, then met their gaze.

"It's midday." Tavelo gave a fiendish smile. "Let's open a few coffins and curtains."

❀ ❀ ❀

Chaos mingled with the smell of burning flesh filled the castle as the human vampires' coffins were flung open, their inhabitants dragged out into the early afternoon light streaming in the halls. Screams of agony created a cacophony of horror. Servants rushed to get clear of the scene, not wanting anything to do with it.

Tavelo stood at the end of the hall, staring deadpan. He felt no sympathy for any of them. When he tired of the noise, he nodded to Armon and his group. They dragged each one of the burnt vampires back into the darkness of an empty room with the windows covered in heavy drapes.

He waited a few minutes until the whimpers died down, then walked into the room. His hair hung loose against the dark silver, almost gun metal, robe over a royal blue Hakata. The wooden sandals made sharp clacks, striking the hard tile.

"I find your desecration and disrespect of my coven unacceptable. You will leave here and go back to your own covens. Make sure to send your masters my regards."

One vampire struggled into an upright position.

"We are not to return unless ordered. You have

not been here. This castle is under the leaders' hands."

Tavelo's eyes narrowed. He scanned the room, seeing defiance and arrogance.

"Take them back out and make sure they're dust."

Gasped of despair erupted. The vampire raised up a hand.

"Wait! You can't murder us all!"

Armon grabbed two vampires and started dragging them out.

"We will leave!" The vampire yelled. "Stop!"

Armon glanced over at Tavelo. He gave another nod and Armon dropped his load.

"You have two days to heal, and out my castle."

He turned and left, feeling dissatisfied. So much rage. It radiated through his whole body and out. He didn't know what to do with the massive emotion.

At the corner of the hall, Adelia stood leaning against the staircase rails. Her unruly hair appeared to have fought back, in protest, in the full ponytail that resembled a blonde shrub. The ribbon holding it together, on the verge of giving up.

"That wasn't much fun, was it?" She sighed dramatically. "I took a few of them out myself and watched their flesh peel back and felt nothing."

"The same." Tavelo eyed her. "Then what? It seems I am no longer considered a coven leader."

"Which is ridiculous since you could annihilate all of them in a single blow." He frowned, walking past her to go up the stairs. "Wanna see?"

He stopped. "What do you mean?"

She gave a sly smile.

"Someone cheated death to get footage of you in Volshin mode." She went past him up the stairs. "Let's just say I have far more respect for you than any of the others. Especially when I heard the Endaga family story."

Do I really want to see?

Tavelo felt intrigued yet terrified. He recalled the bits and pieces of memory he had of looking down at the emperor in Kataling form. The perspective seemed off.

Or was it?

"Show me."

Adelia didn't miss a step as she turned to him and smiled.

"As you wish. Follow me."

He noticed then how much she had matured. Yes, that privileged arrogance remained, but underneath resided the smart, practical woman he knew her to be. As a mother and, for currently keeping his coven intact, a queen.

She led him to the small auditorium of his home theater. He had broken down from requests decades before; himself fascinated with cinema and converted the room.

Each of the stadium's six curved rows held twenty seats to accommodate one hundred and twenty viewers. Deep blue velvet cushions on stainless steel frames. The remote controlled projector set mounted above behind them.

A concession area to the right held a popcorn machine, candy stand, and liquor cabinet with top shelf spirits arranged side by side. The same dark blue covered the floor, accented by light gray swirls. The floor to ceiling curtains used for the screen sat open on the wall.

He approved of the upgrades to the liquor area and a larger popcorn machine. Adelia opened a laptop on the long table against the far wall. She rummaged through the files until she found the right one.

The projector came to life, filling the screen with the computer display as the curtains came together. She brought up the file and clicked the play arrow before sitting next to him in the front row. Trepidation came over Tavelo.

This is a mistake!

He decided not to see. Adelia grabbed hold of his arm as he tried to get up and held him down.

Her strength astonished him.

"You need to see."

In larger-than-life full color, he watched his fight with the emperor. He saw himself on the ground morph, growing exponentially towards the sky. Like a dragon from Earth folklore. His gaze widened at the sight. At some point, he realized he hadn't breathed, and his first intake of air made him choke.

"Impressive, right?" Adelia said, her face almost childlike.

How many times had she watched this?

He noticed Armon and Tesul's presence in the back of the room. Their calmness let him know they, too, had seen the footage multiple times. He had to admit; even he feared his Volshin form. Adelia's words echoed within him.

That's why Pridric kept me in stasis so long. Why I was so hungry when I woke up.

Pridric starved him. Not to death. Eterenia and Yutel would have killed him. Pridric's family, always second or third in profit on their home world, flip-flopped between Callesi and Bryhel. On Earth, with one less family out of the loop, he saw opportunity.

"You will be attending the meeting with me." He blurted. Adelia stared at him in shock. "And you will tell your mother what transpired here. I'm sure none of the others keep her abreast of current affairs."

"She won't be happy." Adelia slumped in her seat and pouted.

"I'm not either!" Tavelo went stiff, sitting erect.

Tesul and Armon glanced at each other. They went down to stand near him. Adelia cocked her head, puzzled.

"What is it?" Armon asked.

Tavelo turned to Adelia.

"Where is your guardian? Lariod." They all snapped straight as boards and looked away from him. "I won't ask you twice." His eyes glowed silver.

Tesul took two steps back from him.

"He tried to stop the takeover. When it was all said and done, they banished him to the dungeons. We don't know where exactly. They wouldn't tell us."

"So that we had no way of retrieving him." Armon added.

Tavelo stood. He fought with every fiber of his being not to morph into his Volshin state. It became such a simple thing to do. Knowing the outcome would not be ideal in this situation. A connection of tunnels throughout the territory created the underground level. For all they knew, Lariod could be closer to one of the other covens.

"You know who they were?" His voice slurred at the end from trying to watch his tongue.

"Of course, I do!" Adelia's body relaxed a bit. "I would have killed every last one if Tesul hadn't stopped me."

"It would have made things worse." Tesul said.

"Find them. We will make them tell us where he is." Tavelo walked up the sloped floor back to the hallway. "This won't stand."

❀ ❀ ❀

Still recuperating from their burns, three vampires from another coven were hauled into a damp cove above the dungeon staircase. The dark stone made the pitch-black cling to their skin. Adelia, Tavelo, Tesul and Armon followed close behind them.

"Lead us to him." Tavelo spoke in a terse tone.

The three glanced back at their tormentors, each flinching at the combination of eye colors glowing at them. Malice in all. They headed down into the deep, using the walls to steady their weakened bodies.

For twenty minutes they walked, and Tavelo noticed the edge of where his castle ended and the entrance to a long stretch of tunnel started that led to another loomed closer. They finally rounded a smooth mound of stone that separated the carved-out path from the dank ruins. The scent of decay and mold assaulted the group. Foreboding set in.

At a five-foot-high cave with a narrow opening, inside resembling a black hole, the three vampires halted. Adelia's face contorted into something hideous. Even Tavelo moved away from her. If the three were smart, they would have, too.

"Give me a torch!"

The vampire closest to her reached over to lift one of the thick wooden torches from its holder attached to the wall. He used a lighter to ignite it and she snatched it from him.

"Adelia," Tesul yelled. "Don't!"

The flames shone onto a naked figure inside the cave secured to the far wall by their wrists and ankles with black iron clamps. Dark, greasy hair, not washed in what may have been years, hung down past their knees, blocking most of their features like a curtain.

Directly below, on the crumbling dirt floor, a dark pool formed where liquid seeped down. Maggots squirmed, delighting in the abundant meal of blood, urine, and excrement.

Before anyone could stop her, Adelia let out a bloodcurdling scream and swiped a taloned hand across to her left. The head of the vampire who handed her the torch went flying backwards, hitting the wall near Armon.

The other two forced their way past Tavelo, but not Tesul, who knocked them unconscious with a blow to the head.

Tavelo watched Adelia ram the torch into the ground and step closer to Lariod. The once magnificent warrior's body hung rail thin, starved. Signs of being bled out little by little. Enough to keep him alive. Pure hatred consumed him, and by the look in Adelia's eyes, it had taken hold of her as well.

"Get him down," Tavelo ordered.

Armon and Tesul went over, each taking a side, and pulled the clamps from his wrists.

Lariod's body jerked down an inch.

"Be gentle!" Adelia screamed. Tears of blood streamed down her cheeks. "Gently," she whispered.

"No matter how we do it, Princess, it will do harm," Armon said.

Adelia's knees buckled, and she almost went to the ground. Somehow, she stopped herself to regain her stance. Tesul cradled Lariod in his arms. Stooping low to exit the cave, he went ahead of them, back through the dungeon, towards the main staircase.

"What do you want to do about them?" Armon asked, nodding towards the vampres.

Adelia turned around, eyes glowing red.

"They are mine!"

"No." Tavelo blocked her advance. "We will take them with us to the meeting." He nodded to Armon, who held up his smartphone, showing the picture of Lariod attached to the wall. "Their coven leaders must explain and suffer the consequences." Her mouth opened to protest. "Your first and only priority is to get your guardian back in good health."

Deflated, she backed off and went after Tesul.

"Suffer the consequences?" Armon's fiery stare locked with his. "We should have killed them all." He kicked the severed head out of the way.

❀ ❀ ❀

Rows of luxury vehicles formed a queue in front of the Sapienti Coven's circular driveway. The massive estate loomed over the sparse wilderness. Servants, now playing valets, wore black suits with stark white shirts. They hurriedly opened the doors of the next vehicle as it pulled up after the previous drove off. Without much fanfare, they ushered the guests through the front entrance.

The Durante's vehicle sat last in line on purpose. Tavelo had requested his group to wait until the last minute to leave in order to arrive barely on time.

He sat uncomfortably in the back passenger seat due to the tailored suit. A deep blue with a satin sheen and a black shirt underneath. The tie and kerchief matched the suit. Hair brushed to perfection; a silver ribbon secured the top half away from his face.

Adelia, in an A-line cut dress in Durante blue, snorted as she glanced over at him.

"What is it now?" He leaned against the window, propping his elbow on the ledge. "I'm not in the mood."

"You look like a Yakuza boss."

She burst into laughter.

He gave her a rude side stare. Out of the corner of his eye, he saw Armon trying to stifle a laugh, let out a similar snort. Tesul smirked.

"Well, in any case. You look authoritative. Not someone to mince words with." Adelia said.

Between Armon and Tesul, who sat facing them, were the two vampires. The others he released were already back at their own covens. They sat mute, their heads down.

Speaking of heads. Tavelo grinned.

Across from them sat a gift box beautifully wrapped in shiny blue paper accented by a wide white glittered ribbon in a bow atop the lid. The rest of the body lay stowed in the trunk in case his master requested it back.

I'm not a total monster.

Ahead of them, the Grieger coven representatives exited their vehicle. Yutel had that grave scowl on his face. It deepened when he looked Tavelo's way. While one servant escorted the group inside, another had already rounded the front of the car, got in and drove it off. Tavelo's driver inched theirs forward to the staging mark.

The servant ran up to the doors.

Before they could reach the handle, Armon stepped out and blocked them. Confused, they looked back at their counterpart.

The other shook his head, a signal to back away.

"Good call." Armon tugged the hem of his jacket and opened the back door all the way. "Lord Durante."

Tavelo stepped out of the vehicle, straightening his jacket as well. He walked to the entrance and waited for the rest of his entourage. Adelia climbed out, holding the box, followed by the two vampires, then Tesul.

In tight formation, the servant led them into the grand hall where the other coven leaders assembled.

The conversation nearly hushed as his group entered. Tavelo saw Eterenia step forward, then change her mind. She looked around the room as if afraid someone had seen her. He could feel Adelia bristle next to him.

Stay calm! He advised her telepathically.

Easy for you! She replied.

A mix of human advisors and vampires, along with a handful of werewolves, were in attendance. That meant they had to play their parts accordingly. Darean came towards him, arms raised at his sides.

"Count Durante!" The rest of the room turned their attention to him. "So good to see you awake. It's been too long."

Is he about to embrace me?

Tavelo stared wide eyed as the man approached and suddenly wrapped him in a bear hug. He didn't return the gesture for a moment, contemplating if he should shove the man off. He tentatively placed his hands on the man's back.

"How was your nap?" Darean snickered in his ear.

"I could eat an entire coven right now," Tavelo sneered back.

Darean released him. They locked in a hostile gaze.

"Now, let's not crowd him," Holnar chided. "He hasn't had much time to recover. Two weeks, is it?"

"Princess Adelia." Darean frowned. "Odd seeing you here at the meeting."

"I wasn't invited before," she snapped.

"Well, that's because you are not a coven leader, dear." He looked around her. "That guardian of yours decided not to grace us with his presence?"

A squeaky, grating sound made Tavelo and Darean look over to see Adelia's talons grip the box.

"I disagree." Tavelo walked past him, slightly brushing his shoulder as he went.

"You will not disrespect me in my home, Count Durante." Darean said softly.

"Is that so? But it's okay to disrespect mine while I was away?"

"That's not true. We have done no such thing." Yutel halted taking a sip of his drink. "You, on the other hand sent our people home still healing from the torture your coven administered. They were only there as guardians and proxies."

"What you did was unnecessary." Holnar leaned back in the loveseat ten feet away. "Have you gone mad as a result from your deep slumber?"

"I'm sure there is a valid explanation for this," Eterenia said.

"You will keep defending him regardless of his actions." Darean turned to her.

"I know him better than any of you! He wouldn't do this without a reason!" Her eyes flashed silver.

Pridric sat farthest away in a single high-backed chair. He eyed Tavelo with disdain then shifted his gaze to the two vampires behind Adelia.

"You seemed to have brought one of my pets along with another." Pridric stated.

"Yes." Holnar also looked over. "That one is mine."

"I am missing one though." Pridric's eyes turned silver as he eyed the box.

He knows. He understands.

Tavelo returned his stare with equal rage.

"You meet, deciding the fate and business needs of your peers without so much as an inkling of how it should be done. My company has been taken over without my consent, my trade contacts eroded. Tell me, my friends," his emphasis on friends grated. "What is your end game?"

Darean's face went flush, and he spun around to find himself staring at Tavelo's back.

"We made sure your trade remained intact!"

"Except for those unfortunate incidents Count Ambrook caused the proxy Queen Erena appointed." Chelayl took a sip of her wine and waved a servant with the hors d'ouvres tray to her.

The room went silent, and she looked up.

"Were we supposed to hide it until later? I thought we agreed we would not shield Count Ambrook from Count Durante's wrath."

Holnar slid a hand down over his face and stopped halfway. Yutel's scowl, which had softened with liquor, returned. Tesul pushed the two vampires forward. They stumbled on their feet, then steadied behind Darean.

"Tell them what you've been up to the last few years in my castle."

Tavelo turned around to face them.

Both became nervous as the entire room focused on them. Holnar removed his hand, looking puzzled, as did the other coven leaders. Pridric balled his hand in his lap.

"It wasn't our idea. The Marchand coven," the first began. "We were told to make sure the coven remained represented for trade purposes."

The other picked up the rest.

"After a while, the Ambrook coven guys said their master needed the castle locked down. There were some discrepancies. When we tried to investigate, the coven rebelled against us."

"We asked what the next step should be. And was told to apply a sort of martial law. No specifics."

"So we, the vampires from the other covens, did it our way." The second man added.

"Princess Adelia would make herself available for business meetings with the proxy and not discuss anything that went on in the castle."

Eterenia went to Adelia and grabbed her face.

"Were you lying to me this whole time when I inquired about your state of mind?"

"I had no choice!" Adelia pulled from her.

Tesul approached her side and gently touched Eterenia's wrist, easing it down.

"I begged her to submit to lessen the damage. We were outnumbered and blindsided." Tesul placed a hand on Adelia's shoulder. "She has the resolve of titanium."

Armon clenched his fists angrily.

"If you won't tell them, I will. They kept the werewolves in a single wing, forcing them to be sentries for them. Not the coven. They were only let out once a month for hunting, essentially starving them."

Loud gasps erupted. Darean went pale. Yutel flashed over to Pridric and lifted him off the chair by the front of his jacket.

"What have you done this time?"

Pridric reached under Yutel's arm, knocking it away, then with one hand pushed him ten feet back. Yutel slid to a stop, eyes red as his fangs and talons protruded.

"No!" Darean ordered. "That will not happen here! Stand down, Count Grieger."

Yutel's personal guard coaxed him away and handed back his drink.

"Lady Adelia and her children were prisoners." Armon continued. "They were only permitted on certain areas of the property. Never near the entrance unless she was going for business reasons."

"Okay." Darean nodded. "We have a serious problem at hand." He turned to the two vampires. "Why bring just these two? Why when they have said it was not them, Marchand or I, ,who started this?"

The two vampires stiffened.

"Go on," Tavelo teased. "Tell me what you've done."

They shook their heads, scanning the room for an escape. Holnar got up. His expression one of murder.

"Do not make me come and ask you," he ordered addressing his vampire.

"The riot," the other stuttered. "We tried to get the Princess back into her chambers. Her guardian, Lariod would not budge."

Eterenia clutched her stomach while also meeting Adelia's gaze.

"He was not going to let us do what was required. It took nearly twenty of us to take him down."

Holnar reached his vampire instantly, talons tearing into the fabric of the man's shirt.

"Where is her guardian?"

In the midst of the storytelling, Armon quietly moved over to the projector used for meetings and docked his phone. The machine whirred to life and the far wall lit up. Everyone turned.

Within seconds, it displayed the giant image of Lariod in the cave. Some of the women screamed. Even Pridric stared at it in horror. Yutel's drink slipped out of his hands and crashed onto the floor. Holnar's grip on his vampire went slack.

"They were the ones who put him there," Adelia cooed. "There were three." She walked over to Pridric and handed him the box. "Here he is. If you want the rest of him, I can go fetch it." Her face scrunched. "I only wish I could have seen his face when his head flew off."

Tavelo pivoted back to the hall doors.

"All of my assets will be returned to me. I know this was to be a collective for negotiating trade with our home world. One of my spies brought me up to speed. He never trusted any of you while I slept." He twirled a finger in the air. "We're leaving."

"The meeting." Darean said slowly. "It hasn't…" He stopped.

Eterenia stepped away from Adelia as she passed by. The look of despair, sadness, and hate made her flinch. Tavelo gave her a forlorn look. They would have to reconnect another time.

Armon disconnected his phone from the projector. He met with Tesul, Adelia, and Tavelo at the doors. Tavelo stopped.

"Oh," he addressed Pridric. "Did you want the other half? We have it in our trunk."

"Yes," Pridric hissed.

An Ambrook vampire followed the group out to retrieve the body.

Collaboration

Metal clanking on metal in a steady rhythm echoed the halls. The wide band cuffs on Emperor Manel's wrist gave little room for movement. The chains connecting them attached to another around his waist. They bobbed against each other as he strolled between a unit of guards.

He wore a long-sleeved, full-length robe. An elaborate one-inch-wide gold design ran from the front collar to around the bottom hem with dark grayish brown embellishments. His hair had grown out into a wild mess of cowlicks just below his ears.

The emperor smirked, his normally red eyes now a soft amber, yet still menacing. Master Jaubro, walked on his right side, with his personal assistant, Desedon, on the left to monitor him. They were on their daily midafternoon walk through the palace.

Some days, the emperor chose to be uncooperative, and this was one of them. Restraints became necessary long ago. They had administered a mild sedative to keep him calmer than usual.

"We received word from Earth." Master Jaubro started the conversation. Emperor Manel's expression wavered, the smile faltering before it returned. "A trade contract is being proposed."

"What could Earth possibly have that we want on our home world?"

"Mostly novelty. I think it a worthy experiment, to see how our people respond to goods so far out of our imminent three systems."

Emperor Manel stared upward, contemplating. Master Jaubro never liked it when he did that. Ideas from Manel's tainted; broken mind bordered on madness. The medical scientists worked daily on multiple remedies to restore what should have been his normal state.

So far, they had corrected a third of his internal features and his Kataling morphing under control.

"And how do you propose doing this without my consent?"

Imprisoned he may be, he still reigned as the emperor. Master Jaubro inhaled slowly through his nose, expanding his chest, then let it out. He felt more like a babysitter than a prison ward.

"I'm conversing with you now for your consent."

"Is that so?" The emperor's eyes shifted towards him. A gleam of malice flashed, then disappeared, replaced by playfulness. "I'll bite." He looked down the massive hall. "What do you want?"

"This would entail the entire royal family."

"How do you figure?" Emperor Manel stopped. The metal clanking silent. "I have no desire to force my family to reconcile with me or my decisions."

"But you should. Our planet's success depends on a better trade. Your actions sabotaged so many connections, we are still trying to recover."

The emperor turned and held up his wrists.

"Then remove these so we can talk like civilized business entities." He smiled wider.

Jaubro's assistant glanced over at him with a warning look. Master Jaubro pursed his lips.

"Hand me the key." One of the guards reached over and placed it in his open palm. He took the small cylinder and touched the sensor in the middle of the bands. "Please remember our deal. I won't hesitate to put you down."

They snapped open with an electronic ping. He removed them and the whole chain link from the emperor's person, passing it to the guard, handing Desedon the key.

"Oh, I haven't." The emperor rotated his wrists and shook his hands. "I hope you're not assuming I take up the task of routing them out."

"They are your family. You need to be on the same page. And besides. It's about bloodlines, is it not?"

"We do not have the same mothers. My father was a sadist and a whore."

"And you're not?" Master Jaubro readied himself for retaliation in bringing up the sore subject. "The things you have done?" He watched the emperor's fingers twitch, his talons growing half an inch.

"True." His brow rose. "I am not much different."

"Then I leave it up to you. You're the only one who knows where you may have imprisoned them in this sprawling palace."

"I've forgotten." The emperor shrugged.

"That's a given. But you have an idea. The trade agreements will need royal decrees and with our contacts stretched out, you can't do all of them at once."

"I understand," the emperor sneered. His amber eyes flickered red for a nanosecond. "What is my timeline?"

Master Jaubro's mouth turned down.

"Hmm. Let's say one Earth year, which is about three of our moon cycles."

"Fine." The emperor's expression became playful again. "Now, let's go outside and stroll the citadel."

❀ ❀ ❀

After a day full of uneventful incidents, Master Jaubro settled into his personal chamber inside the palace and breathed easy. He sat in his lounge chair and closed his eyes, letting his head fall back top.

His assistant closed the doors as he entered and sat across from him.

"Master Jaubro."

"Yes?"

"Those children will be worse than the emperor. They have a deep seeded hatred for their father and him, if I may. It would be like wrangling a herd of deranged baby Katalings."

"You think they are all Katalings?" Master Jaubro raised his head, opening his eyes.

"I don't doubt it for a moment. Seeing how the emperor turned out, we know he experimented with his own DNA. I found five in the royal registry."

"He surely had more than that!"

"He did. They were all destroyed after birth when the tests weren't to his liking."

Master Jaubro winced.

The emperor had done the same as his father during his reign. A vicious cycle inherited through blood. He realized early on that the young emperor never had a chance of living a normal life. The father molded the son in his image.

"Well, our emperor will have to find some sense of compassion and convince his siblings that he is not the enemy. They need to work together."

"For the sake of our planet."

"And themselves. This circle of atrocity must be broken."

"Does this also mean we reunite him with his personal guard?"

"Has he been behaving as well?"

"Somewhat." Desedon leaned forward. "He still thinks we are tormenting the emperor. His deep sense of loyalty is unlike anything I've ever seen."

"Yes. It is disturbing." Master Jaubro sat straight in his chair. "Have him released. He may be the one to keep the emperor out of trouble for a while."

❀ ❀ ❀

Emperor Manel sat on his throne, brooding as he thought about his siblings. The act alone made him feel sour and he wanted to abandon the whole idea. His eyes narrowed, flickering between amber and red. He tapped a taloned finger against his temple while his head leaned against the throne's curved back.

His father had banished two of his siblings to the dungeons. One remained part of his armed guards. He had thrown them down there as well after his coup, assigning them to work as door sentries. The last, a girl of barely fourteen at the time, and the youngest, lost to him in a fight.

Noise from the corridor muffled by the closed doors broke his concentration. The six guards inside the throne room perked up, hands on their weapons, ready to defend. The doors flew open and four guards wrestling with another stumbled into the room. The struggle continued until the surrounding guards were thrown back.

They landed in disarray.

Gallic, his personal guard, stood victorious wearing only a tunic and leather pants with boots. He sheathed his longsword and went to the bottom of the throne. He knelt on one knee and bowed his head.

"My emperor. It is good to finally return to you."

The emperor frowned. "Then explain what that business was about."

Gallic lifted his head.

"They had apparently not received word of my return and attempted to block me from entering. They accosted me as I walked down the hall to you."

"Uhn." The emperor rolled his neck as he exhaled through his nose. He looked at the four guards getting to their feet. "Get out." They stared at him for a moment as if not sure they should obey. "I will rip you apart," he hissed.

They hurriedly regained their resolve and fled the throne room.

Gallic stood before him.

"I am here to be your shield and anything else you need from me."

"I know." The emperor stared down at him in disgust. "We have work to do." He got up from his throne and stepped down to the floor's level. "Come."

"As you wish."

The two walked out of the throne room with two other guards following. They walked the corridor in silence. Emperor Manel worked on containing his feelings of dread as he made his way to the stairs that led to the dungeon entrance. As they stood at the opened door of the stairwell, Gallic finally spoke.

"I was briefed by Jaubro on the agenda. What's the protocol for this?"

"What do you mean?"

"If any of them are indeed hostile and try to kill you, am I ordered to dispatch them beforehand?"

The emperor turned to him. "Absolutely not!" Gallic flinched. "Blood shed won't solve anything." His face softened. "As much as I would like to."

"And who are we going to contact first?"

"My eldest brother."

The emperor descended without any warning, forcing the rest to catch up. He wanted it over with quickly. His feet barely touched the stone steps as he sped down. At the landing, he stopped, faced with four guards standing in a row across the main threshold. Their swords were in front of them, tips resting on the stone floor.

"Emperor Manel." The one on the end at the right greeted him. "We have been told to stop you if you or your guards attempt to assassinate any of your siblings within these walls. Although you are emperor, we must defend the honor of the royal house above all else."

A nasty expression formed on the emperor's face, and he almost lunged forward. Gallic placed a hand on his shoulder.

"That said," Gallic replied. "If you disrespect your

emperor again, I will cut you down."

The four guards looked at him in disbelief. Emperor Manel knew their sentiment. He, too, could only take so much of Gallic's steel like loyalty.

"I will play along." The emperor waved them away. "For now." They parted, the two in the middle opening the doors. "Let's go see my elder brother."

The group moved through the entrance, floating bulbs coming to life as they went. The narrow corridor had no openings, making it feel constricted, claustrophobic. At the end, it sprawled out to an area of iron cages separated by stone walls. They were configured like a labyrinth to deter prisoners from talking to one another. The emperor walked up to the first guard.

"Where is my Elder brother?"

The guard pointed to the left. Taking a deep breath, he walked towards the edge of the first level. There, in front of the entrance to the other wing of the dungeon sat a guard twice the size of Manel.

Wild black hair curled slightly at the ends brushed along his broad shoulders. His tight-fitting uniform hinted at the definition beneath. His red eyes burned into Manel's.

"Why have you come down here?" His deep voice shook Manel's soul. "What prisoner do you have business with in this wing?"

"You." Manel's gaze didn't waver, determined to win this contest.

His brother sat straighter, a look of suspicion emerging. When his elder brother broke the stare first, Manel inwardly celebrated his victory.

"The reason?" His elder brother's fingers grazed the hilt of his longsword attached on a belt at his side.

"Royal family business. Regarding trade with a new world. A different solar system, really."

"So now you want to fix what you have broken?"

Manel balled his hands at his side.

"If that's how you want to put it." He felt his

heart race. "The fate of the planet rests on our cooperation."

His elder brother stood, towering over him. The hostile gaze more intense than before.

"It always has. You are the one who threw our home into chaos."

"Is that it?" Manel smiled up at him. "You'd punish our people over your hatred for me?"

His Elder brother tilted his head back.

"I don't hate you, little brother. I'm merely disappointed." He dropped his hand from the hilt. "I wanted to kill you for your sins." He eyed Gallic in a defense stance. "He wouldn't have fared much better."

"Yes, well, you would have torn him apart." He turned to Gallic. "Stand down."

When he didn't budge, his brother emitted a loud, guttural sound, startling the other guards in the dungeon. Gallic finally obeyed, his lack of fear disturbing. Then his eyes fixed on Manel.

"Then you'll want the others as well. I'll handle that for you. And gather them in a room to meet within the next few weeks."

Stifling his relief at not having to go to each one, Manel nodded.

"I thank you." He smiled, all teeth, like a predator. His brother returned a smile of his own. Frightening even to the emperor. "I will leave you to it."

Manel hurriedly turned around, bumping into Gallic and the others as he pushed his way back to the main corridor. He felt the need to flee. That thing called his brother was why he didn't personally go after him during the coup.

He would have lost his life.

A communications room set inside the palace long ago now acted as a relay hub between the other solar systems for trade purposes. They added Earth after the emperor's downfall. The soldiers working inside wore only their battle suits. No need to have the full cape, helmet, and weapons although, their swords stayed by their sides.

Forty stations in all spanned the room.

Master Jaubro perused the aisles, watching the feeds flood with information. He stopped at the one for Earth. So engrossed in his task, the worker didn't acknowledge him at first. Master Jaubro leaned over his shoulder and the worker jumped, instinctively grabbing the hilt of his sword next to him. He glared at Jaubro as he eased back up, releasing it.

"I would advise you to refrain from that in the future." The worker frowned at him.

"Oh?" Master Jaubro stared back. "Were you, perhaps, going to try your best to defeat me?" The worker went pale, still looking defiant out of pride. "We need to send a message to our merchants on Earth." The look of disgust that crossed the worker's face made Master Jaubro angry. "Are you not up to the task?"

The worker sputtered at the insult. "How dare you…" He stopped, realizing he would make a scene. Some of the others had turned their attention to his station. The overseer glared at him. "My apologies. I would gladly assist. What is the message?"

"Very good." Master Jaubro stood tall, pushing his hands into his pants pockets. "Tell them they need to assess all goods viable for intergalactic transport and revenue. Timeline, one Earth year from date of receiving this message."

The worker touched the icons on his panel that corresponded with the words. A triangular symbol turned back and forth, the send indicator ticking across the bottom until it went red.

"Send complete," the worker said in a huff.

"Thank you. That should give us time to prepare as well." He turned around and locked eyes with the Royal Trade Commissioner who had crept up on him. "Don't you agree?"

In dark billowy robes with puffed shoulders and an ornate black hat, the commissioner resembled a human from the Renaissance era. The similarities in fashion amongst the elite from both races amazed Master Jaubro.

The commissioner's face contorted in aversion.

"That depends on what comes to our shores." He turned around to walk side by side with Master Jaubro. "This is new territory. We've never ventured so far out of our three systems. They may be alike in species, but they are so fundamentally different. That goes for their planetary resources."

"I believe this is a blessing in disguise. A positive after such a tragedy."

The commissioner let out a loud sigh.

"In hindsight, we should have tried to rein the emperor in." He placed both hands into the sleeves of his robe. "He's dangerous."

"That's not accurate. He's merely a product of his upbringing and environment."

"You're being kind."

"I think he can be saved."

They made their way down the main corridor, sparse with servants traveling along the walls to stay clear of them. Their heads were held down in fear. Master Jaubro hated seeing that. The class system on their world had begun to rot. He knew firsthand how much his own family had contributed to the demise.

Nothing as cruel as the Strana family towards the Endagas. He had a suspicion on what that was about. It brought him to his niece on Earth with Tavelo. The last time he had heard from her, conflict had ensued, caused by Pridric.

"What are you thinking exactly?" The commissioner asked.

"Food items, hard commodities, artwork."

"Hmm. I did see various examples. The edible fare may be touchy."

"We're having a collective meeting to consider multiple ways of preserving them."

"Good, good. The metals are interesting as well. Soft compared to ours, but I think they can be used for disposable or everyday things."

"Yes."

An entourage of guards rounded the corner at the end of the corridor, and they saw the emperor with his personal guard in the center. Master Jaubro noted the look of terror from the emperor and wondered what had happened.

As the two groups came together, he placed a hand on the commissioner to be silent.

"Emperor. What have you been up to this day?"

The emperor became enraged, his eyes turning blood red.

"What you asked." He replied through gritted teeth, growing fangs.

This could be bad.

Master Jaubro sent Desedon an urgent message. *Get here. Quickly!*

He gently pushed the commissioner behind him.

"I see you're agitated. Let's remain calm, hmm?"

His personal guard came forward as expected to defend the emperor.

"You have harmed him more than enough!"

He went into a stance, drawing his sword, ready to fight, then sent flying as the emperor knocked him out of the way. Manel's black talons grew thicker and the robe began to tear as he went down into a crawling position, on the verge of morphing into his Kataling form.

The guards behind the emperor were also tossed back as Desedon came barreling forward, syringe gun in hand. He leapt into the air and, nearing the emperor, plunged the tip deep into his back.

Manel howled in rage, swinging his body around to dislodge the assistant. Desedon hit the injection button and the emperor bucked a few times before laying still, mid transformation.

His body reverted slowly.

"Nice timing."

Master Jaubro commended his assistant.

"Your message sounded quite dire." Desedon stood, releasing the syringe. Its tip retracted. "He was doing so well."

"You," Desedon turned to the nearest soldier recovering off the floor. "What happened?"

"He went down in the dungeon to talk with his eldest brother, General Megen."

"Oh." Master Jaubro's lips went thin.

"He seemed terrified of him." The soldier's mouth almost turned up in a smile and he rethought the act. "So were we."

"As you should. Even the emperor could not best him at his strongest." He turned to his personal guard. "Pick him up and take him to his chamber. I will have a medical team there later."

Gallic gave him a hateful look and reluctantly got to his feet. He flipped the emperor over and cradled his body close to his own before lifting him up. The somber entourage went past Master Jaubro and the commissioner.

"Still think he is not dangerous?" The commissioner chided with a smirk.

Master Jaubro turned to him, eyes silver, and the commissioner flinched.

CHAPTER TWO

Human Element

The decreased flow of activity in the Marchand estate correlated with late night meeting. Holnar had ordered most of the staff to retire until it ended. Only a few servants were left to set up the room and wait on the coven leaders.

Chalayl motioned one of the servants over. She whispered in their ear. They nodded and walked off to the spread of treats on the long table against the wall.

"Really, dear," Darean sighed. "I wonder how you have not gained a ton."

She glared at him as she settled into the fancy loveseat with floral embroidery.

"I can only imagine what she asked for," Holnar tsked.

"The whole damn platter, obviously." Pridric sneered. "Like the glutton she is."

Silence. Pridric bristled at the response. Yet again he had somehow crossed a line.

"That was uncalled for," Eterenia snapped.

"As usual." Tavelo walked into the room, Tesul behind him. "He can't help himself."

Holnar raised a glass to him from where he sat on a lounge chaise, his legs stretched out.

"Tavelo! have you come to actually engage in the meeting, or have you brought another gift for us?"

The two men's gaze locked.

Tavelo's not amused.

"Can we not check each other's genitals size? We have more pressing matters to attend to."

Eterenia sat in one of the tall high back chairs, crossing her legs. The maroon maxi dress flowed along them like silk. Her hair pulled back tight and secured with a clip, hung in big curls.

"It's what they do." Yutel's burly body nearly burst against the seams of his suit. "I don't understand when I have the upper hand in that department."

He tossed back the last of his bourbon.

This time, Darean burst out laughing, breaking the tense mood.

"Enough of this," Holnar said. "Sit down, Tavelo. Have a drink." He snapped his fingers, and a servant ran to his side. He turned to Tavelo. "Tell him what you need. Tesul, are you having one as well?"

Tesul glanced at his master who nodded.

"I can." He sat next to Tavelo. "A beer."

"Fine," Tavelo said in defeat. "A gin and tonic."

The servant bowed and went to fetch their drinks.

"Pfft! You're going to need something stronger after this." Holnar said.

They all got comfortable while one of the servants connected the computer feed to relay messages from their satellite. The holoscreen lit up, taking up most of the far wall and the message from their home world spread across it. Lips went thin, eyes narrowed, and no one said a word for quite a while.

"Well." Darean placed the fingers of one hand on his temples. "We did expect this."

"And we should have been more prepared." Pridric slapped his napkin on his lap. "Now you see why I had to take the reins over your slow responses?"

"No." Holnar replied. "That was your greed."

"The pot calling the kettle?" Chalayl mocked.

"Hold your tongue, woman," he warned.

"For food, I say we start with dried goods first. Less chance of spoilage," she said. "Spices mostly."

"Very good," Darean nodded in approval.

"I can handle the metals. We have to make sure they remain stable is all." Yutel undid his jacket as he sat forward on the edge of his seat with both legs spread wide. "I'd rather do finished goods as opposed to raw materials."

"To start, yes." Holnar stated.

"Most of the imports I deal with are still porcelains and teas," Tavelo added. "I feel the same. Not sure such fragile pieces would make it."

"Well, we need to figure out something." Holnar leaned back. "Our reputation and lineage is at stake if we mess up such an opportunity."

"A new trade planet to add to the empire." Pridric seemed far away, his expression, drunk on ambition.

❈ ❈ ❈

The leaders' offspring had taken far too long to come together. They booked a ballroom equipped with a projector and other required hookups to accommodate their party. They opted for the catering service. Tables covered in food and various spirits lined the main wall. Three giant chandeliers high in the ceiling lit the place, giving it a soft ambience.

Calm was the goal for the day.

They filed in, perusing the tables to gather their first round of drinks and snacks then headed to the round tables set up in a cluster. The French vanilla table clothes added to the soothing atmosphere. One table sat a few feet away from the others in the front of the stage. That is where Chase and Baltise sat with Adelia.

Olette, usually all frills oozing femininity, wore khaki cargo pants, a black tank top and an untucked button-down shirt. Worn down combat boots graced her feet. Her twin brother came dressed similarly in a mechanic's jumpsuit. His hair had a raggedy cut that seemed like it wouldn't lie down no matter what.

Falson and his guardian looked exhausted. Both men had dark circles under their eyes. Their suits, once elegant, now appeared old, outdated. Chase felt his heart sink.

What happened to us?

The same appeared true of the others. They had had enough. He glanced at Adelia sitting next to him. She slowly ate from a plate of fruit, as if it were the last meal. Off in the corner, Lariod watched her.

"If you're all ready," Chase called out not too loud, getting their attention. "I think we should get this underway. As you know, our parents have decided to do business with their home world while cutting out the humans, and us."

Some shifted uneasily in their seats. They had gone up against Imperial forces, suffered loss, yet they were terrified of going against their parents.

"My father has been commissioned for a project," Tavelo's son, Tamar, said.

"The Marchand corporation is making plans to build a space port with support from Grieger." Olette brought her feet up onto the edge of her seat. She rested her hands on her knees. "The moment it is up and running, the humans will have no say."

"The revenue alone would be massive," Falson added.

"Aren't we jumping the gun?" Yutel's son, Chiron, asked. "They still have to figure out what goods can be transported. It all stems from the success of that."

"Do you really think they don't know what will and won't work?" Tamar replied.

A silent tension blanketed the room. They all knew the truth of the matter. No need to sugar coat the details. Chase took a sip of bourbon from the crystal tumbler in front of him.

"We;re not in the loop. I'm here to propose a solution." He looked over at Adelia. "Are you with me?"

Adelia stopped eating. She set down her fork and stared up at the others. Her eyes burned silver.

"The Ambrook Holdings company did some dirty deeds, impacting the other families. You all know this from our individual spy networks. That said, Chase is not part of the equation. I trust his judgement again on this matter."

"Right." Falson said. "We were born on Earth, not their home world. It was great to see it, but it is not ours. Humans are flawed. So are we."

"And that is why we will help them behind the scenes."

Chase scanned the room for any concerns.

"While lining our own pockets as well." Olivier raised his glass of wine. "We can establish our own global operation. A new generation in contrast to the old guard."

"You sound like father," Olette chided.

"Bite your tongue, woman." Olivier drank half the wine from his glass.

"My father is not much of a willing participant." Tamar leaned forward to set his folded arms on the table. "I did tell him about our meeting."

Angry protests erupted and Chase stood, waving his hands down to quell it. When it subsided, Tamar continued.

"And he sends his blessings. He warns it will be a hard road. The other leaders won't be hoodwinked for long."

"Our movements will eventually be seen as we go deeper into the business." Adelia picked up half a strawberry. "The backlash from Ambrook, Marchand, and Guillarmo will be fierce. Sapienti and Grieger companies may look at us as not being on the same playing field."

"They will underestimate us," Falson said.

"So, we prove them wrong." Chase took a small sip, his eyes closing to let the harsh liquid course through him. "My father is a Strana. I am an Ambrook. The same for you. These covens were once companies established by humans and run over by vampires."

"This is a dangerous game you're playing."

Chiron slumped back into his chair.

"Who's playing?" Falson and Olette snapped.

Olette set her legs down. "We are being serious."

"So, how do we do it?" Chiron sat straight. "What happens first?"

"We should create multiple companies but have it under one umbrella. Like they are doing." Tamar began. "That way, if they pinpoint just one, it doesn't hinder the rest."

"Which means, we need a scapegoat." Olivier stated. "A dummy corporation."

"I like the way you think." Adelia raised her wine glass still half full, the red liquid sloshing around. "As far as I can tell, De Luce is remaining neutral along with Durante." She frowned. "We can do this."

"Then a toast." Olivier stood, glass in hand. The others did the same. "To our success as independents from our power-hungry elders."

Everyone raised their glasses higher then drank. Chase managed a forced smile.

Let the trade battle begin.

❀ ❀ ❀

Fog rolled in from the ocean, cloaking the docks in a thick mist. The English Channel never disappointed. Tavelo wrapped his long trench coat around him to block some of the chill that came with it. Armon beside him, checked the incoming cargo on a ten inc,h tablet. It had a handle on the back where his hand fit in to balance it easily. A soft breeze swept through, bringing the ocean scent to their noses as it ruffled their hair.

"I was able to intercept a shipment that had been rerouted by Ambrook some time ago." Armon didn't look up from the tablet. He continued to swipe across the screen. "It was to arrive here to be split then redistributed."

"What was its original destination?"

Tavelo almost regretted asking.

"Italy. They were a shipment from our premium line. He won't be happy when it doesn't show up."

"I don't care."

"We're technically on his territory at the moment."

"He's going to have to endure. I won't be stolen from. Profit be damned."

They watched the workers grab hold of the ropes to tie the ship down as it docked. Their footsteps banged on the wooden planks along the wharf as they jumped around, securing everything.

Armon smirked.

"They are efficient." He finally turned to Tavelo and smiled. "The advantage of werewolves."

Tavelo eyed him dubiously. There were many vampires who resented having them around, seeing werewolves as an inferior species. Which was untrue. He marveled at their instincts and natural brute force. Then it dawned on him why the proxy said that.

"Are the vampires not pulling their weight?"

Armon rolled his eyes upward to the side then stared out at the docks.

"The coup wasn't merely contained to the castle and shipments. Your workers were either sent elsewhere or their access revoked."

"What did you say?"

Tavelo narrowed his eyes, seething.

"But, the werewolves are loyal to you more than any of the other coven leaders and they refused to be bullied by Ambrook vampires. When that happened, his workers refused to work with ours." Armon spread his arms wide. "Hence no Ambrook vampires on the Durante side of the English docks."

Stifling his anger, Tavelo took a deep breath, and exhaled slowly. Pridric's explanation of why he meddled in everyone's shipments he found unacceptable. He had heard how Yutel almost ripped his throat out over one of his.

Serves him right!

An off-rhythm clanking caught their attention and they turned to the sound.

"Well, speak of the devil," Armon said in a low, mocking tone.

Pridric walked towards them, the metal tip of his cane purposely struck the iron bands connecting the planks. The vision of a vampire aristocrat, he wore an all black suit and trench coat. His stark white shirt glowed in the fog and his hair hung loose under a black fedora. Chancellor Rayne kept in step next to him in similar attire with a dark red velvet scarf that hung to his waist accenting the look.

Four vampire guards followed.

"Imagine my surprise when I came to check on my docks and heard you were here." Pridric stopped a few feet from him. "There seems to be a misunderstanding regarding a lost shipment."

"Not at all. I misunderstood nothing." Tavelo turned around to face him.

"It's not lost." Pridric slammed the cane onto the ground and used it as a stand, bearing his weight on it. "I meant to evenly distribute it for a broader reach."

"Toldja," Armon said, still working on his tablet.

"Branching out would behoove your limited portfolio," Pridric continued.

"That's not your decision to make." He cocked his head to one side. "Did you think my family was unaware of yours stealing contracts behind our backs while sabotaging some of our business relationships with lies?"

Pridric blanched, stepping back from him.

Chancellor Rayne gave him a sympathetic stare.

"If it weren't for your family, we would have been far more lucrative than we were." Tavelo straightened his head and frowned. "This is not our home world. You will respect me from now on."

Pridric's baby blue eyes turned electric, the irises glowing.

He lifted his chin as if looking down on Tavelo.

"I don't have to do any such thing."

"My lord," Chancellor Rayne warned. "You need to see reason," he whispered to him.

Behind Tavelo, a few werewolves had stopped working, observing the scene. They moved in closer, anticipating a fight between leaders. He saw Armon's hand stop moving as he looked up and shook his head at them.

Thank you Eterenia for a competent ally.

Sensing the change in the air, Pridric regained his composure. He chewed on his tongue and Tavelo knew he contemplated something ugly. He flashed towards him, their noses barely touching. Pridric didn't move.

"Pridric," Tavelo said softly. "Unlike Dakien, I will tear you apart. And it would make us all sad. Is that what you want?" He searched Pridric's face.

"I despise you." Pridric stepped away from him. "More than that whore Chalayl."

"You really don't take rejection well, do you?"

A knowing look of irrational thought came over Pridric, which then made him angry.

"Finish your business here and leave." He turned from Tavelo.

"That shipment isn't coming," the Proxy yelled.

Pridric halted.

"Do what you please. I have other avenues for my gains." He continued walking, Chancellor Rayne and the guards in tow.

When they disappeared around stacks of cargo, Tavelo shook his head in disbelief. He turned back to the docks, and the werewolves resumed their tasks.

"And we thought it would be Marchand to go too far," Armon said. "Turns out he's the one with some sense of reason."

Holnar, that greedy bastard.

Tavelo made no mistake about him. He also knew the merchant valued the collective over money.

They were a tiny community on Earth that needed to stick together. His family acted the same way on their home world even when they ridiculed the Endagas. For every set back they had, courtesy of Pridric's family, the Bryhel's would find a new route or contact for them anonymously.

Or so they thought. Tavelo had figured it out when his father assigned him to handle shipments on the docks.

"What's coming again?" Tavelo asked Armon.

"One thousand porcelain sculptures with a new metal inlay for stronger integrity."

Tavelo pursed his lips at the thought. In his eyes, their initial beauty had been ruined by the process.

"Are they swans? Dragons? Cats?" He asked.

Armon grinned, trying not to laugh.

"They were actually requested by the royal commissioner from your home world."

"Oh?"

"Volshins and Katalings."

Tavelo's expression dropped in stunned silence. He blinked a few times.

"What?"

"To decorate the foyers of households to let their neighbors know who and what resides there. Kind of like a pride piece."

"Ugh!" Tavelo gripped his abdomen as it cramped with anxiety. "That's not pride. It's tacky."

"Oh, I totally agree. I kind of hope they don't make the trip intact."

"We can only be so lucky." Tavelo shivered as his coat opened. He closed it back. "Let's get this over with. I'll await in the office."

"Not going to inspect them? See the quality of the pieces?" Armon mocked.

"I'd rather not."

Inside the office, Tavelo couldn't see much out of the windows due to the fog thickening.

The forecast didn't expect the sun to come out, which meant it would not burn off by midday. He settled in a chair close to the vending machine in the lounge area. The thermometer showed the heat set at a comfortable seventy-two degrees, knocking off the chill. Tavelo drifted off to sleep.

The office door banged open, hitting the other side with a loud crack. Tavelo jolted awake. A strong wind blew in, sending papers flying and tossed small items across the room. He shielded his face from the assault and anything that may come his way.

Outside, a storm was underway.

Chancellor Rayne stepped through the entrance and took hold of the door, forcing it closed. He brushed off his coat and cleared debris from his hair by shaking his head.

"Working has stopped for the day." He walked over to the big metal desk on the other side of the room. "Got everyone tying stuff down."

"Is my shipment still out there?" Tavelo asked.

"No. We got it sealed back up and secured."

"Oh." Tavelo leaned back in his chair, disappointed. Chancellor Rayne noticed and gave him a questioning look. "If you knew what it was, you'd gladly toss it in the ocean and let it be taken."

"I'm not understanding."

"Commissioned art pieces for the royal districts."

"They can't be that bad. I know the royal families have some questionable aesthetics…"

"Katalings and Volshins," Tavelo said. Chancellor Rayne's eyes widened. "Seven feet tall. Porcelain and metal."

"You're joking." He deadpanned.

"On my honor."

Both men sat in silence for a moment.

Tavelo snickered first, then Chancellor Rayne let out a guffaw. They laughed for a solid minute, tears in both their eyes. When they finished, wiping them away, Tavelo set his feet on a chair and relaxed.

"Pridric doesn't despise you." Chancellor Rayne spoke. "His envy runs deep."

"I know."

"Then stop antagonizing him."

"He started this."

"What are you, children?"

Tavelo sighed and let his head fall back onto the window ledge behind him.

"Aren't we?"

Chancellor Rayne came and towered over him.

"Not even close. You're both way past that! Your childhoods ended at your one hundred year ceremonies. You should both know better at nearly three hundred and fifty years old."

"Then how come we don't feel like it?"

Chancellor Rayne sat back at the desk and propped his feet up on its corner.

"You need to figure that out on your own."

"And Pridric?"

"Needs to stop blaming others for his father's mistakes."

The door banged open again. Armon hurried in, followed by Pridric and the two vampire guards.

"Where the hell did that come from?" Armon yelled over the din of wind howling. He shook his hair out and brushed it with his fingers. "It got real nasty out there fast."

The last vampire in slammed the door shut, which muffled the sound. The two moved further in the room and watched the windows rattle off and on.

"I guess we're stuck here for a bit until it blows over." Chancellor Rayne looked around the room. "That means everyone is going to play nice."

Pridric, hair in disarray, his hat in one hand, gave him a nasty expression. He sat on the other end of the room on the same side as the door, far away from Tavelo. Armon eyed the vampire guards, daring them to start anything.

"Sit down," Chancellor Rayne ordered them all.

Tavelo laid his head back on the ledge to rest, closing his eyes. He tuned out the noise in the room and listened to the storm outside.

Its angry growl rumbled, mingling with the wind's whistle as it squeaked through cracks in the building structure. The chill on the windows cooled his head. Pings and scratching from items on the dock being carried across the boards, hitting everything, formed a rhythm that lulled him back to sleep.

His arms went slack at his sides.

Pridric watched Tavelo drift off.

Must be nice!

To be so carefree. Envy consumed him yet again, and he tried to push it away. The Endaga family. A compassionate, loving, and hardworking clan. Nothing like his own. In his mind, it came so easily for Tavelo. At the same time, he felt an urge to protect him from all the awful things in the universe. That's what angered him. He couldn't shake that feeling.

When Tavelo transformed into a Volshin while fighting the emperor, Pridric realized how high the stakes were. That the Endaga family, a line of first generation Volshins, had kept their secret from the royal regime.

Yet, his family sought to ridicule and bankrupt them for the simple reason of sick pleasure. He only wanted to be Tavelo's friend. He truly did. But his father would never allow it. And he started to believe everything his family said about the Endagas.

He felt eyes staring at him and turned. Chancellor Rayne giving him a forlorn look. The proxy looked up from his tablet, shaking his head in pity.

Did everyone know?

Pridric frowned. He brought his attention back to Tavelo and it struck him. Tavelo, beautiful and deadly, looked like a sleeping child.

❀ ❀ ❀

77

The imperial commander overseeing activities on Earth for the emperor watched the variety of goods from each coven leader's business loaded onto the ship that would transport it all to their home world.

A small cargo ship equipped with a flux engine capable of lightspeed. The hull had a matte effect, the sun not glaring on the dull silver. A ramp lay open, protruding from its lower section, letting workers load speedily. The red directional lights were lit, though not needed.

A shorter vortex path had been mapped.

The quicker the goods arrived on their planet and inspected; the faster contracts could be established. Details on how to preserve them from damage were scrutinized before implementation. Each container had its own vacuum seal allowing some items to free float inside or remain compact.

The commander stood akimbo; arms folded, her feet shoulder width apart, atop a staging platform built for the purpose of seeing the whole operation in one shot. She had peeked at some of the items and found them mediocre.

Then again, she wasn't much for material things. Her dark red cape fluttered against the back of her calves from a short breeze. A few wisps of dark hair that somehow made their way from under her helmet whipped across her eyes. She pushed them back in with one finger, going deep to ensure they stayed put.

One of the soldiers came up to her. He had what would probably be described as a permanent scowl. She had never seen the man's expression waver. He stepped up to the landing and placed one foot on the platform.

"We're almost done loading. The manifest is complete." His gruff tone matched his ire.

"Excellent. I will contact the trade commissioner. By the time he gets it, the ship will be halfway there."

"There really isn't much here to make profit on, in my opinion."

"I feel the same. Since we're here, though. We might as well find viable goods."

The soldier snorted. He removed his foot and walked back to the ship. She waited until it closed up before leaving the platform. With the main ship only a half a mile away, she decided to walk and take in the morning scene. Her boots crunched on the dry, rocky ground of the open field.

When her ship landed over a decade ago, the greenery previously there had been scorched bare.

She found sunlight tolerable in moderation and forced herself to stay in it at least a few hours a day to placate the humans. To show the government she was not one of those wretched vampires.

Those things! She shook her head in pity for the merchants crash landing on a random planet so far away and encountering a similar species only to find them inferior.

A small unit of armored vehicles formed in a row on her right sat static, the soldiers relaxing at tables set up in front of them. She glanced over, wondering why they felt so safe around her fleet. If the emperor decided to order annihilation tomorrow, they would all be wiped out by end of day. The report from the first fleet gave her a better insight on humans' sense of superiority.

Her ship came into view quicker than anticipated. Checking her wristband, she saw that twenty minutes had passed. Time went by so fast on Earth. She walked up the open ramp and headed to the command center. The doors slid open to a hushed room. Each station manned with soldiers did their jobs quietly. She stood by the communications tech.

"Send the message to the Trade Commissioner. The cargo will be leaving within the hour."

The technician frowned as he brought up the virtual screen linking Earth to their home world to eye level. The commander caught her reflection in the console below his arms and saw a similar scowl on her face. It never dawned on her that they all looked like that. The tech's arms raised, blocking her view, and she focused on the message being constructed.

"Make sure he knows to follow the unpack instructions to the letter. It would be a waste if the goods were ruined after getting there."

The technician nodded, tapping the icons as he formed the message.

"Are you also not excited for this opportunity?"

"I think we should do as planned in the beginning. Drag our merchants back home and leave this uncivilized planet."The technician replied.

"Hmm. Yes. They are being stubborn and refuse to see reason." She stood straight and sighed. "There is no turning back now. This planet has been exposed to another race. They can't undo it. And neither can we. As Master Jaubro of the merchants said, it's best to make it worth our wile."

"Message complete. Your assessment?"

The commander scanned it, making sure it was to her liking."

"Approved. Send it." The technician tapped the signal icon. While it uploaded, the commander went to the settle in her seat. "Now we bide our time and wait for a reply."

She thought about the previous commander now the emperor's personal guard. His way of doing things proved inefficient. Instead of toying with the humans, negotiating, he should have arrived in brutality and left no question as to his agenda.

Then she thought about what she had observed so far. It made sense. Hunting humans did not make for good sport. Or vampires, for that matter. It would be equivalent to slaughtering small animals.

Planetary Shift

Merchant leaders from across the planet gathered at the docks as the cargo ship from Earth eased into an open port along the wharf. The Trade Commissioner stood near the ramp waiting for it to extend when the ship opened. He noticed the crowd size. It surprised him, not sure why merchant families were interested.

The usual gloom of the sky displayed a comfortable light gray, blocking much of the harsh sun. A few waves rippled along the pier, rocking the smaller ships. In the sky above, two Volshins cruised around in a circle, watching for any disturbance.

Their majestic size and power always amazed him. He looked to his left at Master Jaubro and saw the trepidation on his face.

"Are you not confident in the condition of the goods?" He asked jokingly.

"Are you?" Master Jaubro turned to him, not amused. "This is a crucial moment."

"I agree. No sense in being pessimistic."

Master Jaubro stared at him, stunned.

"That is a reversal of thinking on your part."

"After much thought, I decided to hold my judgement for now."

"You merely want to see those gaudy ornaments you requested."

The Trade Commissioner feigned insult. His mouth opened slightly as his eyes widened.

"I am interested in studying the humans' craftsmanship." He smirked. "Besides, they're not gaudy. I feel our ancient beasts should be respected. Admired. Unlike how the emperor treated them."

The merchant leaders walked up as Master Jaubro turned around. Lord Endaga lingered in the back of the group not really paying attention while the others greeted him and the commissioner. A sense of shame mixed with anger nudged at him. The Endaga family had been devastated the most. Even as the other families tried to atone and help them back on their feet, they felt a lack of trust.

He didn't blame them.

Once the ship opened, the containers were hauled out on the floating pallets. The leaders took possession of the ones with their family crests and had them transported to their holding blocks. The commissioner followed Master Endaga while Master Jaubro went with his counterpart to the Jaubro's. He stood outside the work area making sure to stay out of the way as workers went back and forth.

The container's release activated, venting air. The lid popped open as the hydraulics whined from being locked down for so long. The lid split in two and went down the sides of the container. A wall of creamy figures glinting with metal inlay greeted the audience.

Master Endaga fell speechless as he watched his family workers stare at the things in awe. Not out of admiration; audacity. He couldn't imagine how Tavelo must have reacted when he got the commission for their creation. Only the royal community would display such atrocities in front of their homes for all to see.

His stomach felt queasy.

"Magnificent!" Commissioner Polp exclaimed, startling Master Endaga out of his thoughts. The man turned to him. "May I?" He gestured towards the container.

"As you please." Master Endaga raised a hand and swept it outward.

Commissioner Polp walked up to the container, the workers stepping back, horrified.

As they should be.

Master Endaga had no intention of mass producing them on his watch.

"Such detail." Commissioner Polp traced the outline of one. The clear sealant protected it from the skin oil on his fingers. He leaned closer. "There are a few minor discrepancies in the mold but that gives them their charm. Don't you think?" He turned his head to Master Endaga.

"I think this being their first attempt, it is," he struggled with the word. "Impressive."

One of the family members gawked at him. He shook his head at the member, who then closed his mouth tight.

"I had two of each set aside in the order for your family to have for prosperity."

Master Endaga grimaced, then glanced up at the things. With his hands still down at his sides, he waved them towards the statues.

"Get them ready for delivery to the royal palace." One of the workers handed him the tablet with the custody agreement already up. "Commissioner."

"Oh, yes."

Commissioner Polp pried himself away from his precious cargo and took the tablet. He read the usual verbiage then held his royal insignia stamp over the screen. The image superimposed on the signature line and the form disappeared, replaced by an accepted icon.

"I will be waiting in the transport once all the goods are ready to be loaded."

When he left, Master Endaga didn't move. Thoughts of destroying the statues danced in his head. As if reading his mind, a family member picked up a tool used for breaking apart metal.

"Would this do the trick?"

He hefted it up, gauging its weight.

Footsteps came from behind Master Endaga.

"What you need is a disintegrator," Master Jaubro

answered him as he came to stand by Lord Endaga. "Those are hideous."

"Can you imagine?"

"Sadly, I can." Master Jaubro couldn't pry his eyes from them.

"And what has your niece sent?"

"Textiles. Fabrics of different sorts."

"Anything of use?"

"We'll have to see how long they last on our world." He placed a hand on the side of his face. "Although, the waterproof ones seem promising."

"Oh?"

"How is it that in all these centuries we only protected ourselves from rain with overhead devices when we could have just worn waterproof attire?"

Master Endaga felt his eyes widen in revelation. Then jealousy sunk in. Why hadn't his family thought of that? In the same moment it came, so it went. He chastised himself. That's how the other merchant families thought.

"We have the means for mass production, but your family has the better seamstresses. Would you be willing to take on the order?"

That caught Master Endaga off guard, making him sputter.

"What? Well, yes. Of course."

"We are of one family now. All of us. One cannot and will not push out the others for profit." Master Jaubro turned to him, his hand dropping. "I know you are still hurt by our past transgressions. Please know, we are here for you." He slapped a hand on Endaga's shoulder. "And, we will get to see Eterenia and Tavelo's children along with the young ones in a couple of years."

"That arrogant child who calls himself a general can stay put on Earth."

Master Jaubro laughed. He cleared his throat.

"Yes, that one does not instill joy." He turned to leave. "By the way." Endaga looked over at him.

"My understanding is that Tavelo refused to see the finished product. I wouldn't tell him how bad they are when you send him the receipt notice."

Master Endaga watched him go. He heard a loud clang and saw the worker with the breaking tool stare at the edge of a metal work bench. A small burst pattern where he had struck it marred the surface.

His eyes narrowed.

"Enough. We are not doing that. Put it away and finish repacking it for transport. The faster we get them out of my sight, the better." *My poor nephew!* He walked down the promenade to get away from the scene.

At the edge of the docks, he found Lord Strana leaning against one of the large posts, his blond hair sticking up in the back from the wind hitting it. He inspected a small trinket held high in one hand. Endaga exhaled softly and went to walk past him. The man's leg came up and blocked his path, one foot set on the post opposite him.

"Really, Endaga? Let's not act childish about this."

"I was merely taking a stroll to clear my head."

"Yet, you were going to purposely walk past me and not say a thing. Acknowledge my presence."

That family's arrogance Endagas despised so much angered him. He stood still, not wanting to move for fear he may lunge at the man. Lord Strana set his foot down and stood to his full height of six feet five, only an inch taller, yet it somehow seemed much more.

"My father was a monster. A tyrant who ruled with an iron grip. It takes more than a few decades to remedy that. You need to be more patient with us." He pocketed the trinket. "Let's try this again."

Master Endaga clenched his fists tight, then released them.

"Good to see you. How was your shipment?"

"Likewise." Lord Strana smiled, amused. "Mm," he shrugged. "The quality isn't up to our standards, but the concept is sound." His head tilted back as he gave a playful stare. "I saw that order commissioned by the royal house. You should file a complaint."

"Against who? The Trade commissioner? And for what?"

"That's part of your family's problem." He tsked.

"And what's that?" Master Endaga spat, holding back his rage.

"You have all that clout and never use it to your advantage. Being honest isn't always the best way." He walked back towards his block. "Sometimes you have to get more than just surface dirty."

Master Endaga hung his head. He knew it to be true. His family always worked hard, getting their clothes ragged and filthy. They rarely had a chance to show off the impeccably made suits they tailored for themselves while watching others on the planet strut about in their craft. So many times, his brother could have pushed back on the false claims and sabotage.

But that is not our nature.

Endaga walked off the promenade onto the main road where transports lined up along the streets waiting to be loaded. His family took pride in treating everyone fairly, not causing rifts in the trade. The shriek of a Volshin soaring above made him look up.

Don't let them change you, Tavelo. Stay true.

Building multiple hubs for interstellar trade, though not an easy task, benefitted Earth. Government officials were the main obstacle. A meeting had been called at the start of the project, the coven leaders not bothering to contact them since they owned the property where the hubs were being built.

None of them saw a problem. Military, scientists, and country leaders, all converged on the concert auditorium in France courtesy of the Marchand coven.

Every face coming through the doors scrunched up with sour expressions.

Holnar gave an exasperated side glance to Darean standing beside him. Both men smirked as one of the world leaders glared at them with hateful indignation.

"They are so put out by this," Darean said. "You'd think we were asking for a peaceful enslavement."

"Aren't we, though?" Chalayl asked. "We're taking their sloppy trade system from them."

"They can still do," Darean waved a hand, "whatever it is they do. We are going for bigger fish."

"This is going to go badly," Pridric said as he came to stand with the others. "These humans have no idea how to run something like this."

"Who said they're running any of it?" Holnar asked.

There came a pause of realization. Tavelo crossed his arms, pulling the fabric of his jacket tight across his back. Eterenia continued to watch the humans flood in. With a collective thought, they agreed. Earth would be getting a lesson on how true commerce worked.

What occurred over the course of five hours did not constitute a meeting. More like a hostile take-over. The world leaders wanted incentives; a cut of the revenue for doing business in their countries. The military wanted soldiers used for security to over-see any violations. Every scientist itched to get their hands on anything alien that may come to Earth and wanted first dibs.

They talked over each other incessantly while the coven leaders sat back and watched, occasionally shutting down any of their absurd requests as they came up. When it finally dawned on the humans that they were getting nowhere, the room went silent.

"You will not even entertain the idea of including us in this even though this is our planet, not yours?" One of the world leaders asked. He leaned back in his seat, face flushed pink from yelling.

"You are being paid for goods produced up front. Why do you need to be involved as they leave for their destination off world?" Yutel asked. "The burden is on us."

"That's not the point!" Another leader shouted. "We should be doing our own trading!"

"No one is stopping you." Pridric scanned the room. "If you want to use the hub, pay the transport fees. I can't imagine what you would be sending and to whom."

"Yes," Yutel leaned forward in his seat. "What other planets are you trading with?"

"Please, do tell." Holnar's eyes went wide with anticipation.

The humans looked around at each other. The first leader spoke.

"Once we establish what's out there and what resources they possess that we may like and vice versa, we can start doing that."

"Oh. So, you want us to find other planets for you?" Tavelo said, amused. "I think not."

"How about we see how this goes first." Holnar stood. "You should all go home, sit back and watch how it's done."

❀ ❀ ❀

Goods from all around the world were being shipped to the three main docks. The space ports had been built in record time under two years due to the speed of vampire and werewolf workers. Not many humans contributed, not wanting to be that close in proximity to predators. The imperial fleet on Earth lent out some of their ships for transport until the home world sent interstellar cargo ships along with supplies for the merchant leaders.

Holnar rejoiced in the flow of business.

He stood watch over the assembly line of vehicles hauling product to the ships. The platform rose high above the dock level with metal handrails to hold on to so he wouldn't fall off. His dark grey suit, tailored to his physique, had a slight sheen to it. His celebratory way of expression.

Beside him, Pridric wearing his signature black suit sans fedora, said nothing. A deadpan look on face told Holnar the man wasn't even paying attention.

"You're not going to celebrate such a feat?"

"I think you pat yourself on the back enough for all of us. I just want this over with."

Holnar stared at him, sounding puzzled.

"Are you saying you want to go back home?"

"Perhaps." Pridric blinked, coming out of his state. "I don't mean that."

"I should hope not."

Holnar pitied him like a parent as the oldest with Darean, followed by Yutel. Pridric, Eterenia, and Tavelo, were the youngest. All three living in their parents' shadows.

"You need to establish your own path here. If it still does not bring you what you want, then look towards new avenues." He slapped Pridric on the back, causing him to grip the handrail harder. "Don't give in yet."

The two left the platform and took the stairwell to the communications room on the next level down. Everything was painted grey to match the metal fixtures. Their hard soled shoes made slapping sounds on the concrete steps. They reached the landing and Holnar pushed the door open to a narrow corridor on the other side.

They walked in silence to the end where a door with a panel reader sat. He placed his right hand on the panel. A green light appeared, and the door slid open.

A thousand square feet filled with computer consoles, holoscreens, and wall panels spread before them. Some fifty workers moved around the stations completing their tasks.

Ten humans assigned with keeping track of the shipments wirked inside. Holnar walked up to the manager.

"I need to contact the other hubs to make sure we are on track."

The manager nodded and went over to the main console. He touched a few icons and the holoscreen in front changed from static view to a communications logo twirling in the center. Then it went away, replaced by the inside of the other hubs' command stations side by side.

On the left, Yutel and Chalayl intimidate a worker, the poor human shrinking from their verbal assault. To the left Darean and Tavelo were so far from each other, they stood on opposite ends of the room.

"That's because of Tavelo," Pridric blurted out.

Holnar grimaced, giving him a side glare. Their behavior started to get old. Tugging his jacket down, he loudly cleared his throat to get the others' attention. All four turned to the screen, frowning, and walked towards it.

"Is everything a go on your end?" Holnar smiled brightly. "We have to make sure the launches are co-ordinated so the shipments arrive together."

"A couple of goods were loaded on the wrong ship due to human incompetence," Yutel replied in a raised voice. He pointed to the human nearby.

"I tried to tell him it's not an issue," Chalayl added.

"Correct." Holnar said. "As long as the goods go out, the destination is the same." He saw Yutel get ready to protest. He held up a hand. "I know. You want perfection."

"That's not it!" Yutel shouted.

"Everything is fine here." Darean leaned forward. "Queen Erena sent hers ahead with a proxy. There's a local fire to put out."

"The Prime Minister is not happy."

Tavelo picked at a nail on one hand while the other lay across his chest.

Negotiations

Winter air frosted the glass of the French doors inside Eterenia's chamber. The silent cold weighed down on the room. The giant heavy comforter piled atop the bed covered her and Tavelo, keeping them warm. Her arms had come from under it while sleeping and her body shivered. She pressed her body closer, snuggling her face into his chest. He squeezed her even more. Lilac and musk from his perspiring skin filled her nostrils and she breathed deep. His natural scent always left her in awe, and ecstasy.

"It is a bit cold in here." Tavelo opened his eyes and searched the room. He found one of the doors cracked open by a millimeter. Enough to bring in the freezing temperature. "I can close it."

He moved to sit up and Eterenia pulled him back.

"Uh uh. Stay here," she whispered.

"We have to get up in a few minutes, regardless."

"No." She buried herself further. He laughed softly. "I want you to stay."

Hearing the sadness and longing in her own voice, she covered her face with one hand. When Tavelo didn't respond, she looked over at him. He had a curious expression.

"I have a proposal on the matter." Tavelo propped himself up on his elbows. She raised her head. "I think it will solve all our issues."

"Is that so?"

"First." He kissed her hard, grabbing her behind the head and lifted her up with him. He disengaged and smiled mischievously. "We have to get up."

Eterenia pouted, then hit him hard in the chest, knocking him out of the bed.

"Such cruelty!" She rolled over and set her feet on the floor. "Yesh!" She fell back on the bed, bringing her feet up. "So cold!"

Tavelo went over to the doors and pulled the one shut, making sure it completely sealed. In an instant, the cold air ceased. The glass started to fog on the inside from the heat. He walked back to the bed and pulled Eterenia off. She hopped a few times on the cold floor while he laughed at her. She watched him, barefoot, wearing only a pair of boxer briefs, head to the closet oblivious to the cold.

So beautiful.

"You can't just stand there ogling me like a piece of fresh meat," he said, interrupting her daydream.

"This is my palace. I can do as I please." She threw off the flimsy sheer robe she slept in and went to stand at the closet alongside him. "Tell me your proposal."

They took their time getting dressed. Tavelo had picked out a pale blue shirt with navy slacks. He sat on the bed buttoning the cuffs while Eterenia pulled on a stretch knit maxi dress that hugged every curve of her body. She grabbed a red jacket and tossed it on the bed.

"Our families are blended now." Tavelo began. "And we have the two young ones. Adelia has already proven herself capable of being a leader." He buttoned up his shirt. "My proposal is this. You make Adelia Queen of the De Luce coven. I will have my cousin, Innego, take over mine. Then we can build a home of our own and raise those two demons ourselves."

Eterenia stopped in her tracks, eyes widened in disbelief. She stood stunned for a moment, thinking.

A sound idea. The logistics would work.

"What about Tesul? And my Valkyrie?"

"He would only guard me on outings. It would be like a human job. No reason to be away from his family all the time. And, Adelia has Lariod whether Tesul is there or not."

"The others won't like this."

"I don't' care what they think." Tavelo's tone filled with disdain.

"Where would we go?" Eterenia sat beside him.

"We can find a spot somewhere between our two palaces in the zone. That way we're not too far from either."

"And the covens? Who would be handling the daily agendas?"

"The covens are not synonymous with our business ventures. There's no conflict."

"A place of our own," Eterenia mused. "Together." She laid her head on his shoulder. "That sounds nice."

❀ ❀ ❀

Golden streams of sunlight were lessened in force by a single window high above the long aisle of the Durante study. Floor to ceiling bookshelves of dark wood lined both sides, making the room feel intimate while also vast. A small sitting area near the entrance held a loveseat, two chairs, and a coffee table. The late afternoon lull brought serenity.

Full lips pouting like a disobedient child, Adelia struggled to keep hold of her son Adulfo, Addy for short, squirming in her lap to get free as she made her demand.

"I want a family meal." She said, smacking Addy on the thigh which made him more unruly. "With my father."

Eterenia looked up from the tablet in her hand and set it down on her lap. The cotton fabric acted like Velcro, stopping it from sliding. Tavelo stopped reading and set his book face down on the armrest.

Until now, the serene, narrow study had been a center of calm.

"Why?" Eterenia frowned.

"I just need to do it." Adelia's expression changed to sorrow. Her son sensed the change in mood and stopped squirming. He turned around and placed his hands on her cheeks, smiling gleefully. "I want to know how he feels about me."

"Oh, Adelia." Eterenia lowered her head in guilt.

Of course, she wanted to see her father. Now a mother herself, Adelia needed closure. *And so do I, really.* She had last spoken to him before Adelia's birth.

"That would be one of Yutel's cousins, correct?" Tavelo asked.

Eterenia nodded. Addy abandoned his mother and went to her. She scooped him up, tossing the tablet on the side table, and let him get situated in her lap. Adelia gave him a traitorous stare.

"Before that." Tavelo let his arms lay limp on the armrests, the book going nearly flat at the spine. "How about we discuss this in your mother's personal chamber?"

Eterenia nodded in agreement. Too many eyes and ears around. Tavelo still felt unsure if spies from other covens were lurking. They got up and left the study. On the way, he pulled out his dreaded smart phone and sent a message.

Tesul and his eldest son halted the chess game they had laid out on the folding table near the closet as Tavelo, Adelia, and Eterenia, holding her grandson, came in. The Valkyrie stayed put on the landing of the entrance to secure it.

"Sorry to interrupt." Tavelo sat in one of the chairs. "I know it is last minute. We need to discuss why I summoned you here."

The French doors creaked further open, letting the damp air of afternoon rain in, followed by Tervan in his military uniform, being his usual austere self.

"Yes." He stepped into the room and leaned against the frame of the sliding glass doors. "What is so important that you need your offspring present?"

"Eterenia and I have decided to make a few changes. Since our families are now one, it is only fair that it reflects our new circumstance." Tavelo looked around the room to gauge the mood. "Adelia has been doing well in her role as leader of my coven." He turned to Adelia "We want you to become Queen of the De Luce coven."

The room went still with a startled silence. Adelia's eyes widened as her mouth gaped open.

"You want me," she stuttered softly, "to be Queen?"

"Absolutely not," Tervan said loudly. "She didn't do well. Your coven ended up enslaved under her rule."

"That was not her fault." Tesul stood, his stance showing him ready to fight.

"Sure it is. The entire coven got overrun by rogue vampires. I won't stand for that kind of incompetence in the De Luce coven."

"I didn't see you bothering to come to our aid either!" Adelia snapped. "Your spies knew what was going on long before we did."

"I assumed you would fulfill your role and stop it. You obviously weren't up to the task."

Adelia gripped the arms of her chair as she leaned forward and turned her head to give him a deadly stare. The two siblings locked eyes.

"Enough of that!" Eterenia squeezed Addy close to her as a counter measure so she wouldn't get out of her seat. "I will not tolerate you blaming her for what the others set in motion."

"Where will you go?" Adelia brought her attention back to her mother after easing back into the chair. "If I am Queen, then what happens to you?"

"I will be with Tavelo and the young ones."

Tervan severed his gaze from Adelia and turned

to his father. Tavelo pursed his lips.

"I will have Innego take over the Durante coven."

Sharp gasps erupted. Tervan unfolded his arms.

"Not Tamar?" Tesul asked. "He is next in line."

"And not ready to lead. The last battle traumatized him."

"That's an understatement. That brat couldn't lead an army of rats from the dungeons." Tervan smirked. "Your cousin isn't much better. Didn't he run from the enemy?"

Tavelo warned him with a glare.

"He is willing to act as a personal assistant to my cousin. It will be good practice for him."

"Then who will be running the businesses in your absences?" The Valkyrie's voice rang out higher than usual as she stepped off the landing into the room. "What am I to do?"

"What you always do," Tervan replied. "Be useless to everyone, including my mother."

"Stop!" Eterenia commanded as the two wrapped their hands on the hilt of their longswords.

"Being coven leaders has little to do with running the companies. We will do that from our new home." Tavelo continued to bring everyone back into the conversation.

"What new home?" Adelia asked.

Eterenia and Tavelo nodded at each other.

Tavelo answered.

"We're scouting empty areas between our two covens in the dead zone. That keeps our houses in close proximity in case a situation arises. A small ten-bedroom estate."

"Ten bedrooms?" Adelia yelled in disbelief. "What about if we want to visit? "

"I think that is an adequate..." Tavelo began to explain.

"What about family holiday meals?" Adelia went on. "You need at least twenty."

"What would you do with some tiny ten room

house?" Tervan added.

"It's just Tavelo, the two children, and myself." Eterenia shook her head in frustration. "What more do we need?"

"At the very least, a simple stronghold!" Tervan replied, crossing his arms.

From the corner of the room came Lariod's voice.

"I'm excited to not have a bunch of brats running around. Visiting someone else's abode from time to time would be ideal. I won't have to deal with any children."

He sat in a chair he had carted off to there and remained silent the whole time until now.

"We're not sending ours there, you cretin!" Adelia glared at him.

"Oh. You should consider it." Lariod leaned back in the corner.

"I actually agree with him." Tervan shrugged.

"Tesul will only accompany me when needed. You have Lariod, so there shouldn't be an issue." Tavelo turned to Tesul. "It would be like a day job. You'll get time with your family more than with me."

"You are part of that family." Tesul finally sat down. "My job is to protect you at all times."

"Do you think anyone would get past her?" Tavelo motioned to Eterenia. He looked over at the Valkyrie. "You will still be her personal guard. This way, you can finally promote your second in command to lead your Valkyries to protect Queen Adelia."

The Valkyrie's expression softened, and she stood silent for a while.

"I have to deal with them?" Lariod piped up. "Am I being punished for something?"

That made the Valkyrie's head angrily snap up. No love existed between the guardian and the Valkyries. Both had their own way of protecting their royal charges. Tavelo sighed in defeat. He decided to avoid getting in the middle of that argument.

"See?" Tervan gestured with one hand, sweeping across the room. "This is a bad idea."

"We're doing it." Tavelo said, ending the subject.

"When do I get my dinner with my father?" Adelia brought back her request.

Tervan raised his brow at that. "Oh?"

"Soon." Eterenia pondered the thought. "In the next two weeks. We have to find land to build on."

"Ooh! If you go North, there's a spot near a small body of the water." Adelia suggested.

"Your failed judgement is showing." Tervan said. "They need a better vantage point. To the south there is a cluster of forestation. They can have their home butted right up against them."

"Does he always think in military terms?" Tesul's oldest son asked.

"He only has one braincell. And, that's what it does." Lariod answered.

"Say that again," Tervan warned.

Laughter filled the room. Tervan and the Valkyrie saw Eterenia and Adelia in full laughter with every-one else following suit. Even Addy joined in.

"That's cuz you're mean," Addy said to Tervan, while still letting out an infectious child laugh.

"I'm leaving." Tervan pushed himself off the glass and turned to the door.

"No, you're not." Tavelo nodded to Tesul, who stood and blocked Tervan's exit. "Dinner is only a couple of hours from now. We are all going to sit and be cordial."

The door opened and the other two children came in. They stopped at the landing, hands clasped together with Ethan hiding behind his older brother, Emil. Eterenia waved them in. They advanced a little further until they caught sight of Tervan. He glared at them, hissing.

Addy jumped off Eterenia's lap, ran over to Tervan and kicked him in the shin. He yelped, hopping away on one foot.

"What the hell?" Tervan yelled.

"Bad brother!" Addy said. He went up to Ethan and Emil. "He won't mess with you now."

Emil smiled. Adelia reached around him and dragged Ethan to her. He started to protest, not wanting to let go of his brother's hand. Emil nodded. Adelia got him in her arms and hugged him tight.

"You're such a cutie!" She rubbed her cheek against his.

He relaxed, and Eterenia breathed a sigh of relief. Part of the reason they needed a place of their own revolved around him. Eterenia felt a sense of stability away from the drama of the coven would be best for her child. The others would have to be informed.

Not yet. Her and Tavelo had to time it just right.

Awkward.

That feeling permeated the Durante dining room. Dark cherry wood furniture made the room seem small and dimly lit, despite the giant chandelier that hung above. Candles set on the table subdued the stark white table runner while the fine China plates barely made a statement.

The chairs, evenly placed around the table to accommodate eight, were occupied. Eterenia, Tavelo, and Adelia on one side. Yutel, his cousin Jorsel, and Sully sat on the other. Tesul positioned himself at the end by Tavelo and Emil. Addy confiscated the other end of the table, sitting between his mother and the man now known to be Adelia's father.

Not as large and burly as Yutel, his cousin, Jorsel nonetheless possessed strong features. His six-foot four muscular frame well toned in contrast to his cousin's massiveness. Wavy brown hair that curled at the ends touched his shoulders. Tanned skin, square jaw, and cornflower blue eyes rounded out his looks.

Adelia approved; glad he wasn't some sniveling aristocrat as she thought.

She noticed his nails. Manicured with visible bruising under the nail beds. The tips of his fingers had a roughness that only someone who did manual labor would have. Did he work alongside his coven minions? That seemed preposterous, him being a leader. Surely, he had enough workers. She decided to ask him about that later.

Across from Yutel, Eterenia felt embarrassment. Yutel squirmed uncomfortably in his seat. That may have been the tight suit's fault. She never understood why his tailors never got his measurements right. They were all wearing formal dress wear except the children.

Adelia barely got the Addy into clothes, let alone nice attire. Not to make him feel out of place, Sully forgoed his suit for something casual.

The servants milled around, setting soup bowls atop the China plates. Steam rose from each, sending the aroma of shrimp, fresh vegetables, and Jasmine rice seasoned to perfection into the air. Jorsel breathed it in, eyes closed, and exhaled with pleasure.

"This smells amazing. Don't get this kind of meal often." He lifted the soup spoon from the spread of utensils.

"Why is that?" Adelia asked, confused. "Aren't all the covens profitable enough to eat well?"

Tesul grimaced. Tavelo bowed his head in pity for her. They all realized in that instant that she had yet to deal with the care and feeding of a coven.

"There are many expenses." Jorsel explained. "Profit can only go so far when you have hundreds of mouths to feed."

"Add maintenance to the castle and wages for the workers." Yutel said. He reached for the glass of Sauvignon Blanc set before him. The jacket sleeve strained to contain his bulging arm muscles. "You need to prepare for these things in advance."

"Even then, you can only guess how much money comes in on a regular basis," Jorsel added.

Adelia nodded, taking the information in. She took a sip of soup from her spoon, delighted by the taste, and set it back down in the bowl. Then she looked over at Yutel.

"Why are you not my father if the leaders agreed to the breeding schedule? How is it your cousin has taken your place?"

The four leaders halted their consumption of the fabulous soup. Yutel cleared his throat.

"I knew your mother should have been mated to Tavelo. Even though we are no longer on our home world, I still respected her parents' decision. The others, not so much. But, if she chose to find someone in my family, I would not deter it."

Eterenia sat shocked.

"I had no idea that was why." She looked away in shame. "I went after another to spite you."

"She all but seduced me." Jorsel gave a crooked smile. "I had no choice but to submit."

"I did no such thing!"

"You were relentless. Like an animal hunting prey."

"I may have been a bit angry," Eterenia muttered. Tavelo glanced over at her. She averted her eyes. "Unlike Chalayl, I despised the notion."

"Well, Chalayl is a different story." Yutel scooped up more soup and slurped loudly. "I never looked at the register to see how many she had spawned over the decades."

"Eight," Adelia blurted out as she ate her soup. The room became quiet. Her spoon stopped midway to her mouth, and she looked around. "We saw the registers, remember? I happened to find that number a bit much considering."

Eterenia's stomach did a tiny lurch, forcing her to bring her napkin to her lips anticipating vomit. Tavelo placed a hand on her back and caressed it until her sickness subsided. It would mean Chalayl had laid with every one of the men except Tavelo. He wouldn't have touched her. And Pridric would have out of perceived entitlement even without the decree.

"Okay." Adelia sighed. "Let's not finished that conversation." She looked over at Addy. He smiled mischievously, far more intelligent than he appeared. Adelia returned her attention back to her father. "I want to know more about you."

"Besides the fact that I am the leader of a lower coven with little clout?"

"Yes, besides that. Why didn't your mate join us?"

"Huh." Jorsel snorted. "She finds me repulsive for one. Since I'm not one of the top coven leaders, she feels I'm a failure. When she learned of you being my child, she was none too pleased when I refused to use that as leverage for better status."

"You should have found him a better mate." Adelia pointed accusingly at Yutel. "How could you let your cousin endure such a woman?"

Yutel sat taken aback by her statement. It never occurred to him that the responsibility would be at his discretion. As if reading his mind Adelia fired an accusation at him.

"Of course, it's your responsibility. The coven's happiness and of your family is on you." She frowned in frustration. "I tried to keep this coven together the best I knew how."

Her hands balled into fists on the table. Tavelo covered the one near him with his own.

"I'm sorry, Adelia." She shook her head, fighting tears. "I only wish I could have been here to help."

Jorsel reached over and covered the other hand.

"No one is blaming you for that." His eyes narrowed. "That is on Pridric."

A servant came into the room.

"My apologies, Master Durante. Are we almost ready for the main course? The cook is about to start plating."

Tavelo took a sip of his soup, and the others did

the same. Still warm.

"Give us a few minutes and we will be ready."

"Of course."

She bowed and returned to the kitchen.

"It won't take me long to finish this." Jorsel said as he began shoveling the soup in his mouth.

"It was yummy!" Addy exclaimed. They looked over at his clean bowl. While they talked, he ate. "I'm done."

Adelia laughed. The lingering tension lifted. From there, they had a normal family meal.

❀ ❀ ❀

The quarterly coven leader meeting at the Marchand chateau in Paris was about to start. All the leaders were situated in their chosen seats. This time, even Tavelo opted to sit on one of the loveseats with Eterenia. Servants passed around the usual fare of desserts and spirits, wine the dominant winner for now.

Holnar scanned the room, observing everyone's demeanor, and zeroed in on Eterenia and Tavelo. They were keeping something from everyone. We'll get to that soon enough. He rolled a gold weighted ball in one hand as he watched them. They never could hide secrets from him.

Once everyone had a drink in their possession, Holnar nodded to his personal assistant standing by the projector. The far wall displayed the quarterly earnings. It came into focus, auto adjusting for size.

"It looks like we're doing far better than anticipated. Of course, the humans are angry that they are not getting much of a cut." He turned his body more towards the screen. "We may be able to move on to the next phase."

"Which is what?" Darean sipped the red wine. "Doubling the load?"

"Trade with the other systems," Pridric stated.

"There has been interest." Holnar turned back around and picked up his glass of white wine. "Screening of their goods would have to take place. We don't want anything untoward coming onto Earth."

"No creatures of any kind, for sure." Chalayl said.

They went through the motions of giving updates on products. Number crunching and projected sales went on for another hour.

Holnar sniffed loudly, rubbing the tip of his nose.

"So tell us, Eterenia, Tavelo, what's been on your minds?"

The two looked up at him startled.

"What?" Tavelo's face squinched.

"Really? Spit it out." Holnar leaned back.

They glanced at each other for a moment.

"Fine. We'll tell you." Eterenia said, then prodded Tavelo.

"No one else speaks." Holnar ordered.

He told them their plan without interruption and waited for someone to say something. The room remained silent for what seemed like minutes.

Yutel broke it first.

"Why didn't you tell me this at dinner that night?" He asked angrily.

"We wanted to, but the timing." Eterenia protested.

"And where is this new home supposed to be located?" Darean asked.

"We haven't nailed it down yet," Tavelo answered.

"What could you possibly do with a ten bedroom home?" Chalayl exclaimed. "That's so tiny. What if you had visitors? Or we needed to have a meeting?"

Tavelo shook his head in disbelief. Holnar certainly knew that subject had come up on many occasions and he agreed.

"You must have a bigger estate. It's not up for debate." Darean added.

"It's our home!" Tavelo's fist slammed into the cushions.

"Stop being childish."

Holnar snapped a finger at his personal assistant. "Bring up the dead zone map." The charts disappeared from the screen, replaced by the territories with coven domains. "Zoom in there," he pointed to a space five miles from the Durante castle and a little over eight from the De Luce palace.

"Who are you getting to build it?" Pridric asked haughtily. "I know a few architects."

"I'll get my men on it." Yutel stood and walked over to the wall. "You need professionals. I won't have my family in some half ass construction."

"Is that an insult?" Holnar gave him a side stare.

"Yes, was it?" Pridric tossed back his tumbler of whiskey.

"Since there seems to be genuine concern for their wellbeing, how about we all contribute to the build?" Darean set his glass down. "That way they can focus on getting everything else in order."

"Please, Tavelo, for the sanity of us all, let Eterenia do the décor." Holnar made eye contact with him and saw the indignance. "There is no need to make do any longer. You can have whatever you want or need."

Tavelo's expression fell. He got up and walked out of the room. Holnar knew he had hit a delicate subject. Eterenia stood.

"You didn't have to say that."

Tears brimmed her eyes.

"It's ingrained in him," Darean said. "They weren't poor by any means, but they had limited funds."

"They went years without an updated furnace. They couldn't justify the cost." Yutel added.

"What do you mean?" Pridric snapped.

Yutel turned to him.

"That the Endaga family went along being cold in their home while yours sabotaged them at every turn." Pridric went pale. "Is that enough for you?"

"I never knew that," Holnar said angrily.

"Neither did I." Eterenia dropped onto the loveseat. "Even when we were inside, I never bothered to notice the conditions they lived in."

"Well," Darean picked his wine back up. "We are all guilty of that."

"Then it's settled," Chalayl raised her glass. "We build him a real home." She winked at Eterenia. "And you have to provide the love and support."

"I was going to do that regardless."

Yutel went over to Pridric.

"This is your chance to talk with him." Pridric stared at him, horror struck. Yutel sighed. "Putting it off any longer is ridiculous. Holnar agrees."

"I already told him to stop this foolishness."

Holnar's personal assistant held up a hand.

"Does this mean the meeting is adjourned?"

"Oh, yes." Holnar stood. "Have the servants bring in the hard liquor."

"Of course."

They shut down the projector and left the room.

"Go get Tavelo," he addressed Eterenia. "He can't be off brooding. He's too old for that."

Influx

Chalayl didn't know how to fill the big hole in the Guillarmo coven's morale. She strolled down the stone corridor, her head down as she counted each step. When she stopped counting at one hundred, she looked up to observe her surroundings. Coven members in the halls moved out of her way. They could feel the heat and tension coming off her.

After imprisoning the Kataling leader, Omeron, long ago, forcing herself on him to spawn their son, she never thought about the consequences. Beyond angry on the day she let him go she made matters worse by refusing to let him take the child.

As a result, Caden had not been taught the basics of being a Kataling. The damage done to him by the emperor hurt her more than she ever imagined.

He wasn't ready.

Her determination to do all she could to nurture him after he returned from the battle didn't happen. His father awaited in the castle, livid at the state of his offspring. He wouldn't listen to her explanations or reasons why their son should stay with her.

She made it to the catacombs where the tunnels ran underground connecting the leader homes to the cities. Inside one of the cavernous stone rooms stood the Kataling. His broad shoulders, bronze skin gleaming where the tight fitting grey muscle tee left it exposed, accented the dark wavy head of hair that looked wet as it brushed the nape of his neck. He turned those amber colored eyes at her and glared with disdain.

Such a beautiful creature.

She wanted more of him.

Clenching her thighs tight, she slowed her steps to stand before him. Cedar and musk filled her nostrils as his natural scent wafted off him. Sensing her desire, his eyes glowed almost golden.

He despises me to his core. I don't care.

"You came back. To what do I owe such a privilege?" She smiled sweetly.

"He's missing." His deep voice reverberated in her ears.

"What do you mean?" She squinted at him, the notion unacceptable.

"Three weeks ago."

"Three weeks?" She screamed. "Why didn't you come to me sooner?" She got closer to him and had to look up to meet his gaze. "What happened to make him leave?"

"I thought you might know."

Omeron didn't waver from his position.

His shirt seemed to expand with every breath he took, his muscles barely contained. She wanted to touch his chest. The black cargo pants fit him nicely as well. She realized she was caught up in her own fantasies when he stepped back from her out of reach.

"I have no idea where he would have gone. I'd like to think he would have come home."

"To you?" He snorted. "No, I knew he wouldn't be here. But maybe you knew why."

"Shall I start a hunt?"

"What would you do differently that we can't? We have far superior senses."

"And yet, you still haven't locate our son," she snipped at him.

He had his hands around her throat in a flash,

slamming her into the wall. Her guards placed their hands on the guns at their waist. Chalayl waved a hand at them to back off. She relented in the Kataling's grasp and sighed with desire. So close!

"No need to be so sensitive. My apologies," she cooed. He let her go and moved even farther from her. Miffed that he hadn't tried to throttle her, she continued. "What about the child?"

"Taken with him."

"Hmm. Do you want me to ask the other covens for help?"

"Absolutely not," he replied with gritted teeth.

"Then what?" She asked, confused.

"I needed to know what you may have. It's obvious you have no clue." He turned towards the tunnel entrance. "I will keep trying to track him."

"You're worried." She grinned, tilting her head to one side.

"He's mine. Of course I am."

Omeron left the catacombs, and Chalayl still reeling from the encounter. She could feel the moistness increase as she relaxed her lower body.

All her regrets vanished.

❀ ❀ ❀

Tavelo and Eterenia's newly built home set in a clearing butted up to a cluster of trees. A three-story estate with over twenty-five bedrooms, a library, a meeting hall, home theatre, and an indoor pool right in the center. Six guards covered the property, four of them vampires. The other two came from the Endaga family.

Eterenia could be seen through the window on the far left, where bay doors led into a sprawling kitchen. Her young son she had with Tavelo came up to her and she hugged him. Tavelo followed with the emperor's child clinging to his waist. He rubbed the boy's hair playfully.

Caden watched in the shadows, torn by the scene. His own son lay slumped on the ground next to him, asleep. He got tired a lot due to his illness. Caden didn't want to be seen. The guards left him no choice. It never occurred to him that the house would be manned by more than Tesul.

Birds chirped in the night sky and he looked around to see if he could spot them. The trees were dense, pouring out their green scent. He closed his eyes and breathed in the cold, crisp air, letting it fill his lungs. Twigs snapping behind him made him perk up. He twisted around, his eyes focused desperately on the dark.

"What are you doing?" Tesul asked.

The massive werewolf's yellow eyes peered down at him, and he fell back on his butt.

"I was," he started to explain. He looked at his son whose body had fallen sideways when he moved away from him. "I need to see Lady Jaubro."

Without saying a word, Tesul lifted his son from the ground and walked towards the estate.

"Come. You'll get cold out here."

He obeyed, following in silence. The guards didn't acknowledge them as they passed. A servant from the inside opened the front door. They entered and Tesul led them to the kitchen. He set his son at the breakfast nook along the wall. Eterenia, Tavelo, and the two boys looked over in shock.

"What is the meaning of this?" Eterenia came forward, cupping Caden's face in her hands. "Why have you come here, sweetheart?" She glanced over at the sleeping child. "Is he well?"

"No." He choked up, barely managing the word. "He keeps getting sick." Tears streamed down his cheeks. "I don't know what he needs. I only know he needed to be with you."

Ethan crept up to the sleeping boy and patted strands of hair from his forehead.

"He's hot," her son said.

Tavelo gestured to Tesul. "Get him up. We need to cool him down quickly." He rushed down the hall with Tesul in tow carrying the child. "How long were you outside?" He asked Caden.

"Only a day or two."

Eterenia followed, catching up to him. She grabbed hold of his forearm.

"Why? That's irresponsible of you! Knowing his condition."

"Now's not the time for chastising him, my love." Tavelo called back as they neared the bathroom. "Our priority is this child."

"I know that!" She snapped at him.

Tavelo took the boy's coat off while Tesul set him in the tub. He turned the dial all the way over to cold and opened the spout. Ice cold water gushed out and he placed the stopper in the drain. The moment the boy felt the water, he started to thrash about trying to get out. His high-pitched screams were that of a wounded Kataling. Tesul held him down.

Caden broke into sobs, sliding to the floor by the tub as he took his son's hand. Still small for his age, he was stronger than he looked. Tavelo had to help Tesul keep the boy submerged. Within minutes, the water started to steam. Tavelo pulled out the stopper and started all over again when the tub emptied.

The other two children brought in ice and towels at Eterenia's instructions. By the fourth time Tavelo had to drain and refill, the water went tepid. The boy started to breathe better and his skin no longer hot. This time, Caden removed his clothes, wringing them out the best he could before tossing them in a pile.

"I'm so sorry," he cried, stroking his son's forehead.

His son's eyelids opened. Eterenia flinched at the black pupils speckled with gold amid all red. Dark like rubies and full of pain.

Her and Tavelo's son brought in a giant fluffy towel. Tesul lifted the boy up gently and together with his mother, they wrapped him in it. He closed his eyes and fell back to sleep.

"Take him to the second guest room down the hall," Tavelo said. Caden rose to follow. "No. You need to tell us what's going on."

His shoulders slumped and he simply nodded. The two boys went after Tesul. Eterenia made her way back to the kitchen with Tavelo and Caden. She opened the top of the electric kettle to check its water level. Satisfied, she shut it and pushed the button to start. They all sat at the island.

"So." Eterenia stretched her arms on the counter, fingers clasped. "What's going on?"

"I heard about the trading with the home world. What my mother is involved in. I don't like it. Instead of working to create a remedy for my son with collaboration with the doctors there, she is making something else. A drug that won't benefit mankind in any way."

"Drugs?" Eterenia yelled.

"She promised she'd help me," he cried.

Tavelo leaned over and stroked his head.

"She's a selfish woman. We didn't know you were suffering."

"Damnit, Chalayl!" Eterenia slammed a fist on the counter. She squeezed one of his hands. "We will help you and your son. I can contact my uncle at the royal palace and get some ideas."

He nodded, his head sinking lower onto the counter until he let it settle there. His eyes got heavy, and he fought to keep them open. Tavelo stroked his head. *Please, stop.* He needed to stay awake and take care of his son.

"It's okay. You're both safe here." Tavelo slid him off the stool into his arms. "It's alright."

He submitted to the empty void of sleep, letting his mind go blank.

❀ ❀ ❀

Chase spotted one of his spies coming up the side wall outside his study's window. The vampire pressed his hands and face on the glass and Chase waved for him to enter. He slid the glass to one side and crawled in.

A strong wind rushed in from behind, lifting papers off the desk. The cool air carried the scent of dead leaves. Chase found it refreshing.

"What news do you have for me?"

"Got a sighting on your missing member. The Kataling kid from the Guillarmo coven. Caden."

"Are you sure?" Chase rose halfway from his chair, hands planted on the desk to hold his weight. "This is important."

"I know." The spy shook out his trench coat and sat in the seat across from him. "And I'm sure."

Chase eased back in his chair. "Where is he?"

"At the new Durante De Luce estate. He snuck onto the property, but Tesul found him. Had his son with him."

"That makes sense." Chase felt a sense of sadness for them. "They should have stayed on our parents' home world for treatment."

"Yeah, they're both in bad shape. Queen Celeste has no idea where they are. It may travel to her soon though. She would want him back, not necessarily the child."

Anger filled Chase as he thought of the selfish Queen and her new endeavors. The humans or the home world didn't need a new drug trade. The level of scientists at her disposal could make better things.

"I need to get a message to him. You're not compromised?"

"Nope. What do you want me to tell him?"

"About our plan. I will arrange for him to meet with Baltise."

"Got it."

The vampire got up and left the way he came.

Chase went to lean out the window and watched

him scuttle down the wall. He took a deep inhale of the night air before closing it back. Turning around, he found Baltise standing by the desk.

"You heard?" He sat down in his chair.

"I did." Baltise sat on the edge of the desk, one hand on its surface as she leaned over. "You know I have my own agenda as well."

"And it is a noble one. I'm not sure all the ancient ones will agree with you."

"We have to advocate better treatment for ourselves, or they will continue to use us as weapons and pawns for their treachery."

Her face scrunched in frustration. Chase cocked his head as he admired her. Baltise had become more open, less timid. No longer afraid to show how fierce a fighter she could be. That tiny body from before had filled out from childbearing and toned muscles.

"I will go to him."

Chase sat straight.

"Wait. Hold on." He saw the conviction in her expression. "You can't just show up."

"The Endaga and De Luce covens are neutral. They don't care what we do."

"That's not my concern!" Chase tapped his fists on the desk. "As we have spies on that property so goes it that others may also."

"You sound like some old aristocrat. What kind of millennial are you?"

Caught off guard, Chase blinked at her words and sat back. She snorted, stifling a laugh. He stared at her in awe. She didn't laugh much. When she did, it made his heart melt. Not winning the battle, she finally erupted into the sweet sounds of amusement at his expense.

The hell with it!

If the leaders find out, so be it.

They already had the dummy company in place for that reason.

He joined in on the laughter.

Agreeing that his thinking indeed resembled that of an old man.

That won't do.

❀ ❀ ❀

Caden heard the whishing of movement in the guest room and knew the vampire tried to be stealthy. He sniffed the air and found the familiar scent of one of the indoor guards. They knelt beside the bed and leaned over to whisper in his ear. Caden opened his eyes, surprising the vampire. They reared back, stumbling to the floor. He put a finger to his lips.

The vampire regained his position.

"I have a message from Chase Ambrook," the vampire said softly.

"Whatever it is, I don't want any part of it. My child is more important."

"This will remedy both situations. You should hear what it is regardless."

Caden sighed, his body relaxing further into the soft bedding. He had no patience for any of Chase's schemes. The last one nearly got all of them killed on a different planet. He also knew the vampire took a great risk in delivering the message.

"Fine. What is this plan?"

The vampire whispered the details to him, at times glancing at the door behind him to make sure no one lingered nearby. Caden listened to every word and as the vampire finished, had made up his mind. He would join them. The elders needed to be taught a lesson.

"Baltise will meet with you soon. I haven't been told when yet."

"Alright. Thank you." Caden watched him open the door slowly and peek around the frame, looking both ways. "Be careful."

The vampire turned to nod then disappeared in the dark hallway.

Caden rolled onto his back to stare at the ceiling. The fan blades were off, casting long shadows above him. Muted light from the oncoming dawn crept through the sheer drapes on the bay window. He turned his head to his right. Next to him lay his son, sleeping badly, his breathing not quite smooth.

Baltise.

He had heard through the rumor mills that the hybrid wanted to rally the ancient ones for a tough negotiation with the elders. Twice on Earth they had been used to do their dirty work. Even being revered on the home world, the emperor made them slaves to his will. *That's a whole different can of worms, Baltise.* He understood the passion.

He rolled over to his side and caressed his son's forehead. For him, he would defy anyone.

❀ ❀ ❀

Tavelo stood in the shadows along the hallway ten feet from the guest room. He watched the vampire go in, heard every word whispered, then waited as the vampire left like a thief, scanning the dark and finding nothing. He had long conquered the talent of erasing his presence. The vampires had told them of the technique and his people perfected it without telling them.

He followed the vampire with his gaze and as he rounded the corner that led to the basement where the vampires slept for the day. Then caught sight of another guard eyeing the vampire. Another spy. A human minion from one of the other covens. He had no doubt, they were there to report back to the others.

That's part of the reason why he didn't want a bigger home. Too many ways to be infiltrated. He had learned much about the coup of his castle.

Tavelo decided to deal with the spy another day. Then he saw him move, heading down the stairs. The vampire would be in his assigned coffin by now, with dawn arriving. A sense of dread came over Tavelo. Certainly, what he thought might be about to occur couldn't happen under his roof.

At the last moment, he flashed down the stairs after the spy and saw him plunge a short blade into the barely sleeping vampire's chest. Tavelo hit the spy in the side, knocking him into the far wall. The blade, halfway in, went with him, dripping with blood that turned a sickly purple color.

Poison.

He sent an urgent telepathic message to Tesul.

We have a breach! Get a doctor to the crypt, now!

The estate became a flurry of activity as he relayed the message. Caden came running down into the fray. He stopped cold at the sight of the vampire struggling for his life as the wound festered.

A doctor pushed his way through, his bag already open, with a testing kit in his hand. He took a sample of the curdling blood and dropped it into the meter. Within seconds it beeped, giving him a reading.

"I can reverse this. He'll live." He snapped at his assistant stumbling behind him hauling equipment. "Hurry up!" He turned to Tavelo. "I need you to leave. We got this."

Tavelo took hold of Caden's arm and led him back up the stairs.

"What about the spy?" Caden protested as he tried to wrench free.

"Tesul will handle him." Tavelo tightened his grip.

"You need to kill him."

"That would benefit no one. We need him to report to his master."

Caden stopped struggling. Tavelo glanced over at him and saw the realization on the young man's face. Time for a different strategy.

"You're not angry at us going against the covens?"

Tavelo laughed.

"I'm trying to figure out why it took you so long. Chase is slipping."

"He's of the Strana bloodline. Aren't you worried?"

"No. Because he was born here on Earth. He's an Ambrook first."

"Will I still be able to meet with Baltise?"

"Oh, I have a feeling Baltise won't care about secrecy this time."

Eterenia met them in the foyer.

"What is going on in our home?" Her maddening expression fell on them.

"A bit of pest control." Tavelo finally let Caden go. "Assassination attempt on one of our guards."

"You're joking!" Her eyes widened.

"A human. I think he's of the Marchand coven." Caden shook his head.

"I think I've seen him before. Brownlee coven. They merged with my mother after the battle because of the financial hit from losing so many key players."

"Ah, yes. The coven devastated from the battle." Eterenia squeezed her fists twice. "Come. Since we're all awake now. Let's have some morning tea."

"Tea?" Tavelo raised his brow.

"With bourbon and honey."

Eterenia's eyes flashed silver as she glanced back.

They entered the kitchen. On a stool at the island sat Baltise in female form. She had on a plain floor length dress that did nothing for her figure. A sleeveless dark green fabric that might as well had been a sack. She wore a long sleeved knit shirt beneath it. The electric kettle was on.

"I had a feeling you would show up." Tavelo went up to her. "I hope you didn't harm any of my guards."

"They were preoccupied, so I took advantage." Baltise smiled. That look of innocence lingered.

"How goes the takeover?" Eterenia mused.

"We're not trying to take anything over. We only want a piece of the action, as Chase put it."

"Yes, well, the others are quite stingy. They don't like people playing in their sandbox without their permission. Especially, Pridric."

The kettle light shut off, the lever clicking back up. Steam rose from the tiny slit at the top. Boiling water rolled around in the clear glass.

"Tea?" Eterenia asked. She reached into the cupboard and brought out a tray of teacups laid upside down. Setting it on the island counter, she began to flip them over. "It's special."

"It's hot toddy," Baltise said pursing her lips.

"Whatever." Eterenia dismissed it with a wave. "Do you want some or not?"

"Yes, please." Baltise sounded like a child.

"Good. After this, you two can conspire away." Tavelo sat on a stool. "I have some interrogating to do later on."

❀ ❀ ❀

Caden found himself once again sitting in silence, while he listened to an outrageous agenda. This time he stared at Baltise in awe. She wasn't joking about what they wanted as an end result. Baltise sipped a second cup of tea and waited for Caden to speak.

"So, let me get this straight." Caden had been holding his cup midway, his hands going slack. He set it down. "You want to create a separate class from the others. A higher echelon superior to the merchants." Baltise glanced up, still drinking, and all Caden could see were those perfect shaped eyes full of resolve.

His father had talked about it once. How on their home world over a millennium ago, their kind were revered above all others. The ancient ones who protected the planet from outside foes and internal if necessary. Living like commoners yet treated like kings. They had their own land away from the rest of civilization since they needed space to roam.

On Earth it would be different. The humans had to agree to it as well. For all he knew, they would assemble an extermination group as they did with the vampires. Caden folded his arms on the island counter and contemplated the angles.

"Master Endaga, Tavelo, is on board." Baltise set his cup on the counter. "He is not happy with the way things have gone so far."

Caden remembered being chained up most of the time until forced to attend school. His mother only allowed it to avert suspicion. Lady Jaubro knew about him and would not let her get away with his awful treatment. Then she let him go to the home world where she felt certain he would be killed in his opinion.

Cherished? Who was she kidding?

"Basically, we get leverage over the elders then pull this gem out and hope they don't kill us all?"

"Do you really think they could take on all of us? The home world as well?"

There were twice as many than on Earth. If the humans or the home worlders turned on them, it would be an all you can eat buffet. The oceans would turn a darker shade of despair from the massive bloodshed. No. They would have to submit or die.

"That would be detrimental to their own well-being. Doesn't mean they won't try."

Baltise smiled. "You seem much better now." Caden's lips pressed inward as he blushed. "I'm glad. We were all worried about you."

"Really?"

"Especially Olette and Olivier."

Discontent hit Caden hearing the twins' names. His step siblings spawned from his mother. Not once had they ever acknowledged him. *And they're worried?* He searched Baltise's face for some kind of amused sign and found none. Baltise picked up on his thoughts.

"Their father doesn't want the three of you to be close and your mother would give anything to keep you locked away for eternity. What were they supposed to do? They couldn't expose how they felt."

"You're right." Caden clenched his hands shut then unfolded his arms. "Now what? Where am I to go? Do I leave my son here?"

"You were going to do that anyway." Baltise side eyed him. "We have a hotel we're using as a front. The three floors from the top two are blocked out as ours. We bought them with the first round of revenue."

Caden sat back shocked. This sounded serious. They weren't messing around.

"That's impressive." Then he thought some more. "In that case, switch me for the dummy company."

Baltise's brow lifted in curiosity. "The reason?"

"When they find out which one ate into their profits, they would outright dismiss me as a disgruntled child. Then we switch it back to the original." He saw the wheels turning in Baltise's mind. "Good idea?"

"Brilliant," Baltise whispered.

"You also seem much better." Caden grinned. "I guess we both had to find our voices."

CHAPTER THREE

A Royal Mess

The first meeting of the royal siblings ended in hurt feelings and eventual bloodshed. Master Jaubro had decided not to attend and let the siblings reunite unsupervised. It was a mistake. Too much hostility stemmed from Manel's treatment of them over the decades.

He watched the feed recorded from the mobile eyes planted in the room beforehand.

While the eldest siblings were dark-haired like Manel, the other two were fair skinned with light brown hair. The youngest sister's hair grew wild like mane. No coiffing tool could tame that cascaded to her waist. The mess did what it wanted. The same true for all of them. Something about the texture made it unbearable to deal with. They all blamed their father and his experiments with their DNA as well as his own.

Manel had come face to face with his younger sister, Lenri. Her beautiful features marred by the scar starting near the temple above her left eye and ran diagonal all the way down across her body as she removed her robes in the heat of an argument. A wound he had given her over a century ago out of pure spite. Tears flowed from her blood-red eyes slitted in rage. Manel had stumbled back on the floor with shame and fear.

The elder sister, Maxelia, sat silent on a large cushion, observing the scene while her brothers held the little thing back. Stopping her from attacking Manel. Her gaze met the eldest brother, Megen, and they nodded to each other.

Manel scrambled onto his knees, angered by his own weak actions, ready to strike Lenri.

Maxellia pulled a blade from under the side sleeves of her robe and brought it down into Manel's back, slamming him onto the floor. She pushed it deeper until she felt the tip hit the planks beneath the rug, impaling him. He screamed in fury, bringing his arms inward, and used his forearms as leverage to dislodge himself from the floor.

Gallic rushed in to help only to be blocked by Megen. Still screaming and foaming at the mouth, Manel got free, the act making a sickly wet, ripping sound, the blade tip protruding from his chest. He reached behind him to grab hold of the hilt flush with his back. When that didn't work, the hilt too far out of reach, he raised his hands in front of the tip.

As he readied himself to smash them onto the blade in an attempt to push it out, Maxelia took hold of the hilt and pulled it from him. Black blood splattered onto the cushion and her entire left side. She flinched away from the droplets hitting her face.

"You deserved that and much more."

Her tone deadpan.

To their shock, Manel sat on his knees crying, his head raised to the ceiling. Then he shrieked, morphing into his Kataling state. His wound, ripping further, spewing blood everywhere as he thrashed about in agony and rage. His siblings raced to him, holding him down to stop the transformation and blood flow.

Maxelia leapt from the cushion to apply pressure to both sides of the wound, forcing it closed.

Gallic ran out of the room and got the attention of the guards outside.

"Get the healers! The emperor is dying!"

They went pale and rushed down the hall. Gallic went back in to be by his master's side and, again denied by Lendor pushing him back.

"You're not strong enough to hold him."

A group of healers along with Master Jaubro and his assistant came in. One of the healers immediately administered a sedative while the others tended to the wound, taking over for Maxellia.

"This isn't what we expected. We only wanted to hurt him." She cried, her face horror-stricken.

"Well, you accomplished that." Master Jaubro said seething. "Congratulations."

Finally, Manel's cries died out and his body went limp, reverting to bipedal form. The healers gently lifted the emperor off the floor and onto a floating stretcher. Gallic followed it out with the healers.

Now, with so many moons past since that day, another meeting had been set. Master Jaubro ended the playback and switched to live feed. He would monitor the situation from afar.

The pristine room showed no signs the incident had never happened. Maxellia again sat on the large cushion atop a lounge chaise in the far corner. Lendor and Megen sat across from each other on either side of the room. Lenri, in a flowy pastel peach robe over her black battle suit, sat closer to the entrance on a loveseat.

Manel appeared at the entrance, Gallic by his side, along with two royal guards behind them. Maxellia took in his whole being. Dressed in a simple kefta, with royal scribe down the center and laced sandals, he didn't give off the air of an emperor. His eyes were a dull dark grey like old metal. His hair a longer mess than before.

Is this our doing?

A sadness filled her chest. She knew he was not responsible for how he turned out. Nevertheless, she felt he should be taught a lesson. That plan backfired.

"Are you not going to come sit with us, brother?"

She gestured to the empty high-backed chair opposite her.

"Are you going to stab me in the back again for fun?" Manel replied, not moving from the doorway.

"No. I'm sorry for that." She saw his hands clench and unclench several times. "Conversation would be awkward from that distance, don't you think?"

Manel reluctantly stepped over the threshold and sat in the oversized plush chair. He clasped his hands in his lap and closed his eyes. Gallic stood beside him creating a block between Manel and Maxelia. His hand rested on the hilt of his longsword as he kept a steady gaze on her. She smirked.

As if he could take any of us!

"We have been keeping tabs on the shipments between Earth." She began. "I am concerned about a few things." She pulled a tablet from her sleeve and touched different icons. "The revenue isn't exactly profitable. Their craftsmanship is lacking."

"And not much variety in their goods," Lendor added.

Manel stayed silent for a while then nodded.

"That is the issue." His voice suddenly seemed to sound slurred. "There is another."

"What is wrong with him?" Maxelia asked Gallic.

"He's mildly sedated to stop his transitioning. It's been a hard few days for him."

"The issue you speak of," Lendor continued. "What does it entail?"

Manel's eyes rolled sideways in their sockets until they zeroed in on him.

"The Boresso merchants."

"Ah, them." Megen's eyes narrowed.

"Is there a problem with them?" Lenri asked.

"You were isolated from the rest of the planet so you wouldn't know much about the top merchant families." Maxellia shifted on her cushion to get more comfortable. "Some of them were ruthless, others hard working. Then we had the ones with no scruples.

That is the Boresso family. There were many times we had to apply sanctions and fines for the undesirable dealings they engaged in." She turned to Manel. "Let me guess. Some scientific atrocity?"

Gallic answered for his master.

"On Earth, they have a recreation, albeit mostly illegal, to indulge in chemical mood enhancement."

"I'm not understanding," Lendor said.

"How we feel when consuming fresh blood and meat is the same way they would feel when taking these chemicals."

"I still don't see the problem?"

"The side effects are..." Gallic struggled to contain his frustration.

"Think of the Thembre system." Manel slurred. His eyes went back to looking straight ahead.

That made them cringe with disgust. A system of gangsters who traded in similar fare. The users were prone to theft and sabotage for credits to buy more if they hadn't died from side effects or overdose.

"Drugs on Earth take a worse toll physically and mentally. I believe the Boresso family on that planet is trying to go interstellar with a new strain."

"That's the last thing our three systems need!" Maxellia snapped.

"Then what do we do about this?" Lenri asked. "Finding another planet for trade is great. Only, not if it involves this."

"I agree. We need to get a better handle on it. Our proxies are not enough." Megen said.

Manel's silence alerted them to his sleeping body still upright in the chair, hands clasped together. He looked like a child. Megen walked over to stand over him. Gallic stepped forward about to draw his sword. Maxelia reached over and pushed him back.

With a gentle touch, Megen brushed the side of Manel's cheek. Manel's eyes opened, red as the harvest moon. The sedative had worn off.

He stared at his brother. Neither moved.

Megen finally stood, not severing his gaze.

"You need to get better. We can't have an emperor incapable of defending himself."

"I vowed to defend the emperor at all costs!" Gallic exclaimed.

Megen looked over at him with malice.

"You can do nothing." He turned from them and headed out the room. "I will see what I can get from the Boresso family here."

Maxellia exhaled softly and went back to her tablet. There had to be a way to fix the problems with the Earth goods.

Out of the corner of her eye, she saw Lenri walk slowly towards Manel who had fallen back to sleep. She knelt on both knees before him and simply stared up at him. Her face a sense of wonderment as she unconsciously scratched at her shoulder where the scar ran.

❀ ❀ ❀

Master Jaubro read the message from Eterenia regarding a remedy for Caden's son, Cameron. It didn't surprise him that Chalayl had not used her resources to help the child. Cellaxa healers pleaded with her on multiple occasions to send him back for treatment.

Granted, the ones being used on the emperor were having mixed effects. That didn't give much confidence. He shut off his screen and rose from the communication console.

He walked out of the control room into the main hall. Desedon fell in step with him as he passed the threshold. Royal occupants bowed their heads to them along the way. Gray skies loomed over the courtyard to their left, sunlight scarce.

A handful of royals scattered around the grounds, strolled the paths, admiring the floral displays.

Despite the lack of sunlight, the plant life grew tall and large. Most of the flower buds were the size of one's head, the petals like giant blades bigger than arms. They hung over the paths, staring down at passersby as if daring them to touch.

Groups of small creatures flew above and scurried through the bushes.

"Thoughts?" Desedon broke the serenity.

"I think we should find a cure before Boresso's new drug hits the market."

"But it is specific for what ails the emperor and his bloodline."

"Oh, it can be formulated to be used for other medical needs. That will get more attention than a recreational concoction with a short lived high."

"They are quite vicious if they feel their territory is being tread on."

"The ones on Earth? Yes, I agree. I'm meeting with the main family here to see what they have to say about the issue."

"Are they coming here?" Desedon slowed his steps and Master Jaubro halted. "Is that wise?"

"Would you rather we go to the Boresso stronghold?"

"Actually, yes. We can defend ourselves easily." Desedon began walking again. "And we don't have to deal with running into the emperor inside the halls."

"Fair enough. I will contact the Boresso head and change the location."

They spotted Lenri walking ahead of them. Her slender backside made her seem taller. The red robe of an imperial soldier flowed from her shoulders. She appeared to sense their presence and slowed down, turning her head back. When they got closer, she stopped to face them.

"Princess, why are you strolling the palace alone?" Master Jaubro reached out to move a lock of unruly hair from her face. She flinched back on instinct. He paused. "I would not harm you."

She stood still while he used a finger to push the hair out of her eyes.

"My apologies." She said almost timidly. "I know this. It's a reflex."

"Of course."

She looked away, embarrassed.

"I'm on my way to see Manel. He seems down. His mood is erratic again."

"Please, be careful." Master Jaubro frowned, not happy about that.

"I will." She gave a short bow and pivoted back around to continue her walk.

"Tell me again why we trust his siblings not to kill him at some point." Desedon said.

"I don't." Master Jaubro smoothed the front of his dress jacket. "Nor vice versa."

They continued their walk. Needing a pleasant stroll before tackling the Boresso clan.

❀ ❀ ❀

Gallic made his way to the emperor's private chamber, his pace hurried. the general summoned him earlier, forcing him to leave his master with two incompetent guards. He never trusted any of them to protect the emperor, knowing they would try to assassinate him if they had the chance. The way each one stared at him as he passed in the halls solidified his decision to always keep one hand on the hilt of his sword.

He burst into the room, slamming the door shut then checking to make sure he secured the room. When he turned to address the emperor, he halted.

In a female form, Manel stood naked in front of the mirror attached to a long dresser. He had never seen that before, not knowing the emperor could shift his sex. His eyes canvassed the lean muscle and skin tone.

Not pale; not tanned.

The hair stuck out n disarray from wild sleeping.

Those red eyes turned to him and he saw something animal like in them. Manel didn't smile or speak. Her expression changed to a different kind of fury. Hunger. The small breasts were the perfect size for Gallic's hands to fondle. Surprised by that thought he averted his glance upwards and met her glare.

With slow movements to show he wouldn't run, Gallic started to remove his cape, then armor, and last, his bodysuit. He tossed his boots into the corner of the room and pushed the suit down off his body.

Kicking it near the boots, he moved a few steps towards Manel.

"You can have me any way you desire."

He tried not to tense when Manel advanced, red eyes glowing. She manhandled him, throwing his body onto the bed like a sack, as she climbed atop him in a fervor. He took a deep breath and tried to relax in anticipation of her brutality.

The moment his member entered her, a stinging sensation cascaded through his whole body. Each violent bounce sent him in a state of euphoria. He stared at Manel, riding him like a beast, spittle dripping from her lips. On instinct, he grabbed hold of the soft mounds of her breast for leverage. Her thrusts pushed him farther to the edge of the bed. They would certainly fall off at some point.

A high-pitched wail came from Manel followed by angry tears. Her body slightly morphed and black talons pierced his chest. After a few more cruel thrusts accompanied by the wails, Manel's back arched back, stiffening. Gallic felt his seed being squeezed out of him, gushing forth in the most satisfying release he had ever encountered.

"Aaha!" Manel cried out in what sounded like a child on the verge of weeping.

And then it was over.

Manel brought her head forward and stared down at him with utter disgust.

Her quick dismount with his erection not fully deflated, the motion tugging it harshly, made him wince, not daring to move. A glance down at his nether regions revealed bruising along his pelvis and thighs. Smears of black blood covered his member. The puncture marks in his chest were shallow and blood oozed lazily down to his sides.

Neither said a word as Manel got dressed in the casual robe, not bothering to wash off. Gallic eased up from the bed and walked over to his clothes to do the same. He could smell Manel's feral scent all over him. A shudder ran through him. He liked it. More than he wanted to or should.

He licked his lips, tasting sweat.

"We are late for your meeting with the others," he cautiously reminded Manel.

"Then we go."

Manel walked past him into the main corridor. He followed obediently; his stride not so smooth from his lower body taking a beating. The walk seemed longer than usual because of that. On the way, they ran into Lenri.

"I was coming to see you before the meeting," she called out, getting closer. "I wanted to check on your wellbeing." She came towards them.

Her expression changed to bewilderment.

"Is that so?" Manel tilted his head. "Worried about me?" The way he emphasized me sounded condescending at best. "And your verdict?"

Lenri stared at him for a moment. Whatever she saw, she didn't like it.

"Are you sure you're okay?" She inadvertently sniffed, flinching.

Manel's eyes grew brighter, glowing.

"I am doing very well today."

Lenri glanced over at Gallic as Manel continued walking. Malice. He returned her stare, indignant, and followed the emperor. She slowly did the same, her gaze boring into the back of his head.

The other siblings were already in the designated meeting room. It had finally been stocked with food and drinks four moon cycles ago. Manel plopped down in the big chair and let out a loud sigh. Gallic went over to the table covered in food and picked out a fist sized piece of cured meat with a small fruit cut in half. He handed them to Manel who ate them ravenously.

They discussed business, while Gallic tuned it out, keeping vigil on Manel. after a few meetings, they noted he need not voice his opinions any longer. He stood by Manel's side the whole time, not realizing the conversation had halted.

A break. He looked up and sound returned. Manel had fallen asleep, but her eyelids fluttered rapidly, a scowl on her face.

While the others stretched their legs and perused the table, Megen came up to him.

"I know that look in your eyes." His own glowed red. "I can smell it. You've had her."

Gallic reared back from him, hand on his sword's hilt. To tangle with that one felt dangerous. Megen leaned forward.

"And unlike before when Manel would take you by force, you enjoyed it this time." He bared his teeth, saliva building. "You will never let her do that again. You don't get to have her."

Gallic went pale with fear and acknowledgement. Of course, they knew about Manel. He had not stumbled onto to some unknown secret for him to keep. And the way the eldest came at him meant they were all very protective of Manel, especially him.

Manel woke up when the meeting resumed and struggled to hold a conversation. Something seemed wrong. The others noticed. Gallic saw Lenri get Megen's attention and an unspoken revelation passed between them.

Are they going to come after me?

"Let's stop for the day," Maxelia announced.

"We seemed to have lost Manel's interest."

Manel got up moving awkward. "I'm bored." Manel didn't look at any of them on the way out of the room.

Gallic kept close to her the entire walk back to her chamber. Manel entered in a flash, flopping flat on her stomach on the bed, head turned sideways. Mere seconds passed and Manel fell back to sleep. He pulled a chair by the bed and sat to watch over her.

By the next day, Gallic got worried. Beads of sweat covered Manel's brow. The edges of her hair stuck to the wet skin. He got up and went over to the call icon on the wall by the dresser.

Master Jaubro's face filled the small display.

"What is it?"

"I think the emperor needs the healers."

"I will be there shortly with them." Master Jaubro's image winked out.

He went back to the chair and waited. Which wasn't long. Master Jaubro came as promised with two healers and Megen. Gallic hissed, not sure what to do if that monster came at him. He stood and backed away. The healers took data while physically checking the emperor's body.

"What has she consumed?" The first healer asked, opening one of Manel's eyelids. "It had to have been in the last day phase."

"What?" Gallic asked startled.

The way they casually shifted Manel's pronoun let him know they too knew of her state. So stupid. "I fed her some meat at the meeting."

"This would have been before that." The other raised his tablet closer to his chest. "Something toxic got into her system."

"Yes," Megen turned to Gallic. "Indeed. My brother has an insatiable sexual appetite."

"Well, that won't do. As a female, the emperor is only compatible with certain DNA. All others would make her ill. Like this."

"We'll have to neutralize her system." The other healer said.

Master Jaubro frown with disdain. He knew of the emperor's tastes.

"This is one thing after another." He turned to Gallic. "Keep her here for the rest of the week."

Gallic nodded.

Megen brushed past him. A telepathic message assaulted his mind.

'Keep your hands off what is mine.'

Generation Gap

Holnar paced the length of the Sapienti coven banquet hall where they held their next business meeting. The others lounged, drinking their preferred liquors, waiting patiently for him to utter a word. He had been like that for five minutes, his silence tedious.

The almost full moon glowed in the winter night sky. Clouds had rolled in blocking most of the stars. Frost crusted along the seams of the window, framing them in pale white.

They rattled softly from the small winds.

The leaders had used vampires as guards which meant the meeting had to be after sunset. To make sure their minions were sharp, they set the time for ten o' clock.

Laid across the arms and back of the large sofa in the far corner were the leaders' coats. Various full length wools and furs with scarves and hats separated by their owners. A vampire servant from the Sapienti coven stood watch, specially made ear buds inserted to stop them from hearing the conversation.

Suddenly, Holnar stopped, one hand raised to his chin as his fingers drummed against it.

"Who would have the audacity to do something so dastardly right under our noses?" He glanced over his shoulder. "I mean, it is a bold move. With flawless execution."

"I tracked the finances." Darean picked up his tablet lying beside him. He raised it chest level. "Half of it went to a human merchant company. The other half is still in the wind."

"Always follow the money," Pridric laughed. "It went somewhere." He looked over at Tavelo. "You seem rather quiet about this. Are you not concerned?"

"With competition?" Tavelo smirked. "No."

"This is not just competition," Holnar snapped. "This borders on theft!"

"Now you're being overdramatic." Yutel sipped his drink. "I say we accept the challenge. See who wins the most contracts for shipment."

"We built those space ports, not the humans." Holnar pointed accusatory at him. "Do you know something we don't?"

"Yes, we built them." Darean set down his tablet. "On someone else's planet without their consent. You should have known this would happen."

"I did," Chalayl piped up, shoving a half-eaten pastry in her mouth. "isn't that right, Eterenia?"

"It seems all male species are alike." Eterenia tilted her head to one side, glancing at the ceiling. "So focused on power and greed without factoring in those who would dream the same."

Tavelo gave her an indignant stare.

"I don't think that way."

"Because, you're not as selfish as the rest of us. Though sometimes I think you should be."

"What's that phrase again?" Pridric grinned. "A goody two shoes?"

"I care for others. I will not apologize for that!" Tavelo snapped.

"Nor should you." Yutel sat up from the back of the loveseat. "They will be found. We will punish them. Until then," he raised his glass. "To a healthy and prosperous fight."

Holnar's eyes turned silver.

"Are you not taking me seriously?"

The others stared at him incredulous. His face contorted as if he had been personally targeted. Darean frowned at Holnar's greedy, merciless attitude. The way he looked now, make no mistake, he wanted blood for the alleged crime.

"Are you insulting us?" Darean countered, to which Holnar's expression crumbled. "Do you think we don't see our own margins?"

Regret surfaced in Holnar.

"I, personally, want to see what their next play is." Pridric drained his glass. "Which one of us will they target? Will it be a big haul or one that sneaks under the radar?"

"You seem to be enjoying this," Yutel said to him.

"Oh," Pridric smiled. "I am."

'He knows.' Eterenia sent to Tavelo.

'Of course, he does. It was his spy in our home.' Tavelo reached over to the tiered Lazy Susan and grabbed a wedge of cheese. *'And he won't let any of us know it. Not yet.'*

"How much did we lose again?" Yutel asked.

"About three hundred thousand," Darean replied.

"Pfft!" Chalayl waved it off. "They can have it."

"It's not about the dollar amount!" Holnar balled his hands into fists. "It's the principle."

"It's the money." Pridric's tone oozed venom. "You're not fooling anyone."

"Fine. Think of it this way. They do this multiple times over the next year or two. Tally up our losses then. We will be hit hard to the tune of billions."

"Hmm. That is a problem." Chalayl crossed her legs causing the hem of her already short skirt to creep up to the top of her thighs. Pridric looked away in disgust. She smiled. "Let me look into it on my end. I may be able to attract more information with my honey than yours."

A gagging sound came from Pridric.

They turned to find him hunched over, covering his mouth with a fist as he tried not to spit out the piece of cake he choked on. He regained his composure, and tapped his chest. Sitting straight, he met their stares.

Chalayl's eyes glowed an angry red.

"My apologies." He gave a tight-lipped smile. "Went down the wrong way."

"That wasn't subtle by any means, Pridric." Darean chastised him.

❄ ❄ ❄

High fives went around the table in the hotel suite turned conference room. The offspring celebrated their first victory against the elders. After four attempts, they had finally gotten the right contacts to get their shipments onto the planetary cargo ships that left a month ago.

Champagne bottles littered the table's length, flute glasses with different levels of liquor between them.

Chase sat at the end watching everyone rejoice. One of them came around, patting him the shoulder before heading to the spread of food on the side table. He let them have this moment because the next few rounds would get dicey.

The Marchand coven had already noticed something amiss. Sensing his concern, Olette leaned back in her seat to see him better.

"Don't fret so much, dear leader." She raised her glass "My father is getting what he deserves."

"It's his retaliation I'm worried about," Count Brownlee's son said.

"We can handle that." She eyed her brother across from her. "The man is predictable."

"I'm ready to have a duel with the elders." Caden poured another glass of champagne. "I say in about two months, maybe four, they will find the shell company."

"You have to make it believable," Adelia chided.

"I will fight. No need to worry."

"And if they send your mother?" She asked.

Rage filled Caden's face.

"All the more reason to give it everything I have."

"Who's next on the list?" Tamar grabbed a bottle and slid it towards him. "For my tastes, I think going after Ambrook is too obvious."

"No, not them." Adelia rubbed her lower lip. "Grieger. A small haul."

"Makes sense." Olivier grinned. "He would love the challenge."

"My father won't be as nice as you think," Chiron added.

"Oh, we know." Chase took a sip of champagne. "But he won't come after us too hard."

"Was our human partner happy?" Tamar asked.

"Oh, yeah. The money will keep them afloat for another three months." Chase replied.

"I hate this!" One of the coven daughters slammed a bottle down on the table, shaking all the glasses. An empty bottle toppled onto the carpeted floor and rolled away. "By diverting the flow of trade from the humans, their business and economy are suffering."

"If we don't get it back on track, Earth will end up like our parents' home world." Tamar tipped up the bottle and drank directly from it.

"Really?" A coven daughter glared at him. "Have some class. Get a glass like everyone else!"

"Oh, who cares?" Chiron picked up a bottle and did the same. "We have plenty."

"Today we celebrate. Tomorrow, it's back to business." Chase looked around at everyone. A few nodded in agreement. "Alright. Maestro!" He called out to the person by the audio system. "Music, if you please."

The guy pulled out his smartphone and jacked it into the audio slot. He scrolled through his playlists and found a party mix of popular music and hit play. Music blasted out of the embedded wall speakers. Some of the offspring got up to dance.

The walls vibrated from the bass. They had no cares since the conference room lay between the other two floors they owned.

No one to complain.

❀ ❀ ❀

The Guillarmo office building stood on the outskirts of the business district. A peachy orange colored structure built in the late seventeen hundreds then renovated twenty years ago.

In her office on the top floor, Chalayl took a break from pouring over the financial reports requested by Darean. She spent weeks crunching the data and couldn't put her finger on it quite yet. But did find something familiar about the rogue company's tactics.

She walked around her desk multiple times, taking slow steps as she thought. The low cut long sleeved peach chiffon dress, barely concealing her breasts, flowed to her ankles, showing off gold high heels. The gold necklace with the Guillarmo family crest rested just above her cleavage. A messy bun kept her hair wept off her face.

Cars zipped along the narrow, cobbled streets below, sounding like wind-up toys. The distance muffled people greeting each other. Arctic air filtered through the window opened an inch to bring in freshness to the usually stuffy room. All the windows had foggy borders around the inside.

Her assistant knocked on the door frame and peeked her head around it.

"Did you want to make reservations for lunch, my queen?"

Chalayl stopped and checked her watch. Indeed, lunch time approached.

"Yes. How about that lovely café on the corner?"

"The old world one with the authentic food?"

"That one." Chalayl snapped her fingers."

"I'll get right on it." The assistant left.

Chalayl resumed her walk, this time covering the entire office until she got an epiphany. Ambrook. More precisely, Chase.

What are they up to?

She remembered the smug look from Pridric at the meeting. This wouldn't be the first time the Strana family used underhanded means for profit gains. She frowned. The data suggested the humans were benefitting.

Was Pridric trying to appease both parties?

But you can't have it both ways, you narcissistic piece of shit!

She found how he clung to her supposed betrayal during their courting funny. An agreement between their parents, not her. She found Pridric dull, pitiful, and without his own convictions. His lashing out at Tavelo to stay in step with his family's treatment of the Endagas disgusted her. The Stranas didn't think outside the box. Boresso did.

Should I expose this tidbit of information?

She turned to the window and watched a man get out of his car and hit the hood of the one behind hm. The other stayed in the driver's seat and honked his horn incessantly.

"Get out of the car!" The man said in Spanish.

"Move your piece of shit!" The other yelled out his window, his hand pushing down on the horn.

Neighbors came out to complain about the noise.

"I'll play this game a little longer." Chalayl folded her arms, placing one hand against her cheek.

Her assistant came back into the room.

"Are you ready to go? The car is waiting."

She looked down at the street. One of her men approached the two cars blocking the road. It would be cleared soon enough.

"I am. Let's go get some yummy food." She smiled sweetly as her assistant handed her coat over. "I'm starving."

❀ ❀ ❀

So many workers went running back and forth through the Greiger estate that Yutel's cousin and personal secretary, had to maneuver around them as he too walked briskly down the halls. He rubbed his forehead, his fingers coming off covered in sweat.

A problem with one of the shipments had Yutel livid. He gave the workers a fire and brimstone speech.

After Yutel left for his office to let off steam, his secretary went to every department to handle damage control. He now made his way to see if the boss had calmed down. Yutel's office door sat ajar. He could hear things rattling in the room, shaking from Yutel's pacing, stomping really, from one end to the other sans jacket with the shirt sleeves rolled up.

"Are you upset?" He asked cautiously.

Yutel stopped, turning his head towards him.

"Not in the slightest. I knew this was coming."

"Your recent outburst claimed otherwise."

"I had to make it look convincing." Yutel smiled. "It went well?"

His secretary let out a long sigh as his shoulders slumped forward. He relaxed his body and bent over until his head almost touched his knees. Yutel stared down at him, dubious as to what that accomplished.

A sense of calm, you behemoth!

The secretary straightened his posture.

"Yes, you did well." He walked past Yutel to stand by the windows. "That said, you can't allow those brats to get the upper hand so quickly."

"Oh, they get to have this small taste. I'm sure they are rejoicing."

"Indeed. Holnar and Pridric will come down on them with swift vengeance."

Out of the corner of his eye, he saw Yutel bristle. The Dakien and Endaga family were least respected of the merchants. He always wondered why when both had the most solid clients. The others were constantly looking for new vendors and goods.

Yutel adjusted his rolled sleeves, tightening them.

"That will not happen on my watch."

The secretary playfully raised his brow.

"Are you going to protect them, too?" He glanced back at Yutel. "Do you really want to go up against those monsters?"

A page with messy hair and disheveled clothes came to the doorway. Fresh bite marks were on her neck. She had gotten away from the clutches of a stressed out and greedy vampire. The secretary shook his head in disgust. The vampires seemed to lack restraint as of late and preyed on the human help despite the rules against it.

"Are you alright, dear?" He asked, not moving forward. Her body language showed her on edge and leery of anyone's intentions. "Take your time."

"My apologies for appearing to you like this, sir." She answered in a jagged voice. She bowed to Yutel. He waved a hand for her to continue. "We were able to trace one of the accounts."

Yutel and the secretary turned to her in shock.

"First." The secretary said. "Who else knows this information?"

"Just myself, and the finance counselor," she replied with a nervous smile.

"Let's keep it that way. Now, what did you find?"

She took a deep breath and stepped back from the door a bit.

Uh oh. It must be bad.

"It appears one of the Boresso children heads it."

"Oh?" Yutel turned to face her. She flinched yet stood her ground. "Which one?"

"Caden, sir."

Now there's a shocker.

The secretary knew immediately, the significance of that information. Yutel seemed to have figured it out as well. Mustering up a stern face, he looked down at the woman.

"I want this handled discreetly. Make sure Queen Celeste does not get wind of this until I say."

"Yes, sir. Lord Grieger."

She bowed again, remaining.

"Is there something else?"

"From our spy reports, it seems the Ambrook coven may be involved as well."

"Is that so?" Yutel asked, nodding. "Keep that under wraps as well."

"Of course, Lord Grieger."

She did a final bow before turning to leave.

"And clean yourself up. My head of security will have a talk with the one who mauled you."

She simply nodded, barely tilting her head, and hurried down the hall.

"So, he's making a move against her." Yutel smiled wide, baring teeth.

"Which one? Pridric has never missed an opportunity to smite her. As for Caden. She's ging to lose her mind. That child may be in danger from his own mother."

"He may be young, but that Kataling boy is very dangerous. She would do well to be careful."

The secretary cocked his head, staring out the window. That was true. He had seen the footage. Heard the stories from the fight on the home world. Chalayl had no idea what she had spawned.

Serves you right.

He caught Yutel's reflection in the glass.

And you haven't seen my cousin's true wrath yet.

A raid?

Caden almost laughed at the scene as brutes from Marchand and Sapienti barreled through the doors of his dummy company's dock office in England. With the docks being run jointly by De Luce and Ambrook, he could only imagine the fight that would take place when they found out what went on at that moment.

He could smell malice in the sweat coming out of every pore as the thugs smashed the cabinets and equipment. They all wore heavy three-quarter length coats made of wool and tweed slightly damp, the scent mingling with the cold air being brought in.

Keeping his distance for a bit, he watched them manhandle some of the workers, demanding the name of their boss. One brute snatched a skinny young man in dock overalls. The man looked like he couldn't have been a hundred pounds wet. His body lifted a few feet off the floor, his feet dangling.

"Who's in charge here?" The brute yelled in the terrified man's face, shaking him by the neck like a ragdoll. "I'll snap your fucking neck if you don't start talking!"

He can't talk if you're strangling him.

Caden let out a sigh and took a step forward. One of his proxies grabbed hold of his arm.

"Wait!" His proxy hissed. "There's too many!"

"I can handle them," Caden scoffed, wrenching his arm from him.

"What? You're going to morph out on the docks and bathe it in blood?"

Caden frowned. Not really the plan. He knew his actions would only make things worse. They had to keep up the illusion. Make sure his role remained a distraction while the others went for the kill behind the scenes.

"Fine. I won't go all ancient on them." He continued to advanced. "But I won't let them kill anyone on my watch."

He went to the broken doorway, careful not to let

the piece still swinging on its hinges hit him. The thugs closest to him turned in surprise. The other's, holding the skinny man, expression shifted, scrunched with disgust. His brow wrinkled into thick, tight ropes while his eyes narrowed into slits.

"You?" His tone dripped with the same malice Caden sniffed from him. "This?" He tilted his head indicating the office. He tossed the skinny man to the back of the office. His body landed on an overturned filing cabinet. Caden fought his instinct to wince. "Think you can compete with the elders, do ya'?"

Caden smiled. He blocked the doorway, making a stance with his feet shoulder width apart. His eyes turned red, resembling skinned cherry tomatoes, then grew darker. His black pupils became pin dots. The brute and his associates stopped cold.

"You need to leave."

Caden kept his voice even; calm.

The workers crawled further to the back of the office. They were a mix of human and vampire. And they wanted nothing to do with the fight about to start.

"Are you threatening us, boy?" The brute asked, incredulous.

"That depends." Caden exhaled. He dropped his shoulders. "I don't want senseless bloodshed."

"Hmm. You steal from the elders," he started.

"I didn't steal anything."

"And expect us to brush it off?"

The brute continued.

"Only negotiating fair market prices."

"Nah, you need to be taught a lesson."

"So you come here and start killing people on a dock your leaders don't own and think there will be no consequences?" Caden saw a flicker of understanding. The brutes looked around at each other hesitant to finish their task.

"Yes," the voice of Eterenia's proxy came from behind Caden. "I'm going to need all of you to stand down and vacate these docks." Armon stood with four other vampires flanking him. "Unless you want to personally explain to Queen Erena what you're doing here?

His open full-length black coat showed off the tailored black suit with a satin red tie and handkerchief. He wore a red fedora sporting a black band. Caden's mouth turned downwards, approving the new look.

"Is that right?" The brute pointed to Caden. "Then why is he allowed to do business on the docks?"

Armon moved Caden gently out of the way and walked past him into the office. He assessed the damage and shook his head.

"The same reason other companies can. He has a permit for goods being transported."

Can't argue with that. Caden nodded.

The situation appeared to de-escalate.

"Now," Armon turned to him. "to be clear, you are technically stealing customers."

As he faced Caden, his gaze shifted over his shoulder and grew wide. The brute Caden argued with earlier stood stunned immobile behind him, then raised his hands, waving them in an X.

"No!"

Caden felt a sting followed by his own blood gurgling up his esophagus. He looked down and saw a small harpoon tip coated in blood protruding from his chest. He stared at Armon coming towards him.

"Caden!"

He held out a hand, gesturing for him to stop.

Snapping off the harpoon tip he pulled its broken shaft from his back, then morphed into his Kataling form. The doorframe splintered apart to accommodate his size, forcing the rest of the office's structure to collapse. He turned towards the assassin, his tail decimating the inside of the room, as he launched.

The assassin didn't have a chance to flee. Caden chomped down on the left side of the man's body, his grip like a vice and snapped his jaws shut, nearly severing his prey.

A projectile thudding against his thick skin stopped him from biting deeper to complete the act. He opened his jaw to let the brute's body fall out onto the ground. Caden's body whipped around in the direction of the attack. Armon and his guards were fighting a group of brutes that had come in as backup while another focused on him.

He zeroed in on the one holding a large gun. The brute stepped back, realizing his weapon was now useless against a Kataling of that size. He charged, and let out a guttural scream as he flipped the notch on the clip to empty it. Caden hit him full on, sending the brute into the air. He landed on the roof of the adjacent building followed by the sound of bones snapping.

"Enough!"

The loud bellow cut through the din of fighting. Caden swung around, ready to attack again when a tranquilizer dart sailed into him from behind. He staggered, shocked by the sting, then fell with a thud that shook the ground.

He reverted to bipedal form, tears streaming down his face as he forced out an anguished cry. The wound from the harpoon began to bleed out. Caden's proxy, no longer able to stay in the shadows came running to his side.

Chancellor Rayne snapped a finger. Two of the Ambrook vampires went to help them seal the gaping wound until they could get him to the coven house nearby.

"I don't know what the hell any of you were thinking, but it will not be tolerated." He glanced around at the combination of Marchand and Sapienti. "This is not how we do things."

Armon brushed dirt off his coat as he stood arfter being pinned to the floor. His attacker backed off.

"I was trying to handle it."

"You failed." Chancellor Rayne replied bluntly. "How am I supposed to explain this mess?" He looked around and his gaze fell on the half-eaten vampire. He gestured to another of his men. "Get him stabilized and transported to the crypt. Sapienti will have to deal with it."

Caden used all his strength to stay conscious. He saw Chancellor Rayne's legs come up to him then the man bent down so he could see him.

"You've been a naughty little shit. That said, we can't have your mother going full monster on us." He pulled a syringe from his inside jacket pocket and stuck Caden in the neck with it. "Get some rest."

"You can't do this!" Caden's proxy shielded his body from Chancellor Rayne's men coming to lift him off the ground. "He comes back with us."

Chancellor Rayne grabbed him by the throat.

"I wasn't asking." He hissed, baring fangs.

"Are you really going to try and take him by force?" Armon pushed two of the Ambrook vampires out of the way and stepped between Chancellor Rayne and Caden's proxy. His movement forced him to release the young man's neck. "You need to let them be."

"Do not interfere!" He looked around at the scene and saw hesitation in everyone's eyes. "He needs medical attention and the Ambrook coven is the closest facility."

"After what happened to Master Durante?" The proxy yelled. "We don't trust you!"

"Stop being stubborn! You're acting like ignorant children."

A loud, high pitched shriek made Chancellor Rayne's blood run cold. He cringed in shock and fear, not daring to move in the event he may get gouged, as a Volshin swooped down from above the fallen office structure. It snatched Caden's body up, causing a mighty whirlwind before taking off to the skies with its prize. It took all of Chancellor Rayne's strength to not succumb to the forcible wind.

Most of the thugs, along with some of the De Luce and Ambrook men weren't so diligent. They went flying in every direction, landing on debris and hitting the sides of nearby buildings. Which gave the assistant time to signal his group. They fled the scene, leaving a stunned Chancellor Rayne. The thugs not gathering their wits fast enough to catch them.

"Well." Armon shook out debris that had flown in his hair. He straightened his suit jacket. "That solves that problem."

"No." Chancellor Rayne glared over at him. "This little stint is going to cost him. The council will want to drag his ass in for some hard questions."

"Seriously?" Armon scoffed. "How much did any of us actually lose over this? A couple of million? The amount is negligible compared to the quarterly revenue."

"It's the principle of the thing! Don't act like you don't know that."

Armon rolled his eyes, shaking his head. He whistled at his men and they gathered around him.

"I'm leaving. I have to report the damage to the office area of the docks and get a crew to repair it by the end of the week." He smirked. "We look forward to your payment of half the cost." He looked over at the thugs. "That goes for your covens as well."

One of his men handed him his hat. He flipped it in his hands and placed it on his head. Chancellor Rayne stepped out of his way, not without giving him a disgusted stare. Armon's entourage walked off the docks towards the lower street level.

The Volshin slowed its descent as it neared a large house built into the rocky hillside. Two Katalings guarded the entrance of the sandstone structure. The dark birchwood double doors opened for Omeron who walked out onto the landing, his eyes narrowed in concern. Hovering above him, the Volshin gently released Caden into his arms. His father caught him and carried him into the house.

The remains of the Volshin's clothes, tattered from the transformation, fell to the ground when he reverted to human form. He hadn't time to stuff them in the satchel around his neck before morphing to save Caden. He brushed long blond hair from his face, pulling it back, then followed stark naked.

Omeron went down a long corridor and kicked open the last door at the end on the left. He went in and laid his son on the bed. The healer from the home world came in. Omeron ripped open Caden's already ruined clothes to expose the wound. He sucked air through his teeth as his eyes glowed silver with rage.

"Step back." The healer moved forward and he obeyed. He placed a hand on the wound and pushed gently around it. "Looks like whatever it was went through some scar tissue from a previous wound near the area."

"Can you fix it?" Omeron began to pace the room like an anxious animal. He glanced over at the Volshin. "Loaman! What was it?"

Loaman pulled on the pair of leggings a servant handed him. "A mini harpoon. Seems they liked the way the imperial soldiers used them in the first battle on Earth."

Everyone in the room stared at him in horror. They remembered the giant harpoons launched from the Imperial dropships, cutting down Volshins in the sky and impaling Katalings to the ground.

"Who?" Omeron stopped pacing a few feet from him. "Which coven did this weapon come from?" Loaman shrunk from him. "Tell me!"

"A Marchand thug had it." Loaman locked eyes with him. "You shouldn't be surprised."

"I'm not." Caden's father turned from him. He addressed the healer. "What do you think?"

"Whatever sedative they gave him is super powerful. It's a blessing. He will be out for days while I fix this mess."

The chiming of a cell phone echoed in the room.

Loaman pulled it from his small satchel.

He answered with a swipe of his thumb across the bottom.

"What is it, father?" He kept silent for a moment then nodded. "Yes." Then looked at Omeron and Caden. "You would need to see for yourself." More silence and nodding. "Of course." He swiped his phone again to disconnect the call. "My father is on his way. He's in the backyard. Saw me flying in with a body in my talons." He shrugged.

While the healer set his tools on the side table, Luamis, the Volshin leader, walked into the room. A sloppy, dirty blond braid twisted past his shoulders. He wore a loose cream tunic and leather leggings. Thick soled sandals graced his feet. Small dirt stains were on his forearms and under his nails. He smelled of ripe tomatoes, a blending of herbs, and earth.

The sight of Caden on the bed with his chest splayed open stopped him in his tracks at the foot of the bed. Everyone in the room could see him struggle to contain his internal rage. He stood rooted, silent, as he scanned Caden's body.

"Explain this." Tension tinged his soft tone. Loaman leaned over to whisper in his ear. When he finished, Luamis' eyes turned blood red, almost glowing. "This is the last straw."

"I agree." Caden's father moved from the bed, the healer shooing him away with the waving of his hand. "We need to bring this secession to fruition. Either that or we start killing all of them."

"That is not ideal." Luamis replied. "I know you harbor deep feelings against them, especially that Boresso female." He indistinctly ran a hand over his shoulder. "I too, have no empathy for them."

Omeron grimaced at the motion, knowing the scar beneath Luamis' clothes ran diagonally across his body. A deep wound from the massive harpoon that shot him down over a century ago. He felt a rush of nausea come, bending him over.

His eyes started to sting as if he were on the verge of tears. He fought it back as he clutched his abdomen then stood straight.

The healer gave them a quizzical stare, halting his work on Caden. Omeron glared at him and he went back to his task. His first assistant kept the machine suctioning blood and loose tissue stable while the other helped with repairing the wound.

A house member came to the doorway, followed by Caden's proxy. The young man barely contained his grief as his gaze landed on Caden. Anger replaced it. He walked up to Omeron and placed the broken piece of the harpoon in his hand.

"He'll want it as a souvenir." The proxy sniffed, wiping the bottom of his nose with a finger. "They tried to take him. Chancellor Rayne and his men. To Ambrook coven."

"Contact Baltise. And Lord Endaga." Luamis leaned against the wall near the doorway. "It's time to make the family heads understand our position."

"And theirs," Omeron added. "They no longer get to do as they please with us."

Forced Unity

Holnar slammed the car door shut as he exited the vehicle, his face scrunched in disgust. He straightened his three-piece suit; a charcoal grey with black silk accents and accessories. His bodyguards came around to meet him so they could walk into the stone house in a tight formation. He didn't trust not one ancient. A glance at the surrounding area let him know they had the advantage.

"How dare they summon us like servants?" He spoke more to himself, yet receiving nods of agreement from his men. "And blindfolded. As if we couldn't find them otherwise."

"Griping already?" Darean stepped out of the car parked behind his and tilted his hat to him. "We have to keep an open mind and see what it is they want."

Holnar stared at Darean's deep maroon over the top suit with matching waistcoat. He looked like he had stepped out of a period movie.

"What's with the getup?" He pointed at him.

"Oh, this?" Darean grinned. "I figured this meet would be some sort of farce or unrealistic demand. I wanted to feel nostalgic."

The slam of a car door from the other side got their attention. Yutel stepped from his vehicle and passed them in a huff. Pulling his jacket together, to force it around his bulk, he barely got the buttons in.

"You're an ass," he said loudly at Darean as he walked across the front lawn.

"I'm going to concur with that," Pridric said. He came into view ahead of them. His signature black suit with silver pin stripes and black tie set off by his hair pulled tight in an austere ponytail gave a vibe of authority. Chancellor Rayne kept in perfect step by his side. "For all we know, they've lured us here to eat us."

Holnar stopped walking.

"That's not amusing. Pridric."

"Who said I was being funny?"

Chalayl sashayed up the middle of the lawn from her vehicle wearing a skin hugging dress made of a stretch material that moved with every curve. The coral color made it look like she wore nothing but a tan when the light hit it just right. Her hair hung loose, the giant chocolate brown waves cascading around her shoulders and falling to her waist.

Pridric made a scene by softly retching while turning his head. Yutel turned his head to look behind him at the rest of the group. He glared at Pridric. A warning. Holnar did the same. Pridric straightened his posture, staring at the sky in exasperation.

"Oh, dear!" Chalayl laughed. "Are you still miffed I won't let you climb into me like the petulant child you are?"

Pridric turned on her only to have Darean grab him by the arm and wrench him back forward.

"Don't you antagonize him!" Holnar yelled. "What is wrong with you?"

"Let's go."

Darean forced Pridric to walk with him and his entourage. The Ambrook vampires followed behind in silence. "Ridiculous."

"Where is Eterenia and Tavelo?" Holnar looked around. He spotted another set of vehicles on the side of the abode. "Ah. They beat us here, apparently."

Yutel frowned at that.

He didn't voice it, but he felt Pridric's immediate caution and tension. It may well be an ambush. Too late to turn back now.

Two house members led the group into the home, with another two behind them. There would be no escape. The décor matched the outside. Shades of neutral whites, yellows, and tan made the place feel comfortable, relaxing. The group felt anything but. Each leader stayed on full alert. They turned a corner and came into a massive sitting area with oversized cushions laid strategically along the floor.

In the far end at the center were the Kataling and Volshin leaders. Omeron had his usual scowl while Luamis sat stoic. Ancient ones, with mutually angered expressions at the merchant leaders' presence, sat scattered throughout the room.

Tavelo and Eterenia sat on a pile of cushions to the left. They already had drinks in their hands and looked apprehension.

Chalayl seemed to shrink as her gaze fell on Omeron. She hurriedly looked away, fearful he might come at her. The other merchants, except for Tavelo and Eterenia, stared at her in awe, not knowing why. She kept her distance, heading for a set of cushions on the other side closest to the doors.

Pridric connected the dots in an instant. He had heard snippets about how Caden had been conceived.

"So that's the one kept in chains while you climbed on him against his will. Caden's origin." He tilted his head as he saw the animosity for her in the Kataling's eyes. "How fortunate for you to meet again."

"This does not bode well," Yutel whispered to Darean. Holnar glanced over at him. "Still think you should come off authoritative in this situation?"

"Take a seat." Luamis commanded. The issue not up for debate. "We have much to cover and you need to be silent."

Holnar sputtered, ready to argue.

He saw Tavelo and Yutel shake their heads at him. His face flushed with frustration, he found a place to settle with his one bodyguard. They were only allowed one in the room with their merchants. The rest they escorted to an adjacent one.

The ancient ones waited until all the merchant leaders were settled with drinks in hand before they turned to the head Kataling and Volshin. Despite the quiet, everyone waited on edge. If a fight broke out, it would be a massacre.

The merchants on the losing side.

"We will no longer be treated as pawns for your bidding." Luamis made sure to make eye contact with each merchant leader. "For centuries our kind have protected and coddled you. Obeying out of pity."

"Because the alternate would be to annihilate you," Omeron added.

"As of this day, going forward, we are declaring our ties severed." Luamis' eyes turned a gradient shade of amber, green, and red. "Any assistance we provide for you will be on a voluntary basis."

"We've had enough of your foolish ideals."

Omeron leaned forward to emphasize.

"You may now speak." Luamis leaned against the sides of the giant cushion that enfolded him. When no one spoke, he exhaled loudly through is nose. "I insist."

"I understand." Tavelo set his drink down. "It's no surprise, really."

"Oh?" Holnar bellowed, with eyes bulging. "You knew of this little coup?"

"That's a bit dramatic," Darean address him.

"The hell it is!" Holnar stood from his cushion. "Your kind has been in service to our families and the royal house for a millennium and now you're, what, dissatisfied with the arrangement?"

A Volshin flashed to his side and whispered.

"Sit down."

The color drained from Holnar's face.

He didn't dare turn around. Instead, opting to slowly ease back into the comfort of his cushion. Tavelo stared at him in disappointment.

"That being said," Darean spoke up. "If you wish to stay here on Earth, the situation poses a different dilemma. There is no way, humans are going to let you roam the surface unchecked."

"We know." Luamis raised his head. "You are going to assist us in negotiation."

"And why should we do such a thing?" Pridric asked, swirling his glass of whiskey. He didn't look up at any of them. "What's in it for us?"

"You live." Omeron answered.

Pridric finally looked up and found the other merchants and himself surround by a room full of beastly eyes from half morphed ancients. His mouth downturned.

"Noted."

The meeting ended swiftly. With nothing more to say, the servants ushered out the merchants along with their entourages. Tavelo and Eterenia stayed behind. Omeron led them to the room, where Caden rested fitfully under a mild sedative while his wounds healed.

"What do you wish to do?" Tavelo asked Omeron.

"You need to take him with you. He's safer at your home." His face softened. "And his child is there."

"True. How about tomorrow? I think he should rest more."

Eterenia stroked the top of Caden's head. She had a worried look. Tavelo sighed.

I get it.

"Do you think we were too forward?" Luamis asked as he came into the room.

"Not at all. In fact," Tavelo smiled. "I think you came across as quite civilized."

"But, do you really want to stay on this planet?" Eterenia asked.

The ancient leaders paused, not sure how they wanted to answer. Many of the younger ones were born on Earth. They knew no other home. Whether it was the right choice for their kind lingered.

"Let's save that conversation for another time." Tavelo sat down in the chair by the bed. "First we find out how the humans react to the proposal."

❀ ❀ ❀

Architecture machines flooded an entire swath of land situated between the royal houses and the docks to make way for a new district. Whispers spread across the planet with guesses as to what the emperor may be up to in the area. Foundation grids were being carved out nonstop day and night. Imperial soldiers stood guard at every access corner to prevent prying eyes.

Emperor Manel sat on his throne with his head resting on one hand as he leaned against its side. The royal historian bustling around nearby to ensure a clean live feed. Maxellia glanced over at him.

"Are you sure this is wise, brother?"

Maxelia frowned.

"I will not allow this to continue any further." Manel blinked a few times to alleviate the stinging in his eyes. He felt tired. "Our ancient brethren are not to be slaves for this planet."

"And yet, you made them so for nearly two centuries." She flinched from the stare he turned on her. The untethered rage in those red eyes let her know the level of guilt he had. "My apologies."

"We are ready, my lord," the historian announced.

Emperor Manel sat straight on his throne and stared into the monitor lens.

"I have a decree." He spat out bluntly.

His siblings and the guards winced.

"All ancient ones in servitude are not obligated to submit. Family heads must negotiate contracts for reasonable pay and boarding and send them to the royal recorder for review."

His eyes became fleshy, turning a deeper red. The lens zoomed in on his face. The historian stepped further back from the throne. He saw how the framed image made Emperor Manel look primal.

"Once it is approved, any violation of the agreement will be met with royal justice. Mine. There is no alternative. This is not a request. You have until the third moon to respond."

The monitor shut down and the historian hastily broke down the equipment with the help of his two students. While they gathered it all in their arms, the historian approached the throne.

"Will there be anything else, my lord?"

"Get out." Manel turned away from him and waved a hand towards the doors.

The historian and his students bowed then fled out of the throne room.

"You have created an even more hostile situation." Lendor said, leaning forward in his seat next to Maxelia. "The merchants may have no qualms to comply. The other business families, I'm not so sure."

"It would be in their best interest to not go against Manel. Look what happened last time." Megen walked to the doors. "I will send a patrol out to alleviate the chaos you just incited."

As he left marching down the main corridor, Manel slumped in his throne. He propped his elbow back on the armrest and laid his head in the palm of his hand, closing his eyes.

Maxelia cocked her head to one side. A grin formed on her lips. About time. She wondered when her father's instructions would take effect. From the way Manel seemed to have less energy the past weeks, she assumed the royal physicians under their family's obligation had begun the process.

Gallic stood unwavering at Manel's side.

She frowned. He's an obstacle.

Watching over Manel's sleeping form inside her private hamber, Gallic pondering if he should call a healer. She had started convulsing and shifted to female form in an agonizing fit. She now lay still in a deep sleep.

He caressed her forehead, pushing stray locks of unyielding hair from her face to no avail. They bounced back obstructing her eye lids. He settled back in the chair he had dragged to the edge of the bed and decided to wait until morning.

With daybreak came a flurry of activity in Manel's chamber. Gallic barely had time to unlock the doors when two royal physicians, Master Jaubro, and the two eldest siblings barged in.

Manel awoke, hostile at the intrusion.

"This is madness!" Master Jaubro said.

The first physician went towards Manel to check his vitals and she pushed him into the adjacent wall.

"Do not touch me!" Manel pulled herself upright.

"There is no need for violence." The other physician stepped cautiously forward. "As you know, your father spoke quite adamantly about increasing the family bloodline. He manipulated all of his offspring's DNA to find a suitable remedy."

Gallic felt his insides churn.

He remembered Megen telling him that Manel was his. The first physician got up and stayed near the wall.

"We administered a drug to force ovulation. The one compatible to create a pure bloodline is the eldest son. Maxellia is to facilitate the sessions and make sure there is no interference."

"Wait." Gallic raised a hand to his chest, palm out. "You want to breed the emperor like some experiment because the former emperor willed it?"

"This is not of your concern!" Megen seethed

"Oh," Master Jaubro's assistant said. "But, it is. He is the emperor's personal guard."

The siblings frowned at that inconvenient fact.

"So I do not get a say in this disgusting ritual?" Manel tilted her head down as she stared up at them.

"This is for the good of the kingdom." The second physician replied.

"And will stop you from engaging in behaviors of sexual depravity," the other added.

"Hmm?" Manel smirked. "Is that so?" She stared at Megen. "You think I will just lie still and let you violate me without a fight because father wanted it?"

The room went silent.

Gallic saw a sinister gleam cross Maxellia's face. Megen looked about livid. Manel would not let him have his way without leaving bloody reminders. The physician nodded at Manel and began his checkup when she didn't move. The siblings waited until he finished before speaking.

"Is her body in decent condition?" Megen asked. "I won't waste my seed if the attachment is not viable."

"Is there a regiment for optimal time periods? How close between pregnancies is safe?" Maxelia added. "Please send me a proposal."

The two followed the physicians out of the room after they were done. Manel sat still, hands clenched in her lap as she stared down at them.

Her eyes conveyed conflict.

Master Jaubro looked ill. Gallic didn't blame him. He too felt like they treated Manel with disrespect. And they both knew when it came to the previous emperor, Manel's loyalty fluxed. She would comply to a degree because their father still had a hold on all of them, even in death.

Manel walked, surrounded by Maxelia's imperial guards, down the main corridor to a room on the far side of the palace. She had summoned her there with instructions to leave Gallic behind. Which she refused as an option.

Gallic fell in step with her, taking on the furious stares of the guards. They approached the entrance to the room, and the doors flew open.

Maxelia frowned at Gallic.

"You will wait outside with my guards." She addressed Manel. "Come in here." When Manel didn't move, she let out a sigh. "Don't make this difficult."

Megen came to the doorway and grabbed hold of Manel's wrist. He pulled hard, tossing her into the room. Maxellia slammed the doors shut.

Manel landed on the bed set in the far left corner. She rose to attack. Maxelia wrestling her down on her back in a flash. She locked Manel's arms above her head by wrapping her own around them. Manel kicked and screamed, trying to get loose.

Megen grinned at her despair as he removed his tunic and leather pants. He climbed onto the bed and gripped her legs, running his hands up until he reached her hips. She continued to struggle, spittle forming at the corners of her mouth. He slapped the side of her buttock so hard the sound lingered in the room.

Manel stunned by the assault went still for a moment, allowing Maxelia to take hold of the hem of Manel's dress and pull it completely off to make a bondage tie at her wrists.

"Don't fight me. I'll hurt you." Megen leaned closer and their eyes met. Without warning he forced himself into her. Maxellia muffled her cries by clamping a hand over her mouth. "You will give me a spawn every third season until I'm satisfied."

He thrust into her roughly, like an animal, partially morphing at times. Manel continued to resist even in their sister's iron grip. Tears streamed down her face from humiliation and pain. She felt his seed flow into her as he finished with a guttural howl.

Drenched in sweat, he leaned over her, his hair dripping onto her.

"That wasn't so bad. Hmm?"

He wiped the tears from her eyes and sat up.

"If this won't take, we'll try again in a few weeks."

He slid off the bed and went into the bathing room on the other side of the room. Their sister felt Manel go slack and looked down at her. Guilt hit her. An invisible boulder sized weight plowed into her soul. She shook it off.

No. This was fine.

Manel deserved to feel helpless. Deserved harm. That said, she didn't want to see what lay beneath her. A broken doll.

She unraveled the dress at Manel's wrists and pulled it off. Their brother came out of the bathing room and stopped in the doorway. His gaze landed on Manel. His expression turned to horror. Deep gouges from his talons ran along her sides.

Bruises already formed at her pelvis and thighs. Blood smeared across her body.

"I didn't mean to…"

Their sister carefully slid from behind Manel and gently lifted her off the bed.

"You are a monster with no restraint. Why else do you think I had to hold her down for you?" She nodded at the bathing room. "Move. I need to clean her up. We'll have to deal with Gallic."

He stepped out of the way so she could enter then turned to the bed. Blood and sweat stained the covers. He pulled them off into a heap on the floor for the servants to retrieve.

I'll be more accommodating next time.

Manel would always fight unless he eased her anxiety.

He didn't wish for this to be a vengeance for the harm Manel had caused them. Merely a task to be completed. Once done, there would be nothing to tie them to their father's deranged instructions. His sense of satisfaction became short-lived seeing Manel hurt. He fantasized daily on how to make his younger sibling suffer.

Not like this.

Shuffling on the other side of the main entrance alerted him that Gallic had heard what had transpired over the past hour. He could almost envision his sister's guards subduing him every time he tried to break into the room. Not wanting blood shed so early in the day, he flung the doors open.

"Commander Gallic!" The guards stopped their assault." You will wait obediently until emperor Manel is brought out. These guards," he glared at them. They released Gallic. "Will escort you back to the emperor's chamber where you will make sure she is not disturbed for the next few weeks. Is that understood?"

He saw Gallic fight back tears. His loyalty knew no bounds. Which was part of the problem.

"Bring her to me." Gallic regained his military composure and stood in the doorway ready.

"Good." Megen turned towards the inside of the room and saw his sister redressing a comatose Manel. When she was done, he took Manel from her and carried her to Gallic. He placed her gently in his arms. "You are dismissed."

Gallic turned away, Manel cradled in his arms, and walked down the corridor with the guards close behind. They rounded the corner at the edge of the sector and disappeared out of sight. Megen turned around and grabbed his sister by the throat.

"Don't you ever let me do that again." His voice hissed out through gritted teeth, his eyes burning red. "This is not what I wanted."

She wrenched his hand away and stepped back from him.

"This is your doing, not mine! Learn to control yourself. It's not my job to do so."

"No." He moved closer to her. "It's your job to assist and make sure she is not harmed." She flinched from him. "If you cannot fulfill your duty, maybe Lendor can facilitate in your place."

"That's not necessary!" She spat. "I'm leaving." She pushed past him and walked out the room, glancing at the pile of bloodied bedding as she went. "I'll have the royal physicians check on her condition tomorrow."

"Yes. You do that." Megen plopped down in one of the chairs by the door. "I hope it took." He didn't want to try again in only a few weeks. Manel would not have healed by then. And he couldn't guarantee his level of control.

❀ ❀ ❀

Dock workers scrambled towards the newly built passenger ship with the Jaubro logo emblazoned on the side of its hull. The ramp came down at a thirty-degree angle, connecting to the stop chocks on the ground. Master Jaubro and his secondary assistant, Stawen, walked down to the docks, followed by their own workers who veered off to unload the cargo.

Master Jaubro stuck both hands in his pants' front pockets. His opened mustard tan long coat swayed behind him, showing off his tailored attire.

Stawen kept in close proximity, glancing around the area for threats. He wore the usual black suit with a white tunic underneath. A mid-level Volshin and devoted worker, usually stationed at the homestead, performed high risk missions for the Jaubro family when needed.

His shiny black boots clacked against the planks. The docks were bustling like normal, but something seemed off. The Volshins patrolling the air didn't screech, yet their presence was menacing. Merchants conducted business in a sort of quiet.

"Something rotten is afoot, my lord."

Stawen stood at the edge of the boardwalk.

"Yes. I agree."

Their family's personal vehicle waited on the street with the driver leaning against its side.

The moment he spotted his charges, he pressed the door sensor. The panel slid open for Master Jaubro and Stawen to settle inside. He shut it behind them and went around to the operating seat in the front. The vehicle eased forward, gaining speed as it left the industry district.

Entering the residential sectors, the scenery changed drastically. Even from inside the vehicle, Master Jaubro could feel the hostility. He saw several families walking with stern expressions, their service ancient one following behind at a safe distance not caring.

Traffic came to a halt ahead. The vehicle stopped. Master Jaubro leaned forward to gauge the situation.

"Lower the viewing shields," he commanded the operator. "I want to hear."

The window on his side disappeared, letting in the moist air. He took a deep breath, then focused on the drama unfolding.

A high classman floated in the stream next to the overpass. Algae covering his head also ruined his suit. He struggled to stay above water. On the overpass, a woman, clearly his wife, screamed for their guardian to help him.

"How dare you!" Her face contorted in rage. "There was no cause for you to throw him in there. Your kind are just monsters when not on a leash."

The ancient one's talons extended. The woman backed away.

"If he didn't want retaliation, he shouldn't have struck me with his cane. I won't tolerate it."

"He's drowning! Do you wish him to die?" Her voice reached a fever pitch.

The ancient one cocked his head to one side. The woman blanched.

"No. But why should I rescue him?"

"Because it's your duty!" She yelled astonished.

"Then fire me. Cancel my contract."

The ancient one shrugged.

Bystanders stood witness in disgust at the scene. Then Master Jaubro corrected his assessment. The family members were aggravated. The ancient ones in their service were not.

"Please." Then the woman's expression changed to sorrow. "We're sorry. Just," she slumped to the ground. "Save my husband."

The ancient one became a blur as he flew to the man and scooped him up, planting him in his wife's arms. She held her husband close while their servant stood over them with not a drop of water on him.

"When you have both recovered yourselves, I will assist in getting him home."

"Thank you," the woman whispered.

The ancient one pushed them out of the street so traffic could resume flow. The onlookers went back to their strolls. Tension filled the air.

"This kind of thing happens all the time," their operator said. "I think the high classmen got it all wrong. Ancient ones were never meant to be our slaves. Treating them like so was a mistake."

"I agree. This will take time for them to adjust."

"They better get it together soon. The emperor's eldest brother is losing patience. He has called for swift and stricter punishment for offenders."

"Then the palace will be our first stop. Home will have to wait."

"As you request." The operator tapped the display to select the palace coordinates already programmed in. "Course set. I will send a message to Lord Desedon to meet you at the royal entrance."

"Thank you. Once you drop me off, make sure Stawen gets home."

The operator acknowledged with a nod. Along the way, Master Jaubro saw more incidents of strife between families and the ancient ones in their service. What a mess.

❀ ❀ ❀

Master Jaubro and Desedon maneuvered their way through the bodies laid along the walls of the royal chambers' corridor. A mix of the unconscious and those struggling to regain control of their bodies moaned in agony. Bite marks from what appeared to have been a rabid animal were on various parts of the skin.

One royal guard tried to reach out and grab his assistant's leg. Not having the strength, his arm fell to the floor as he went face down. His assistant stepped out of the way staring at the pitiful man.

"Looks like the emperor is expecting again," Desedon spoke nonchalant. Master Jaubro stared over at him in confusion.

Lendor walked forward to greet them. His gaze darted around, taking stock of the situation as he strolled. When both parties were a few feet apart, he stopped in the middle of the corridor, away from any of the fallen.

"What has happened here?"

Master Jaubro swiped an arm before him.

"Manel is quite ravenous while ready to spawn. None of us dare get in the way."

"As I have said before, this is indeed madness." Master Jaubro heard, with trepidation, a groaning woman on the floor, inch closer to them. "I don't recall this happening on such a scale the first time."

"Well," Lendor shrugged. "We did keep Manel secluded for that reason. She ate more food than an army. We had to find a way to stop the bloodshed. The reservoir cube had been a third drained by the time she gave birth."

"And this is the remedy? The reservoir cube is essential, yes. But there has to be a better way than letting her attack the palace residents."

"The emperor is also quite angry. Hostile at her condition." Desedon used one foot to nudge the groaning woman back against the wall. "This seems," he hesitated a moment. "Spiteful."

"That too." Lendor turned around to lead them the rest of the way. "Our eldest siblings are settling into their roles during this time."

"Which I do not agree with."

"What would you have us do?" He glanced over at Master Jaubro. "Manel is not fit to run the empire. Megen is merely acting emperor while also taking control of the military. Maxellia will handle all the administration."

"And what is your role again?" Master Jaubro frowned, knowing the answer. He wanted to hear the royal brat say it.

"To keep Manel in check." Lendor's tone tensed.

"Yes, well, you've failed." Master Jaubro gestured behind. Once they rounded the corner ahead, they would no longer see the carnage. "Here, I thought, things would be handled accordingly while I was away on business." He turned to Desedon. "And you should have reported this to me."

"My apologies, Master Jaubro." He stopped to bow his head, then resumed walking.

The corridor veered to the right, then headed into the curve that opened into the main hallway of the palace. They continued in silence. At the throne room, the guards halted them. The doors opened from the other side to let them in.

On the throne dais sat Maxellia stood next to Megen in full military uniform.

"Welcome back, Master Jaubro," Maxellia greeted him, smiling.

"Yes, how were trade negotiations?" Megen asked.

"I would be doing much better," Master Jaubro replied as he stepped before them. Lendor went to join his siblings. "If I hadn't witnessed an attempted mass genocide in the halls."

Maxelia clutched the arms of the throne. Her lips twitched into a thin line.

"I was not aware another such event occurred." She nodded to one of the royal guards near the door.

They rushed out of the throne room. "It will get cleaned up immediately."

"You are the royal family. I have no claim over any of you. My only task is to be a bridge between this palace and the citizens. At the same time, keep the emperor from harm. Whether it be self inflicted or otherwise."

"We understand that." Maxelia replied. "And we appreciate your wisdom."

"Thank you. Now." Master Jaubro clasped his hands before him. "About the other mess I saw while traveling through the citadel."

"There have been some escalations regarding the last decree." Megen looked down at him. "I am going out momentarily to patrol the hot spots. Violators will be brought here for punishment."

Master Jaubro pinched the bridge of his nose and closed his eyes. He took a few slow breaths. Calm, he reclasped his hands and stared at the royal siblings.

"As long as you are not executing them, I won't interfere. You're dancing on a delicate balance. The emperor did no favors these past centuries." He dropped his hands to his side. "After I check on Manel, I would like to accompany you on your rounds."

"Do you not trust us?" Lendor asked, playfully tilting his head.

"You ask me after initiating such a disgusting breeding order set in place by your father for the sole purpose of securing a pure bloodline?"

The siblings' eyes turned red. Megen looked ready to strike. Master Jaubro's assistant stepped in front of him prepared to defend.

"That decree also applies to you," Megen spat.

"Oh, do not fret. Our contract is in order." Master Jaubro said.

"My employment has always been of my own will. I serve Jaubro." Desedon stood firm.

His unwavering stance put doubt on their faces. Megen seemed to back down.

It was as if they couldn't put their finger on why he instilled fear in the Kataling brood. Even Master Jaubro had no idea. Partly why he appreciated his assistants choosing to remain in service.

With one swift move, Manel threw a naked Gallic onto the bed. She straddled him like an animal in heat. Her swollen belly not yet prominent to obstruct her view of him. Her ravenous hunger didn't stop with food. Since being confined to certain areas of the palace, she could only alleviate her sexual appetites with him.

The moment he came in to check on her and saw that look in her eyes, he knew to strip down and let her do what she pleased. She had been in a state of troubled sleep when he left. To ease the suffering, he went to the healers for a sedative.

Now he lay still, trying not to let his feelings of lust overcome him. Manel eased down on his already erect member and gasped. Her eyes rolled back, then focused on him, red as blood. She rode him hard, and he endured, enjoying the short-lived ecstasy. The last time he had been able to have her was a few weeks after she gave birth the first time.

By the next moon, Megen wated no time impregnating her again.

He despised the eldest siblings. All of them, for that matter. They took satisfaction in seeing Manel in pain and being desecrated against her will. The tightening of Manel's womb around his cock snapped him out of his thoughts. Her talons dug into his chest as her back arched as his seed emptied into her after being squeezed from his loins.

Manel's head flopped forward, angry tears streaming down her face. He waited for her to control it. He understood her frustration. Manel did not like being toyed with.

Her role as a pawn in someone else's game started at the moment of her birth. Gallic served under her father's reign and regretted not making himself more available to Manel.

The tears stopped. Manel wiped her face with the back of her hand and sniffed. She seemed almost childlike. Her body tilted forward, eyelids slowly shutting. Gallic carefully switched their positions and laid her down. He reluctantly let his member slide out of her and rescind into his crotch.

He stroked her unruly hair.

To throw off any suspicions, he wiped her clean with one of the bathing cloths then dressed her in one of the casual gowns. He threw the blankets over her and went to wash off himself. If Megen came near him, he didn't want a drop of her scent detected. Maxellia frightened him more. Her adamant reason for no one else to touch Manel seemed a mystery.

Gallic got dressed in his uniform and went to his station by the entrance. A high-back chair shoved in the corner so that he could see if anyone so much as cracked the door open. Within minutes of getting settled, he heard movement on the other side of the door. A small tapping followed.

"It is Master Jaubro and I. We wish to see emperor Manel." Desedon's muffled voice said.

He got up and opened the door. Desedon stepped aside for Master Jaubro come in. Gallic gestured both of them to enter. They went to the bed.

"How is she doing?" Master Jaubro asked. He looked up at Gallic. "Truthfully."

"Not well. They let her rampage in the courts. I had offered to find her more food elsewhere. And her sleep is anguished. I am not sure what they're thinking."

"That's not true. You know exactly what they want."

"But why antagonized the people and the royal courts? If they wanted to overthrow the emperor, then do it. This game is…"

Gallic halted in frustration.

"That." Master Jaubro finished for him. "A game of foolishness. They want to hurt Manel, politically and psychologically."

"I won't let them." Gallic said tersely. His hands became fists. "I will defend her with everything I have."

"Oh, I know. Everyone knows." Master Jaubro placed a hand on Gallic's shoulder. "And that is why you are in as much danger as the emperor."

Gallic nodded. He knew all too well. There were a few failed attempts on his life. The culprits underestimated him, seeming to have forgotten his title as a battle commander before he became Manel's personal guard.

No longer gorged from pregnancy and back in male form, Manel relished in his power. He knew Megen would get a hold of him in a few weeks' time for the next round of implanting his dirty seed in him. The last had not taken. After days of trying while Manel lay beneath him, unphased by his efforts, his brother decided to take a break.

For the third time since the beginning of his reign, Manel held another planetary announcement. Imperial soldiers were dispatched across the planet to make sure the holoscreens in each district functioned properly.

People still ran from them, despite having changed his ways. Distrust ran rampant throughout the lands. In the capital, the citizens cowered in fear of what may come.

Manel walked through the side door of his throne room and settled into his seat. The sides of his hair had been forced into double cornrows secured by metal rings on the ends.

Each strand threatened to unravel from the tight knots, creating a mohawk of unruly hair, the back touching below his shoulder blades.

For the special occasion, he wore his black battle suit with a red cloak clasped to one side with an over-sized golden crest. Gallic stood next to him on the left and his siblings to his right. They all wore variations of black and red attire. The gold-colored tapestries on the walls behind the throne completed the aesthetic.

The historian once again took the helm of the feed controls. He ordered the imperial guards into position away from the viewfinder, so only the royal family were in the frame.

The emperor had been talking in length with the historian over the decades. His new decree stemmed from the man's teachings. Manel had demanded their sessions be kept secret the more he learned. After fussing around, checking the equipment, he stood before the emperor.

"We are now ready, my lord." He bowed and stepped back to operate the feed.

"Greetings, citizens." He tried to smile, then abandoned the idea. His eyes smoldered. "As you have seen over the years, we have established new districts and regulations for guardians. Instead of a new dawn, this will be a rebirth of the old."

Some people on the streets began to whisper.

"Is he going to implement his father's agenda?"

"Are we going to be enslaved like before when he took over?

"What does that even mean?"

Manel faintly heard their complaints from briefly enhancing his hearing. He understood their trepidation and knew they may revolt once he announced the decree. He also knew that rebellion would be met with swift punishment.

"As of now, all Volshins and Katalings will be categorized as Elite status. They will no longer act as guardians in servitude. The new upperclass district is their domain alone. No citizen is permitted without their expressed permission."

He could hear the muffled outrage from the capital, imagining the same occurrence happening around the planet.

To suddenly be forced to let go of their pet ancient one and treat them better than royalty must sound preposterous in their minds. That their guardian's now decided if they wanted to stay with the family they protected or part ways to live freely.

"All Volshins and Katalings will move into the new district and claim their homes." Manel dropped his head as he stared into the lens. "Any citizen found to engage in coercion or continued enslavement of an ancient one will be punished as the royal court sees fit." This time he did smile, like a demon.

The feed cut and Manel leaned against the side of the throne, one elbow propped up on the armrest with his head in his hand. He grimaced, unhappy, knowing the situation to come.

Megen stepped in front of him.

"I will send out a unit to each region to ensure everything goes accordingly."

"Nothing will go as we please!" Spittle flew from Manel' mouth as his body tensed with anger.

"It had to be done." Maxelia stroked his hair. It went flat as her hand ran down then shot straight back up like a porcupine. "The situation was getting out of hand."

Manel recalled seeing a man get angry with his family's Volshin guardian. He came out of the home with a giant bullwhip and lashed at the guardian relentlessly. The Volshin did nothing. They all did nothing because that meant killing a lesser being.

A waste of energy, time, and life.

He had his soldiers stop the assault. The Volshin begged him not to slaughter the entire family. The look of shock and rage, as the patriarch realized his life fell in the hands of the beast no longer forced to serve him, made Manel almost rethink his decision when he granted the Volshin's wish.

"I beg your pardon, my lord." The historian came forward. "Will you not be explaining why you have made such a decree?"

"My word is absolute. What need do I have to explain myself?"

"To, um," the historian raised his arms up. "Lessen the bloodshed?"

Manel glared at him and nodded at Megen to go. The smell of blood already wafted in from the capital.

It had begun.

####

Tavelo understood Earth's vastness. Even so, he still couldn't bring himself to imagine Volshins and Katalings roaming it undisturbed. A meeting with every human faction had been called and here he sat in a giant auditorium waiting for them all to take their seats.

The other coven leaders nervously milled around. Humans had not really encountered the ancient ones. Explaining what they were and why they should be left alone would not go easily.

The infighting between them, their offspring, and ancients didn't make matters better. Baltise managed to get Omeron to back down in an earlier fight but Holnar, Chalayl, and Darean would not be satiated.

Tavelo rubbed his face with both hands causing his skin to flush pink. Long arms wrapped around his waist. Soft breath brushed his ear.

"Stay steady, my love," Eterenia whispered.

He covered her hands with his and leaned back into her. He closed his eyes, taking in her scent.

"This could go badly." He took a few deep breaths then removed her arms from him. "I'm not sure we can trust the others, let alone the humans."

"You leave in a few days for the home world. Take it at pace."

He turned around so their foreheads touched. The tension in the air almost suffocated him.

"Come, Tavelo." Darean said tersely. "Our audience awaits us."

"I want this over with." Holnar spat out.

The coven leaders entered the main section and climbed onto the stage. A set of tables in the center, connected in a row, had seven chairs and wireless microphones at each seat. They all sat and looked down at the humans in the seats below.

"We thank you for coming." Eterenia began.

"Get on with whatever farce you have going!" A human called out vehemently.

"Our time is more precious. So, don't waste it on pleasantries, you monsters!" Another said.

Eterenia reared back in her seat in surprise. Then her eyes burned, flashing silver. She knew the others had as well. The humans went silent, their faces pale, realizing they took the situation a step too far.

"No need for civilized communication, is it?" Holnar leaned forward. "I hope they eat every last one of you. I don't care anymore."

Murmurs of what he could be talking about filled the room. Tavelo, furious at the humans after all his kind had done for them, cleared his throat to get their attention. When they quieted done, he finished what Eterenia started to say.

"We have a rank within our species, referred as ancient ones. Volshins are what you may describe to be flying dragons. The Katalings are akin to giant bats with bull like features. They reign supreme. Some of them are here with us."

"Worse than any of you?" A military leader asked.

"You have no idea." Darean spoke.

"Only if they are provoked!" Tavelo bellowed. "If left alone, they do not seek out destruction."

"Why are you telling us this?" An American asked.

"Some would like to stay on Earth since a few of their children were born here. The only way that could happen is if there are safeguards in place."

"You want us to harbor these creatures and not be afraid they might decide to go on a feeding frenzy?"

"As I said…" Tavelo curbed his frustration.

"We heard what you said!" The man shouted. "That won't cut it!"

"All they need is a place to themselves away from society. But they should still be granted the option of having a life like any other being on this planet."

"You want those things to also have citizenship?"

"Are you not letting other alien beings live here?" Darean snapped.

"That's different!" A world leader replied.

"Explain it to me." Tavelo's gaze sunk into them. He saw a lot of humans fidgeting in their seats. "Please, I am waiting."

"What do these ancient ones do? What skills would they have?" the military leader asked.

Tavelo stared at him, confused. He turned to Eterenia who shook her head.

"What do you mean?" Yutel stared, curious as to what they were getting at.

"Can they work? Are they, I don't know."

The military leader didn't finish.

"I am one." Tavelo stared them all down. "So I am not sure what you are implying."

Sharp gasps echoed. The diplomat and the military leader looked away in shame.

"The way you initally described them." A renown scientist piped in. "They sounded like beasts with no communication skills or rational thought."

"Because you didn't let me finish." Eterenia scoffed.

"So, a safe haven," the world leader said.

"That is correct."

"And you guarantee they will not harm us?"

"We don't guarantee that we won't harm you," Holnar stated. "Why would you think others, including the aliens visiting, do?"

"Hell, another human for that matter." Pridric laughed. "You have a saying that fits for this. Don't poke the bear and you won't get eaten."

The humans stared in horror as all the coven leaders' eyes turned pure silver. They saw pure rage.

Tavelo didn't find jump seating in the cargo ship ideal. The only other option would be to ride in cryo with the goods strapped to a pod. Another no for him. He took his seat between the pilot and navigator and attached the resistance strips to him. Once they hit the jump point, he would drop into cryosleep in the cockpit's comfort.

The journey would take sixteen months this time. So much had been shaved off due to better technology from another race. He liked the shorter ride. When they arrive, he will wake up back on his home world. Eterenia traveled in a different ship with the children and Tervan as her bodyguard. They would arrive a few days after him.

He had an idea why the emperor summoned him. Talks of a decree regarding the ancients coincided with his meeting. He took what the insane emperor said with a grain of salt. He could never figure out what that monster was thinking, so he braced himself for travel. They were near the jump point. The ship shot forth, winking out of existence into the stars.

Dock workers guided the cargo ship to the empty slit along the wharf. It backed up against the docks, stopping a few feet from the edge. The ramp doors opened, and it protruded forward, hitting the platform with a deep thud.

Rain coated the ramp, making it slick. Tavelo walked towatds the manifest holder. His body ached from being in cryo for three quarters of the journey.

The man held his tablet at waist level while walked, swiping a finger across it every now and again. He didn't look up from it once yet, his footing planted firm. Tavelo felt a pang of envy. By no means a klutz, he had not gotten his bearings, stumbling as if drunk. Part of the reason he hated space flight.

Rainwater ran off his tailored brown suit made from waterproof material. It came down in a slant, getting under the floating cover above him and the manifest holder. The tips of his hair got damp. They plastered on the jacket shoulders. He finally got his legs to act right and straightened his posture.

The Trade Commissioner waited at the ramp's end along with representatives from each merchant family. His uncle from his mother's side, the new Master Endaga, one hundred years his senior, waited in the back. The other merchant members kept their distance from him. He wanted to know the meaning of that.

"Tavelo Endaga!" Trade Commissioner Polp greeted him loudly. "Welcome home."

"I thank you. I hope all is well?"

He looked beyond the man towards his cousin. The Commissioner followed his gaze. The others flinched, turning their heads from him.

"Or not."

"Please rest assure, everything is fine." Trade Commissioner Polp met with the manifest holder. "Let's see what Earth goods we have today."

Tavelo moved from under the cover briefly into the rain then under the one where the merchant representatives stood. They all went tense, looking around at each other before kneeling, heads bowed.

Except for Master Endaga who stood under his own cover staring at them with disdain.

"What is going on?" Tavelo demanded.

Startled, they all rose. The Bryhel rep stepped closer to him. Her wide brimmed hat peeking from under the cover caught drops of rain.

"A lot has happened. The emperor's decree went into effect. A sort of uprising occurred. Now both parties are at a stalemate."

"They can't kill us all!" The Callesi rep snorted.

"Who?" Tavelo asked, impatient.

Master Endaga motioned for him to come over. He made his way through the reps and once again went from one cover to another. The two stared at each other for a moment.

Without warning, his uncle embraced him tight. Squeezing Tavelo with such might he tapped the man on the back.

"That hurts! I can't breathe." Tavelo sputtered.

"I'm sorry." Master Endaga released him. "It's so good to see you." He gripped Tavelo's arms then let his hands slide off. "These are trying times."

"What kind of decree?"

A royal entourage of four Imperial guards came marching down the docks. They stopped before the two men. The leader bowed at the waist and abruptly back up.

"The emperor is waiting for you." He moved to the side and raised an arm out. "This way."

Tavelo and his uncle walked towards the end of the docks, flanked on all sides by four guards. The leader brought up the rear, making sure they weren't being followed. On the street, business owners glanced their way, frowning. Except for the sounds of floating lifts hitching onto loading vehicles and sliding in, quiet blanketed the area.

A few feet away, the royal transport sat with its doors open, surrounded by more guards. Tavelo got in with his cousin and settled on the cushioned bench seat. The four guards accompanied them. The leader rapped a fist on the overhead and the transport doors closed. It lifted off the ground and sped towards the palace.

Tavelo couldn't see much due to their traveling speed. What he got a glimpse of, he didn't like.

Families strolled about. Some in fear, others were indignant. Not an ancient one in sight. He turned to his uncle. The man looked away.

In record time, they arrived at the palace and were led into the main hall. There they took the lift to the throne level. The doors opened to the gaudy golden floors and tapestries that flowed all the way into the throne room.

Emperor Manel sat lazily on the throne, looking put out as usual. Tavelo could immediately see the big difference in the emperor's condition. A sickness came over him as he thought about that creature climbing atop one of their subjects to engage itself in sexual depravity. They went and stood before the emperor. Tavelo almost bowed.

His uncle stopped him.

"No need for that nonsense." Manel pushed herself off the throne and stepped down. "We have much to discuss." She clapped her hands twice at an old man, tall like a reed with a beard that touched his chest. "Historian, if you please." Manel joined the three men. "Walk."

The four guards stayed behind them as the group made their way down the promenade that opened on the left to the courtyard garden. Royal citizens perused it at their leisure. Tavelo realized he had never gone into the greenery to explore.

"Tell us a story, historian." Manel finally broke the silence.

"My apologies, my lord, but I think it best if you tell it. I will chime in if necessary."

"Very well."

"Emperor…" Tavelo started.

"Manel." The emperor glanced over at him. "I am not your emperor."

Tavelo blinked in shock, his eyes widening. His uncle nodded at him.

"Let's see. In ancient times, there were two rulers. They each kept the planet in flux with the others in three systems. The palace was split as far as throne rooms. One ruler watched the East, the other the West. The sun and the moon."

Manel looked over at the historian for approval. She continued.

"One was a Kataling whose kind roamed the surface, making sure the land was being used wisely. The other was a Volshin. They ruled the skies, watching over the oceans and alerting the Katalings if they saw anything out of place."

"This planet was ruled by the ancient ones?" Tavelo asked incredulous.

"Yes. They were royal. Revered by all."

The historian answered. He conceded to Manel.

"Here comes the good part." Manel smirked, her tone dripped with sarcasm. "There was an invasion. We won of course but the main ports on the Volshin side were destroyed. So many deaths meant not enough workers to handle the cargo coming in on the Kataling side, let alone rebuild the other port.

With the focus on keeping the planet from going into ruin, the other side languished. No one patrolled it much since shipments had been rerouted."

"I truly believe this could have gone better if the workforce had been evenly split." The historian came into the conversation. "The time to recover would have been longer but we would still have the two ports."

Tavelo and his uncle took in sharp breaths as they understood at the same time.

"That's what lies on the other side of the dead lands!" His uncle exclaimed.

"Correct. The ships never fly over it, always coming in from the West." The historian nodded to Manel.

Manel rolled her eyes then exhaled before she continued.

"The Volshins abandoned their side to help the other, as they would. Both ancient races blended into the workforce while the Kataling ruler stayed in place on the throne to keep a royal presence. Over time, both nearly died out and the citizens began to see the ancient ones as obsolete."

"And a reliable labor source. What better creature to haul their goods and defend their families than an almost extinct species who would be grateful for any charity?" The historian pursed his lips.

Tavelo's head swam with from information overload, combined with a tinge of rage. He had known of too many ancient ones mistreated by their masters. Or, in the emperor's case, starved and forced to act as a military weapon.

Manel somehow sensed his thoughts.

"I made a mistake." Manel shrugged.

"You became a monster like your father!" His uncle cried. "You don't get to be forgiven for that."

"True." Manel seemed to not care. Tavelo shook his head in disbelief. "Moving on."

Tavelo noticed they had walked far past the known parts of the palace. The area grew grey, shadows everywhere. Their footsteps made the only sounds on old stone floors covered in sand and dust.

Up ahead lay a staircase, its walls filled with cobwebs. One of the guards pulled a flame thrower from behind his cloak and sprayed the stairwell.

Hand sized insects scuttling on four pincer legs flooded out, running along their feet. Tavelo tried to kick them away. A couple got hold of his cousin's pants and started to crawl up. He knocked them off, his hands getting bloody from hitting the pincers.

"Move!" The guard ordered.

They all got out of the way as he sprayed the floor. Loud shrieks erupted, followed by the cracking of the insects' shells as their innards popped out from being roasted to death. It died out. Dark blotches covered the floor.

"You may want to have that cleaned." Manel said snidely. Tavelo glared at her. Manel smirked and gestured to the stairs. "This is where you go alone."

Tavelo looked to his uncle, who tilted his head sideways from him with an expression that told him he wasn't volunteering. He took a deep breath, exhaling slowly, then went up the dark stairs. The smell of burnt insect carcass invaded his senses, making him gag. His footsteps echoed around him. He ran his fingers along the cold stone walls, feeling the emptiness within.

A blurry square of dim light appeared, filtering some of the darkness into a dull grey. Wind carried the scent of dead earth and stale ocean. He stepped into the light and found himself on a balcony that spanned fifty feet out and wrapped around equally from both sides. He could see far into the horizon.

Nothing. Barren land with decayed structures turned to ash blending in the sand. He adjusted his eyesight, gripping the ledge. His evaluation put him at least twenty stories above ground. A jolt of memory flooded through him as his hands tightened their hold on the stone. The scenery began to change. These are not mine.

He saw a young man with chestnut hair pulled back in a messy ponytail. The wind whipped the curled ends around his shoulders. He wore a white puffed shirt and plain brown pants. A land full of trees and homes scattered as far as the eye could see. The man stripped naked and morphed into a giant Volshin, his shrieks carrying out as his wings flapped, lifting him over the ledge.

Tavelo felt himself tilting over the ledge, though he knew it wasn't his body. With great speed, the Volshin launched forward, shooting through into the air like a bullet. Even at that speed, he could see the activity below. A woman, hanging out laundry, looked up to the sky and smiled. He passed a few more homes and came to a village where everyone waved at him.

The land ended at the edge of a beach.

Without stopping, the Volshin flew a quarter mile

out and dove deep into the water.

It enclosed him in a shielded capsule. He felt the coolness of it permeate every part of him, its color a vibrant swirl of blue, green, and purple. He surfaced, forming a typhoon that spiraled beneath him. The swirl suspended midair for a nanosecond before it fell back into the depths from which it came.

Wings flapping slowly, the Volshin hovered in the sky, letting the wind dry him off. He turned around to the left. The Eastern docks, filled with cargo ships, sprawled out like a city. Its workers hustled to get the goods to the merchant ports on the platform.

He rotated more and his gaze landed on the stone balcony of the palace.

Tavelo choked on his own breath as he inhaled too hard. He fell back, holding his throat as he tried to regulate his breathing. His other hand slipped from the ledge and he went down on one knee. Coughing, he stared back out into the deadlands. Recovered, Tavelo stood, taking one more look before heading back down the stairs.

His entourage still lingered around the staircase. Manel gave him a questioning stare. His uncle also looked at him strangely.

"Did something happen?" The historian asked. "You look pale."

Tavelo placed a hand on his cheek, feeling the cold skin from standing too long in the wind.

"I had a vision. Of the past." He felt his body sag. "I'm tired."

"Tavelo!" His uncle caught him before he hit the ground.

His eyes wouldn't stay open. He let the darkness take him.

❀ ❀ ❀

like bookends on one side of the table, as a protective shield from Manel and the siblings across from them. Tavelo already assessed his dislike for them.

He decided to address only Manel.

"I was surprised to see you are of dual sex, Manel."

Manel stopped drinking from her chalice and set it down.

"Are you saying, if you knew, you would have wanted me?" Manel smiled mischievously.

"No," Tavelo replied tersely. "I was merely…"

"Hmm. Maybe if that were the case, your pure blood would have trumped my father's breeding decree and I wouldn't have to carry my brother's spawn every third moon cycle."

Eterenia's spoon fell from her fingers onto the table with a soft thud. Tavelo stared at Manel for a moment then scanned the siblings. They seemed to tense up at Manel's blunt response.

"What?" Tavelo sat straight, not feeling hungry.

"Oh," Manel picked up her chalice. "Did no one tell you? My father wanted a pure bloodline so he tinkered with our DNA so I could mate with my elder brother." She raised her chalice in a toast. "To royal dominance!" She took a gulp of her drink and slammed the chalice on the table.

Tervan wiped his mouth with the red napkin and tossed it next to his plate. He turned to look at Ethan, Eterenia's teenage boy fathered by Manel. His older brother tentatively caressed his back. He sat silent and demure. His hand clutched a spoon as it hovered over the bowl before him.

The room's atmosphere became heavy.

Manel leaned forward and stared at the boy until he raised his head. They locked eyes.

"Don't ever let anyone use you like a pawn. Take what you deem is yours. Kill any in your way."

"That is not acceptable!" Tavelo pointed a finger at Manel. "There are better ways."

"Hmph." Manel sat back in her seat. "I already

pushed out two of those things." She turned to her Megen as she patted her belly. "One more to go?" Her eyes turned red. "Or were you going to breed my like an animal for all eternity?"

Megen slammed his fist on the table. "Stop." He glanced over at her. "I didn't want this any more than you. This is the last."

Tavelo noticed Maxellia perk up as if surprised.

As if that was not agreed upon.

What is your agenda in all this?

The other two siblings seemed almost relieved by the declaration. He changed the subject, the topic too awful. Eterenia finally regained her composure. She picked up her spoon and proceeded to go through the motions of eating, her heart no longer in it.

Can't blame her.

"This decree regarding the ancients." Tavelo met Manel's gaze. "Why haven't you expanded the residence further into the deadlands? It seems to stop miles from the start of the Eastern border."

"I'm leaving that to your discretion. I have no idea what kind of home front you want."

"Why? I have no say in this. It's your decree." Tavelo braced himself, knowing what came next.

"Because you are the East Emperor. Did you not understand that the first time?"

Utensils clinked to a halt. Tavelo's cousin wiped his face in a downward stroke with one hand. The siblings raised their heads and turned towards him. Tavelo felt his body sag in defeat.

"I did. I just couldn't bring myself to say it."

His young son with Eterenia pursed his lips.

"If you are the other emperor, what does that make us?" He asked in seriousness.

Manel gave a wide, sinister smile as she stood with arms wide.

"Royalty!" Manel exclaimed.

Tavelo watched Maxellia frown. Gallic, sitting on the edge next to Manel met his stare. A plea for help formed in those eyes. It dawned on him then.

Manel was not safe.

Master Jaubro led the royal entourage, based on the historian's previous directions, through the royal estate, down into a cavernous room filled with archives lit only by candlelight. Old books bound in tough animal hide with synthetic twine sat on dusty shelves. Their weight made the structure bow slightly. On another shelf, cracked parchments were stacked atop each other, some of them rolled up in scrolls. The dust made Tavelo's nose twitch.

The historian felt a tinge of embarrassment for their race. There should have been better upkeep of the archives. He too, stifled a sniff, not wanting to breathe in the acrid scent of aged paper mingling in the air. His role had not been utilized much over the past few centuries.

A wall of clear slabs etched with data glowed the palest blue further in on the right. They could be read on the machine standing next to them. A long-gone technology, only a few still knew how to operate. It beacme a necessary thing to make sure recorded history remained.

The historian watched Lord Endaga scan the area while Tavelo and Eterenia gasped in surprise. Manel appeared bored. The historian nodded. They moved around the room, touching the ancient artifacts. Careful not to disturb much of it.

Eterenia ran a finger along a piece of parchment hanging over its shelf ledge and frowned. Her fingers lifted off, covered in grime. She rubbed them together before wiping the residue on the side of her dress.

"Let's begin," Master Jaubro said. "I believe we should start where you left off." He addressed the historian.

"I don't understand."

Eterenia stood in front of the slabs.

"Why has this been passed down to our family? Why not the Endagas?" No one answered her.

The historian perused the large books and pulled down one from the second level, hefting it close to his body to accommodate its weight. He slammed it down on the heavy wood table in the center of the room. Dust curled along the sides up into the air. With slow movements, he opened it and flipped through the pages.

"Ahh! Here we are." He tapped the third page in. "This is part of what I found."

They all gathered around the table, leaning forward to get a look at the words. Lord Endaga placed his hands on the edge of the table and settled his weight on them. His eyes moved rapidly back and forth as he speed read the text.

The historian summarized for the others.

"After nearly a century of the Volshins helping rebuild, the emperor decided there may not be any need for them to return to the palace. His family ruled the planet just fine. So, he made a decree."

"Volshins would become servants of the people." Lord Endaga's disgusted tone broke the mood.

"Yes." The historian looked over at Master Jaubro. He nodded for the man to continue. "The Volshins were not happy about this. A rebellion started and the royal family were hunted down. Any Volshin who aided them also received punishment."

"They went into hiding," Eterenia added softly.

"And that is when the royal Volshins came up with a plan." The historian walked over to the slabs and used a finger as he glanced through them. He stopped at one further down on the fourth row. "There!" He slid it out with delicate ease and held it at an angle as he carried it to the bulky machine.

He tilted it towards the horizontal slit at its face and guided it in.

A quarter of the way, the machine grabbed hold

of the slab and slurped it up. It made a loud chirping sound. Lights came along its sides and a fuzzy display appeared on the front.

"Many of the adults were slaughtered, leaving a slew of orphaned children. Only one royal family clan already hidden among the masses survived; the Endagas."

"I see." Lord Endaga glanced over at Tavelo. "A necessary evil."

The machine sputtered.

The historian gave his attention, touching icons and pushing its buttons. When the noise stopped, a projection shot out onto the wall across from it. They saw footage of children clustered together in what appeared to be a small dungeon.

Filthy, malnourished, and frightened.

"These are the royal children left after the fall." The historian stepped off to the side so everyone could see the image. "They were fed into the adoption pool for the higher class."

"Because who else could care for such poor souls left orphaned during such trying times?" Lord Endaga said in a huff. He sounded more than angry.

"Yes, well." The historian pursed his lips.

"I find it genius." Manel smirked.

"The children selected into those families had monitors assigned to them. At a certain age they would be arranged to marry an Endaga. The set up was the key. The adopted parents rarely saw their new charges as part of their bloodline, so had no qualms about marrying them off to a lower-class family."

"Wait." Tavelo raised his hand, confused. "If we were royalty, how did we become lower class?"

"Oh," Master Jaubro interrupted. "That's easy enough. The Endaga clan was on the lower end of the royal house and not well known. They entered themselves as a merchant class to avoid detection. Since they had been working on the docks to help with trade, they blended in quite well."

Eterenia's eyes went wide, as did Tavelo's. Master Jaubro gave them a tight-lipped smile. Their two families had intermingled over the centuries. How they were related would have been hard to trace.

"But over time, the people made an observation." The historian resumed. "Having Volshins was all well and good. They also needed muscle for the heavier work. Another uprising occurred."

"To appease the masses, the emperor caved and allowed Katalings to serve as well." Lord Endaga snorted. "Did he really think it was going to be so one sided?"

"And that decree has remained for centuries." Manel moved away from the table and found a chair hidden deep in a corner near the door. She plopped herself down on it. Tufts of dust plumed, forcing her to fan them away as she coughed. "I kept it because it would be a hassle to undo it."

"And now this is atonement?" Tavelo asked. "You see what's happening? It will take more than this to fix."

Manel's furrowed brow conveyed her answer.

The historian touched the pads on the machine's display, ceasing the projection. He pushed a button, and a strangled grinding erupted. A few seconds later, the slab got pushed out of the front slit. A slow and painful process the historian had to endure as he held the edge of the slab and moved his hands up the more it came out so it wouldn't fall.

He felt the other's stares and turned to them.

"It doesn't get used often. You have to give it some pittance." The slab fully out, he carried it back to its housing along the wall. "Did this answer your questions?" He turned around to face them.

Lord Endaga pushed himself off the table to stand straight. He looked over at the slabs, narrowing his eyes. Tavelo seemed to know why. Master Jaubro let out a sigh and caught Eterenia's gaze.

"How many are left?" Lord Endaga asked.

"I'm sorry?" The historian squinted.

"Royal Endaga children. Their offspring," Lord Endaga snapped.

"Oh!" The historian smiled. "I have no idea. It's been centuries. If Lady Jaubro did indeed know the secrets, she herself may have been one. Her records could be somewhere in the family estate."

Eterenia slapped a hand over her mouth, stifling a cry, the implication not lost on anyone in the room. It answered her question. Manel even perked up at that, leaning forward in the dusty chair, causing more particles to fly outward. Master Jaubro walked over and placed a hand on Tavelo's shoulder.

"This is now your destiny. What will you do with all this information?" He asked.

Tavelo met Manel's eyes and the two stayed locked in a staring contest. Finally, Manel relented and stood. She brushed off her backside.

"Come, Emperor Tavelo. We have much to do."

CHAPTER FOUR

Divided

The Cellaxan interstellar transport eased through the clouds on its approach to Earth's trading hub. Its sleek, elongated oval design's thrusters protruded from the center of the underbelly as opposed to near the aft. The silent running engines created a faint hum.

Ships from different solar systems occupied every other dock on the space station. Workers went about loading and unloading of their cargo. The passengers in the main cabin of the ship, stayed strapped in.

Tavelo leaned towards the viewport to watch the activity, no longer feeling good about the ordeal. Humans deserve to have a say in what happened on their world. The merchant families had essentially turned into conquerors. Invaders with their own agenda.

He felt Eterenia's head rest on his shoulder. They had talked about it in length during the journey and he knew what needed to be done. The other merchant families would no doubt disagree. Especially Chalayl and Holnar. Even still so far away, he could see the vampires moving goods with inhuman speed while the handful of humans were being berated for their slowness.

"It's not right."

He raked his fingers through her hair.

"I know." Eterenia closed her eyes.

"We have to remedy this soon." She added.

The designated slot for their ship loomed below.

"Prepare for docking." The navigator's voice came over the commlink. "ETA thirty seven minutes."

Tavelo turned to the other passengers, merchants from other planets delivering their products, settle in their seats. The ones in the center seats had gotten up to check out the station. They begrudgingly went back and strapped in.

A particular group of merchants caught his eye, making him frown. Not quite reptilian, they had an air of deceit about them. A combination of thick hide and armor covered massive, mammal-like bodies. Half the race's population were military rank.

Weapons.

That's what they traded throughout the system.

With the ship secure and the lines vented, the passengers were allowed to disembark along with the cargo. Tavelo walked down the ramp behind the weapons dealers, keeping watch.

At the bottom, Armon and the Valkyrie waited with six coven minions. Tavelo grimaced at the show of force. No one would attack him or Eterenia at the docks. No sane person, anyway.

The alien merchants went to the side of the ship to check on their goods. Tavelo's gaze followed them. He zeroed in on their conversation and could barely hear them.

"Troubles?" Armon raised his brow.

"Maybe." Tavelo stepped onto the platform, his boots striking it with a soft clack.

"Arms dealers," Eterenia explained.

"That doesn't sound good at all." Armon shook his head.

"Let's just keep an eye out for now." Tavelo waited for the entourage to fall in formation before moving forward. "I will take it up with the others later."

❀ ❀ ❀

Holnar slammed his crystal tumbler on the top of the maple wood coffee table. A loud knock emitted on impact. Chalayl pursed her lips at his silly outburst. Yutel merely sat back in the sofa he occupied and rested a finger on his temple.

"They have made a deal with the aliens!" Holnar could barely contain his rage. "Not only have our own children turned against us but they facilitated a meeting with the enemy. Cutting us out, effecting our profit margin."

"You don't have proof of that. I would tread carefully or you'll turn it into fact." Darean chided.

Holnar raised his brow.

"Oh? You don't believe me?"

"That's not what he said!" Yutel snapped. "Until we see it, there's no reason to interject."

"Fine." Holnar leaned forward in the cushioned chair. "Come down to the trade district at the Eastern hub. You'll see."

Darean let out a loud sigh, raising his glass to his lips. "We will indulge you on this." He took a long sip, swirling the hard liquor around in his mouth before swallowing. "If what you say is true..."

"Then we have much more to worry about than lost contracts," Pridric finished for him.

"I got word from Tavelo about a few merchants who didn't sit well with him." Chalayl chewed on a mini cake. "This could prove detrimental for both us and humans."

"So, you're suggesting we spy on the humans at the hub?" Darean asked.

"It's not spying! We own those spaceports! Not them." Holnar sat back in a huff. "This isn't how I thought it would all go."

"Yes, well," Chalayl shrugged. "We've never tried taking over a planet before."

Darean drained his glass. He set it on the nearby table, and slapped his thighs.

"When do we go observe this supposed tragedy?"

"The sooner, the better." Holnar tapped his lower lip. "Next month. There's a shipment coming in so it won't look suspicious if we are going to inspect it."

"Alright." Yutel stood. "Give us the time and we will meet you there."

Pridric remained silent. He sat in the corner of the room deep in thought. That made them all uneasy.

❁ ❁ ❁

As usual, merchants from different quadrants of the galaxy crowded the docks, bringing their wares and negotiating with the coven proxies assigned to handle the particulars. The fight to keep humans out had been lost already. They stood by interpreters, hoping to break the language barrier and gain mutual agreements.

Holnar positioned himself on the platform above a sector, along with the other merchant leaders. They watched each human conduct business; the proxies frowning in frustration. He shook his head at the scene. The humans were stubborn and, because of the hostility between their races, refused to listen to reason.

Tavelo spotted a group of four humans with two military and two government leaders chatting up the arms dealers from before.

"There they are." He pointed towards them. "This does not bode well."

Yutel leaned forward over the railing, focused on the alien as it turned from the storage cube, brandishing a mid-sized projectile weapon. A foot long, it had a wide barrel, with the control panels flat against its shell. One look at the proxy's horrified face told him what it conveyed.

"We need to get down there."

Yutel turned away from the rail and headed to the lift. The others followed. As it made its slow descent to the main level, he turned to Tavelo.

"You should have told us immediately. We can't allow this."

Tavelo frowned, opening his mouth to object, ready to defend himself, when Darean chimed in.

"That's not the problem, Yutel." He flicked his nails together. "How did they know to come here? Who would invite arms dealers from another planet to trade with humans?"

"You don't think our children are that naïve?" Chalayl asked. "I know we're giving them a hard time, but surely they wouldn't retaliate this way."

"Let's hope not." Eterenia placed a hand on her abdomen. "It would break my heart."

The lift stopped and opened for them to vacate. They made their way to the dock station.

"We should spread. Only two of us are needed to confront them." Darean suggested.

"Good idea." Holnar cleared his throat. "Yutel, Tavelo, you're up."

With that, they veered off in different directions while the two went directly to the group. Tavelo laid a hand on the new proxy's shoulder, startling the vampire. He turned to stare over at Tavelo.

"Lord Durante! What brings you here?" His voice came high and shaky.

He's scared!

Yutel towered over the humans. They stepped back a few feet from him, giving him access to the alien merchants. He pivoted to stand face to face with the one holding the weapon. The interpreter remained calm as he rounded his shoulders, waiting to resume his duties.

"We have not sanctioned the trade of weapons on this planet," Yutel said. "How were you given access?" He let the interpreter relay his words and waited for an answer. He listened to the harsh grunts of the arms dealers. "I blame this on your gullibility." He addressed the humans.

"This is our second round of sales on Earth," the

interpreter spoke. "We're here to demonstrate them in person as a courtesy at the request of the humans. They needed a means to combat your oppression."

Tavelo's eyes went wide. He turned to the humans who returned his stare with rebuff.

"We are not the enemy!" Tavelo exclaimed.

The government leader's face flushed pink and his brow furrowed.

"Aren't you?" He bellowed. "You built space ports on our planet, cut us out of intergalactic trade and expect us to lay down and take it? We have every right to defend ourselves against you!"

The docks went quiet. All the other merchants and customers in the sector stopped what they were doing and focused on the scene.

"What else have you purchased from this race?" Yutel demanded as he faced the military leader closest to him. "Where are they?"

The military leader scoffed, smiling mischievously. "Wouldn't you like to know. You don't want us to reap the rewards. You don't get to know what we do."

"This isn't the time for your defiant games!" Yutel stepped closer to him. To his surprise, the man didn't flinch. "You have no idea what you're dealing with."

Tavelo gently moved the proxy aside and stood before the interpreter.

"Tell them to pack up their weapons and prepare for departure. I want them off this planet in the next four days."

The interpreter spoke to the arms dealers and a round of angry grunts came at the group. One of them produced a tablet with the screen locked on a document. Tavelo leaned close to peer at it.

"The hell!" He raised his head in anger.

"It appears they have the correct documentation to trade other goods as well until the end of the week." The interpreter addressed Yutel who seemed confused by Tavelo's outburst.

"If you'll excuse us," the first government leader said. "We need to finish conducting our business."

Yutel straightened his suit jacket and turned backwards from the group so that he could face them. Tavelo tapped the proxy in the middle of his back.

"I need you to find out how this happened," Tavelo whispered in the proxy's ear. The vampire nodded. "Good. Now, ensure this doesn't go badly."

Yutel and Tavelo walked away from the dock station and met back with the others. Holnar had a scowl on his face, already assessing their retreat.

"No talking sense into them, huh?" He asked.

"They have certified documents," Tavelo replied.

"Although," Yutel wagged a finger. "It's only a generic one for any and all goods. Which is not how this works for something like weapons."

"They should have been declared," Chalayl said. "There's no way we would sanction this."

"And here I thought this was right up your alley," Pridric said to her. "A worthy fight with humans to satiate your appetite."

She whirled on him.

"What is wrong with you?" Her eyes burned red, making him step away from her. "This is not some silly ploy to laugh at. Fight with the humans? Where would you get such a stupid idea?"

"Yes, that's not our agenda." Darean gave Pridric a puzzled look. "We don't want them on equal terms. They're a much weaker species. Having advanced weapons won't make them stronger."

"On that note," Eterenia nodded at the proxy. "We make sure delivery is not processed. That way, a refund will be triggered."

"Good idea." Holnar began walking down the main aisle. "We also need to know what the humans already have in their possession."

"And then what?" Pridric asked.

Tavelo glanced over at him as he followed Hosltrin. "We pray no tragedy occurs."

The mood went sour, the merchant leaders all frowning at the thought. Tavelo took one last look at the humans with smug faces as they continued their talks with the alien arms dealers. Fuck!

❀ ❀ ❀

The government leader and his associate sat in his study lounging on the loveseat while drinking twelve year old scotch. Both swirled their glasses, sniffing the contents before taking a sip.

"This is good stuff."

His associate smacked his lips.

"Nothing like old fashioned liquor, no matter what era." The leader's lips stretched in a grimace from the bite of the alcohol. "Technology ain't got nothing on this."

"I'll drink to that!" His associate took another sip. "Those coven leaders were pissed at the docks."

"Serves them right. Our military friends seem happy about the trade."

"Those two, maybe. The other world militarys think we haven't thought this through."

"Wars aren't won on half ass plans." The leader set his glass down on the oval, ornate table. "If we had better weapons, we wouldn't have seen ourselves in the predicaments from before."

A knock at the door made them both look over to see a messenger in the doorway. His suit fit a bit loose, indicating a lack of tailoring. He seemed to be in his mid-twenties. Intern.

"Excuse me sir," the young man addressed the leader. "I have some rather bad news."

The leader gestured for the man to enter the room. He stopped short of the loveseat.

"The goods paid for at the last trade have had their delivery blockaded by the coven proxy."

"Say what?" He sat straight. "For what reason?"

"Investigation of the document granting trade of

weapons found it invalid. Apparently, it should not have been issued."

"That's not our problem!" His associate turned to him. "We bought a product. Simple as that."

"From the interpreter's relay from the dealers, the coven leaders are going to take possession of the weapons and plan a siege of the local government. Force us into compliance of their rules."

The leader squinted, dubious. "That doesn't sound right. Where did you hear this? Was it from the interpreter directly?"

"Third party chatter sir. It supposedly happened when the military liaison went to acquire the goods."

His associate went pale. "Who has heard of this?"

The intern looked down at the floor. He clasped his hands before him before lifting his head.

"It seems to have spread already through the ranks and some of the heads of states."

"Shit!" The leader stood. "We have to nip this in the ass." He glared at the intern. "I want a message sent out to every last one of my people to not even think of doing anything stupid until we get to have a meeting. Is that clear?"

"Yes sir."

"Get to it, then!" He waved the intern out and plopped back onto the loveseat. He let out a huge sigh. Picking up his glass, he paused it at his lips. "For fuck's sake." He took a sip.

"I had a feeling this may happen." His associate leaned back, glass in hand.

"What?"

"The trade of alien weapons. Think about it. Would we have granted something like that if it was on our side?"

"Hell no!" Then it struck the leader.

This is real bad!

An Ancient Dilemma

Tavelo nervously paced his castle's main hall. Servants already bustled around making sure all the food and drink stations were well stocked. Mostly spirits, per his request. He opted to hold the meeting there, instead of his new home, which worked best. He had no idea how the other merchant leaders or the ancients would react when he told them about the dual rulership.

Not even Tesul and Armon were aware yet.

Eterenia advised him against it for now. He didn't want them to be blindsided by the news, so he opted to tell them ahead of the meeting. Eterenia would handle Adelia, the Valkyrie, and Lariod. The two bodyguards walked in amid the flurry of activity and stopped a few feet from him.

"You look like you're about to be ill, my lord," Armon said.

"Is everything alright?"

Tesul frowned, scrutinizing Tavelo.

Realizing he had been biting his thumbnail, Tavelo wrenched it from his mouth, letting his arms drop to his sides. He stopped pacing and turned to them.

"I wanted to tell you what this meeting is about. Eterenia and I are not sure it is the right thing to do, telling the others this news."

"You're going back to the home world."

Armon hung his head as he spoke it.

"It's not just that." Tavelo saw Tesul's inward struggle. "Walk with me."

He went to the side door that circumvented the main corridor. They followed in silence for a while until they were led far from the din of noise. Tavelo halted and turned around.

"There used to be two rulers on our world. One Kataling and one Volshin. The system collapsed over a thousand years ago. Emperor Manel has chosen to reinstate it. Only those pure of blood can rule."

Tesul and Armon's eyes went wide.

They understood immediately, having heard conversations about his DNA being ancient.

"You?" Armon whispered. "Are the other ruler?"

Tesul seemed to go rigid. His hands flexed, clenching and unclenching. "This is a bad idea," he finally said.

Tesul looked over at Armon who met his gaze.

"I agree. Telling them now, at this juncture." Armon shook his head. "They will come at you."

"We will protect you at all costs." Tesul folded his arms.

"Which is a given," Armon added. "But, make no mistake, they will not be pleased."

"Can you hold off for a bit longer?" Tesul asked.

"I need to get this done so I can see who wants to leave or stay." Tavelo leaned against the stone wall. "Something tells me it will be more than expected. Those who want to go home."

"Adelia will not like this." Tesul bowed his head. "I don't like this."

"With the new routes, we can visit our families every few years. It's not a deal breaker."

"Still." Armon pushed his hands in his pants pockets. "I'm not sure the two of us can handle a room full of angry merchants and their entourage. Let alone the ancients."

"This will get ugly. Fast."

Tavelo placed his hands over his face and exhaled slowly. He dragged them down, stretching his skin.

"Suggestions?" He asked, dropping his hands.

"Yes," Tervan's voice echoed in the gloom. "Either keep your mouth shut or have one of my units guard the proceedings."

"I'm trying to avoid bloodshed, not cause it." Tavelo glared at him. "And stop sneaking around the castle."

"This is to show you how vulnerable you are. These two didn't even know I was nearby."

Tesul and Armon smirked at him. Armon cocked his head to one side.

"We knew. There was no reason to acknowledge you. It would ruin your fun. Which makes us happy."

Tervan's face scrunched in anger and Tavelo laughed. They all looked over at him.

"Serves you right!" Tavelo continued to laugh, bent over in amusement. Done laughing, he finally stood straight. "Fine." He addressed Tervan. "Keep it discreet. I don't want any of them thinking this is an armed insurrection of some sort. Especially Holnar."

"Oh, that's not the only one I am worried about." Tervan turned back to where he came from and walked off. "Be careful, father."

"I'm regretting this already." Tavelo gestured his guardians towards the main hall. "Let's get this done."

They walked back, again in silence, the tension thick as mud.

The small event room, already packed to the gills with the merchant leaders, the heads of each coven house, the ancient leaders and their subordinates, resembled a palace harem.

Plush, brightly colored pillows, decorative throws, and sheer fabrics covered the area. His guests settled on cushions with drinks and hors d'oeuvres in hand.

Tavelo saw Holnar's eyes track to where he spotted Tervan and his soldiers snaking around the outer perimeter of the seating area.

He knows something is up.

Tavelo slumped his shoulders, then straightened his posture. No need to back out now. Armon and Tesul followed him through the room to the raised section on the far wall where large cushions were piled. Tavelo eased down onto them.

A servant came with a drink already made for him. He took it, bowing his head to them as they blushed before running off. The room became hushed. All eyes veered towards him. He sipped his drink, tasting the hint of blood. Setting it beside him, he forced himself to make eye contact with his audience.

"I thank you for coming at such short notice. This is a dire matter, believe me." He waited for the murmurs of doubt to subside. "As you know, I went to the home world at the request of the emperor. I will tell you what my visit entailed."

Armon and Tesul seemed to change their stances. Almost defensive. He could see Tervan place a hand on the hilt of his longsword. Yutel and Holnar sat up a little straighter, sensing the shift in mood.

"The royal historian told us of the ancient rulers. A dual empire with Katalings on the West and Volshins on the East. Two emperors." The volume in the room rose. "Ancients were not a species in servitude. They were revered as royalty."

Cries of outrage and disbelief broke out. He saw the ancients in the room simply nod.

"For the emperors, only those of pure blood could hold the throne. This is why the royal house is ruled by Katalings."

"Then what of the Volshins?" Luamis asked. "If it was to always be a dual rulership, why only the Katalings reign supreme?"

"There was an invasion." Tavelo had to speak louder over the angry voices. Armon and Tesul stared down the guests and they quieted down. "Both sides were devastated but the Volshin side was hit the worst. It is now what we call the wastelands."

"I don't understand," Darean said. "You need to clear this up, Tavelo."

"That's what I'm doing," Tavelo replied. "Give me some room." Darean frowned and waved a hand for him to proceed. Tavelo took a deep breath. "There were two merchant docks." That shut everyone up. "Since it would take longer to rebuild the one on the East, the Volshins left it to help the Katalings on the West. We couldn't have both ports inoperable." He sighed. "That's not why I invited you here."

"Oh?" Pridric swirled his glass of liquor in one hand. "Then what, pray tell, are we here for?"

"As I said, the emperors are pure of blood. Emperor Manel is because the Kataling ruler made it a priority to continue the lineage. I have found out that the Volshins had also done this except in secret."

Holnar immediately sat upright on his cushion, eyes wide in terror. Like a tidal wave, the rest of the room appeared to have the same realization.

"The emperor was looking for a pure blood for some devious breeding agenda," Darean said.

"And thought it was the Jaubro clan," Yutel said.

"Not quite." Tavelo braced himself. "The Jaubro family did know of the secret. But it was to protect another clan." Hostile glares turned to him as he said, "Mine."

"You?" A high class clan member jumped up from her cushion. "You are to be an emperor?" Her irises turned red. "Some lowly merchant family who never even reached the heights of profits is to rule over us?"

Others voiced the same ire, while the ancients seemed to deliberate amongst themselves. She nodded in approval, glaring at her family matriarch, Chalayl who met her stare with a smirk. The sudden stunned silence made her look around the room.

She saw the merchant family heads standing along while Tervan's soldiers moved towards the center.

"Sit down, you insufferable twit."

Chalayl's command made her slump down hard

in her seat, frightened by the scene.

Pridric's expression soured. He eyed his drink as if it were a nemesis. Yutel moved first, heading straight for Tavelo. Darean and the Volshin leader followed. Tavelo glanced at Eterenia sitting a few yards from him. She gave him a reassuring smile.

"If that's the case," Yutel said, stopping before him. "Then I guess congratulations are in order."

"I can't say I'm pleased by this." Darean stood next to Yutel. "It seems the decision is out of our hands."

Luamis walked past the two and clasped Tavelo's hands in his.

"You are frightened. That's good. I will accept your rule." He let go and went to stand by Darean. "May your reign be glorious."

All three went down on one knee and bowed their heads. Slowly, others did the same. Except for three coven heads and their court members. Eighteen in all, they scrunch their faces in disgust. Holnar stood silent while Chalayl and Pridric returned to being seated.

"Oh, hell no!" The fifth house coven leader yelled. "I will not bow to that sniveling wretch." He pushed his way forward, knocking down a few who still kneeled. Others were ready to follow. Tervan moved to block his advance. "We didn't crash here only to backslide into old regime doctrines!"

Tavelo motioned for everyone to rise. He did as well, stepping down to the floor. His irises glowed silver.

"I wasn't finished." His back rippled from his wings trying to sprout, and he fought them back. The people in the room parted, making a beeline for the coven leader. "If you wish to stay on Earth, that's fine. For those of you who wish to go home, that will be arranged." He got closer to the man. "And those who defy me can die."

Eterenia flashed in front of him.

Tavelo saw Tervan turn around to see her place a

hand on his chest. He struggled with an urge to tear the coven member apart.

"*It's not worth it,*" she said to him telepathically.

He breathed in through his nose and exhaled from his mouth. The tension in the room lessened. He stared at the man, unfazed by his own near death. Almost like he dared Tavelo to harm him. To prove something. What?

"Emperor Tavelo." Pridric spat out his new title like venom. "That's all we need, isn't it?" He drained his glass and slammed it on the small tray beside him. The impact of glass on metal made a loud ting that rang out though the room. "I won't bow to you. Not ever."

Tavelo turned around and the two leaders locked eyes. Holnar grimaced at the display. He understood the other coven leader's frustration. This feud was getting tedious.

"I never expected you to." Tavelo severed his gaze.

"We're not done!" the coven member bellowed.

"Oh, but you are." Tervan nodded to his soldiers. They began to usher the dissidents out of the room.

"This is how you rule?" The man said. "No tolerance for opposition?"

"Oh, shut up, and leave!" Chalayl turned to the woman from earlier. "And take her brood with them."

The guards removed them in protest; the woman screeching obscenities at the soldiers manhandling her. When all the naysayers were gone, Tavelo went back to sit on his cushion. He let out a deep sigh and picked up his drink, relieved no bloodshed occurred.

"You think this is over?" Omeron asked. His eyes bore into Tavelo. "They will not stop here. A target has been placed on every inch of you."

"I know," Tavelo whispered.

I know.

❋ ❋ ❋

Holnar listened to his page relay the information about the covens storming the government building with confiscated weapons. He sat silent, then burst out laughing. Darean and Yutel were seated a few feet away from him.

"Preposterous!" Darean rolled his eyes.

Bloody tears streamed down Holnar's cheeks, and he wiped them away with shaky hands. He took a few deep breaths, still chuckling. Yutel shook his head in disbelief.

"That message get sent to the others?" He asked the page. The boy nodded. "You're dismissed." When the boy left, he sat on the edge of his seat and composed himself. "That was the most asinine thing I've heard yet."

"Which is dangerous, considering what the outcome may be." Yutel stared him down.

Holnar met it with indifference at first, then his own expression grew serious.

"They wouldn't dare."

"I wouldn't put anything past these humans." Darean reached for his glass of wine on the coffee table. "They can be quite irrational."

"Tavelo may have information soon on where the document came from and who granted it."

"Good. Whoever it is needs a royal ass kicking." Holnar nodded at Yutel.

"Glad to oblige when it comes to that," Yutel said.

Darean's phone pinged. He lifted it out his jacket pocket. For a moment, he stared at it, not speaking. He glanced up at Holnar, then to Yutel.

"We need to get to the space docks." He set his half empty glass of wine down and stood. "Right now."

Yutel simply nodded, rising from his seat. Holnar sat rooted, dumbstruck, before rising to his feet.

"No," was all he said.

"The information is at least two days old. Those arms dealers are due to depart soon," Darean said.

"They plan to leave us, and the humans, with a

debacle on our hands," Yutel added. "Retaliation for the block."

"Let's go. The others will probably be there before us. Especially, Tavelo."

They met at the entrance of the spacehub, finding Tavelo already there, as expected, with Eterenia. A young proxy working under Armon stared at Pridric like hot garbage. Holnar almost didn't approach them. His assistant tapped him on the shoulder and handed him a tablet. The look on his assistant's face told him the severity of the outcome.

"It has not been divulged yet, sir," his assistant whispered in his ear. He glanced at the proxy. "I think he is biding his time so we can stop a massacre."

"Is that so?"

"Brace for it, sir."

Holnar snorted then looked down at the tablet. He sucked air through his teeth, hard, the coldness hurting his teeth. He stared at Tavelo. *Shit!* Chalayl and Pridric arrived with their entourage. Darean gave him a puzzled look.

Holnar grabbed hold of Yutel.

"Get over there to Tavelo and don't let him move," he seethed.

Yutel frowned. He walked over to Tavelo and stood by him.

"What are you doing?" Tavelo asked, leaning away from him. "Why are you so close to me?"

"Precaution."

"For what?" Tavelo snapped.

"No idea."

Pridric stiffened at the proxy's glare. His gaze fell on the tablet in the man's hand then at Yutel. He moved backwards towards his vehicle, bumping into Chancellor Rayne.

"What are you doing, my lord?"

Holnar walked over to Pridric, Darean following. "You stay put!"

The proxy loudly cleared his throat, getting every-one's attention.

"We were able to sift through the data and found the official documents the arms dealers were able to obtain." His eyes narrowed, turning red. "Authorization was approved by the Ambrook Group under direct recommendation from one Lord Pierce Ambrook."

Darean did a sharp intake while Chalayl clamped a hand over her mouth and started to laugh. Eterenia turned to Tavelo. He moved towards Pridric. Yutel caught him mid flash step and wrestled him to the ground on his back, to stop his wings from sprouting.

"Get off me!" Tavelo's eyes went silver. "I'll kill him!"

"No" Yutel put all of his weight onto him. "That cannot be allowed."

Chancellor Rayne turned to Pridric, eyes wide in disbelief.

"You did this, my lord?" Pridric stepped away from him. "Why? What possible outcome were you looking for?"

"Yes." Darean, about to go to him, got held back by Holnar. The look in Darean's eyes just as deadly as Tavelo's. "Explain yourself!"

"You stupid, greedy, little man," Chalayl erupted. She dropped her hand and her expression changed from amusement to rage. "This is why I despise you."

"Enough!" Holnar struggled to keep Darean, still trying to get loose, at bay. Yutel had not moved off Tavelo either. "We have a more serious issue at hand. The humans have sympathy from the arms dealers. This needs to be remedied. Now!"

Yutel stared down at Tavelo. Their eyes met, and he felt Tavelo relent. He stood, helping him up. Holnar let go of Darean, who didn't avert his gaze from Pridric.

"Let's go." Holnar slapped the tablet against his assistant's chest. The man took hold of it and followed his master towards the spacehub. "We will settle this debacle after we finish this one."

The coven leaders, along with their entourage, walked in tight formation up the space dock's ramp leading to the lift. They piled in, not minding the closeness for once despite the tension and rode it up to the main level. No one said a word. No need. Considering the now dire situation, they put the time to clean house on the back burner. Pridric pressed himself against the corner in the back of the lift, not daring to look at anyone.

The lift doors opened. Chaos.

Screaming flooded the sector in conjunction with laser fire zigzagging across the aisles. Bodies were flung in the air, landing on cargo. The coven docks took the heaviest fire further in. They all focused to the left of the docks and saw the alien arms dealers handing out weapons to humans. But it wasn't just humans being slaughtered.

Every species in the space hub is in danger!

The leaders didn't have time to ask questions. Like a blur of light, they moved as one towards their docks and began to take out insurrectionists. Yutel and Tavelo headed straight for the arms dealers.

They seemed surprised to see them, halting their distribution. The four humans waiting for their weapons turned around. Seeing them, they tried to flee. Yutel grabbed them from behind and smashed them together like an accordion.

Before the humans hit the ground in a heap, Tavelo reached the first arms dealer. His eyes glowed silver, his talons glistening black.

"I warned you. This is the last time you set foot on Earth."

It raised one of the weapons at him. He swiped his talons across the barrel, slicing it at an angle along the width. Sparks flew out. The dealer tossed it away as it exploded, landing at a nearby dock. The occupants were blown out, their skin singed on one side.

Yutel leaped over the barrier that divided the dock from the main corridor and went after the other two arms dealers behind the first. At last, the leader came from inside the cargo hold, brandishing what Tavelo could only imagine to be more lethal than the other weapons.

The larger barrel's wide mouth iris glowed blue and white, building energy. Tavelo calculated the alien getting the first round off, but he could stop the second. A loud crunch echoed on his left. He saw Yutel let go of an alien's head, now twisted the wrong way. The other already on the ground dead.

A swath of blinding blue light whisked past his head, singing some of his hair. He could smell the burnt shampoo scent mingle with its natural oils. The shot went in a straight line, tearing through every dock in its path, destroying goods, structures; and killing merchants.

The hand cannon glowed for a second fire.

Angered, Tavelo morphed into Volshin form. He kept his size manageable at nearly ten feet. With one swift motion, he snapped his fangs onto the top of the alien's head, sinking them deep into the dome.

The weapon went wild as the alien's body shook violently. It dropped to the ground, still active. Yutel stomped on the barrel, crunching it shut, making it resemble a bigmouth bass.

Tavelo sucked the life out of the alien arms leader. Finished, he let the husk fall. The translator lay on the ground a few feet away, a nasty gash on his forehead.

"I tried to stop them. Told them they would be banned and or killed for such an act." The translator gently touched his wound. "There's more on the ship." He nodded towards the open ramp connected to the loading dock. "They won't be happy."

"That suits us just fine," Yutel said.

On the other side where the coven docks, Holnar confronted the humans attacking them. He recognized a few members from factions of the government and military. Grunts, really. Which he expected. He knew damn well the higher ups weren't going to get their own hands dirty.

"Your kind is partly to blame for this!" One of the soldiers yelled. "Those civilian and other deaths are on your hands."

"Oh, I think not."

"If you hadn't cut us out of this whole thing, we wouldn't have had to retaliate!"

Darean gave them a wild-eyed stare.

"You're blaming the murder of innocents at a spacehub where you knowingly took possession of deadly weapons of unknown technology and used them in a crowded area on us?"

He looked over his shoulder at the number of wounded on the ground and the destroyed dock platforms. "Are you being serious?"

The head of security came towards them, his anger towards the humans visible in his expression. Behind him were four government leaders and two military generals. The shame on their faces said plenty.

"Lord Marchand, these men were at the main hub demanding entry. I felt it necessary to bring them only after we had established a safe route."

Holnar glanced around at the carnage. The atmosphere had indeed settled. No more weapons were being fired. Debris floated down. The Prime Minister of France came forward, hands wringing.

"Lord Marchand. Please believe me when I tell you this wasn't our objective. Loss of life is unacceptable." The soldiers' eyes bulged in disbelief. Holnar could tell. *They were going to be the scapegoats. Serves you right.* "We only wished to," he licked his lips nervously, "persuade a new deal."

"You failed."

Darean's blunt response shocked the man.

"This can be taken care of on your end, correct?" Holnar asked Darean.

"Of course. We will assess the damage. You go

help Tavelo send those arms dealers packing."

Security forces surrounded the arms dealers' dock area and the ship. Holnar went to stand next to Tavelo. Back in his original form, the front of his clothes drenched in a purplish black goo, he still exuded rage. Yutel appeared untouched and clearly miffed about not getting more out of the fight.

Two alien arms dealers came onto the dock platform followed by a unit armed to the teeth. Holnar raised an eyebrow at that. *What did they think was about to happen?* The translator brushed himself off and stood. The alien on the right began yelling in its tongue, pointing at Tavelo.

"We had legitimate business here," the translator conveyed. "This is the human's planet. We gave them what they wanted."

"Which was against our trade policy." Holnar shook his head. "Whether you had documentation or not, you should have clarified with security."

The other alien pointed to the empty husk of their former leader. Its tone and expression angry.

"You murdered our commander." The translator let out a sigh of exasperation.

"He killed a lot of innocent species in this hub." Holnar nodded to the head of security who came up behind him with a tablet. He took it and began tapping icons. "As of now, you are banned from Earth. You will not come near this system. No trade is allowed." He looked up from the tablet. "You will depart immediately and take all of your goods with you."

A group of security agents arrived with a net full of confiscated weapons. They dropped them at the edge of the dock platform. Two of the arms dealers broke rank and retrieved them, carrying them up the ramp into the ship. The first alien got huffy.

"We know of your kind." The translator frowned. "This will not go unfinished."

The alien arms dealers turned around and headed back to their ship.

"Make sure they're cleared for fast departure." Holnar gave the tablet back to the head of security. "I've registered their information for future reference."

"Very good, sir. We will make sure they are gone before the day is over."

With that, the head of security and his unit went to start their task.

"I need to see the damage to our docks."

Tavelo came face to face with Holnar.

"Fine." He glanced back at Yutel, who nodded. "As long as you behave."

They walked together towards the ruins of their businesses' bays. Nearby, Chancellor Rayne yelled orders to his men to remove any dangerous debris. Inside the hangar, Pridric roamed around, staring at the rafters as parts of its railings swung down, ready to break loose and impale someone.

The Chancellor stopped yelling, seeing Tavelo approach. He held out a hand as if to stop him.

"I need you to be calm and not confront him." Tavelo's eyes burned into his. "This is not the time for retaliation. He knows he needs to explain himself sooner than later."

"Be patient, Tavelo." Darean came up behind him. "We will make sure he answers to this."

"Hmm." Tavelo sidestepped Chancellor Rayne and headed into the hangar. "Sure. Promise."

He got past the threshold and waited for Pridric to acknowledge him. Tavelo knew he could feel his presence. Pridric halted his pacing and turned his head towards him in a sideways tilt. His expression changed from blank to apprehensive.

You should be afraid.

Tavelo glanced behind him at the other leaders chatting away, their gaze flickering between the docks and him.

Slamming a fist onto the side panel of the hangar, he hit the door release. The metal shield came down, locking into the side clamps with a loud clank.

Tavelo and Pridric stood far apart, staring at each other for a while. They could hear the panicked shouts from the leaders on the other side of the door. Pounding commenced, rattling the hinges.

Tavelo slowly walked to Pridric, who turned to face him. *Good. Don't run.* He left less than a foot of space between them.

"Tell me why I shouldn't, Pridric." Tavelo kept his voice steady.

"Honestly?" Pridric lowered his eyes.

"That would be best."

"It was partly a test for the humans. And," he sighed. "A way to anger you, knowing there was nothing you could do about it."

"I don't understand." Tavelo's eyes began to glow.

"Your family never got its hands dirty with any of this!" Pridric looked up at him. "Refusing to do business and profit from the black markets."

"Why? Why do you constantly come after me when I have done nothing to warrant such rage?"

Tavelo stepped closer. Pridric tried to move back and Tavelo grabbed both sides of his face. Tears formed in Pridric's eyes. Pridric turned his head to release Tavelo's grip, with no luck. Tavelo didn't let go, forcing Pridric to let him watch his tears slowly spill down his face.

Tavelo kept his hold firm.

"Why?" He asked again.

"It's because I love you!" Pridric cried. Snot dripped from his nose. "More than my brothers. Or my family. I wanted so much to at least be your friend. To be by your side as an equal." He sniffed to stop more snot from dribbling out, his face a mess. "You have such integrity and conviction that I could never attain!"

Tavelo sighed heavily as he used a finger to wipe some of the tears from Pridric's right eye.

"I'm sorry!" Pridric cried.

"I know. I get it." He cupped his face in his hands.

"And because you love me, you know to brace yourself." Pridric's eyes went wide. "For I'm going to hurt you."

Tavelo's eyes turned silver. His wings sprouted from his back and flapped once, causing a strong wind that knocked over nearby crates. Fear filled Pridric's expression. *Endure this.* Tavelo morphed, his high-pitched shriek filled with anger and sorrow.

The screams didn't just filter through the metal doors of the hangar out to the docks. They pierced the minds of everyone in the vicinity. Many cried out in pain, clutching their heads as they fell to their knees.

Fighting past the brutal psychic assault, his body instinctively bending towards the ground, Chancellor Rayne stood straight. He clamped a hand over his left ear, already dripping blood from the canal.

"Damn you, Tavelo!"

He cursed himself for being so naïve to believe Tavelo would not harm Pridric. His promise disingenuous. Holnar and the proxy regained their composure. They gave him a knowing glance. The screams continued, followed by what sounded like something thrashing against the inside of the sealed hangar.

His heart sank, fully aware Tavelo showed no mercy with Pridric's body.

"Get that door open!" He yelled at his minions.

"Help them!" Holnar ordered his men. "Hurry!"

The proxy ran up to the three-foot-thick shutter and pressed his hands to it. The screams seemed to muffle up close.

"Even with all of us, it would take ten minutes."

He turned to Holnar and Chancellor Rayne.

"I don't care!" Chancellor Rayne charged. "The quicker we get this open, the better chance we have to save him!"

With the combined strength of forty vampires and coven family members, they struggled to lift the door out of the groove, locking it into the ground. It came up slowly, inch by inch, letting the sounds of Pridric's demise intensify with each increment. Their irises turned red from the strain of using all their power and the deep anguish of knowing a family head lay on the other side, hell bent on destroying another.

When the door rose high enough to allow them under, they all ran in. Four of the vampires went to secure the door so it wouldn't drop back down. The silence made them halt.

In a small beam of dusty sunlight on the floor, Tavelo cradled a bloodied Pridric in his arms. He turned his gaze on them. Blood splatter peppered his hair, across his face, and covered much of his clothes.

"How could you do this after you said you wouldn't?" Holnar cautiously stepped forward. "Was his apology not enough for you?"

"This is unacceptable!" Chancellor Rayne took a step. Tavelo's stare stopped him.

Tavelo caressed Pridric's forehead while he looked at him. Pridric's eyes fluttered open, bloody tears streaming across his cheeks. The two locked eyes and stayed that way for a while. Chancellor Rayne stood confused, not sure how to proceed. Holnar raised a hand in the air, signaling him to wait.

"He needs to get into the crypt." Tavelo finally spoke. He went on one knee and lifted Pridric up. He stood pressing him close to his body. "Lead the way."

"Get our leader and take him to the castle," Chancellor Rayne ordered.

Tavelo's eyes turned silver. "Don't touch him." The men backed away. He looked down at Pridric. "It's okay. I got you." Pridric closed his eyes.

Chancellor Rayne caught Holnar's stare and the other nodded. Defeated, he turned to the hangar door already rising so they could exit easily.

He headed to the Ambrook coven's main vehicle and flung the back door open for Tavelo who didn't let go of Pridric as he settled into the seat. Chancellor Rayne felt unnerved by it. The two leaders were nearly the same age yet for some reason Tavelo now appeared older, wiser.

233

CHAPTER FIVE

234

Hostile Visitors

Tavelo startled awake, clutching his chest as he gasped from a dreamless sleep. A perpetual darkness had consumed him that he couldn't sever. He vaguely remembered returning to the home world; His mind in a haze as he walked down the ship's ramp.

The satiny bed coverings slid down his naked body, bunching at his waist. Searching for his clothes, his gaze landed on Manel sitting in a chair across from the bed. An animal-like expression of lust relayed on her face. Tavelo didn't dare throw the covers off. He had no idea what might happen if Manel thought he condoned being mauled.

Manel smiled deviously. "I already took a peek." She licked her lips. "A small taste too. Delicious."

"Don't ever touch me again without my permission." Tavelo kept his tone even.

"Why won't you create a hybrid with me? Half Kataling, half Volshin?" Manel tried to seem nice.

"Why would you want to create such a creature? What need is there for it?"

Manel pouted, her eyes red.

"Curiosity? A super being?"

Tavelo looked at the ceiling, shaking his head. He tested fate and tossed the covers aside, swinging his legs off the bed. His feet sank into the plush carpet as he stood. Manel scrutinized every inch.

Tavelo felt violated. He spotted his clothes on a changing rack in the corner and got dressed. All the while checking to make sure Manel did not move.

"That means nothing to no one except your father. Why are you continuing his horrible experiments?"

Manel frowned.

Tavelo wondered how much the old emperor had ingrained in the broken Kataling. He had read some of the reports from Master Jaubro about it. And then there were Manel's siblings. He began to feel differently about the emperor.

"Don't you dare pity me!" Manel leaned over in the chair, hands turning dark from the death grip on the armrests. "I am not broken!"

Tavelo watched Manel fight back tears. He felt guilt. Shame. He knelt before Manel and cupped her face in his hands.

"I'm sorry. I shouldn't have thought that."

Manel's expression changed abruptly.

"Then you'll let me have you for my hybrid?"

"Absolutely not!" Tavelo stood, backing away from her. She pouted. "Stop that!"

"You're no fun."

Manel settled back in the chair, leaving Tavelo to contemplate running from the palace. Which was moot. His memory flooded back, and he felt his body slump. More had left Earth than expected. He wasn't surprised, really.

Earth no longer held the same appeal. Adelia continued to struggle with her decision to join them at a later date.

They transported Pridric in a suspended state. Tavelo refused to leave him there. Grateful, Countess Ambrook came to care for him when he awakens.

Both stayed within the palace. Tavelo refused to entertain the Strana's invitation to let him recuperate at their homestead. They'd caused more hurt than anyone else.

The silence startled him out of his reverie.

He turned to Manel and found the emperor asleep, a face that of an innocent child. Her presence diminished somehow. If only that were the case. Tavelo checked his attire to make sure his robes were in place. Satisfied, he turned to the double doors.

Running footsteps followed by softer, steady ones from the corridor on the other side got closer until they stopped at the door. It swung open, waking Manel. Eterenia stepped in while her young sons clambered around her and entered the room.

Ethan suddenly halted, his eyes fixated on Manel.

They locked stares. Manel sat with her head rested in the palm of one hand, her red irises gorged.

"Hello, little one." Manel dropped her hand and leaned forward. "Aren't you a delicious morsel."

To everyone's surprise, Ethan's eyes turned red and black talons grew from his fingertips. He reversed course in an instant at Manel's murderous gaze. Ethan stepped back, bumping into his older brother, who held him tight against him.

Manel looked amused as she sat back.

"No need for that. I won't harm you." Manel's fingers gripped the armrests. "I wouldn't do that."

"You can't blame him for being defensive," Eterenia said. She caressed the top of her son's head. "You were nothing short of a monster." She tilted her head. "For all we know, you still are."

"Hmm." Manel got up and walked past them, addressing Tavelo. "Make sure you're at the meeting before evening meal." The moment she set foot outside the door, four royal guards fell in step with her.

"So," Eterenia breathed. "It has begun." She ran a hand along the fabric of his outer robe. "Endaga colors. Fitting."

"My family has been getting unwanted attention since the announcement. DNA testing has started to see who else in our bloodline is a dormant Volshin like me." He looked over at his son. "There is no doubt you are."

"And none that this one," Eterenia ruffled Ethan's hair, "is a Kataling." She moved around the room, inspecting it. "I will have them stay with Countess Ambrook while we attend the council meeting."

Tavelo nodded. Their children seemed to ease her pain, not being able to cuddle her grandchildren, still on Earth. The woman had become gaunt, not eating, or feeding as she should.

"Come. Let's go find my uncle, and yours." Tavelo ushered her towards the door as he saw her face scrunch in disappointment at the room. "You too." He turned the boys around and pushed all three out into the corridor.

❀ ❀ ❀

Master Jaubro heard them approaching as he sat in the study adjacent to his private quarters. Desedon stood off to the side nearby, unmoving, silent in his stark black suit with a white tunic. In the chair across from him sat Lord Endaga, wearing a navy suit accessorized by an almost teal satin ascot. His jet-black hair teased the tops of his shoulders.

Even more exotic in appearance than our clan.

Master Jaubro snorted.

Lord Endaga looked up from his raised teacup. "Is something amusing?" He glanced around the room, searching for the reason. Steam from his tea wafted in front of his crystal blue eyes.

"No, no." Master Jaubro waved a hand. "Just an observation." He waited until Tavelo and his brood were close to the door. "I was wondering why it took you so long to come see me."

Tavelo entered the study and sat down in the chair next to his uncle. Eterenia leaned over and kissed the top of her uncle's head. He raised an arm and squeezed her close to him before releasing.

"This one still laid in that tiny chamber getting ready." Eterenia eyed Tavelo.

Lord Endaga set down his tea and opened his arms for the boys, who rushed to him. Master Jaubro breathed a sigh of relief at seeing the Kataling child show affection. He turned to Tavelo.

"Was the morning long? Why were you in there?"

"I think I requested it after arriving. My mind's a bit fuzzy." Tavelo sat not far from the small cocktail table as a servant came and filled more cups with tea. "I really don't like traveling."

"I heard you brought young Strana back home."

Tavelo's reach towards the table slowed to a stop. He hesitated for a moment then picked up one of the teacups. He leaned back into his seat.

"Yes. I decided for his wellbeing, that home was the best option."

"He retirned in a rather odd condition." Lord Endaga sipped his tea. "What happened on Earth to put him in that state?"

"That would be my fault." Tavelo hurriedly sipped his tea, immediately regretting it as the hot liquid burned the roof of his mouth. "Ahh!"

"Oh?" Master Jaubro let his arms flop over the arm rests of his oversized chair. "Do tell."

"I'd rather not," Tavelo mumbled."

"Let's just say, Pridric did something dastardly and paid the price." Eterenia answered.

"As Stranas are known to do," Lord Endaga said.

"We warned him he would get no help from us against Tavelo's wrath."

"Well, they like to learn the hard lessons." Master Jaubro sighed. "What of the others?"

"I think they'll eventually return as well," Tavelo replied. "As much as we relished in creating trade for ourselves on Earth, the work was not as fulfilling."

"And much harder to build from the ground up," Eterenia added.

"I think you did remarkably well, considering." Lord Endaga smiled. "You managed to strive despite being targeted by the emperor."

"Speaking of which." Master Jaubro tilted his head towards the door. "I have not seen Emperor Manel since yesterday."

"Well," Tavelo pursed his lips. "She was in my room leering at my naked body while I slept." This time he slowly took a sip, wincing in anticipation of the heat.

Master Jaubro's shoulders slumped in invisible defeat. Lord Endaga grimaced. Ethan, sitting on the floor, clung tighter to his calf.

"You asked about Pridric. I am not ready to divulge the details but I can tell you the end result." Tavelo decided to change the topic. "On Earth…"

"Ooh! I want to know too," Manel cooed as she entered the room. She flopped into a chair while Gallic kept his distance at the entrance. "Do tell."

A servant came over to pour her a cup of tea. Her mouth turned down in mild resentment at the drink. Tavelo gave her a warning stare. She smirked.

"Arms dealers from our third quadrant showed up on Earth selling their goods." Tavelo continued.

"That's…" Lord Endaga lowered his teacup.

"Disturbing," Master Jaubro finished the thought.

"And that means what?" Manel reluctantly took a sip of the hot liquid, making a face.

"They threatened retaliation," Tavelo replied. "That they know where our home world is."

"Let them come. They will see what real might looks like." Manel sat back in her seat.

"We have no idea what they are capable of or how they would attack."

"I don't care!" Manel snapped. "If they're stupid enough to attack a planet of carnivores, they deserve annihilation."

Lord Endaga's head tilted up as he sighed, his tea lingering in mid air by his fingers. Master Jaubro glanced over at Manel and shook his head sternly.

"Emperor Manel," Tavelo said. Manel's eyes narrowed. "Are you implying that the enemy will have free rein to terrorize our people should they infiltrate?"

"That's not what I said!" Manel shot up from her seat as did Tavelo. The two rulers stood face to face. "I am merely saying, regardless of how they show up, I will end them."

Eterenia let out a loud yarn, breaking the tension. They looked over at her. She stared at them with disinterest and continued to drink her tea.

Manel turned her head.

"Hmph!" She sat back down in a heap.

Embarrassed at his own behavior, Tavelo also sat. He understood what Manel meant. That's not going to cut it. They needed a plan to ensure their military forces were ready. He didn't like surprises and Manel certainly didn't either.

❀ ❀ ❀

The council meeting wasted time in Tavelo's opinion. None of the royal advisors had anything meaningful to add. Manel's older brother, more hardheaded and stubborn than him, cited the same argument when the arms dealers' retaliation topic came up. He left feeling exhausted.

Eterenia kept a hand on the small of his back as they walked. Close by, Tervan wore a sour expression. He, too, felt mildly disgusted with the meeting.

"Small steps, my love." Eterenia tried to comfort him. "This is a new dawn, and no one knows how to navigate it yet."

"Common sense should prevail," Tavelo replied curtly. "I see now why they say the royal government is useless."

"And you're here to help steer it on the right path."

Tavelo rolled his head to the side and closed his eyes for a brief moment. He felt the weight of his responsibility already and he hadn't done anything yet.

Opening his eyes, he straightened his head and caught sight of Countess Ambrook.

She kept the title for now because of her children. The Strana family seemed none too keen to embrace them. That alone made Tavelo angry.

"Countess Ambrook," he called to her.

She turned to him in surprise. Her pale grey gown, made of many sheer layers, flowed to the floor. Her blonde hair with the slightest of curls hung loose down her back. Bloodshot eyes with dark patches under them greeted Tavelo. *She looks bad.* He didn't know what he could do to ease her pain.

"Dania is fine." Her voice barely rose above a whisper. Then her face scrunched. "Oh, you're an emperor now. I'm sorry for my insolence."

Tavelo looked at her in horror as she began to bow. He ran to her and stopped her midway.

"Don't." Tavelo held her as she rose. "I think we've known each other long enough to not resort to that." She smiled weakly. "Come. What's wrong?"

"The physician says he will awaken soon."

"That's great news," Eterenia said. "Is it not?"

Dania lowered her head further. Her shoulders slumped.

"I don't know what happened. No one will tell me much of anything. You hurt him so bad." Tears streamed down her cheeks. "And I know you had a reason." She raised her head and sniffed hard. "He did things. Horrible things. I'm not sure if when he wakes up it will be any different."

"Oh, it will be." Tavelo squeezed her shoulders. "He knows better. Don't worry. Our fight is over."

"Was it really a fight, though?"

Eterenia tilted her head in amusement.

Seeing that, Dania let out a small laugh. Tavelo let her go and stepped back.

"I did hurt him." He replied in a somber tone, making her look up at him. "I regret it more and more each day that he slumbers. A reason? Not to warrant what I did." He bowed to her. "I am sorry for causing you and your family such heart ache."

"It's fine," Dania whispered. "I'm glad it was you and not someone else."

There it is.

That also crossed Tavelo's mind. If that had been the case, he would have killed them, even if it turned out to be another merchant leader.

The royal guard on duty at the command center monitoring the outer realm of the stratosphere leaned forward in his seat to scrutinize the small blip on his screen. He watched it start to warble then spread a few miles from the nearest satellite. With calm and ease, his fingers typed in the emergency alert code while keeping his eyes on the object. Right as every screen in the observation hub lit up with the battle signal, the object blossomed into a blurred splatter.

The other operators reared back from the battle symbol at their stations as if assaulted. Stunned, they looked around at each other. An already awkward hush made worse, as if everyone in the room held their breath. When it sunk in that the planet would indeed be attacked, they went to complete their tasks.

He switched to the live feed and witnessed a vortex opening between the early response weapons and the planet. So close. And intentional. Such calculations meant the enemy knew where to hit first. A slew of ships shot out in quick succession, piercing the atmosphere. Even with the silent alert going out, ground forces would be short on time in preparing for a fight. The royal guard tapped the icon for the release of his duties.

A servant came into the room, making a swift beeline towards him. He stood, grabbing his sword, helmet and cape at his feet under the station. The two men switched places without one word. Outside the observation hub in the main corridor, more royal guards assembled.

The sound of boots striking the tiled halls echoed all around. Servants and members scattered around in a panic, their voices slightly raised.

"Was that really a battle signal?" A female house member whispered to a male counterpart. "Who in their right mind would attack us."

"Hmm." A man nodded. "We haven't had invaders since the emperor came back and the Jaubro family renegotiated with the trade organizations."

"Who are these mongrels?" The woman's face scrunched in fury, irritated by the thought.

That question flowed through the palace.

A hundred years ago, this would've been one of many normal occurrences caused by the strife the emperor's actions caused merchants across the five solar systems.

The royal guard frowned.

This is because of Earth. I'm certain of it.

The commander of the royal guard came towards the soldiers lined up, his stony face set with a grim expression. He stopped a few feet from them and scanned their faces.

"You will form a perimeter around the palace and strike down any enemy that dares to reach its steps," he yelled. "I want no excuses for failure." He turned to the royal guard from the hub. "What did you see?"

"An anomaly in the fifth quadrant. At least one hundred ships heading straight for the docks and the palace. A widespread force. They know our planet."

"Any recognizable markings?"

"No." The royal guard pursed his lips. He felt useless not being able to identify the enemy.

From the far end of the corridor, he spotted the newly affirmed emperor, Tavelo, walking towards them. With a sour expression he went to stand by the commander.

"I fear, I know who they are." Tavelo tried to force a grin.

No go.

"They're arms dealers from the fourth system. They use a mediator from their sister planet to negotiate."

A few of the soldiers took sharp intakes of air. The commander's face became unreadable.

"Why have they come?" The commander asked.

"They caused much damage and carnage on Earth. We banned them from trading on that planet."

I knew it! The royal guard gave Tavelo a dark stare. When he met it with one more menacing than his own, he flinched. Tavelo is not one to toy with.

"That is part of trade," the commander snapped. "This is asinine!"

"We also banned them centuries ago from this planet. They sold under a different corporation's umbrella."

"Oh?" The commander tilted his head to one side, intrigued. "So they haven't learned their lesson?"

"Apparently not." Tavelo addressed the royal guards. "Show no mercy. For Manel nor I won't if you fail."

The royal guards snapped to attention, their fists slamming to chests as they shouted in unison, "As you command!"

The commander turned his back to them and began the march down the corridor. The royal guard from the hub could feel Tavelo watching the guards move in step behind the commander. He felt targeted. No matter. His hands itched to grab hold of his sword. It had been a long time since he shed blood on a battlefield.

Enemy ships slammed into the docks, destroying an entire bay and crushing a third of the walkway. The wooden planks shredded as they splintered, the sound like giant trees being snapped in half. One side of the bay collapsed; metal on metal grinding as it made a slow descent into the water causing large ripples. Workers cried out in frustration, not fear, as they scurried to save what goods they could muster.

Within seconds, the hatches opened to let a horde of armed aliens spew out onto the workers. Volshins soared in the air, pitting themselves against more ships coming down.

A ship aiming for the other end of the docks met with a Volshin nearly equal in size. The giant creature flapped its wings to stop within range and kicked the side of the ship with its taloned feet. The hull caved in from the blow as it got knocked out of the sky into the ocean.

The Katalings on the ground moved in to protect the workers. And the enemy didn't prepare for such an onslaught. Compared to them, the Katalings were five times their size. The blasts from the weapons they used seemed to piss the creatures off instead of doing harm.

An enemy soldier continued blasting a Kataling that bore down on him. He let out a barrage of screams as he fired. The Kataling tilted its head and chomped down from the side, nearly engulfing all the enemy's body. Juicy crackling cut the enemy's screams off as the Kataling pressed down, draining the life fluid from him, crushing every bone.

Master Strana, Pridric's eldest brother, and Master Dakien, Yutel's third uncle, arrived at the edge of the pier, eyes gorged red with blood. A small group of their family members followed them.

"Can you believe it?" Master Strana asked, while removing his full-length navy coat as he walked.

"Not really." Master Dakien had already tossed his coat on a nearby post, pulling his ascot off. "But," he smirked. "I don't mind at all. It's been so long…"

"Since we've had fresh kill," Strana finished for the both of them.

With talons and fangs extended, they ran into the fray to get their fill.

Manel stood in the streets on the outskirts of the palace watching black smoke plume from enemy ships crashing into the upper wings of the structure. The transport he had been riding in with his entourage lay a twisted piece of metal, its insides charred. They were able to clear out a split second before a volley of blasts hit it.

He cut a glance behind him; his ruby red eyes gleaming with malice at being surrounded, as his royal soldiers engaged in battle. Gallic, along with his personal guards kept their distance from him, forming a line of defense.

The sound of angry footsteps advancing flooded in. From his gauge, possibly fifty enemy combatants. Among the carnage and bloodshed swirling around him, he turned to face them.

Gallic drew his sword along with the other royal guards, ready to protect the emperor. Ten in all, they were prepared to get their hands dirty. The enemy leader of the assault halting the stampede less than a few hundred feet away surprised them.

His massive biceps flexed as his mouth spread across his face before opening to a sharp toothed grin. Two rows of thick needle canines already stained with blood. He wielded a large weapon resembling a battle axe, black like coal, nearly six feet.

"You are emperor of this planet?" He frowned. His grin returned a split second later. "I remember. We heard you murdered the previous one. You are the son." The leader's slitted eyes narrowed further. "Trash."

"Hmm?" Manel tilted his head in amusement. Although, he clearly wasn't.

"Your kind always interfere in our business. Who are you to stop the buying of our weapons?"

"Warmongers," Gallic breathed out.

"No matter. We take this planet and create new cornerstone for our merchandise." The alien did something that may have been a smile.

Gallic stared at the enemy leader in disbelief as the enemy pointed his weapon at Manel.

"First, we get rid of you."

The already crowded battlefield grew stifling. The enemy stepped forward to resume their stampede. The royal guards stepped one foot back, crouching into a defensive stance.

A guttural yell emitted from Manel. His mouth opened wide, saliva dripping. Manel's eyes became like ripe peeled tomatoes, the pupils, black slits in their center.

Terror gripped the enemy soldiers further back. The line behind the leader moved up to block Manel.

With lightning speed, Manel grabbed a sword from the nearest downed soldier and shot into the horde. The enemy's first line of their defense, no match for his precision, were cut through as Manel killed twelve and wounded eight in seconds. He held an unconscious enemy by the armpit as he sucked the life out of them while keeping up his assault.

Finished with the body, he tossed it aside and made his way to the leader. His talons grew long and pierced beneath the chin of the first enemy that stepped in his line of sight. Two of them protruded out from the top of the enemy's head like glistening horns. He yanked them out and slurped the blood off. His eyes turning pure black.

Gallic and the other royal guards were left rooted in place, unable to move as they watched in horror as Manel morphed into Kataling form and started devouring the enemy. The rest of the horde fighting his soldiers abandoned the battle and tried to retreat.

That no longer seemed an option. He crushed them with his size and weight, making them easily accessible. The leader shrieked in a panic as he tried to get away, taking advantage of his soldiers, using them as shields.

Manel stopped in front of the small group of five ready to protect their leader.

In a flash, he morphed back into human form, tossed the soldiers aside and skewered the leader. He pulled him close, making sure his talons were secure in the leader's gut.

"You think covering our planet with your puny forces was capable of ending my reign? How dare you come here and insult me!" Manel's face contorted conveying the rage of his tone. "This is my domain. All bend to me!"

Gallic and the royal guards flinched at the vitriol.

"You will leave my home and never return," Manel seethed, baring a full array of sharp teeth.

He lifted the enemy leader off the ground and threw him to the side, his talons releasing him. Using the crook of his elbow, he wiped his mouth and turned to his entourage.

"No one will conquer this world while I live."

Gallic dropped his stance and stood straight. He could tell from the demeanor of the other soldiers what they were thinking.

What are we here for?

Manel's attack took out an entire horde in mere minutes. None of them had a chance to act. Only a handful had known of his battle skills. And now they had every reason to fear their emperor. Which led to the next thought that would invade their minds.

Monster.

❀ ❀ ❀

The palace shook with outrage, being bombarded with a constant barrage of attacks. Inside, the enemy had free rein, scouring the halls, engaging whoever they came across. A large group of them rounded a corner and entered the row of personal chambers. The guards formed a semicircle, protruding their fangs and talons.

"Lots of guards," the enemy in front said. "Must be someone important."

A loud rumbling followed by a crack above in the ceiling distracted them, and they all looked up. The entire thing split into multiple pieces all the way in past the double doors behind them and came down.

Seeing an open, the enemy attacked, not caring if they too got caught in the falling debris. They forced their way through.

Past the doors, two soldiers accompanied Lady Dania. Behind them lay Pridric's coffin, with him still asleep inside. The quake had jostled the container, knocking it off its platform and broke the latches.

The slats beneath it went lopsided, forcing the coffin open, exposing Pridric. His blond hair splayed loose over a white shirt and black leggings. His hands lay across his waist.

"What heathens have come to desecrate our home?" Lady Dania seethed. Her eyes turned red as she struck the first enemy to enter the room. "This is madness!" The soldier a few feet from her grappled with an enemy. Anther closing in on the coffin.

The crack in the ceiling widened. Lady Dania glanced over at the coffin sitting too far away. She knew the enemy wouldn't let her turn back. Their leader zipped past her, getting a good look at her sleeping mate.

"The traitor. Yes. This will do."

The enemy raised a long, quarter inch thick spear, black as pitch, with the tip sharpened to a fine point. It would pierce Pridric with ease, skewering him to the coffin and the floor. He went to ram it down with delight. A blurred flash came between the spear and Pridric's body. The second soldier pushed the coffin off the rickety slats onto the floor. And took the blow.

Like liquid, the spear went through him and the floorboards. Lady Dania gritted her teeth to stifle a scream. Then witnessed the most karmic thing she had ever seen. A chunk of the ceiling came down and crushed the enemy. His body lay beneath, a blob of crushed flesh and bone.

No time to rejoice. Enemy soldiers kept coming, and Pridric remained vulnerable. Lady Dania vowed to finish them at the door.

Then she heard the impaled soldier speak.

"Please, Lord Strana, wake up."

Movement. Lots of it. Pridric felt like he had been taken a bad roller coaster ride. He struggled to open his eyes to see past the black. His body felt heavy; weak. A tiny voice said his name.

Who is that?

Then his body hit a hard surface, forcing him to wake. Pain flared in his side. On instinct, he reached out a hand to grab hold of something and found the edge of a shape he knew well. A coffin.

His eyes burned from the sudden onslaught of light. He pulled himself up halfway to see what awaited on the other side and came face to face with a young soldier, one arm still stretched out.

With eyes bulging, the young soldier whispered, "I made it." He gave a small smile. "You're safe."

Pridric watched the young soldier's arm lower to the floor. His gaze fell on the spear. Rage filled him.

"Don't you dare die," Pridric admonished him.

He took his first deep breath. Blood. All around him. It drifted out far and wide. His vision cleared, and he saw his wife and another soldier as the lone blockade against an onslaught of intruders.

He recognized them.

"You can't be serious," he whispered vehemently.

They really came to the home world to retaliate?

His legs didn't want to cooperate, but he willed himself to his feet right as an enemy broke through, heading directly towards him. Pridric caught hold of the enemy's neck with one hand before he could strike.

"That," he squeezed, listening to the alien struggle to breathe while trying to get out of his grip, "is unacceptable."

Even in his weakened state, Pridric proved stronger than most. He pulled the enemy towards him and bit into his exposed neck. He drank hard and fast, nearly draining his prey. His eyes glowed silver.

"More." His barely audible voice made everyone in the room go still. "Hungry."

He had been asleep for far too long.

His wife immediately turned to shove the other soldier to the side, taking herself with him. *Good girl.* The enemy backed out of the room.

Oh, I think not.

Pridric flash stepped into the fray. He would feed enough to at least function properly. And that would take all of them.

"What a disappointing battle." Master Jaubro brushed debris from a collapsed wall off his suit. He glanced at Megen. "Unless that suited your taste."

The oversized brute frowned in disgust. His face had purple blood splattered on one side. He licked the corner of his mouth, tasting its acrid flavor, and spit it out. The smell of alien blood going sour filled the air.

"Such stupidity." He straightened his stance and sheathed his longsword. "Their planning was poor."

Master Jaubro wagged a finger.

"They had the numbers. That's where their false confidence lay."

"All they did was give us more food to consume."

A muffled grimace from behind made them turn around. Desedon used a finger to wipe his lips and stared at it with disdain.

"Not very tasty."

Master Jaubro let out a small laugh. He agreed. Maybe for an emergency ration. And even then, he would probably just skip a meal than consume these creatures. Out of the corner of his eye, he saw four figures coming towards him.

He squinted, not able to see clearly and realized some of the enemies' blood had gotten in there. *Well, damn.* He rubbed his tear ducts, trying to get them to dilute and flush it out.

After a few blinks, he deciphered the group. Lady Dania assisted Pridric with walking. A soldier carried another covered in blood. What looked like the scraps of a drape tied unreasonably tight around the fallen soldier's abdomen.

"What is this?" Master Jaubro asked, gesturing to the wounded one.

"The enemy had a formidable weapon."

Lady Dania held out her hand.

Master Jaubro sucked air in through his teeth as he finally noticed the large black spear she had been carrying. Megen took it from her and weighed it in his own.

"Indeed."

Healers came running down the corridor. Master Jaubro stepped out of their way.

"This one needs immediate care," Pridric called out. He leaned away from his wife and whispered in the wounded soldier's ear. "You will live. You understand?"

Two healers came and took him from the other soldier's arms, whisking him away in a hurry.

"So, this is what it took to wake you up?" Master Jaubro snorted.

"Not my ideal plan." Pridric staggered.

Lady Dania tightened her hold.

"How are you still weak? Didn't you consume enough?"

"I drained about ten of them." Pridric frowned. "None of them were satisfying."

"Oh, I agree completely. Such lovely color, yet disappointing in taste."

"Where's Tavelo?" Pridric looked around.

His answer came in the form of a blood-curdling shriek that had them rooted to the floor.

They all looked out the open frames of what used to be windows and stared at the sky.

Tavelo felt his body morph and surrendered to it. This would be the first time he remained conscious of every cell moving, rearranging. He needed to know what his full form entailed. It had never occurred to him to practice, mostly out of fear. That got shoved aside with the invaders raising havoc on the planet.

At first, it seemed heavy. Like lifting a living mountain. Every muscle strained from the weight. He forced himself to endure it. Then there came a lightness. He could feel gusts of wind whip around him as he floated into the air, letting it embrace him. Cool to the touch. Loving. The smell of the ocean wafted in his nostrils.

In that same moment, his rage took over.

The audacity of the enemy to come to his home world and cause so much chaos. Anger became all consuming, erasing rational thought. His attempts to keep a hold of his senses didn't work. He reverted to a primal state.

Everything went black.

Rising in the air, a Volshin of size none on the planet had ever seen, blocked out what sunlight peeked through the clouds. The wings expanded to nearly twenty feet. Every swish of its tail caused a gust of wind that rocked the docks below. Multicolored flesh like tendrils and flaps enveloping it, giving the illusion of flowing hair and feathers.

"Beautiful," Master Endaga breathed as he stood covered in enemy blood.

All eyes focused on the Volshin, including the enemy, who hastened their retreat upon seeing it. The planet seemed to fall into a hush. The only sound created from air being forced around by the Volshin slowly flapping its wings. Looks of terror and awe graced it.

The enemy ships were taking off.

Except the flagship that had descended earlier in preparation for an expected victory. Its main cannon glowed bright yellow, aimed directly at the Volshin. The sound of its energy building up whirred, breaking the silence. The Volshin let out another cringing shriek.

Its large kaleidoscope eyes shined like prisms.

The main cannon unleashed a wide stream of destruction, scorching the air, making it hot. People could feel its heat push down on them.

Master Endaga let out a gasp and instinctively moved forward. Dakien grabbed his arm to stop him, holding him firm. Both never took their eyes off the Volshin.

With one hard flap of its wings, it created a wind tunnel that stopped the blast midway, forcing it to concave. The energy displaced, licking around the edges with nowhere to go. The Volshin folded its wings back, releasing the blast. Before the energy could come back together, it dove straight down the middle of the blast, pushing it back towards the ship.

In a desperate move to dodge its own assault returning, the ship maneuvered into an upward tilt. Too slow. Master Endaga watched the Volshin plunge into the front of the ship and disappear into it. The sides of the ship began to bulge all the way to the aft, with orange glows bursting out through the cracks being made. A loud crumbling erupted.

From the end of the ship, the Volshin shot forth, followed by a funnel of flames. Its angry screech echoed out into the horizon. Stopping a great distance from the ship, it turned, hovering in the air, to watch its demise.

Smaller ships spewed out of the burning carcass and fled to the stars. Abandoned, the ship exploded on its way down to the ocean. The waters swallowed it whole, flames slowly flickering until the deep snuffed them out. The enemy gone.

The Volshin descended onto the street along the pier, morphing back into its original form. Master Endaga wrenched free of Dakien and ran towards it. Halfway through its transition, the Volshin slammed into the pavement.

"Tavelo!" Master Endaga frantically slid to his nephew's side.

Tavelo's body writhed in pain as he tried to rise on all fours. His wings convulsed as they retracted. The one he landed on, crooked from the fall.

"I got you." Master Endaga held him tight. He grabbed the edge of the broken wing and bent it back into place.

"Ahhh!!" Tavelo screamed.

An audible snap emitted.

"How do you not know how to land?" Master Endaga chastised him. Tavelo took sharp, short breaths between cries. He slumped against his uncle's chest. "It's okay. We'll get you back to the palace, and the healers will take care of you."

Dakien went to kneel beside them. People had gathered around, keeping a safe distance, to see the identity of the massive Volshin.

Even he stared, awestruck.

And this is why he is to be an emperor.

Master Endaga met his gaze. They both understood. Tavelo was dangerous. To himself and others.

❀ ❀ ❀

Master Endaga met Master Jaubro inside the East palace's main corridor as a group of royal guards carried a half conscious Tavelo towards the hallway, leading to his personal chamber. Scattered royal members made a path for them, continuing to gossip, and replay their non-existing near-death experiences.

Master Jaubro followed the group, along with Master Endaga.

256

"I saw the feed." He patted Master Endaga on the shoulder. "He did well for one who has no idea how to use that massive form."

"It was reckless!" Master Endaga's face flushed with anger. "He could have just fought in his regular form, like the rest of us."

"If he hadn't…" Master Jaubro didn't finish.

"We would have taken care of it." An unfamiliar voice rang out from the other side of the busted-out panes of the garden to their left.

A male and female stepped over the broken glass as they both pulled the rest of their bodysuits over their shoulders. Volshins. The group reached Tavelo's chamber and dumped him onto the bed. A healer, already on hand, entered with an injection gun. Tavelo's eyes glazed over once the sedative took hold.

"What was the meaning of that horrid display?" The female Volshin inquired. "Clumsy at best."

Eterenia came running to Tavelo's side. She went around the other way, steering clear of the healers so they could work without interference. Caressing his damp hair, she answered them.

"He has never morphed into his full Volshin form on his own. The first time was during his fight with the emperor. His body transformed on its own as a defense and out of fear."

"He's worse than a newborn, then." The male Volshin shook his head. "He needs training."

"Well, there was no time for that since the enemy decided to invade without notice," Eterenia spat.

"No need to get upset, my child." Master Jaubro raised his hands before her, motioning as if putting on brakes. "We all understand the situation. Merely stating a fact."

"He is not allowed to do so again without proper supervision." Master Endaga faced the Volshins.

"Agreed." The female Volshin nodded to her counterpart. "Our emperor needs guidance. We will consult with our leaders to find the best candidates for his training."

Eterenia leaned over Tavelo's sleeping form.

"You impatient creature. I should punish you somehow." She let out a small cry. "I don't really have the heart to do it though." Tears slid down her cheeks.

"Leave them be." Master Jaubro said to the others in the room. "We have much to do. Tavelo must rest."

Everyone except the healer and Eterenia left.

Master Endaga took one last look back.

It's true. All of them are still children.

Children sent away with no parental guides.

Birds chirped. Their high-pitched songs carried through the open window next to Tavelo's bed. A warm breeze fluttered the sheer curtains. He took short slow breaths before opening his eyes wider than the tentative slits; the light of day and the over-heads hurting his retinas. His body felt heavy. Which didn't surprise him as he remembered the invasion.

At the foot of the bed stood Manel, in male form. His blank stared bore down at him.

"That … was the most spectacular landing I have ever witnessed." His deadpan delivery made worse by the strange pursing of his lips. His eyes showed… what was that? A half-assed smirk? *Is he teasing me?*

Manel turned away and exited the room without another word.

Tavelo felt his face heat with anger. He knew how bad his form looked. It wasn't like he didn't try to land properly. His bulky Volshin form shifted faster than he thought. Movement on his left startled him.

Pridric sat cross-legged in a chair beside him. His blonde hair hung loose, crudely chopped at the middle of his back. He wore a plain white tunic and black leggings with short boots.

He glanced over at him.

"You're finally awake." Tavelo heard the roughness of his own voice. It felt raw, too. Ack. "I'm glad."

"I didn't really have a choice. Those idiot arms dealers tried to impale me while I slept."

Tavelo started up and regretted the movement. He settled back down.

"Dania?" Tavelo knew she guarded his body. No way she wouldn't fight to protect her beloved. "Is she alright?"

"Pfft!" Pridric snorted. "If anyone was alright, it was her. She took out most of them herself."

Tavelo managed a small laugh. *Ouch!* His chest ached. "Good."

Pridric turned his head to meet his gaze.

"Tavelo." Tavelo gave him a curious look. "I love you dearly. But I need you to live up to my expectations a little better, or I can't brag about you as an excuse for abandoning my family."

"What does that mean?" Tavelo asked, alredy defensive.

"The whole planet saw the feeds. There was great awe in your Volshin form and then…"

"Don't." Tavelo's mouth downturned in disgust. "What is being said?"

"Not necessarily disappointment," Pridric said. Tavelo's eyes narrowed again. "A confusion. And maybe a lack of confidence in your upcoming reign."

"Great." Tavelo let out a long sigh. He finally managed to tolerate the stiffness and pull himself upright, leaning against the headboard. "What was Manel doing here?"

"If I were to guess. To make fun of you. Gloat?"

"Ugh!"

"He took out an entire enemy force alone. His guards, and even Gallic, were left to stand by the sidelines and watch."

"That's because he has no sense of restraint. It's all or nothing with him."

"He is better than before." Pridric frowned then smiled. "Oh! By the way. You'll be getting a Volshin trainer."

"Say what?" Tavelo yelled in surprise.

"Not only at the recommendation of your uncles. Manel insisted. He refuses to have an emperor not equal in might."

Rolling his eyes in protest, Tavelo crossed his arms. No denying that sentiment.

True Devotion

Four moons after giving birth to the last decreed child, Manel stayed in female form simply because it unnerved the palace. She maintained her muscular lean physique, now deadlier than her male state over the years.

In her usual black battle suit with the red cape flowing over it to one side, its hem brushing the floor, she resembled a walking menace. Her hard-soled boots clapped down on the marble with every step. There was nothing to do about her hair. She gave up on it after the stylist did the same.

Gallic alone walked by her side. He wore the modified version of his uniform at her request to distinguish him from the others. Maxellia's royal guards were assigned elsewhere. She smiled crookedly. That meant she could ravish him to her hearts content whenever the need arose in her.

Which seemed to happen more often than not. She couldn't understand why. And her body kept changing, affecting her mood.

Despite her build, her breasts were now larger, softer. With every pregnancy they had remained barely there. Small mounds, not much to fill a hand, then reverting to mere humps afterwards. This time they were different.

Even her thighs started to touch, becoming thick.

Gallic like the change.

One person didn't. Maxellia seemed none too happy with the ending decree, citing Manel should simply volunteer her body for the sake of the bloodline. Maxellia encountered strong disagreements, eyeing Gallic with contempt.

Manel found the most noticeable difference in her eyes. They no longer remained gorged with blood. She didn't go into a manic frenzy whenever she became enraged, morphing uncontrollably. To be honest, she felt relief. She told no one about the excruciating pain. The constant torture she suffered her entire life.

Maxellia never once took that into consideration when she sided with their father during those examinations. Her entourage of royal guards came towards them. *And, the demon persists.* Manel's lips curved. Six in total flanked her like a protective glove.

She towered over them, the scene comical.

"My dear sister," Manel cooed. "How does one fare on this glorious day?"

Her soldiers halted in step with her as she glared.

"Is that supposed to be genuine?"

"Of course! Why would I not greet my sibling?"

Manel's expression darkened.

"Hmm?" She tilted her head to one side, a crafty grin emerging. "In that case, join me for an afternoon drink. Tea? Something stronger perhaps?"

Manel tsked.

She had walked right into that invitation. *Well played.* She smiled wide.

"Yes, let's do that." Her tone, full of mocked joy.

Her sister also gave a disingenuous smile. She motioned for her guards to advance. They engulfed Manel and Gallic as they turned to walk beside her.

❀ ❀ ❀

Chains rattling on the other side of the large doors at the bottom of the dungeon stairs drifted into Tervan's ears. They must be giant metal rings for their sound to carry so far and through what he deemed a stronghold of an entrance. Heavy metal doors with two rows of rivets across the front sat before him.

A guard in all black entire, including his armor, stood sentry. Tervan sized him up. Massive frame, bulging muscles beneath the metal plates, and a grim expression border lining on disdain.

Tervan placed a hand on the hilt of his longsword in its sheath attached to his hip. He also wore an all black body suit that hugged every inch, accessorized by his long cape clamped onto the shoulders and calf-length boots that no longer shined after descending the dirty stairwell.

He glanced at the nearly seven-foot-tall soldier, meeting his gaze.

"I figured I should introduce myself. I am Emperor Tavelo's son, and general of Eterenia Jaubro's army."

The guard gave no indication of listening or that he even cared. Wait. No, he does. Wrinkles formed on the soldier's brow. Not really a frown. Annoyance?

"State your business." The guard's demanding, deep voice burrowed through his skin.

Tervan forced himself not to shudder at its vibration. A fight would not end well for either of them. Not to mention the strife it would cause with the two houses.

"In light of the recent invasion," Tervan began. The guard turned his head to spit onto the concrete. Tervan's eyes widened as he followed its trail before continuing. "There is speculation that more enemies may arise. I wanted to get a look at the holding cells to be familiar with the setup here."

"There is no need. We are efficient in our capture and imprisonment of enemies."

"So," Tervan took a step back, not sure how the guard would react. "Who or what is exactly being held in those cells? If I am correct on the history, there hasn't been a hostile event in nearly a century."

The guard moved from the side of the door to stand directly in front of it.

"You need permission from General Megen to enter this area."

"Hmm?" Tervan smirked. "Not the Emperor?"

Hesitation. *Ahh. Got him.* The guard stepped back to his position. With one arm reached out, his hand grabbed the metal bar of the door and pulled. It wheezed, making squeals as it was pried open. Tervan stared deep into the room on the other side before proceeding.

"Thank you. I will make sure to let the emperors know of your cooperation."

"You have until sunset. I will have my soldiers retrieve you by force if you are not back at these doors by then."

Tervan turned to rebuke him, but the door slammed shut, causing a gust of debris to fly into his face. He shielded himself in time to stop most of it from going in his mouth. Still, he sputtered in case he missed some.

More guards in black stood watch at holding cells configured like a maze. He marveled at the way no one cell faced another. Total isolation from the other prisoners despite having no doors. Energy bars crossed the entrances. Their faint, almost invisible light shimmering when they flickered every so often. A reminder of their existence.

Inside the occupied cells, Cellaxans huddled in despair. After better scrutiny, he counted four alien prisoners. *Now why are there royals in the dungeon?* The dirty rags the Cellaxan prisoners wore were made of high quality materials. Such decay meant they had been down there for years, decades even.

Checking his chronometer embedded in his armband, he saw he had been perusing the dungeon for nearly two hours.

How big is this place? He still had another hour or so before his favorite guard sent the horde. He rounded another jigsaw corner and came to a dead end that split right and left.

"I heard Emperor Tavelo's ambitious son creeped around the palace, investigating every crevice."

That unmistakable voice. Tervan inhaled slowly, closing his eyes to calm himself before letting it out. He turned to face Megen. The behemoth towered over him; eyes red with contempt. His cape, not on his uniform, exposed the giant sword hanging from the belt. There would be no need for that. He already had his black talons extended.

"How else am I to protect my mother and the emperor if I don't know the lay of the land?"

"The dungeon is my domain."

"So I've heard." Tervan glanced at his talons. "Is it really that serious?"

"All I can say is that you met your demise in the invasion and that's why no has seen you for this long."

"Oh." Tervan smiled. "You plan to murder me? Are the guards joining in to handle your light work?"

Before Tervan could react, Megen pushed him into the wall behind him. He felt the impact through his whole body. Bricks crumbled from where he landed. As he slid downward, peeling away from the wall, Megen came at him in lightning speed. Tervan managed to dodge sideways.

Megen's talons went through the wall where Tervan's head had been a second before. While he pulled them out, Tervan nailed him in the ribcage with a swift kick. It only angered him more. With no time to cover, Tervan took a punch to the side of his face that had him seeing black for a moment. He staggered away from him, leaning into a back bent as the second blow came.

Not to be denied, Megen grabbed Tervan by the ankle and swung him into the air. Tervan landed in the section he had come from and into a cell's energy barrier. He smelled his suit burn as the bars sizzled. The prisoner backed further away, frightened by the scene. The guards didn't flinch. They stayed at their stations. No intention of interfering.

Tervan realized why. This was no rare occurrence. He could only imagine the harm that ensued when trying to stop a monster like Megen in such tight confines. His domain indeed.

He looked up in time to see Megen mere inches from him and slid down to the ground. He punched upwards and felt resistance as his talons tried to puncture flesh. They got a few millimeters. Megen pivoted his body and grabbed hold of his wrist.

Oh shit!

He felt the pressure of his arm being twisted, holding him in place, as Megen slammed his elbow down onto his forearm. He heard and felt the bone break. Not willing to give him the satisfaction of a scream, he gritted his teeth and waited for his arm to go slack.

Tervan took that opportunity to swing one leg up between them and kick Megen directly in the face. He saw his head snap back, his eyes squinted shut from the blow. Blood flew from the corners of his mouth. His grip on Tervan's wrist released, and the monster fell backwards.

He recovered quickly, spinning onto all fours, his eyes gorged with blood. His fangs protruded. Tervan pushed himself up to a kneeling position with his one good arm. *This monster is about to morph into Kataling form? Here, in the dungeon?* The way the guards finally moved from their post let him know this normally happened.

The two squared off, ready to resume what Tervan figured to be a fight to the death.

So be it.

"I don't know what you two think you're doing," Tavelo's voice rang out. "But it ends right now."

"Really, brother?" Manel's voice dripped with

disgust. "Did you think you could kill him and not suffer the consequences?"

Tervan looked over at the adjacent corridor and saw the two emperors blocking the hall with six royal guards. He was certain more waited further out. The flickering hover lights cast a glow around them. *This must be what they mean by divine intervention.*

Megen tsked as he rose from the floor. His eyes turned to normal; fangs and talons retracted. Tavelo went over to Tervan and stared down at the broken arm. His eyes turned pure silver. Frightened, Tervan struggled onto his feet.

"Father. It's fine. It's just broken. That can easily be fixed and healed…"

Tavelo flashed before Megen, his talons deep in his abdomen. Megen gagged, choking on his own blood. Tavelo leaned closer to whisper in his ear.

"No one harms my children."

He ripped his talons out creating a stream of bloody arcs flying into the air. Megen staggered backwards holding his abdomen tight to lessen the blood flow. His eyes burned with hatred. Manel raised a hand to his mouth and snickered.

"Serves you right." Manel flash stepped next to Tervan and snapped his arm back in place. This time, Tervan couldn't help letting out a sharp cry. "Better? Good. You should see a healer."

Manel walked back to the main hall, four of the royal guards following. Tervan stumbled towards his father, one hand keeping his limp arm steady.

"Come away. Please."

Tervan turned to him and reared back from the bright silver. His father did as he asked. Megen locked eyes with him and, to his shock, sent a telepathic message to him.

This isn't over.

Tervan snorted. He smiled, the gesture throwing the beast off.

Bring it, you monster. I'll end you.

Leaving the dungeon, he trailed his father along with the remaining royal guards. Tervan cursed inwardly. He had shown weakness in the face of his father. Fighting back tears of rage, he fell silently in line. His arm throbbed, going numb.

❀ ❀ ❀

The smell of blood and antiseptic assaulted Maxellia's nostrils the moment she entered the private medical wing. A small chamber draped in semi darkness that could hold ten patients. The overhead lights were set to a minimal glow hovering in the corners and the center.

Four scientists, distinguished by their dark blue suits, mulled around checking on their projects. A group of healers tended to three patients lying in the examination section.

She found the two scientists who assisted with the breeding decree. They stood together watching a clip on the vidscreen before them. Their arms were folded, one hand raised to rest against the edges of their lips. Sensing her presence, they turned.

The first one frowned.

Maxellia felt the same about coming to talk with them. If she had the choice.

I'd kill them all.

She smiled at them as she approached.

"Doctors. I came for an updated report on Manels' offspring."

The second scientist leaned against the edge of the raised surface where the vidscreen attached.

"And what exactly do you want to know about them?" He glanced over at his associate.

"Nothing special, really. Just their genetic make-up and how they're faring."

The one who frowned gave her a dubious look. He went over to a nearby workstation and pulled up a screen with the children's data.

"If what you are searching for is if they are pure blood Katalings," he turned to face her. "The answer is yes and no."

"Excuse me?" She squinted at him in confusion.

The other straightened and walked over to them.

"What he means is that the first child is indeed a pure blood, as expected. And a Kataling."

"Though not as strong or efficient as he should be when he reaches maturity."

"What does that…" She shook her head trying to decipher their assessment.

"He won't be of much use in a battle. Self defense would be more his speed." The second one said.

"The other two are not Katalings." The first added.

"Say what?" She yelled, teeth gritting.

"The last child showed only eighty-five percent purity. Lower than the second child whose blood came close to pure, ended up short."

"How can this be?" She balled her hands into fists, her gaze shifting from one to the other. "Was all that preparation for nothing?"

"It's because a third party gene was introduced." The first one replied.

"The DNA was muddled," the second added. "I would say the experiment wasn't successful. Manel is a product of multiple manipulations. He would never produce pristine, or even sane, spawns."

"A third party?" She whispered. Then her eyes turned red. "So it made things worse."

The two scientists stared at each other.

"That's not…" The second one started to explain.

She would have none of it. With a hard pivot, she turned to the doors and exited the chamber. Her guards fell in line behind her into the main corridor. She had tolerated Manel's sexual depravity because she felt it did nothing to interfere with her plans and the decree.

I was mistaken!

The report would be released to the royal descendant advisers. They would have a say about it. First things first. She needed to rid the palace of the rot. Gallic.

Master Jaubro waited for Maxellia to clear the main corridor as she barged from the royal medical wing. He could tell she was on a mission. And nothing good would come of it. He walked to the scientists still stunned by the workstation. They regained their composure as he walked over to them.

"I was able to hear most of that. No need to relay it again." He held up a hand to stop them. "When you say third party and muddled DNA, what were you implying?"

"If that monster would have let me finish." The second one muttered.

"The third party DNA is not making Emperor Manel worse." The first said. "It is actually repairing any damaged or mutated cells."

"Gallic's DNA is healing Manel?" Master Jaubro asked incredulous, his brow raised.

"That is correct. It overrode Megen's with each pregnancy."

Master Jaubro frowned. He knew Maxellia had forced the decree out of spite along with a fondness for her father's horrors, being more like him than the others. A given that she would go after Gallic. He also thought she now had a reason to kill Manel. The emperor's usefulness in her plans had expired.

"If the emperor were to ever spawn a child with this third party," Master Jaubro eyed the two men.

"It would reverse nearly seventy percent of the issues. Manel won't be completely without ailment but functional as a regular being of his caliber."

"Was this part in the report sent to the advisers?" They both shook their heads. "Good. I need you to keep this to yourselves." He put his hands in the front pockets of his slacks. "I fear that scenario will come to pass sooner than we'd like."

Every curtain in Manel's private quarters, drawn shut, blocked out any light that creeped through the windows. Not yet bright, daybreak had arrived. Gallic sat up in the bed, head against the board. Manel's lay on his chest, her hand in a half grip on his bare skin. She looked at peace. No nightmares had occurred. He gently ran his fingers through her unruly hair.

The small mound of her belly pressed against his hip, and he wondered if that was okay. He wanted to make sure no harm came to the unborn child growing inside. Gallic had finally convinced Manel to change up the style of her wardrobe to hide her condition.

Those who knew of the decree would assume it was another round of pure blood. Her siblings would know otherwise.

He also saw the major changes in Manel. How would the people and the royal family feel about a newly sane emperor? It certainly wouldn't fulfill their narrative. Everyone wanted to blame all the planet's strife on Manel when it had been declining long before his birth.

Emperor Mallen had no love for the people. He just had the sense to maintain trade while dappling in horrors only seen within the palace walls. Manel brought it to the masses for all to see.

Manel's eyes flew open, and she jerked upright, sitting on her knees beside him. He let his gaze roam her naked body. She looked down at him in short-lived disgust. A sort of playful grin formed as she slid on top of him. At the same time, she leaned to kiss him, engulfing his mouth with her own, he felt his member enter her with ease. He loved when she woke up this way.

Maxellia stood outside Manel's quarters, honing her ears to hear inside. Her mouth turned downward, her eyes hooded, as she listened to the sounds of mating. She heightened her sense of smell and flinched, blowing sharply from her nose. The stench of sweat and bodily fluids drifted forward.

She stepped to the door and slammed her fist twice on it. At first, nothing happened. The sounds and stench continued. She readied herself to pound on the door again when the sound of footsteps emerged. Minutes went by, trying her patience. The door opened, revealing Gallic in his sloppily donned uniform. He had attempted to brush his hair back, but it still looked bedridden.

"Princess Maxellia. What brings you here so early to call on the emperor?"

"That is not of your concern." She pushed him out of her way into the room. "I am your superior and you do not question my actions."

A sword came to her neck. Her guards placed their hands on their hilts, ready to draw.

"I only serve the emperor, protecting her from all enemies, regardless of status. You may be royalty. In my eyes, you are also a threat."

"Don't slit her throat. She's not worthy of dying by your hands." Manel slid off the bed wearing a long, flowing robe. Its billowy fabric hid her features. She addressed her. "You need to answer his question." Manel's eyes narrowed in anger.

They aren't gorged with blood!

The usual air of hostility missing as well. Maxellia pursed her lips.

"I received the report on the offspring you spawned for the decree."

"Oh?" Manel sat in the chair near the foot of the bed. "Do tell."

"They were not viable to the decree's standards. Only one is a pure blood Kataling."

"A weak one at that," Manel scoffed.

"You already knew this?"

Maxelia contained her shock.

"Of course. The moment I laid eyes on it, I pitied the creature."

"In that case, the decree has not been honored. It needs to be remedied."

Manel rose from her seat. This time, the malice permeated the room. Maxellia smirked.

Yes. Attack me you failed experiment.

"Absolutely not!" Lendor came into the room. He pushed Gallic's sword away from her neck. He stepped between her and Manel. "The decree is done. I don't know what you're trying to accomplish," he said to her. "But I will not allow you or the advisers to desecrate Manel any further. Find a new hobby." His red eyes conveyed his conviction.

"The whole purpose of the decree!" She sputtered.

"Was to fulfill our father's sick obsession with creating flawed beings to control under his thumb." He raised a hand towards her, palm out. "If that is all you came for, leave Manel to enjoy this day as she sees fit."

Maxellia's eyes became slits. She peered at him for a moment. Both in a silent battle of frustration. She wanted chaos at the expense of Manel. Lendor wanted to play devil's advocate when no one abided by the rules.

"My apologies for interrupting your morning." She bowed her head to Manel. "I shall take my leave."

Gallic placed his sword on the mantle behind him. His stare never wavered as she backed out of the room, then turned to face the hallway. Another set of guards with purple capes attached to their body armor were positioned around hers.

She forgot Lendor had his own royal soldiers. Her guards stood from their defensive stances and followed her down towards the dead end that veered to the left.

Her body felt hot. She seethed with rage. Another smell mingled with Manel and Gallic's. A scent she had become accustomed to over the years. Manel was with child. A devious plot ran through her mind. She let a genuine smile spread on her face.

Tavelo stared at Gallic sitting silently then shifted to Manel. His insides tensed with fear for them. He could see the concern in the soldier's expression as he sipped from his glass. Worry lines etched his brow while Manel seemed unbothered, eating the fresh slices of warm bread and meat on the plate before her. Beneath the oversized black kefta embroidered with gold design down the middle, he could make out her protruding belly.

How reckless.

When the royal advisors came around to talk about his own bloodline and accidentally divulged Manel's current state. By the way Maxellia started to act, he concluded her response bordered on disdain. He didn't trust her.

Master Jaubro also raised concerns.

Metal utensils clanked against the plates.

Everyone at the breakfast table had no desire to speak. Tavelo sighed heavily, spearing a piece of raw meat with his fork and shoving it in his mouth. He chewed slowly, savoring the spices sprinkled on it. Eterenia glanced over at him with a questioning look. He shook his head. Not now. She resumed eating.

From across the table, Pridric couldn't take his eyes off Manel. He could also tell, and his eyes were wide in awe of the situation. Stop that! His telepathic command sent louder than he wanted. Pridric's eyes shifted to land on Tavelo. He reluctantly averted his gaze to his meal.

"You need more protection." Tavelo blurted out. Everyone halted eating. "Gallic is not efficient." He heard the sound of utensils dropping hard on a plate. He looked up at Manel. "From now on, you will be assigned a detail from the East. I don't trust yours."

Gallic appeared to deflate with relief. As if sensing it, Manel became livid.

"What are you saying? My royal guards have been loyal to me always. Gallic has protected me all this time! I don't need your…"

"This is not up for debate." Tavelo met his gaze. "The royal guards are loyal to the throne. They will turn on you at your siblings' command."

Manel's demeanor faltered. Her hands fell to her sides. Gallic reached down and clasped her hand beneath the table so no one could see. Tavelo felt a tinge of trepidation. Something sinister hung in the air of the West palace every time he visited.

❀ ❀ ❀

For weeks, Maxellia tried to catch Manel alone, or at the very least with Gallic to eliminate them both. She lurked in the hallways after meetings. Followed them whenever they broke from the newly assigned guards from the East.

Damn that meddling Volshin!

That was the main reason she couldn't get any closer to either of her prey. Six East imperial guards surrounded Manel everywhere she went.

Lately Manel only came out of her chamber for the rare, occurring mandatory meetings. Hiding her condition took priority. Whispers floated throughout the palace about the decree and if this last one saw its end. Maxelia gritted her teeth, still angered by the whole account.

Lying in wait by Manel's chamber, her guards previously dismissed, she held a dagger in hand; hilt in palm with the blade resting along her forearm. The East guards had already departed. She overheard Gallic saying he and Manel would take a stroll to the banquet hall only a few corridors away.

Gallic would be the first out the door, anticipating any attack from the waist up. She planned to take him down at the legs first and slit his throat while down, negating Manel's chance to save him. A pregnant Manel would be slow to react. She smiled at the plan.

Footsteps approached the door from inside. She steadied herself to strike. Her eyes widened, and she froze in her stance as she felt a presence behind her. Not one, but two. She had heard nothing. Standing tall, she turned her head to see who dared interrupt her right as the doors opened.

Master Jaubro and his cringe worthy assistant watched her with expressionless stares. Chalking the incident up as a mere blip in the day. Disappointing on the entertainment level. She wasn't worth their time. Gallic stood in the doorway, his sword in hand, unsheathed. He tilted his head to the right, giving her a sideways glance. Proving her right, Master Jaubro addressed Gallic without acknowledging her.

"Is Manel up for the short walk? I figured we could enjoy a midafternoon break together."

Gallic diverted his focus between the two.

"Yes. We are about to leave."

He tentatively fingered the hilt of his sword.

"And put that thing away." Master Jaubro pointed at it. "There's no need."

He walked past her and stood on the other side. Manel came out of the room. The two siblings made eye contact. Neither spoke. She could tell Manel knew her reason for being there.

"Are you joining us as well, sister?" Manel gave her a warning stare.

Not to be intimidated, she laughed.

"Why, thank you for the invite. I will." She slid the blade back up her sleeve into the hidden sheath. "Please, lead the way."

Gallic sheathed his sword. He gestured for her to follow Master Jaubro and Desedon. Manel stayed by his side, bringing up the rear. No trust. She grimaced at the situation she found herself in.

The small meal break proved to be a grueling experience. She smiled sweetly and played nice for nearly an hour before excusing herself to attend non-existent work. The moment she reached the main corridor, she hurried to the other side of the wing to her quarters.

She flung open the doors and rushed into her bedchamber. Her fists slammed on the vanity dresser, shaking everything on it. A few items toppled to the floor. She felt her body tremble with failure.

"I forgot to tell you, sister."

Lendor's voice invaded her ears.

She turned to see him inside her room. His calm demeanor belied the red storm of his eyes.

"How dare you come in…"

"If you harm Manel in any way, I will personally come after you."

She stood. Amused, her face contorted into a grin. She let out a loud, "Hah!" She stepped closer to him, towering over his medium sized frame compared to hers. "You? Think you can punish me?"

"You are not invincible, dear sister." He turned away from her and walked to the still open doors. "I warned you. That's all I needed to say."

She followed him. The moment he set foot outside her entrance, she slammed the doors shut. Leaning against it, she let her head bang then laughed.

There was always plan B.

Healers ran around the private royal birthing room getting ready for Manel's delivery as she lay on the table screaming in pain. An unusual situation since the previous births were uneventful with Manel barely making a sound. Gallic guarded the entrance, cringing at Manel's cries, yet held his position.

"Hurry!" The first healer called to his counterparts. He rushed over to Manel and checked the crowning. "It's coming now!"

Like a blossoming flower, her womb opened wide. Blood streamed down the sides of her inner thighs. The healer paid no heed to that. He focused on the tiny head, forcing its way out.

A healer behind him awaited with swathing cloth in hand while another stood with the mist sprayer.

A sick, ripping sound came with the newborn as its legs cleared. The healer hosed it down with the gentle spraying of cleansing antiseptic. The other quickly wrapped the child. Manel screamed more. The first healer watched the womb retract.

"My stars, there is another!" The healer, checking Manel's vitals, exclaimed.

The one holding the child looked around in confusion, then set the child in a nearby clear basin. They ran to the other side to get another swathing cloth. Shocked, the first healer saw the head of a second child poke its way through. More blood spewed out faster.

The other healer made it back with another swath cloth before the first healer caught the child in his hands. Once sprayed off, they wrapped it up like the other and set it inside next to its sibling. Manel thrashed about, writhing in pain as her gaze fixated on the entrance. Blood went everywhere.

"Hold her still!" The first yelled.

"I am trying!" The healer grappled with Manel. "Gallic! Come!"

He needed not ask as Gallic, already at Manel's side, struggled to hold her down.

"It's alright. You did well." He saw her eyes filled with tears, frightening him. Manel looked terrified. "Shh. I am here. Please, be calm."

An arrow sailed through the throat of the healer catering to the newborns. He fell in a heap. Within seconds, four royal guards came crashing into the delivery room. One went straight for Gallic while as another sliced the first healer and positioned his blade over Manel.

Gallic yelled out in desperation, feeling helpless. His enemy relentlessly swinging his sword, not giving him an open to unsheathe his own. The blood drained from his face when he saw the remaining guards raised their blades over his newborn children.

"The Royal blood has been tainted!" The first guard shouted. "These abominations will be cleansed!"

In her manic state, Manel managed to catch the blade coming down at her. She used every ounce of strength she could muster to twist the soldier's wrist until it snapped. He howled in pain. Manel cut it short when she rammed his own blade under his chin. The tip protruded from the top of his head and his body fell backwards to the floor.

A long sword blurred before the two guards ready to murder the infants. Blood arcs flew in the air. The guards hit the floor, but not before dropping their blades. Both went straight down in the basin into the two crying babies. Manel saw the plight of her children and let out a shriek unlike anything Gallic had ever heard.

The sound almost made him faint.

Megen stood over the newborns along with Master Jaubro. Other guards lay on the ground from various arrays of hurt administered by Desedon. In the flurry of events, Gallic and the healers had not noticed more enemies flooding in.

Lendor came towards Gallic and pushed him out of the way. He stabbed Manel with a large needle, hitting the plunger as it went deep. Manel wailed weakly, her strength spent. Her body went limp.

Master Jaubro removed the blades from the basin. They had struck the children and fallen to the sides. Blood seeped through the swath cloths. Healers from the other sections came running in. One stopped at the basin to inspect the newborns.

"The wounds are shallow. We will get them cleaned up and apply sealing gel." He caressed both their heads. "It's alright little ones. You're going to be fine."

Megen remained rooted in place, his eyes gorged with blood. His stained sword hung from his hands. Master Jaubro's lips went thin.

The first healer grabbed hold of the edge of the delivery table and pulled himself up. A large gash on his shoulder spread open as he did so.

"We have to stop the bleeding." His voice rattled. "The emperor. She's dying."

"I figured she may be bleeding from an attack." Lendor came to the healer's aid. "I gave her a powerful sedative and anticoagulant."

A loud animal like sound erupted. They all turned to see Gallic slump to the floor, choking on his own saliva as tears ran down his face. Rage, despair, and sorrow showed through half squeezed eyelids.

"We need another for him," a healer advised.

Gallic's head shot up and he glared at everyone in the room.

"Don't touch me." His tone evoked fear with a tinge of madness. He used the edge of the table as leverage and pulled himself up. "I'm not leaving."

Four healers came to tend to Manel. The others were helped out to the main medical sector for treatment.

"How did this happen?"

Master Jaubro raised his hands at the scene.

Megen's expression shifted to rage. He gripped his sword's hilt, his knuckles tense.

"The royal advisers," he seethed. "Those monsters are to blame."

"I should have kept a better eye on them," Lendor said.

Master Jaubro seemed to deflate inwardly. Tavelo had to be briefed on the incident.

❀ ❀ ❀

The royal advisors sat comfortably in their lounge, located along the throne room's corridor. All five lay on plush chaises six feet apart, arranged in a semicircle. Their robes draped lazily over the edges, brushing the floor.

Servants were on hand to fan them with giant feathers and hand feed them fruits. The hover lights had been dimmed to create a relaxing ambience.

They had not a care in the world.

The doors flew open, causing a bang as they hit against the adjacent walls. The servants stopped their duties and ran to the sides of the room. Royal guards of the East palace marched in surrounding them. Two in direct line of sight sat up, their expressions full of outrage. Until they saw Tavelo enter the room. Both seemed to go pale. Two other advisors sat up in fear.

The one on the end gazed at him with disinterest.

"What is the meaning of this?" The first advisor regained his composure. "This area is off limits even to the royal family."

Tavelo paid him no mind.

"Which one of you ordered the murder of Manel's children?"

The four advisors flinched at the accusation. The fifth glared at him.

"And what would you do with such information? Kill them? Lock them in the dungeon? None of those remedies produce a satisfactory outcome."

"No," Tavelo hissed. "But, I would feel better."

"If that is the case," the first advisor said. "Maybe the death of those creatures was for the best."

The advisor next to him gave him a disturbed stare while shaking his head. At first confused by the gesture, he then he frowned.

"I didn't say which children." Tavelo spoke calmly, despite his red eyes. "That you knew Manel was in labor is most interesting."

"It means they had planned all along to kill the newborns." Lendor stepped into the room. "Now," he drew his sword. "Answer Emperor Tavelo."

"No need." Tavelo held out his arm to stop him from advancing. "I will cull them all."

Two of the advisors morphed into Kataling form. The others picked up their swords that lay at the side of the chaises. Tavelo smiled with glee. The servants ran from the room and the guards stepped back to give some space between the monsters. Lendor sighed. Another palace chamber on the path to destruction.

❀ ❀ ❀

Dania used a finger to gently poke the chubby stomachs of Manel's twin boys sleeping peacefully. The room had been soundproofed so no outside noise would disturb them. Ethan roamed farther in the room. He took a small blanket off the stack by the bed and brought it over to her. She arranged it around the two infants, tucking in the sides.

On the bed lay Manel. Her bosom rose and fell in a slow rhythm. She had been sleeping most of the hours of the day for weeks. The healers explained she needed to regain her full strength after spending nearly all of it that day in the delivery room.

Gallic went out to run an errand, entrusting his children and Manel to Tavelo. Dania gladly accepted the duty when he asked. On a spur-of-the-moment decision, she brought Eterenia's son with her. He had been sitting around in the private quarters doing nothing except reading.

"They are quite adorable." She rubbed each of their cheeks. They stirred, then settled back in. "I know you may feel awkward, but they're essentially your brothers."

"Not at all." Ethan sat next to her on the bench seat positioned close to the basinet. "It is no fault of their own, nor mine, who they were spawned from." He brushed tiny strands of hair from the baby closest to him. "I hope they'll grow up safe."

"With this royal palace, that may be wishful thinking."

Dania looked over at Manel.

She had seen the changes in the emperor over the

years and wondered what she would be like when she awakened. No doubt, still arrogant and hostile. But, maybe having more empathy. A sense of compassion. She watched Ethan care for his new siblings.

One could only hope.

With the events of Manel's birthing session kept under wraps, Maxellia roamed the palace untouched by the backlash. The advisors had not drawn her into the fray, even though she had known about the plot. She made sure their decision did not bloody her hands. Her own plan ready to set in motion. Where the advisors had failed, she would succeed.

For now, they kept the twins' paternal lineage secret. Only those in the inner circle knew. Her four guards followed in silence, always on alert for any disturbance. She had been attacked numerous times by factions who despised her way of ruling since her release from exile.

Her boots striking the floor echoed in the empty corridor. Most of the palace had gone for the usual midafternoon activities. A stroll in the gardens or to the cities. She preferred the silence it brought, giving her time to think.

To her surprise, up ahead, Lenri leaned against the side edge of a window, staring at the sprawling city below. Her pretty features marred by the scar Manel had given her. She turned her head towards Maxellia and her brow scrunched.

"Sister," Maxellia said, soothing. "Why have you not gone out with the others for fresh air?"

"The same could be asked of you." She tilted her head. "Sister."

Ah! So, we're playing that game.

"I like a bit of peace and quiet every now and again." She halted a few feet from the younger.

"And I like to keep an eye out for schemes."

"You sound like Lendor," she laughed. "What for? You hate Manel."

"I do not." Lenri glared at her. "I know what he did to me. I also know why he had no remorse."

Had? That perplexed Maxellia.

"Then your capacity for forgiveness is greater than mine."

"No matter what, Manel is still my sibling. Our father was a monster." Her eyes narrowed as her head titled downward, still locked on Maxellia. "Is your goal to be just like him?"

Maxellia brought her head high. A slight grin tugged at the corners of her mouth.

Perhaps.

❁ ❁ ❁

Gallic entered the dimly lit chamber and peered around until he found a figure seated in the far left corner. The silhouette of long scraggly hair with a pronounced nose reflected against the wall behind them. Nothing held in their hands or on their lap. They simply sat in silence.

"Father." Gallic walked further into the room to stand before the man. "I have come to talk."

He took stock of the small chamber.

Minimal furniture and amenities. Enough to keep one comfortable and in check. His father's wounds from the first years of Manel's reign never quite healed, thus he got assigned to palace duty. Even then, they limited his work. Gallic heard he started assisting in training the royal guards fifty or so years ago.

His father leaned forward to look up at him. Grey eyes, narrowed in disdain, greeted him. The two locked into a staring match until his father relented.

"I heard you were the emperor's pet these days."

His father's tone drip with venom.

"Were you not one as well?" Gallic clenched his

fists. "You gladly did his bidding after he murdered Emperor Mallen."

"That was my duty!" He watched as his father struggled internally. Sadness fell over him. "I know now how wrong we were. Our planet suffered for it."

"I came to tell you something that's been kept secret."

"There's enough of those in this place," his father snorted. "I steer clear of the main palace."

"I know. You never agree to meet with me. Which is why I made the guards of this wing bring me here."

"What is so dire that you disturb my solace?" His father asked, visibly angry.

Gallic took a deep breath. He dragged the empty chair from the other side over and set it before him. Plopping down, he met the man's gaze.

"I have sired two children." His father frowned. "With Emperor Manel."

His father's eyes widened in disbelief. His mouth gaped open as if about to speak, yet nothing came out. He grabbed Gallic by the shoulders and squeezed.

"Ahh!"

Gallic tried to wrench away from his death grip.

"Have you gone mad?" His father seethed. "You mated with that creature?"

"Don't." Gallic got loose, smackingd his father's arms from him. "I won't allow you to say that about the mother of my children."

His father slumped in defeat. Gallic suddenly felt pity for him. His mother rarely came to visit, opting to stay at the family home near the city. He had not seen her either in ten years. Loneliness. It permeated the room.

"I want you and mother to meet them when it's deemed safe."

"What does that mean?"

"There have been a few attempts on our lives. Mine, Manel's, and our children." Gallic tried to contain his rage by mentioning his infants. "I wanted to kill all who were involved."

"What did you expect?" His father whispered. "The emperor is hated throughout the land."

"I know that." Gallic hung his head. "Would you," he hesitated, "come and be guardian for them?"

"Are there not guards assigned to the emperor who can do that?"

"I would rather have family at my side."

An awkward silence ensued. Both men sat trying not to convey their embarrassment.

Leaving his father's chamber, Gallic made his way back to the quarters he now shared with Manel. Inside, he found her sitting upright in bed, her hair a tangled mess. The twins slept in the basinet at the end. He wiggled a finger on their cheeks.

"Where have you been?" Manel swung her legs off the edge of the bed and stood. "I woke up, and you were gone."

A bit of sorrow sprinkled in her voice.

She pulled on a robe hanging off the nearby chair. Placing both hands on the vanity, she put her weight onto it while staring in the mirror. Her expression bordered on anger. He understood why. She considered her current state a sign of weakness.

"Brought something for you." Gallic pulled a necklace from his battle vest's inner pocket.

A medallion with deep blue, yellow, and red jewels, arranged in a crest, dangled from the gunmetal chain was. Its scalloped design frame made an irregularly shaped oval. Manel frowned at it.

"This is my family crest. I know you are required to wear the imperial seal but, I figured you could also wear this." Held it out. "As a symbol of our bond."

He steeled himself for an assault, holding the necklace tight in case Manel tried to knock it from his hands. She stared at it for a moment. Her face softened, then she reached out and took it from him, holding it up for inspection.

"I didn't know your family was important enough to have one." Her sarcasm fell flat.

"My family has served the royal palace for generations. We took great pride in that."

"Past tense?" Manel scowled. "Since my reign?"

"No." Gallic met her gaze when she turned to him. "Your father's."

Manel's eyes narrowed.

Her body tensed as if ready to fight an unseen demon. Gallic gently removed the necklace from her fingers and placed it around her neck. It clinked against the larger imperial crest she always wore before sliding further down below it. If she kept it tucked in under her robes, no one would know she had it on.

Sensing she had come to the same conclusion he let out a small breath of relief. Manel fingered the jewel. A tiny smile crept up.

"A secret, then. For only us." She let it drop back down into the robe.

Gallic rejoiced inside.

❀ ❀ ❀

Tavelo tapped the armrest of his chair. He sat in the library of the main palace, along with his uncle and Pridric. A tea set in the center of the table had three cups with steam drifted from them. Gallic stood next to an empty seat, his head tilted down, visibly mad.

"Absolutely not," Tavelo finally said.

Gallic frowned. "As long as you provide the guards, I will protect Manel and our children." He balled his hands. "My mother has the right to see her new Doljas."

"I get that," Tavelo snapped. "I don't trust the royal guards who will have to go along with mine."

"Becoming a Dego is a great honor," Pridric piped up in Gallic's defense. "Not knowing my grandchildren would have crushed me."

"As I said…" Tavelo huffed.

His uncle raised a hand to stop him.

"Denying Gallic from seeing his family is not an option." He templed his hands over his mouth, thinking. When he lowered them, he turned to Gallic. "Tavelo's concerns are valid. You understand that better than most." He averted his gaze to Tavelo. "However many royal guards are assigned, you should match it. "

Defeated, Tavelo leaned back in his chair. "When are you planning to do this family outing?" He glanced over at Gallic. The soldier almost appeared ecstatic, yet holding back celebration.

"Next moon cycle. That would give me time to prepare a safe route around the main roads."

"Yes, we don't need any witnesses to an imperial procession," Pridric chided.

"Manel has four royal guards and four from his eldest sister. If you match that…" Gallic stopped.

"That is a lot of escorts," Master Endaga said. "Royal procession two-fold."

"I'd rather they have too much than not enough," Tavelo retorted, still unsure.

"A secret outing." Pridric sighed. "Good luck."

"I suggest you tell no one until it is time." Tavelo reached over and picked up his tea. "Your siblings seem to have a lot of spies." He took a sip and felt stares. Looking up he saw the trepidation on their faces. "Especially Maxellia. Tread carefully."

Gallic gave a quick bow and exited the room. Tavelo watched him walk briskly down the hall, in a hurry to undoubtably give Manel the news.

"Are you really going to allow it?" Pridric raised his brow. "The whole time you said that, your face told otherwise."

"I'll send four East guards with the entourage."

"Only four?" His uncle asked, surprised. "Not matching the numbers?"

"I said with the entourage." Tavelo took a sip.

"Where are you sending the other four?" Pridric searched Tavelo's face for a hint. "Tavelo."

Master Endaga pursed his lips. Tavelo gave them both a sideways glance.

He had no intention of revealing his plans.

Two servants, each carrying a basinet hefted them into the transport structured like a carriage similar to the ones seen on Earth in the turn of the previous century. Except this one had no need of horses to pull it. Inside, the plush bench seating faced each other. Burgundy velvet lined the walls with gold and black trim. Its exterior top sat flat while the sides bulged out to accommodate the seats.

A small ramp extended, lay flush on the ground.

Daylight barely creeped in, the sky turning a light grey. A breeze sent fallen leaves rustling and robes to billow softly. Gallic nodded in approval of the weather. Manel walked down the steps of the palace side entrance.

While Gallic wore his usual royal uniform, Manel chose a different attire. A short-sleeved kefta embroidered to death with gold brocade on deep red fabric. The shoulder sections moved independently to allow ease of movement when Manel raised her exposed arms. Her muscles bulged as she reached to scratch the back of her head, further messing up her hair. The bottom of the robe opened enough to let one peek at her well-toned legs in the black leggings.

Her boots struck each stone step with force.

"Be gentle with my spawns or I'll kill you all." The tone of Manel's calm voice sounded anything but. She meant it.

The two servants nodded, securing the infants before climbing in beside them. Instead of twelve guards, there were ten. Maxellia removed two after hearing about the outing only hours ago. She felt no need since Tavelo assigned his own to accompany them.

It felt too easy. Gallic had a sense of anxiety. Manel seemed to feel the same, scrutinizing the area for anything out of place. Still on pins and needles, they walked up the short ramp into the transport and settled on the bench opposite the children. Four royal guards, two from each palace, came in after them and sat in the corner seats.

The ramp retracted as the carriage lifted off the ground to hover while the pilot checked his gauges. Slow and steady, the transport made its way down the cobbled streets behind the palace. When it reached the back roads, it maneuvered around a bend then sped up.

"So." Manel smirked. Crossing her legs, she placed both hands over her knees. "What is your mother like?" Gallic cocked his head in thought. "I know of your father. The disappointing failure he is."

"Don't." Gallic looked up and met her eyes. His change in demeanor startled her. "He has always been loyal to the empire."

"My apologies," Manel mumbled. "I was only…"

"Trying to rile me up. Force me to back out of the visit because you are afraid my family will hate you."

Manel's eyes turned red, then reverted. She let her arms flop by her side as she pouted, proving him right. Watching her relent to that truth relieved him. If her psyche were still damaged like before, she would have torn apart the carriage in a rampage.

"Relax. My mother is more forgiving than even I give her credit." He slumped against the back of the bench. "If anyone should be nervous, it's me." The guilt seeped into him. "I have not seen her in so long."

He could sense Manel staring at him. Out of the corner of his eye, he saw the two imperial guards glance at each other. The exchange lasted only a nanosecond. Long enough for Gallic to go on alert.

The carriage stopped in front of a dark grey stone structure. It was six stories high and from the outside looked to be in shambles. The heavy wooden door set deep in the stone entrance had seen repairs over decades. Makeshift pieces embedded in the original sealed the broken areas. Tiny plants grew through cracks in the chipped driveway.

The lack of sun and the high humidity added to the surrounding dampness. Manel and Gallic exited the carriage. The two servants followed carrying the infants. Manel glared at the homestead, not liking its state.

"It's better on the inside," Gallic laughed, trying to lessen the mood. "My family aren't merchants, so we rely solely on royal stipends." Manel swirled around to face him, eyes glistening with rage. "All of my brothers and sisters of combat age are employed in the royal palace."

Before Manel could respond, the door creaked open. The metal brackets holding it in the stone whined in protest, disappearing into the dark behind it. A tall, slender woman wearing an eggshell-white robe stood holding a lantern. Its lighting elements flickered, crackling, as if the power was about to fail any moment. Her chestnut brown hair hung loose past her waist, not yet combed.

"Gallic?" Her high tenor voice almost sultry. "Is that you, my son?" She peered out at the entourage, her eyes falling on Manel. She suddenly faltered, dropping to her knees. "Emperor Manel. Please forgive my insolences."

The way she went down, Gallic could see her exhaustion. She hasn't slept! He went to help her up when Manel pushed him back and did instead. She knelt before the woman and lifted her chin so their eyes met.

"No need to bow. Stand." The two rose together.

Gallic's mother clamped a hand over her mouth and turned her head towards the dark.

"Quickly! We have visitors." She paused. "The emperor has arrived." From the darkness came the sound of feet rushing around. She turned back to Gallic and Manel. "Please, I welcome you. Do forgive the squalor of our abode."

"Wait here and let no one near this road," Manel ordered the guards.

Manel, Gallic, and the servants followed her.

She found the inside indeed better than expected. The hover lights came on, brightening the corridors to reveal a modest aesthetic. Muted colors blended with the rustic sandstone walls in complete contrast to the dark stone outside. Every room they passed had plush furniture and minimal accents.

Servants rushed back and forth between them from the center of the home, careful not to brush against Manel. They arrived at the great room and Manel's face turned to that of a small child. Her eyes widened with glee and her mouth gaped open. Realizing her expression, she immediately regained her royal composure, clearing her throat.

Food arrived on the massive table. Water and blood carafes were strategically arranged down the middle for easy reach. Gallic felt a sense of nostalgia. They were led through a narrow hallway until they reached a small, dimly lit chamber. His mother set the lantern down on the one rickety table, giving more light to the room.

"I'm sorry," she began. "There's so much to be done in the morning hours. This room is private. And I assume you are here for a purpose."

"You would be correct." Manel unbuttoned the kefta as she sat in the chair opposite the woman and heard the mother gasp.

"You are," Gallic's mother spoke through fingers covering her mouth. "A shifter? The emperor."

Then she noticed the servants and the bundles they carried. She turned to Gallic.

"Yes, mother. These are my sons that I have sired

with Emperor Manel."

A brief moment of elation faded as her face tensed. "This is a great secret, isn't it?" She asked, forlorn.

"For now, yes."

Gallic sat on the bench built in the wall.

"Then you and those precious children are in great peril." She bowed her head. "Your father knows?"

"I told him. He too feels concerned."

"This is of no concern," Manel blurted. "I will protect our spawns, regardless."

Gallic sighed.

"Manel, please. We have discussed this."

"Is that?" Gallic's mother pointed to the exposed medallion. "Our family crest?"

Manel touched it then held it up for her to see. She had removed the imperial seal from her neck in the carriage before arriving. Tears welled up in Gallic's mother's eyes.

"That is good. I'm glad you accept us."

Her words took Manel aback. She expected it to be the other way around, turning her head in shame at her previous thoughts. Gallic's mother stood and leaned over the two bundles set on the other sturdier table. She used both hands to caress their faces.

"I have new doljas." Her shoulders raised as she hunched over, peering at their faces for a closer look. "Welcome little ones. I am your Dega."

Her smile seemed to brighten the room. Manel inadvertently shielded her own eyes at the sight.

Gallic's mother carried one of the twins in her arms as she gave a tour of her home, the other fast asleep in Gallic's. Manel felt awkward among the energized atmosphere. Children ran around laughing and shrieking, playing catch me, much to the chagrin of the adults yet never chastised.

The introductions were a blur. Too many of them. Manel tried to clear her head. House members praised Gallic's mother for being an elevated Dega.

Manel forced herself to remain calm while other people handled her children.

The dining area almost equaled the size of the palace's private royal one. Manel could see why after losing count of the occupants. Including the children, there were at least forty household members. They made room for Manel and Gallic at the main table. The servants sat with the others at another nearby.

Manel's face lit up, smelling the four large loaves of freshly made bread set in the center, piping hot, cooling on wooden planks. She had never gone into the palace kitchen to see her food prepared her food.

By the time any of it came to the royal table, the temperature had lessened. Meats were lukewarm, fruits and cheeses as well. She could feel her mouth salivate at how much better the food before her would taste.

A servant came to stand between them with a multi-slicer. She held it over the nearest loaf.

"Thick or thin?"

"Thick!" Manel replied ecstatically.

The servant rotated the dial on the side, making the separator's blades widened. In one downward motion, it cut the loaf into eight slices. The ends fell over onto the plank. Steam rose, filling the air with more delicious aroma. Manel breathed deeply.

Gallic laughed. Manel turned a warning glare at him. He didn't pay it any mind.

"You're like a child waiting to be fed."

Manel frowned and returning her gaze to the bread found the other children were indeed doing exactly what she had. Her face flushed. Four of the adults arrived at the table halfway dressed in royal guard uniforms. They rubbed the heads of who Manel concluded were their own children before settling in their seats.

Gallic's mother stood at the head of the table and clapped her hands. Everyone stopped talking and gave her their attention.

"We have been graced this day by the emperor's presence. And my son, Gallic, has brought me twin doljas. I cannot express my happiness." She addressed Manel. "I hope this meal is to your liking. Please enjoy our humble fare." She made a gesture for her to go first.

Manel looked around. Everyone waited for her to start the meal. She grabbed the first slice of bread and hurriedly bit into it. The hot, moist texture made her taste buds explode in satisfaction. Her eyes squeezed shut. When she opened them, chaos had begun.

A flurry of hands reached out to grab various portions of food. Gallic quickly stood and attacked a platter of meat with the two-pronged serving fork. He speared two big pieces and plopped one on each of their plates. Within seconds, the rest of the platter sat empty. Fearing she may not get anymore, Manel snatched two more slices of bread.

The din of noise rose to deafening decibels. Only when most of them were chewing, did it die down for a moment. Gallic ate calmly, comfortable in the environment. Manel had heard many times that she had no idea how the people of her planet lived. That she lived in a privileged bubble. Narrow minded and lacking empathy.

The scene before her made that observation hit hard. They were right. She never bothered to find out either. Safe in the palace walls, dictating decrees that she knew negatively impacted them, yet not caring about the consequences. She stopped eating a piece of large fruit midway, her eyes stinging from the threat of tears.

No, no! I don't want this!

She gripped the fruit harder, forcing juice to drip. *I'm not a monster.*

Gallic placed a hand on her back, startling her upright. He didn't look at her, but she understood he tried to ease her pain. She finished the fruit and moved on to the last slice of bread on her plate.

After what seemed like a long visit, Manel and Gallic got ready for departure. His mother reluctantly gave up the twins sitting in her lap to the servants who placed them back in their carriers. Manel found out the four royal guards at breakfast were Gallic's cousins. Still new to the fold, their assignments didn't allow residence at the palace.

It shouldn't be required to begin with. The way his father explained it to Manel, the royal guards should be grateful for the separation from their families. Their only focus served the royal house. Thinking about it now, after seeing the family dynamic, Manel felt ill.

The twins' servants walked towards the carriage while Manel followed a few feet behind. Gallic mother caressed his cheek, smiling lovingly in the doorway. He turned away from her, embarrassed.

An arrow flew into his chest, punching through his breastplate and out his back.

The diameter, twice the normal size, had a honed metal needle tip. He faltered, his mother screaming. The two servants still standing inside the carriage were hit with smaller arrows right as a blast flipped the carriage on its side.

One fell, losing her grip on the carrier. The infant tumbled to the ground while the other managed to hang onto hers. The arrow went through the carrier and into her abdomen. She pulled it out, splattering blood over the infant.

Right as Manel turned to where the first shot had come from, one of the large metal arrows struck her in the right shoulder. The excruciating pain felt like her arm had severed from the rest of her body. She saw the basinet with the arrow and let out a shriek.

Her eyes gorged with blood. Two smaller arrows hit her in the left side of her ribcage and her right thigh. She went down to one knee, seething with rage.

From the edge of the trail, a group of royal guards emerged. Maxelia's two guards were on the other side of the carriage and made their way around heading for the fallen infants. They didn't get there. The East royal guards brought them down.

Gallic's mother dragged her son back into the home. His four cousins blocked the front entrance. The horde of royal guards rushed forward, taking advantage of the chaos.

"You dare to come for me and my family?" Thick, bloody saliva dripped from Manel's mouth, baring sharp teeth.

With a horrid screech that made some of the guards hesitate for a brief second, Manel removed the metal arrow, throwing it aside and morphed into her full Kataling form. Twice the size of the carriage. Massive, weakened, but no less ferocious. She went after the first row that came at her. The crunching of bone as her teeth chomped onto three enemy soldiers at a time echoed in the air.

The four cousins defended the homestead, not letting a single enemy pass them. Inside, Gallic tried to get up and join the fight, but his wound and his mother held him at bay. Blood flew from Manel's wounds with every step. Despite the replenishing of blood from her kills, they didn't heal fast enough.

Gallic pushed forward out of his mother's grip and through his cousins. He got to his crying son lying on the ground unprotected and used his body as a shield as more arrows flew, striking him in the back. The royal entourage had been overrun.

Flashes of white swirled around the enemy. Ribbons of blood came forth as they moved among them. Where the flashes slowed, the silver and blue robes of the East palace became visible. Manel registered them in her diminished state and suddenly felt tired.

Her large body staggered backwards and fell with a rumbling that shook the ground. Her eyes fluttered as she morphed back to normal, covered in blood.

Twenty East Palace guards brought the attack to

a halt. The battle scene went still. The leader of the guards walked over to assess the damage. A transport pulled up next to the downed carriage. Healers came out and rushed to Manel.

"No." She barely whispered. She smacked the healer's hand away. "My children...first." Her eyes closed, yet she stayed conscious.

"There are enough healers for everyone," the leader answered. "Whether you like it or not, you are the priority, Emperor."

Tears streamed down her face. She let out a weak cry, her mouth filled with the mix of enemy blood and her own. Lendor's guards sheathed their blood soaked blades and came to aid the healer with Manel.

The leader held out his left hand. A blue sphere emerged from a tiny device in his palm and hovered.

"I'm sorry, Emperor Tavelo. We should have followed closer. We had no idea an arrow brigade had positioned themselves on the other side of the trail."

Tavelo's voice came through as if inside an echo chamber.

"You're not to blame. I should have known better than to underestimate Maxellia."

"We are bringing in the wounded."

"Emperor Manel?" Tavelo asked tentatively.

"It's bad. All around."

Tavelo's face contorted. "The children...Gallic?"

"As I said, Emperor. It's bad."

The holoscreen winked out.

The leader proceeded to check on Gallic. He bent down and saw the infant clinging to his father. He no longer cried. The child simply stared at into the air. Gallic's chest heaved slightly as he struggled to breathe.

A healer knelt by his side.

"We have to remove those arrows." The healer took out a vial of red solution. "The best way would be to dissolve them one by one."

"Wouldn't that cauterize the wounds as well?"

"Yes. That's ideal."

"And that?" The leader stared at the giant metal arrow still protruding from Gallic.

The healer turned to another in the transport.

"Bring the cutters." He looked over at the leader. "Once we removed the bulk of it on each end, we can lift him."

The leader nodded and walked over to the four cousins who were trying to stop Gallic's mother from going out into the carnage. He bowed to her then met the distraught face of a mother fearing her child's life. He addressed the cousins first.

"Your assistance in this fight will be commended."

"There is no need," the tallest of them replied. "We were only defending our family and our home."

"Your duties for the day are suspended."

The leader went to turn away.

"No. We will not abandon our cousin."

The leader stopped. He pivoted back around. All of their faces conveyed a steel sense of duty.

"In that case, you will escort Gallic's mother to the palace and guard her along with the royal children."

Relief combined with purpose replaced their stern stares.

"As you command," they replied, bowing.

The leader went to brief his men on the situation. *This is madness.*

He almost felt a twinge of pity for Maxelia. Well, not even that much.

Unspeakable rage filled Megen as he burst through the royal healing room's double doors. Healers rushed about, some with bloodied rags that were used to stop bleeding. To his right near the far wall were two hover beds three feet apart. Healers went back and forth checking the wounded bodies that occupied them.

On the first bed, Manel's anguished loud wailing, followed by soft mewing, reached into Megen's soul. He approached the right side of the bed and leaned over her. The wounds were worse than he imagined. Her body looked nearly torn apart yet somehow she miraculously lived.

What startled him the most were the tears of sadness and fear. She stared up at him.

"I'm sorry," her voice ghostly, barely above a whisper. "I'm sorry." Her arm extended towards the bed next to her, hand reaching. "Please."

Megen turned his head to look behind him. Gallic lay unconscious with a blackened hole in his chest, the result of it being cauterized, exposing the tissue. Blood seeped from beneath him.

"Please," Manel rasped. "I…"

His brother brought his focus back to her and clasped Manel's hand. She began to cry, the tension further opening her wounds.

"I should have protected you better." He bowed his head. "I am the one who is sorry."

A healer came over with an injector to administer an anesthetic. The front of his grey robes darkened with blood that turned a charcoal tint.

"Her pain threshold is extraordinary." The healer pressed the injector against Manel's neck and hit the button. "It's probably a result of all the experiments the previous emperor had done on her."

Manel's eyes slowly closed, the tears dripping down the sides of her face then landing on the bed. Megen wiped them away from her eyelids with one thumb.

"I will fix this." He looked at Gallic. "I promise."

A group of healers converged on the two beds. He stepped out of their way then walked over to the healer at the intake station near the entrance.

"Where are the twins?" He kept a hand on the hilt of his longsword out of habit.

The healer stared at the sword then him.

"They luckily only sustained minor scratches and bruises. I believe royal guards from the Eastern palace escorted them along with their Dega."

"Their…?" Megen stood stunned. He knew about the outing but only the transport navigator knew the location. "Gallic's mother."

He left the healing chamber, seething. His guards were waiting for him in the hallway. They faced the direction of the throne room. He went to his second in command.

"Get my siblings and have them meet me in our royal lounge. "

"As you wish, sire."

The guard bowed then headed off in the opposite direction towards the living quarters.

Megen led his group to the advisors' wing. He knew for certain what his sister had been planning, even if she hadn't voiced it. *Was Manel wrong to kill their father?* He felt unsure. They all condemned the emperor for his indiscretions, deciding Manel to be no better and should be put down like the monster their father created.

He balled his fists tight, swinging his arms straight at his sides. A scowl formed as his eyes narrowed. The offspring he had fathered with Manel were flawed, pitiful creatures who deserved a family free of manipulation and strife.

We are merely continuing a cycle of despair!

It ends now.

He would make his conviction known.

Tavelo marched down the main palace corridors surrounded by an entourage of eight royal guards, Master Jaubro, and Pridric. The merged sound of their boots striking the floor thundered.

People parted, creating a wide berth for them to pass. Mostly out of fear, seeing Tavelo's murderous expression. His deep blue robes with silver trim flowed around him, kissing the floor as he moved.

They rounded a corner and came to the hallway that led to the royal family chamber. He made no announcement, pushing open the doors, causing a whine as they were forced apart.

Inside, the royal siblings were already in the throes of a heated fight, with Lenri standing tensed up in anger.

"Why?" She yelled. "Why would you send out an assassination squad after Manel?"

"This is unacceptable!" Lendor added. His uniform had blood spatter on it from handling the wounded when they came to the palace. "What kind of madness is in your head?"

Maxellia leaned forward on the cushion she sat on atop the raised platform. Her eyes glowed red as she bared fangs.

"I will not have our bloodline tainted by some low-life parasite that lacks ambition with altered DNA!"

The doors hit the adjacent walls, making a loud bang as the force shook the room. They all turned to the entrance. Megen raised a hand towards Tavelo as he approached.

"Stand down, Emperor Tavelo. We will handle this ourselves," he managed to get out before being overtaken.

Tavelo hit him in the solar plexus with one hand, sending him into the far wall. Cracks formed around his body on impact. Maxellia stood from her seat on the raised platform. Tavelo flash stepped to her, his hands already around her neck. Her eyes grew redder as she struggled to remove his fingers, her air cut off.

"Tell me why I shouldn't." He shook her like a rag doll. "What did you hope to gain?"

"Let's not be rash." Master Jaubro clenched his hands. He turned to Pridric and whispered, "You need to talk him down."

Pridric stared in disbelief and shook his head. Lendor took it as a cue to move slowly towards Tavelo.

He kept a hand up in defense, just in case.

"I understand your rage. We all do. She will need to atone for her actions." He got to the platform. "You want to know the reason why you shouldn't? She is of royal blood. Regardless of how we all feel."

Tavelo already accepted that.

Knowing the answer, he hoped to get their agreement to end her life. In defeat, he released his grip. Maxellia dropped to the edge of the platform, holding her neck, gasping for each breath.

As she looked up at him, a sinister grin on her face, he changed his mind about doing no harm. He punched her with talons extended in the chest, the upward motion going under her ribcage. In the same motion, he lifted her high, then tossed her across the room to the opposite side.

Megen fell to the floor, coughing blood. He looked over at his sister plastered to the wall, eyes rolled up, showing whites. Her embedded arms spread wide. A moment passed where everyone stood still. Her body finally relented to gravity and peeled away, sending her face down on the floor. Blood spreading from her wound stained the plush carpet.

"I will hold you to that." Tavelo flicked his hand. Blood speckled onto a nearby chaise. "Make sure she does not leave her quarters for the duration of the moon cycle." He turned to them, eyes burning silver. "Or I'll kill her."

He turned away, exiting the room. His guards stood on both sides of him until he passed. Pridric followed with the guards falling in line. Master Jaubro stayed with the royal siblings. He had a bone to pick with their handling of the situation when it started.

Grasilda, Gallic's mother, walked around the small chamber taking in every corner, every detail. Pale peach walls with burgundy plush carpet were accented by sheer fabrics on the windows, and furniture. Two chaise lounges, a bench covered in pillows, and four beds occupied the space.

Near the center, on the left side of the wall, sat a basinet with the sleeping twins tucked inside swathed in clean cloths.

The welcome amenity of quiet for being far away from the main corridors. She adjusted the top of her one shoulder dress that cascaded to the floor. Its soft, cream material fell in waves, the bodice cinched at her waist. She had her hair down. A servant brushed it earlier after offering the dress. The bloodied one surely went into an incinerator.

She took a deep breath to ease her nerves. Her hands busied themselves playing with each finger of the other while she paced. A knock on the door made her stop. She exhaled slowly, smoothing her hair, then stood in the center of the room.

"Please, enter."

The door opened slowly.

One hand gripped the frame until the entrance revealed the visitor. Her husband stood filling the doorway. She suppressed a gasp at his appearance. His drawn features and matted hair made him look older than his age.

A black short, thin jacket with no buttons worn over a black bodysuit that saw better days. Old leather sandals graced his feet.

She held out her arms. He hesitated at first.

"Come," she urged.

"I never wanted you to see me this way," he said softly.

"I know. Nevertheless."

She gestured with her arms again.

He went to her, wrapping his arms around to hold her tight. She enveloped him like a lost love.

She could feel how slender he had become. They held each other for a long time. The sound of a baby cooing broke their embrace.

She wiped her face, realizing tears had fallen.

"They're awake." She waved a hand. "You need to say hello."

They stood over the basinet. Both infants were looking around, taking in their surroundings. Gallic's father rubbed their cheeks. they enjoyed the attention.

"They are precious." The corners of his mouth lifted slightly.

"Have you decided? His cousins were assigned to me and the children for now. It may become permanent if necessary."

Her husband turned to her. His eyes burned with conviction.

"I'll protect our son, our doljas, and the emperor."

"I'm glad." She rested her head on his shoulder. "Our family is once again whole."

Another knock on the door startled them. She gasped, clamping a hand over her mouth. Her mate frowned at her.

"What is it?" He placed a hand over his short blade concealed at his hip. She shook her. "I don't understand."

She removed her hand.

"The other children," she said. "That's why this room is set up this way."

"Other children?" His brow furrowed.

"The emperor's." She walked over to open the door wider.

A servant along with four royal guards accompanied a group of young beings varying in age. The tallest two, possibly the oldest she assumed, looked ready to fight some unseen battle. Their features varied from having different mothers. The same was true of the other younger two.

She counted seven in all. The three little ones she understood to be the products of pure bloodline decreed by the former emperor. Thinking about it made bile threaten to come up.

"Come, children. It's alright." She smiled. "I am not the enemy. You are safe here."

They all trudged in and spread out taking to whichever area suited them. The little ones huddled together on a bed. The two oldest plopped down on separate chaises while the younger two sat on the cushions in the center.

Her husband shook his head in disbelief. He turned around to the door and saw the royal guards leave the servant. She bowed her head.

"Is there anything I can bring to assist you with the children?"

Grasilda looked around and found the empty food tables. She pointed to them. The servant nodded, not needed to say a word, and went to fulfill the need.

In her place came Eterenia with Ethan. Already half her height, his eyes had a tinge of red rimming the irises. Grasilda flinched. Eterenia raised a finger, wagging it as a deterrent. Then she turned to the other children. They too had various forms of abnormalities in their eyes.

"Will you be alright?" Eterenia asked Ethan.

He responded by walking into the room and headed straight for the twins. He reached in to tickle their stomachs, grinning at their giggles.

Looking around the room, he sighed.

"I'll be fine." He eyed the other children. "No matter what agenda the royal advisors or our Dinas have, we are all siblings and will protect each other."

The two oldest turned their heads, seemingly ashamed. Grasilda could only imagine what they were thinking when they saw the other children. They had all been living separately from each other being raised by servants. They saw Manel annually by decree of the royal advisors.

She went to stand by Eterenia.

"Will this really be okay? They don't know each

other." She clasped her hands at her bosom. "And the way they were spawned. It hurts me inside."

"I know." Eterenia placed a hand on her back and caressed it gently. "But I believe this is the best remedy to fix it. Caden will be here soon with his son of Manel's."

Grasilda turned to her with wide eyes, mouth gaping. Her expression crumbled into sadness, and she looked away.

So many damaged children.

"I will leave you to it." Eterenia backed out of the entrance then headed down the corridor.

Gallic's parents were about to coral and address the children when a ruckus outside caused them to turn back to the doors. A yelling match between the four cousins assigned to guard the room and Gallic's siblings erupted. Both sisters and the two brothers were face to face, squaring off with them.

"We should have been told!" The eldest sister snapped.

"He's our brother!" The younger brother added.

"We have more right to protect them!" The eldest sister yelled.

The older of the cousins stepped closer to her.

"But you didn't." He snapped, harshly. They all went silent. "We defended our home."

The second cousin relaxed his stance.

"You have assigned posts in the royal court. We are fill-ins with no sectors. It makes more sense to put us under our Dina's command."

The younger sister turned, pushing her siblings aside. "This is stupidity."

She entered the room, followed by the others who decided to end the fight. They all stopped in their tracks at the scene. Their father gave them woeful stares. The eldest ones looked embarrassed by their actions.

When reports of the incident found its way to their squadron, the siblings went along with other soldiers mocking Gallic's plight. Even going so far as letting them cite unfounded rumors about how his own family had no care for him.

Labeling him a failure. A royal pet paraded on a leash.

The eldest sister gave her siblings separate looks of guilt. They would not allow it any further.

CHAPTER SIX

Mending Wounds

News of the invasion reached Earth. The coven leaders who remained were floored. It never occurred to them that those arms dealers would keep their word and carry out the threat. They called a meeting at the Sapienti estate in Italy. In the dead of night, they converged on the home resting on the outskirts of a small town.

Chalayl had come alone, hitching a ride with Yutel and his cousin, the secretary. To their surprise, she dressed modestly in an empire dress with her hair in a tight bun atop her head. She almost looked wholesome. Holnar's vehicle pulled up next to theirs.

He came out wearing a casual grey suit followed by his two bodyguards in similar attire. Dakien pulled his own casual jacket closer to his chest, it only going halfway due to his massive chest. He hardly ever got his nontailored ones to close.

Ahead of them, Adelia and her two guards were already at the main door with Tesul and Armon. Over the past few years she had matured more than the other leaders had expected. A touch of guilt and shame came over them.

"Shall we?" She giggled, without looking back. "Can't wait to see what deliciousness the Sapienti cooks have whipped up for us."

"I'm certain, it being so late in the night, it won't be too heavy," Holnar replied.

"Watching your figure?" This time she looked over her shoulder at him. "You are getting a bit plump."

Holnar's face flushed. Chalayl laughed heartily.

"Oh, that's funny!" She gave all the men side stares. "And I'm the one always criticized for eating too much. Take that, fat man."

Holnar moved towards her. Dakien yanked her out of his way and pushed Holnar back.

"Stop being childish!"

The door opened. Two servants stood on each side of the entrance and gestured for them to enter. They silently moved through the hallways, ending at the lounge where Darean brooded in a high-back chair.

He appeared dazed, a glass of dark liquor held at chest level, his fingers wrapped around the center. His focus left the glass and finally took notice of his guests. With a startled jump, Darean set his drink down and stood.

"I did not hear you come in. My apologies." Darean smoothed the front of his button-down shirt. "Please, get comfortable."

"What has you rattled?" Holnar sat in the chair opposite Darean's. "Those thugs didn't try invading Earth, so we're good."

"Are we?" Yutel plopped down onto the love-seat, taking up most of it. "I beg to differ."

"How so?"

"I'm sure if you think about it for a moment, you will understand Darean's dilemma and my concern."

Chalayl's face scrunched up as she sat further away. She didn't take off her coat, instead pulling it closer around her. Adelia raised her brow questioning.

"I built this." She whispered angrily. "All of it. It's mine."

Holnar sat up straight, realization hitting him. Then his expression changed to defeat.

"I get it now. You're right."

He turned to Darean who had eased back into his chair. "Our families are probably laughing at our small feat."

"We were ambitious." Darean said.

"And greedy," Yutel added.

Adelia cocked her head to one side, deciphering their conversation. When she got it, a sadness came over her. She looked over at Tesul and Armon. They too had figured it out.

"We came here by accident and at first did what we needed to survive." Darean began. "Somehow along the way we thought ourselves to be gods compared to humans."

"And turned into wannabe conquerors." Tesul finished for him. "Even werewolves didn't think so highly of ourselves to try suppressing humans."

"Nor vampires," Armon said. "We just fed off them and tried to blend with society."

"There is only one solution." Adelia turned to Chalayl. "You're wrong." Chalayl rose her head up and gave her a hostile stare. "Your empire was not created by you alone. That said, your moral compass is broken, making all that you have built incomplete."

"How dare you say that to me, you useless twat!" Chalayl stood, ready to attack.

Yutel got between her and Adelia in a flash.

"Sit down, Chalayl!" The two locked eyes. Yutel's glowed red to match hers. She relented and fell back in her seat. "You and Pridric made a bigger mess than the rest of us."

"There are others who need to be here." Darean gestured to the far end of the room. "I invited them as well."

They followed his outstretched hand towards a group sitting silently in the back of the lounge area, watching them with pity, some with disdain. The Kataling and Volshin leaders, sat on floor cushions along with their entourage with drinks already in hand.

"How did we not notice they were here?" Adelia asked incredulous. She stared at Tesul.

"I saw them," he said. "There was no reason to point them out." He tilted his head slightly. "Or so I assumed."

Chalayl's angry expression shifted to something unsavory as she eyed Omeron with lust. He returned one of disgust. She smiled meekly. Yutel grabbed her by the front of her dress, pulling her close.

"This is not the time for your nonsense. Show some restraint!" He seethed, in a low, hateful tone.

She forced her way out of his grasp and flopped back against her seat.

"We weren't supposed to be on this planet in the first place." Darean raised his glass and took a sip. The two servants finally came around with the drink carts to take requests and serve them. "It's safe to say we've overstayed our visit."

"Is that why Chalayl is lashing out?" Adelia asked. "Are you proposing to go back to your home world?"

Chalayl hissed, bearing fangs. Yutel turned from her and sat back on the loveseat.

"Not just us," Holnar answered. "Everyone." He addressed Adelia. "Including you."

"Oh." Adelia let her body slump against the large sofa. She stayed like that for a long while. No one said a word, waiting for the rest of her response. "That makes sense." She took a sip of her vodka tonic. "There are other alien races on this planet now and humans need to run it themselves."

"I've always wanted to go home." Luamis spoke. "With the emperor losing his mind and destroying trade on our world, I could not fathom doing so."

"Well, Tavelo has gone to fix it along with Master Jaubro." Yutel gulped down a swig of his whiskey. He smiled at his cousin. "From my secretary's reports," he paused, "they're definitely disappointed."

He lowered his glass with a pained expression.

"But, how?" Adelia pursed her lips.

"We only have two ships. And would everyone from the home world go?" She glanced at Tesul. "What about my werewolf?" Tesul raised an eyebrow at that. "Or even a human vampire." She gestured to Armon. "Is it safe for them to live on Cellaxa?"

"Of course, it is!" Holnar snapped. "The question is, do they want to?"

Armon and Tesul lowered their heads, appearing to contemplate. Adelia seethed.

"Don't you even think of not coming with me!" Her eyes glowed red at them.

They both looked up and flinched from her.

"How many are we, in total?" Yutel asked Darean. "With the amount of offspring, I would say we have tripled in number, maybe more."

"We'll have to do a census." Darean drained his glass and set it on the nearby table. "My estimate would be we need about four ships." He turned to the ancient ones. "Will all of you go?"

"Without question." Omeron leaned forward. "We don't like it here and the humans have made it clear, they would rather have other alien races to accommodate than us."

"Yes, they were very reluctant to agree with our compromise." Holnar adjusted himself so that he sat sideways facing Darean. "I am not happy about this outcome. But, I know it is the right thing to do."

"We must have a meeting with the world leaders."

Glass shattering cause everyone to stop. They saw Chalayl standing in heated anger, her flute glass in pieces along the window ledge where she had chucked it.

"I will not leave! I," she poked her chest repeatedly, "have an empire to run. My products are profitable because they come from Earth's hub. No one else can claim it but me!"

Yutel's cousin rolled his eyes in exasperation. Holnar merely stared at her. When no one bothered to engage, she threw off her coat, eyes burning silver.

"Oh, really?" Adelia frowned. "Is she serious?"

Before Chalayl could take one step towards them, Luamis advanced, pushing her. She went flying over her seat into the window behind her. It spider-webbed from the Impact. Darean didn't take it lightly.

"You!" He pointed to her as he rose. "Will be the first to go and explain to your elder brother what you've done." Chalayl went pale. "We sent a report on your so-called empire to the home world."

Her bun loosened yet stayed intact. She slowly got her composure and lifted away from the cracked window. Eyes now red, Chalayl went back to her seat, her anger palpable.

"Is it that bad?" Adelia asked.

"Oh, the Boresso family does many uncouth and shady things." Holnar wagged a finger. "That being said, they have a certain amount of integrity. One thing they do not tolerate is the dealing of drugs."

Adelia's eyes suddenly went wide.

"I was born on Earth. I've never been on another planet."

Tesul laughed. "Neither have I." He cupped her face in his hands. "We'll be fine."

❁ ❁ ❁

Bigger than the others, the Durante castle could accommodate the large number of coven leaders crowded in the main ballroom. Chairs arranged in a semicircle around the throne platform now held a long table draped in silver and teal cloth with four seats positioned on either side.

Conversation remained low, almost hushed. To bring everyone together on such short notice meant something urgent. And not a drink in sight. Servants stayed along the walls like statues. No alcohol meant the meeting could get ugly.

Holnar, Darean, Yutel, and Chalayl entered the room from the side with sad and weary expressions as they sat at the table. Anticipating a fight before the storm, all four wore black.

"We have a decree." Holnar bellowed. The loud chatter died, and all eyes focused on him. "As you know, we have done many things on this planet that we found ourselves on nearly two centuries ago. And during our stay, we have caused much harm."

Darean cleared his throat and leaned forward, crossing his arms on the table.

"The fact is, we were not supposed to be here. And it has become clear we shouldn't be." Murmurs erupted. He raised a hand to quiet them. "We understand that many of you saw this as a new beginning. That you have offspring who were born here."

"But we must go home, now." Yutel's sorrowful tone filled the room. "Earth is not our home. We have behaved like invaders, forced them to do our bidding while saying it's for their own sake."

A vampire rose from her seat.

"Then what? You just abandon the covens and we pick up the aftermath?" Rumbling agreements began to go around. "Your kind came here and took over. Killing our leaders and queens because you deemed yourselves superior."

Now that an uproar had erupted, Yutel let out a sigh. Darean pinched his nostrils. Chalayl rose from her seat, surprising the others who looked up at her.

"Yes!" She yelled, causing the loud objections to halt. "You need us to coddle you. Before we took over, your kind wallowed in despair and disorganization. We made you prosperous. There's not one among you that can take the reins and replace us."

Yutel turned his head away from her, amazed at her audacity. Holnar sat back hard in his chair, one arm dangling while the other lay on the table. The frightening silence in the room made every Cellaxan in the room tense, awaiting the outcome.

A slew of Vampires rose from their seats, some tossing their chairs.

"Give us our covens back!"

"Go back to your home world!"

"We were better off without your rule!"

"Invaders!"

"Monsters!"

Chalayl looked around the room, confused by their reaction. A chair came sailing towards her and she dodged it, bending sideways to let it go past her head. It crashed against the wall behind her. She glanced over at Holnar, Darean, and Yutel. They sat watching the scene in distress. What could any of them possibly do now to alleviate the situation?

Then the tide turned. Vampires cowered away from the center towards the door. The servants moved to block the entrance. Every merchant family member's eyes glowed red, focused on the vampires.

"They forgot," Holnar said.

"We are the superior race." Yutel banged his fist on the table, getting their attention. "Unless you want to be wiped out by the end of the day, I suggest you calm down and listen to reason." He turned to Chalayl. "Have a seat, instigator."

"Go to hell." She reluctantly fell back in her seat. "I only told the truth."

A merchant family member glared at her.

"Your timing stinks, Boresso."

❀ ❀ ❀

The assembly building came into view as Darean's vehicle exited the freeway tunnel. Early morning fog drifted along its lawn. Sunlight barely peeked through the grey clouds. A perfect day in his book. Too bad it won't last. He sighed, knowing within an hour, the sky would turn blue.

Saturday Traffic in the corporate district was light as usual. Most of the government workers and office rats were off. The area resembled a ghost town.

Holnar and Chancellor Rayne accompanied Darean in the back seat. The others rode in the vehicle directly behind them, following close. If he focused his hearing, he could make out the arguing going on inside. Holnar pushed his window button to lower it a quarter of the way down.

Fresh, moist air invaded the vehicle. Its coolness brushed their faces. Each breathed deep, exhaling to ease their tension. One hurdle down. Two to go. He really wanted Holnar to take the reins, but he refused to handle this mess they found themselves in.

To their surprise, the emergency meeting they requested with the world leaders two weeks ago had been granted in record time. As the two-car entourage got closer to the federal building, Darean could see the long line of diplomatic vehicles being queued at the front entrance. Armed soldiers flanked the steep stairway.

"Well, I hope we all have our game faces ready." Holnar leaned against the door, peering upwards.

The sound of a helicopter off in the distance closed in. Men in suits stood waiting on the helipad atop the building's annex.

"Does it matter?" Chancellor Rayne scoffed. "This will be a hostile meeting. They all want to sling their disgust at us before even listening."

"Can you blame them?" Darean hit his window button, letting it down enough to create a cross breeze. "We forced them into galactic trade and took away their claims to it."

"Now, whatever happens in our absence will be their burden alone to bear," Holnar said.

The driver pulled up to the security gate.

A soldier in a double-breasted full-length coat with a rifle slung across the shoulders came out of the shack and stopped by the door. Anger etched his face as he got a glimpse of the passengers when the driver rolled the window down.

"Names." The soldier demanded.

He produced a tablet from the holder on his side.

With his teeth, he pulled off his free hand's glove and touched the screen to wake it up. He frowned at the driver.

"Names."

Holnar bristled at the harsh tone as he leaned forward. His brow furrowed. Darean reached across Chancellor Rayne and gently laid a hand on Holnar's chest. Steady.

"Lord Andrea Sapienti, Lord Theodore Marchand, and Chancellor Omaris Rayne as proxy for the Ambrook Holdings."

The soldier tapped on the tablet. He found the information and stepped back.

"Proceed to the end of the line. When you reach the loading area, your doors will be opened by the guards. Immediately exit and go into the building." His eyes narrowed further. "Do not stop or take your time."

"The vehicle behind us is also ours." The driver gave the soldier a dirty look. "Do you need me to state their positions too?" His tone dripped with ire.

"No." The soldier stood straight. "I have to log each vehicle. Please, move forward."

The driver raised the window back up and did as instructed. He glanced in the rearview mirror at Darean.

"That was a bit uncalled for." Chancellor Rayne removed Darean's hand from Holnar. Embarrassed, Darean brought his hands into his lap. "As I said. This is going to be a shit show." He surprised himself using the less than civil term.

The seats in the assembly hall's rotunda curved in a semicircle along the main platform down at the bottom. The podium had been placed in the center between two long tables with black tablecloths, each with three chairs. Name tents sat in front of each chair, accompanied by a microphone.

Two pitchers of ice water sat on either side with glasses already filled.

There were more than world leaders present, grabbing their seats, and talking amongst themselves. Military and scientific leaders had answered the call adding fuel to the fire. They were not necessary in Darean's opinion. He concluded the humans wanted to make a statement, showing a united front.

But we all know that's a lie. He snorted.

Yutel, Chalayl, and Adelia came to stand by them at the staging doors adjacent to the platform.

"All I see is an angry mob of inferior pests," Chalayl spat.

"How about you keep that to yourself today?" Yutel turned to her.

"She's not wrong." Adelia shrugged. "No one should be surprised."

"Let's get this over with." Darean proceeded to the tables and found his place.

The room went into a hush as the others followed suit. Looks of rage, discontent, and curiosity tracked them and stayed even when they were seated. An awkward silence followed. In an attempt to save face, many of the humans averted their gaze and resumed conversations.

After a while, everyone took their seats.

The Prime Minister of England walked out of the side entrance from the other end and stepped to the podium. With a frown, he let out a small cough. The sound echoed through the audio system speakers. Knowing the meeting would be presented in English, foreign leaders not fluid in the language inserted their translator buds. Their interpreters stood by for any questions that may arise.

"Ladies, Gentlemen, esteemed colleagues. Good morning and welcome to what we all assume is a meeting of dire events." The Prime Minister looked to both tables. "The coven leaders who we have learned are merchants from another planet have called this assembly." He gave Darean a nod. "You have the floor."

Once again, Darean stared down at Holnar until he finally gave in. Holnar straightened the front of his jacket, then changed his mind and unbuttoned it. He leaned forward, his arms relaxed on the edge.

"When we created the interplanetary trade hubs on your planet, the goal was to establish our names while also bringing Earth on the map."

"You wanted a conquest!

"It was for greed! Nothing more!"

"Flaunting your superiority to keep us as slaves!"

Adelia reared back at the onslaught of hate. Her face went flush. Yutel grabbed her wrist under the table. She turned to him, and he shook his head. Holnar exhaled loudly.

"Conquest? Slavery? Absolutely not." His eyes went red. "Greed? Of course." The world leaders went momentarily silent, astonished at his candid reply. "We wanted to prove to ourselves that we could surpass our families' status and prosperity."

"That's just an excuse to take what is not yours." An interpreter relayed calmly for their charge. "Our people are being forced to work these hubs and each country only sees a small portion of the profits."

"What is that if not slavery?" Another foreign leader added. "How do you plan to remedy that?"

"By leaving," Darean blurted.

"What?" The reply came from multiple people.

"What do you mean by that?" The Prime Minister of England shot from his seat, enraged.

"I am relieved that you asked." Holnar turned to Adelia. She sat startled at his implied stare. "Queen Adelia of De Luce and Durante will continue." Darean gave him a warning glance.

Adelia pulled her hand from Yutel's and rested it on the table.

"As much as we like how Earth has adapted to intergalactic trade, we are still beholden to our home world. Recent events in the past few years have shown the error in our plans. The goal is to turn all of this over to the human race and hope you have had enough preparation to keep it afloat."

Yutel's mouth went downward as he nodded, impressed, his head tilted to one side. Holnar's brow raised in shock. Chalayl glared at her.

Another diplomat stood, shaking with fury.

"You force this on us, make us work as slaves, and now we have to maintain it? Continue on as if nothing happened while you reap the rewards on some far-off planet?"

"Hmm?" Darean cocked his head. "She said no such thing." Looks of confusion followed. He shook his head in frustration. "We are leaving it to you. How one profits is your concern."

"We will no longer be involved. The humans working for the covens and its leaders are responsible for their companies' trade." Yutel leaned away from his microphone, hearing his voice boom. "If we happen to have something to trade with Earth, it will be under your regulations."

"I suggest keeping the regulations established in place for a few decades," Chalayl interjected. "If you start dismantling them, one or more of the alien races you allow to stay here with gladly give their input."

"And they won't be beneficial to Earth, I assure you." Holnar finished.

A constant barrage of accusations flew in for nearly ten minutes. The six coven leaders sat silent, taking it all in, not engaging. No one had any desire to fall into shouting matches. The humans surely didn't want a response. When it became apparent to the humans that they were causing a scene all by themselves, the vitriol died down.

The Prime Minister of England left his seat and came to the edge of the platform.

"So, what are the next steps, then?" He glanced back at the other leaders.

Holnar straightened his posture and gestured for

the man to sit back down. Darean rubbed the side of his neck. He looked bored now.

"Documents are already being drawn to reflect the transfer of power. Also one for ownership of the dock areas." Holnar clasps his hands together. "Each Earthbound entity will retain their respective docks. Your security teams can regulate the temporary ones for incoming traders doing long-term business."

"That seems fair enough," the second diplomat who shouted our earlier said. "Then, I take it, another meeting will be forthcoming to go over these documents and have them authenticated."

"Correct." Darean took a sip of water. "All should be concluded within a year's time."

The room went hushed again. Whispers floated around amongst the humans. The President of the United States leaned towards his microphone.

"Are you really leaving? All of you?"

The humans' stares fell on them. Yutel grimaced at the scrutiny. Adelia took up the question.

"That is the only way. This was not a decision we came across lightly. Do you not think there isn't strife concerning this issue within our own ranks?"

"In that case, we will wish you Godspeed on your departure." His chilling tone not missed on them.

Yutel led the way out of the building with Chalayl, Adelia following. Darean, Holnar, and Chancellor Rayne brought up the rear. They were all exhausted. Their anger slowly subsiding.

"Three hours," Chancellor Rayne said. "And they had nothing constructive to say."

"We knew that was going to be the outcome," Holnar added. "You can't possibly be surprised."

"Oh, I'm not. Like I said. A shit show." He smoothed the front of his waist coat with one hand. "I feel a bath is needed after this."

This time they were escorted to the side entrance away from the media congregating at the main entrance. No one outside of the leaders knew about this meeting. Someone must have received a tip that all the world leaders were gathering for some emergency.

Their vehicles were already curbside, passenger doors open. The drivers were behind the wheel, assuring a speedy take-off. Armed soldiers surrounded them, blocking the view from the street.

The leaders climbed into the vehicles they came in, the last person closing the door.

The security gate buzzed, and the arms lifted. One soldier ushered them through. They followed each other in close procession. The two vehicles eased out onto the street, circumventing the mob of press berating world leaders as they came down the stairs. Turning onto the main road, the drivers gunned it, making haste towards the freeway tunnel.

Chalayl looked back through the rear window and saw a few press take notice of their departure. She saw one of them tsk in frustration, knowing they could not catch them. Her eyes darkened. This is not what she wanted. Schemes to hide on Earth danced in her head.

"You are going even if I have to drag you kicking and screaming into that cryochamber myself," Yutel threatened, leaning close to her ear. Chalayl stiffened. "You've done enough harm."

❀ ❀ ❀

Dock workers ran along the Cellaxan ship while awaiting departure from Earth's hub. Its downed ramp allowed the passengers and remaining cargo to enter. Exhaust hissed as it escaped onto the dock floors as transport carts zipped around. Security guards yelled at cargo loaders and traders went about their deals.

This would be the first of three ships to leave for the home world. Only Volshins and Katalings were on board, except for Chase and his children. Baltise kept close by with Caden and his son. A few ancients stayed behind to act as defense guards for the other two ships.

Omeron waited for them at the top of the ramp. He wore a black bodysuit that hugged every part of his muscular frame. His permanent scowl appeared more pronounced. The aesthetic alone jarred Chase.

I'll never look that menacing and cool.

"Is this not a joyous occasion for you?" Chase asked as they approached him. "Is home not ideal after all?"

"I am eager to leave. We are behind schedule." The deep tone resonated. "Hurry."

He turned away, leading them onto the ship. Chase breathed a sigh of relief. Grateful to Chancellor Rayne for staying to clean up loose ends. It also made him a little giddy anticipating the reunion with his parents. For a long time, he had rebelled against their rules.

With them gone the past five years on a different planet, with no easy access, he realized how much of a brat he had been.

I've matured, I think.

He glanced down at his youngest daughter.

Maybe.

Inside the main cabin, rows of cryochambers had been assembled. There were smaller ones for the children. Chase let go of his daughter's hand and she ran from him to the nearest chamber.

"I guess she's also ready to go." He turned to Baltise. "Excited?"

Baltise blinked a few times, thinking. Chase felt a sense of unease.

"Excited, no." Baltise smiled. "Just glad to be leaving and be with our own kind."

"Ahh. I get it." Chase threw an arm around her shoulder and squeezed. "It will be a steep learning curve for me since I was born and raised on Earth."

"You'll be fine. I promise."

"Get in." Omeron's gruff voice interrupted their moment. "We depart in two hours."

Baltise went to help their children get hooked up in the chambers. Caden led his son to the next one in the row. Chase could feel the apprehension coming from both of them. They were going back to what may be a kind of hell for Caden. Sensing the hesitation, Caden's father loomed over them, eyes dark and brooding.

"No one will harm you ever again." His father grabbed the boy under the arms and lifted him into the cryochamber. "There is no need for fear."

He reached out to Caden and brushed a hand across the top of his hair. Caden nodded in defeat. His father walked away, leaving Caden to undress his son and put his clothes in the storage slot underneath.

"Think of it this way." Chase patted Caden on the back after the chamber sealed his son inside. "You get to see everyone again and roam the planet without a care in the world. No dungeons or caves."

"That does sound nice," Caden whispered.

"Then get to it like your father said. We have a new home to greet."

With the passengers finally on board and secured in chambers for departure, the pilot settled into his station on the bridge. A monitor above showed each cryochamber, the ones sealed, turning green when activated. His navigator sat to his left, engrossed in pre-check procedures.

"Start main engines," the pilot ordered through the commlink.

"Engines engaged," the engine room technician replied. "Commencing countdown to one hundred percent."

"Course set for Cellaxa. Awaiting all cryochambers green before cabin lockdown," the navigator said.

The pilot watched the monitor.

We're going home!

He realized he had a grin on his face and tried to mask his enthusiasm. His navigator glanced over and smirked. Oh well. He sat back and relaxed. The last cryochamber sealed right as the engines came online at full capacity. Strapping himself in, he touched the initiation icons on the panel.

"You are cleared for departure," the tower tech announced. "Please proceed forward."

The clamps holding the ship in place released, and the ship eased out the dock into the afternoon sky.

Lady Dania scurried around her living quarters, rearranging pillows and small items on the shelves. Pridric watched, amused by her flustered expression. All for the grandchildren. He didn't understand what she fussed about. They wouldn't care about anything in the room. Her energies were more useful setting up Chase and Baltise's quarters. Of course, they would make it their own when they arrived.

"The ship doesn't land for another five hours, and it would take another two for them to get here." Pridric wrestled himself up on his elbows. "Come sit down. Rest for a bit."

She turned to him lying on the bed in nothing but leggings and frowned.

"Unlike you, my love, I refuse to be lazy on such an auspicious day."

"Oh?"

"It's not only them who're arriving. A ship full of ancient ones are returning home. Do you even know the significance of that?"

"I do." Pridric sighed. "And we can do nothing until they land."

Her shoulders slumped.

"I know. I'm so anxious. The children will be ten and twelve. I wonder how big they are now." She flopped onto him, pushing him back down flat. He caressed her hair. "I want to squeeze them to death."

Pridric gave her a wide-eyed stare.

"Pretty sure that is not ideal." He saw her pout. "And, I'm sure they're at least taller. We're not exactly small, my dear. Our genes run deep."

A knock on the door made them both lift their heads. Lady Dania crawled off Pridric and went to answer it. She flung the doors open for Tavelo and Eterenia, standing on the other side.

"Fretting?" Eterenia gave her a sly grin.

"You have no idea," Pridric answered. He slid off the bed. "She rearranged the room four times in the past hour."

"Well, you need to get dressed." Tavelo pointed to his near naked form. "We have preparations to make."

"Hmm?" Pridric cocked his head.

"Did I not tell you?" Tavelo smirked. "You are now designated as one of my cabinet members."

Pridric frowned. He raised his arms, moving his fingers through the thick mane of blonde hair and pushed it up to the top of his head in a messy pile. His eyes turned red with indignation. Tavelo laughed at his display.

"You want to. Stop being childish. You're older than me." Tavelo shook his head, smiling.

Being called out, Pridric dropped his arms, and let his hair fall back down his back.

"Not by much. And, no, you didn't tell me." He turned away, heading to the wardrobe. "What is my title, then?"

He rummaged through his clothes, waiting for an answer. His choice depended on that.

"Palace Ambassador. I think you'd fit better in that role than jumping back into trade negotiations with your family." Tavelo's expression darkened. "Your elder brother has held a firm grasp of the reins so far."

Pridric didn't turn around, hiding a faint smile. Once again, Tavelo understood his feelings.

His fingers landed on a worthy outfit. He glanced over his shoulder.

"Are you going to watch me get dressed?"

Eterenia's face scrunched up. Lady Dania looked offended by it.

"I'll pass on that," Eterenia replied.

She walked off down the corridor.

Tavelo let out a laugh. "I will see you in the main lounge." He winked at Lady Dania. "Sorry, Eterenia only has eyes for me."

####

All Cellaxa had eyes on the incoming ship from Earth as it docked at a port close to the pier. People lined the boardwalk, and holoscreens floated in the air across the planet for those who couldn't be there. Giant robot arms reached out and pulled the ship into the holding clamps. They locked down with a loud bong. Dense clouds of condensation spewed out as the ship decompressed. The ramp extended. And the people waited in anticipation.

On the platform at the bottom of the ramp stood Tavelo, Pridric, Master Jaubro, and Master Endaga. Representing the emperor, Lendor looked around, apprehensive. Tavelo smirked. Something shady about him he didn't like. Pridric went stiff, his body a living statue. He would be facing Luamis. Tavelo exhaled slowly. A battle to take on another day.

"What do you make of the welcoming committee?" He asked Master Jaubro.

"The crowd does seem agitated." Master Jaubro scanned the lines of people along the pier. "They know the ancient ones 'population has been stagnant for centuries."

"Yet, on Earth they bred like rodents. Untethered." Master Endaga's brow furrowed.

"That's a bit much." Pridric tilted his head back in shock at the remark. "They woild be slaughtered or enslaved if they stayed. Their increase in numbers helped us beat back the imperial guards who showed up on Earth."

"My apologies." Master Endaga exhaled. "I know that." He turned to Pridric. "Your anxiety is noted. But you should also know that the leaders of your ancients are near the bottom of the food chain compared to the ones who remained here."

Tavelo's eyes widened with realization. Everyone on the ship centuries ago were children of elders. Including the ancient ones. The passengers began to debark. On cue, the air filled with shrieks, followed by a thundering stampede from both sides rattling the wooden planks. Tavelo looked up.

Ten Volshins circled the area above the ship. They configured themselves into a swirling multiple layer ring, their colors creating streaks of blurred rainbows. The crowd let out hushed sounds of admiration. The largest one exited the spinning circle, and the rest followed, diving towards the docks in a straight line.

The same count of Katalings skidded to a halt, surrounding the four men. Five on each side, their massive frames blocked the entire pier from view. Tavelo lowered his head slightly to look at them. He could sense Pridric go rigid while Master's Jaubro and Endaga went into defensive mode.

Ancient ones on the ramp slowed their descent, not sure what to make of the scene. At the top were the two leaders. They stared at the display of might. The Volshins landed directly behind the Katalings, forming an assembly of giant chess pieces facing each other on a board.

A sharp gust of wind came with them, nearly knocking everyone in the vicinity over. Tavelo spread his legs further apart to keep himself rooted to the ground.

Each ancient one wore a tiny necklace. As one, they all morphed into bipedal form.

Twenty naked bodies appeared before the masses, their hair whipping in the ocean breeze. The necklaces were no longer tiny satchels, but hand-sized pouches connected to expandable cords. They all opened them, producing bodysuits that they immediately donned unabashed.

The largest Volshin, a female, stepped towards the bottom of the ramp and stared up at the leaders from Earth, who hadn't moved from their position. Her hair, a mix of brilliant blonde and shell pink, flowed down her back in feathered waves. She had a lean muscular body with her breasts and backside proportionate to her frame.

A tall, beautiful creature who exuded power.

"Get down here." Her voice seemed to echo. The red eyes demanded they not play around.

The man who led the Katalings stood beside her. His dark, brooding stare looked more menacing than Omeron's. Deep auburn hair past his shoulders, swished softly across them. He also gave the two a steely red glare.

The passengers slowly emptied the ramp, heads down in trepidation as they moved to the side, away from the ship. Luamis and Omeron glanced at each other, then at the horde below. They walked down the ramp side by side, not looking ahead, theiri eyes downcast.

Once they stood on the platform, facing the two ancient ones, an awkward silence fell on the docks. Tavelo dared not moved, darting his eyes from left to right to see if the other ancients would.

"So, you have finally come home," the Kataling leader's voice boomed.

For the first time, Tavelo saw Omeron struggle with his emotions. His face twitched as he seemed to fight back tears that moistened the corners of his eyes. The Volshin's stare softened and she opened her arms wide. Luamis finally looked up. Tears streamed down his face.

Not holding back, he rushed towards her.

Her arms closed around him, pulling him tight.

"It's alright, my son. I am here." She stroked his unruly hair, not styled after awaking from deep sleep. "Shh."

Omeron finally relented, moving towards the Kataling leader. His father roughly grabbed him, then brought him to his chest, causing a thud as their bodies collided.

"You will not be sent away again. Good to see you again, my son." With that, he embraced him.

For a moment, Omeron didn't respond, his arms dangling. His hands balled into fists, and he reached up, returning the gesture. He cried silently, tears slowly dripping onto his father's shoulder.

"Welcome home, ancient ones," Master Jaubro said, bowing. Tavelo and the others did the same, along with the crowd. "You have been missed."

When Tavelo lifted his head, he spotted a group at the top of the ramp. Chase and Baltise were staring slack jawed at the reunion while trying to keep their children at bay. He glanced over at Pridric smiling up at them, winking. Behind them, Caden and his son emerged.

A feeling of malice brushed against him, and he turned to see both ancient leaders staring at the two. They would never forgive the emperor for what he had done.

The spectacle of Ancient Ones reuniting died down, allowing Chase and the rest of the passengers to debark. He watched the scene with bated breath, not knowing if a fight would break out. The menacing red eyes of the horde gave him the chills.

Seeing Luamis break down in his mother's arms reassuring him. Omeron and his father's reunion shocked everyone. He didn't think the creature had any emotions other than anger and rage.

"Stop squirming!" He chastised the twins. "We're going now." He turned to Baltise. "A little help would be nice."

Baltise looked deadpan at him. He should have known better.

The twins went running down the ramp to their grandfather. His father threw his arms wide. A genuine smile spread across his face. Chase sighed in relief. He worried what state his father would be in when they arrived. Their eldest daughter calmly exited the ship. Her poised demeanor almost made him laugh.

She's putting on airs.

"Grandfather!" The twins exclaimed, crashing into him. "We missed you."

"And I missed you." He squeezed them tight before releasing them. "You know who misses you even more than I do?"

"Grandmother!" They replied in unison.

Chase stood before him and waited until the twins moved out of the way.

"Father. We made it."

His father gave him a forlorn look. He could see the mix of shame and regret in his eyes.

"Chase. It's good to see you." Both stood in tense silence. Without warning, his father embraced him. "I'm so sorry. I know you're disappointed in me. I will make you proud this time."

Chase returned the hug in a stunned response. He gave Baltise a wide-eyed glance as he patted his father's back, hoping to signal a release.

"Can I please greet my grandfather as well?" Their oldest daughter asked.

He disengaged from his father and stepped to one side. He did a small bow, swiping one arm towards him,

"At your leisure, my dear," Chase teased her.

She puffed her chest, exhaling loudly, then dove into her grandfather. Her head bent to his chest and her arms closed around him like a vice. His father gasped at the sudden assault, his arms pinned to his sides from her embrace.

"You're hurting me, child!"

"I don't care." Her voice muffled against his jacket. "You deserve it anyway."

He rotated his arms up and he got a hold of her shoulders, prying her off.

Laughter erupted. Chase saw Tavelo, Master Jaubro and Endaga attempting to cover their mouths. He nodded in approval.

This is good.

The ancient leaders from Earth were recovering from seeing their parents alive. Luamis wiped tears off his face and mustered the courage to get a good look at his mother. She still stood slightly taller, with a faint diagonal scar running from her temple to the bridge of her nose. On instinct, he clutched his chest, wincing at the memory of his own scar. She laid her hand over his.

"Do not fret, my child. This is now over." She pressed harder, as if trying to feel his scar through the fabric. "The emperor has been tamed. None shall harm you again."

He nodded, then suddenly locked eyes with her.

"I have a son." He looked around and found the young Volshin lingering about fifty yards from him. "Come." He gestured with one hand. His mother dropped her hand from his chest. The son came to stand next to him. "This is my son, Loaman."

"It is an honor to meet my father's creator."

His son gave a short bow.

Her expression turned to shocked amusement before she erupted into laughter.

"Oh, he is precious." She grabbed hold of the Loaman's chin and lifted his face. "You look like a fighter. I may accept you for now." His cheeks flushed pink with embarrassment.

Omeron took it as a cue and looked to see find Caden. He found him keeping himself at bay. With a terse stare, he beckoned him. Caden took hold of his son's hand and they approached. He held up a hand to his chest, palm up towards them.

"I present my son, Caden, and his child, Cameron."

His father glared at the two, making him go into a defensive mode. The Volshin leader wrinkled her nose at them as well.

"He reeks of Boresso blood," she said.

"You mated with one of those despicable whores?" His father's voice boomed louder.

Everyone in the vicinity who heard it stopped, turning stunned looks at them. Tavelo took a deep breath, ready to intervene if necessary. He glanced over at Pridric, stifling a smirk. The Masters pursed their lips.

"It was not by choice," Omeron muttered.

"And that child is clearly the emperor's spawn," his father continued.

Caden's eyes turned red as he pushed his child behind him. His father became frightened, glancing between the two.

"I may not have been a product of mutual respect or even love." His talons grew. "I am merely a child, compared to you in size and experience. That said, I will not let you say those things. She has treated me like a thing to be caged, not showing me affection, but she is still my mother. Regardless of how bad you hurt me, I will defend what little honor she may have."

The Kataling leader, taken aback, turned to his Volshin counterpart. She, too, looked stunned like everyone else. He met Caden's red gaze. No hesitation, yet a glimmer of fear mixed with resolve.

"You are correct." His expression softened. "It is an unfortunate situation. I should not judge my son or you." Caden's eyes went back to normal. "And who is the mother of this child?"

"Chalayl Boresso." Omeron replied.

Both Ancient leaders hissed, sucking air through their teeth.

"I guess we can discuss this later. There are new consequences regarding her and that family." He reached out to Caden, who flinched. "I will not harm my own blood." Caden barely relaxed as the leader placed one hand on the top of his head and the other atop his child's. "Welcome home."

The tension in the air cleared, replaced by the crowds' resounding cheers that rang out. There were shouts of encouragement, clapping, and welcome home greetings.

Tavelo went to stand between the two parties.

"As the newly appointed emperor of the East, I welcome our ancient ones home." He bowed to them, then grew serious. He turned to the Volshin leader. "Please make sure they are taken to the palace before letting them into the new region. It is better if they see it from above first."

"As you wish, Emperor Tavelo." The Volshin gave a slight bow and turned away, along with her children and the Kataling brood. "Let us depart."

All the elder Ancient Ones formed two rows and brought up the rear, creating a long procession that made its way to the edge of the pier onto the boardwalk. Tavelo exhaled, relieving the nervousness in his chest. So far, so good. Pridric came and whacked him on the back with one hand.

"It won't be this easy when the rest of our families arrive. I would take your victory lap now and brace for the nastiness to come."

Tavelo turned his head to one side and glared over at him. Pridric came around to stand beside him.

"I know that! You don't have to throw a cloud over the occasion." He saw Chase and Baltise talking with Masters Jaubro and Endaga. "I will keep you safe from yours, no matter the cost." Pridric's brow furrowed. "I mean it."

"I know," Pridric whispered.

The Ancient Ones split into two groups when they reached the loading area lined with transport vehicles on the other side of the boardwalk. Two large ones sat, ready for boarding. The leaders and their family entered the first while the rest climbed into the other.

Each twenty passenger vehicle had plush seats. The first six split into two rows facing the front. The rear seats mirrored that configuration. Four seats in the center on each side faced inward, the backs against the view ports.

Luamis sat in a front window seat closest to the doors, Loaman beside him. Directly behind them, Omeron sat alone. Caden and his child were in the next row. On the other side were the elder ancient leaders. The vehicle sat for a long time.

"What is the problem?" His mother asked. "Why are we not leaving?"

The pilot leaned sideways to address her.

"We received a message from Emperor Tavelo to wait for Lord Strana's group. The royal transport with the emperor and his party will board shortly to ride ahead of us."

"That makes sense." Luamis propped his elbow on the view port ledge and rested his head in the palm of his hand. "We can't really enter the palace without them."

Twenty minutes later, Chase and his family came hurriedly through the doors. Baltise slowed down, taking in the two leaders as she passed them. She seemed to shrink from their presence. Luamis understood. If they considered Chase a child by Volshin standards, Baltise and Caden would be nothing short of babies.

Even the rambunctious twins settled down, growing silent to their surprise. The eldest daughter avoided eye contact. When everyone took their seats, the doors sealed, emitting a sound of compressed air.

Overhead lights came to life.

The vehicle lifted off the ground.

From the side came the royal transport.

It maneuvered in front of them, then took off, their own immediately following. Theirs only a few feet behind. The scenery rushed by in a blur of colors until it reached the edge of the pier. Luamis could imagine Tavelo chastising the pilot of the royal transport, telling him to slow down so the new arrivals could see their home.

He stared out the window and tried not to show his joy. The buildings along the main roads had been upgraded. No longer the corridor of dilapidated businesses barely keeping the sections from sliding into the adjacent waterways. The palace looming on the horizon. Forever majestic.

Something about it struck him as odd, then he realized the surrounding landscape had changed. Over the ages, certain areas of the structure had been neglected. He flew over it numerous times before. Always marveling at the care taken to keep the front facet immaculate while the East wings, hidden from the view, were left to fall apart.

Not anymore. With superior sight, he made out the new construction on the far side. The stones had been replaced and greenery expanded from the main garden to wrap around it.

"Ahh! Wow!" The twins exclaimed.

They were out of their seats, clammy hands pressed against the view ports. The eldest daughter remained stoic; her gaze glued to the scene. A tiny smile crept along the corners of her mouth.

The reflection in his viewport revealed Caden's hooded expression. His hands gripped the sides of his seat, knuckles drained of blood. Cameron fared no better.

An entire unit of royal guards advanced onto the East wing's courtyard as they arrived, settling at the foot of the steep stone stairs. Matched in splendor with the West, it had a different color scheme.

Where Emperor Manel kept his side drenched in reds and golds, Endaga blue with silver covered the East. Even the flora matched among brilliant green shrubs lining the walkways.

The transport doors opened for everyone to exit. Tavelo glanced back once, then headed up the stairs with Pridric by his side. The Masters veered off in the opposite direction.

"We are to follow Emperor Tavelo," his mother announced.

The group climbed towards the entrance. Inside the palace, Luamis gaped at the arrangements and immaculate structure. All of it quite new, and it showed. He had never been in the palace but knew this side had all but crumbled centuries ago, small creatures similar to earth spiders covering it in thick webs.

They reached a narrow staircase, forcing them to go single file until they reached the open air above.

For as far as the eye could see, the land sprawled out, ending in a large body of water. He could hear the rush of its waves. The mostly barren land below, had a few scattered newly built homes. Tavelo stepped out of the way so they could all stand at the balcony's edge and get a good look.

"This is the new home for the ancients." He said it so proudly, the leader balked.

"Are we being excommunicated from the population?" He glared at Tavelo and his mother.

"No." Tavelo seemed confused by his outrage.

"Exalted," his mother said. She spread her arms wide. "All this is ours to build as we see fit."

"This was once our home. We ran the other docks on this side which has a massive lake only a quarter the size of the ocean." Tavelo placed both hands on the ledge and leaned forward, closing his eyes as a breeze rustled his hair.

"We're rebuilding the port."

The Kataling leader pointed out to the horizon.

"It was run by Ancient Ones, mostly Volshin.

The Katalings ran the other that is currently the main hub."

And then Luamis knew their home would come back to life as it should have been. He remembered hearing the history of the great war. Their planet was invaded and the trade network nearly destroyed. He began to piece together the rest from what he could see. By Omeron's expression, he also figured it out.

"To build as we please," he whispered.

"Of course, we would greatly appreciate it if you found an area closer to the palace." Pridric stood next to Tavelo with his back against the balcony ledge. Both elbows rested on it, his hair flowing in the wind. "Especially you," he addressed Baltise.

"Unless you prefer living in the palace itself," Tavelo suggested. "There is that option too."

"That is only benefitting Dania. There would be no end to it." Pridric sighed heavily.

Luamis suddenly sputtered, clamping a hand over his mouth to no avail. A laugh escaped.

Tavelo tilted his head.

"That's better. I was so worried you wouldn't understand."

"I'm sorry." Luamis removed his hand. "I know now that you are trying to fix it the best you can." His eyes narrowed. "But you can't expect us to simply turn a blind eye to Emperor Manel's sins."

"Nor would I ask you to." Tavelo bent over so that his forearms laid on the ledge. "I only ask that you keep an open mind and realize why the emperor was that way."

"Was?" Caden gave him a dubious stare. Luamis concurred his sentiment with a nod.

"That is for a later date. For now…" Pridric slapped the stone wall and pushed himself off. "It is time for a royal feast in your honor."

"Yay!" The twins threw their arms in the air and headed towards the stairs. "Food!"

Pridric eyed Baltise.

The Volshin registered no emotion, refusing to address the stare. Luamis snickered. Those children are gluttons like their mother. He hoped the palace had enough food to accommodate everyone else.

A Tense Return

Flags of every color affixed to the tops of holding blocks and posts lining the boardwalk flew along the docks. More were attached to hover drones drifting in the sky. Holoscreens around the planet showed the live feed of the giant transport ship returning from Earth for the last time.

The heads of all ten merchant families waited on the main platform of the docks. Dressed in their best attire, they stood out among the workers. The prominent seven lined up front with Tavelo, Eterenia, and Pridric. A large group of royal guards surrounded the outer perimeter, creating a safety bubble for them.

Volshins screeched high above, circling the ship as it eased down onto the dock for landing. Tavelo felt his body tense. The gravity of the event hit him. They had all come full circle. Barely adults when they fled their home world, each had grown exponentially out of survival. Even with that, in the eyes of their elders they were still considered too young to fend for themselves.

The first to walk down the ramp were Adelia and her brood, followed by Lariod, Armon, and to everyone's surprise, the Valkyrie. Hard to miss, she stuck out like a sore thumb, wearing full armor. Tavelo's face squinched, the right corner of his lips raised. Perplexed as to why she would don all of that.

Is she preparing for a fight? Eterenia smirked.

Addy, now half Tavelo's height with a slender muscular build, locked eyes with him. Tavelo tensed. *He's going to be close to Tesul's size in another ten years.* Tavelo marveled at him, briefly taking his gaze off the boy's face. That was a mistake.

With one flash step, the teenage boy came mere inches from him.

"Grampa Tavo!" He slammed into Tavelo, knocking him back two feet. Master Jaubro, who stood behind him, managed to stop them both from hitting the ground.

"Child! What are you doing?" Adelia walked faster, glancing around nervously in embarrassment. She reached the large group. "I am so sorry." Glaring down at her son. "Let go."

He didn't turn his head to acknowledge her, keeping his grip on Tavelo. "No." He looked up at him and smiled. "I missed you."

"What title is that?" Master Callesi asked. "What is a Grampa?"

Tavelo finally got his hands around the boy's arms and pried him off. "Behave." He addressed the group. "It's what they call Dega's on Earth."

"Oh." Callesi' brow raised as his mouth down-turned in amusement.

"Sounds ridiculous," Master Bryhel added. Her eyes were hooded under the black, wide brimmed hat that went with her black suit dress. The lapels laid flat unmoving in the small breeze. Tailored to perfection. An Endaga design. "You need to make them use the proper terms."

Tavelo turned, ready to berate the woman when Eterenia stepped in.

"They may call him whatever they choose," Eterenia said in a tense tone. "They were not born here and have no obligation to conform."

Soft hisses of air sucking through teeth and small gasps made them look towards the ramp.

A cluster of people were coming down. At first, Tavelo couldn't make out what caused the reaction. Then he saw Yutel struggling near the center. Holnar had his hand covering Chalayl's mouth while Darean and Yutel carried her in a tight grip. They literally brought her kicking and screaming. Tavelo stared at them in amazement.

He caught a glance of Master Boresso, frowning in disgust. The other merchant heads shook their heads. *Oh, Chalayl. Stop this foolishness.* As if hearing him, she got free of her captors and stood. She pulled the front of her suit to straighten it out, her eyes red with fury.

"Don't touch me!" The bun at the top of her head had come undone, hanging lopsided. "I will walk on my own."

"But you weren't," Holnar countered.

Behind them were the twins and Yutel's cousins. They all had pursed lips, not bearing to look at her.

Sensing the mood in the air, the former merchant children turned to face their families. Holnar drew in a breath as his gaze fell on his older sister, left behind on the ship with their parents. Tears welled up in his eyes and she tsked, turning away to hide her own joy at seeing him.

Tavelo kept his mouth shut, exhaling through his nose. *So disingenuous.* Fear seemed to grip Chalayl, and he knew for good reason. The reports of her ventures on Earth were not flattering. Darean's pace had slowed to almost a halt. Each step calculated so he wouldn't reach them too quickly.

"Tavelo!" Yutel bellowed. "Or, should I call you, Emperor?"

"Don't you dare," Tavelo hissed.

With brute force, Yutel removed Addy and wrapped Tavelo in a bear hug, squeezing tight. Addy frowned in defeat. Tavelo tapped Yutel's shoulders.

"You're suffocating me!" Tavelo managed to breathe out. He held on for a bit longer then released him. Tavelo gasped, stepping back from him. "You're such a menace."

"Hmm." Yutel went over and slapped Pridric hard on the back, forcing him to bend forward. "Are you being reasonable these days?"

Pridric gave a dirty, side glare, standing straight. "What's that supposed to mean?"

He adjusted his royal robes.

Workers transported cargo from the ship to larger crafts bearing each merchant family's logo. The loads were set in their respective holds. Tavelo watched them closely as more people jam-packed the ramp. Some were delighted to be home.

Others, particularly the Boresso's and Strana's, appeared put off by the return. They observed their belongings being shuttled out and understood the done deal.

The Valkyrie stopped before Eterenia and bowed low, her body a perfect ninety-degree angle.

"My Queen. I have come to be your guardian, as I promised centuries ago. Please accept me once more."

The merchant heads balked at her as Eterenia's expression changed to exasperation. She whacked the Valkyrie atop the head, stunning the woman.

"Stand up!" Eterenia snapped. "You should've said you wanted to come. What were you thinking?" The Valkyrie rose, holding the back of her head. "Of course, I accept you. When have I not?"

"My apologies, my Queen."

"And stop calling me that." Eterenia huffed.

She glanced away.

"Empress then?" Darean asked, reaching them.

"Sister!" Holnar ran to Master Bryhel, grabbing her into a hug. She tried to break free. "I am so over-joyed you're alive." He glared over at Tavelo and Yutel. "Why didn't you tell me?"

Yutel shrugged and turned to Tavelo. It never even occurred to them to do so. Tavelo felt a twinge of guilt. He should have, as a courtesy.

"I'm sorry." Was all Tavelo could muster.

"Unhand me, you boar!" Master Bryhel took hold of his forearms and tried to push them off. When he refused to relent, she gave in and sighed. "You're still such a child."

Holnar released her. He met her gaze, and they stood silent for a while.

"I'm an adult now."

He managed a smile, despite his tear stained face.

"That's debatable." She went into a dignified stance. "You have a lot to answer for."

Holnar lowered his head. "I know."

"You all do," Master Boresso said, cutting the niceties. "Did you really think you could conquer another planet? Create a new trade on your own? A bunch of children?"

"Let's not do that here." Tavelo turned to him with red eyes. "We know the mistakes we made. There's no reason for you to bring it up and berate us."

"Yes." Pridric moved away from Yutel. "This is supposed to be a celebration of our return. Why are you not happy to see all of us home?"

Indignation and shame. Tavelo could see and feel it coming from the merchant heads. There would be tense moments going forward. Especially when it came to trade.

He vowed to change the system.

❀ ❀ ❀

While the majority of the families stayed at their homesteads, bound to be overcrowded to say the least, Tavelo had the merchant heads escorted to the palace. The rest rode in the royal transport with Tavelo, Eterenia, and Pridric. Darean, his mate, Holnar, the twins, Yutel and his cousins. Adelia and her entourage, including the Valkyrie. His son, Tamar, stayed close to Innego.

Both not meeting his stares.

They remained silent halfway. Darean ended it.

"So, Emperor Endaga." Tavelo winced at the title. "How has the royal life been treating you?"

Holnar burst into laughter. "Don't tease him." He wiped a tear from one of his eyes. "You know he's not used to it yet."

"There has been some strife over the past few years," Eterenia answered. That perked the Valkyrie up. "We're in the process of militry reorganization. With the influx of our own forces from Earth, we should be able to diversify the assignments better."

"What strife?" Chalayl frowned. "We only heard of the invasion. Was there another?"

"Internal," Pridric replied. "The West palace has their own demons to sort out."

"Emperor Manel?" Darean leaned forward in his seat. "What is that monster up to?"

"Believe it or not, Manel is no longer an enemy." Tavelo rested his head in one hand as he leaned against the window. "A lot's happened. I will fill you in later."

Chalayl resumed sulking in the back of the transport. Her body slumped in the seat with her head languishing over the top of it. Chestnut hair splayed all over. Her bun gave up the fight and unraveled.

She looked like a child exhausted after a temper tantrum, her eyes showing fear.

Servants rushed towards the transport right when it settled before the East palace. They swiftly carried the luggage up the stairs through the entrance. Tervan and Dania awaited at the top. Pridric walked quickly to Dania and kissed her. She caressed his face.

"How was it?" Her eyes showed concern.

"Tense. There are hurt feelings all around."

"That's a given," Tervan scoffed. "You didn't expect a hug session, did you?"

"There were a few of those."

Pridric turned to Addy, then met Dania's stare.

"Oh!" She raised a hand to cover her mouth as

she let out a small laugh. "Grampa Tavo?"

"Indeed."

The young ones gaped at the East palace. Sully tried to stay reserved, though his face said otherwise. Addyon the other hand did not hold back.

"It's huge!" He ran up the stairs and took in the horizon. "Wow! A real castle!"

"What do you mean?" Adelia asked in a huff. "We lived in a real castle."

"That one's tiny now," he replied bluntly.

Darean's mate snorted. She too covered her mouth, stifling her laugh. Tavelo sighed. He walked up the stairs. Reaching the top, he turned back to see Tamar and Tervan locked in a staring match. He couldn't tell if it was hostile or indifferent since Tervan antagonized all of his younger siblings. That needs to stop.

"Come. We have a royal feast to attend in a few hours." He stopped a nearby servant as they walked past. "Have the merchant heads been settled?"

"Yes, Emperor." He bowed his head slightly. "They arrived an hour ago and are awaiting escorts to the banquet."

"Thank you. Please make sure everyone is comfortable. Especially our new arrivals." He gestured to everyone coming out of the transport.

"Of course." The servant bowed again and continued to his task.

Tavelo addressed his guests.

"I have something amazing to show you after the main festivities." He grinned. "You'll love it."

❀ ❀ ❀

A royal feast meant to be a joyous occasion turned into a royal mess as the merchant heads fought with their returned family members and each other. Tavelo sat at the end of the overly long table, used to accommodate the large group, staring in fury at them. Eterenia, sitting on his right, held his arm down while on his left Pridric pressed his fingers down into Tavelo's thigh, preventing him from standing.

Masters Jaubro and Endaga were able to briefly steer clear of the fight. They eventually got sucked into the chaos, and clearly not happy about the outcome. Servants moved closer to the walls, anticipating a brawl.

A thunderous bang echoed. The table jumped a few millimeters off the floor, causing the glasses to topple. Dishes spit out portions of their contents onto the white linen tablecloth. Spilt food and drink ran like rivers along the surface, some of it veering off to land on pristine laps. Many jumped up to avoid the stains. Others wiped off the mess.

Near the center of the table, two merchants stared up in terror. Megen's armor gloved hand rested. His massive frame seemed to fill the room. Wearing full battle gear, his dark hair flowing around him in its usual disarray, his eyes conveyed the disdain he had for everyone in the room.

Tavelo went rigid. His anger seeped out, replaced by fear. Tervan, not paying much attention to the infighting, raised his head to stare at the behemoth.

"I could hear your prattle all the way in the main corridor." Megen's voice came through gritted teeth. Saliva formed at the corners of his mouth. "If you can't talk like civilized beings, go home."

He slid his fist off the table.

"Who of all the gods is that?" Master Callesi cried.

Tavelo realized no one had seen Manel's eldest brother, save the people in the palace. When in battle, he wore an armored mask. Master Jaubro took the reins for Tavelo, and he exhaled in relief.

"This, my merchant friends, is Emperor Manel's eldest brother, General Megen of the royal army." Master Jaubro swept a hand across towards him, as if presenting a prize. "He's quite sensitive to disruption these days."

Eterenia and Pridric removed their iron grip from Tavelo so he could finally stand.

"My apologies for the vulgar display." Then he frowned. "What brings you to the East palace?"

"Manel wishes to join you later for a nightcap. I advised against it."

"Would it be better if I came to the West palace?"

Megen's face struggled with the right expression.

"He insists on coming here." *There!* Tavelo saw trepidation. So, things aren't getting resolved as quickly as they liked. "Which is ideal, given the situation."

He turned and walked out of the banquet hall, leaving the occupants stunned.

"The eldest brother?" Master Dakien whispered.

"I rescind my assessment of Emperor Manel," Darean said. "That is a true monster."

"You're never more right than that," Tervan agreed.

Tavelo's anger returned.

"If you're all done throwing baseless accusations at each other." He scanned the room, meeting their shameful expressions. "Can we continue to eat like the family we are supposed to be?"

Family. It struck them all like a hammer. The breeding lottery on Earth blended each merchant family to the point of them all being related. He could tell the three lower merchant houses were relieved to have averted such a fate.

"We must find common ground in our newfound situation."

Master Strana sat with clenched fists resting along the sides of his plate on the table. He turned his head to stare at Pridric. Such malice. Tavelo didn't understand the reason for it. Pridric visibly flinched. The frightened look in his eyes told Tavelo plenty. Pridric's older brother terrified him.

Eterenia spoke to him telepathically.

"Baby steps, my love. This won't be easy."

"I know," he replied. "We're in for the long haul."

The banquet resumed, mostly in silence with a few conversations popping up every now and again. No one seemed to enjoy the meal. Except Tervan and the children. Addy gave Tavelo a big grin, showing teeth covered in food and blood from the fresh meat. He had absorbed every word said. Tavelo felt the boy would become a great strategist soon.

With dinner complete, with most of the guests softened from indulging in high content liquor, Tavelo's royal guards ushered the merchant heads, including the ones from Earth, out into the main corridor. Tamar and Innego aimed to follow when Tavelo gestured with a tilt of his head for them to come. A separate set of servants arrived to cater for the children.

Adelia, Armon, and Tesul exchanged stares, then stood to join the departing group. Tavelo smirked to hide his amusement. Of course they needed to see as well. That was a given. His uncle side eyed him. He knew the man didn't approve. Except, he found no way to keep it a secret any longer.

The group walked the halls until they came to the steep, narrow staircase that led to the balcony. They went single file, careful to not stumble on the slippery stone. Everyone had a hand placed on the walls for leverage. Out in the open air, gasps erupted.

Homes already in full use by ancients, spattered along the barren lands. A main blood station set off center acted as a central hub for the region. The cube would be installed by the end of the season. Tavelo stood aside allowing the group an unobstructed view.

"This is the area where all the ancients have made their home. Many are still looking at builds and hope to have their abodes constructed soon."

"Why the isolation?" Master Callesi asked.

"It's not." Tavelo leaned against the ledge. "This is where they've always been since before the great invasion."

"Is that so?" Master Bryhel placed her hands flat on the balcony. She scanned the area then froze. Her eyes focused on the horizon. "What is…"

The others followed her stare and Tavelo heard intakes of breath. *Oh, It is.* He grinned, watching them became mesmerized by the rushing water beyond the territory. Everyone knew of its existence. Merely overlooking it since they had no reason to acknowledge it.

Master Boresso hunched over, straining her eyes to zero in on the shore. She stood straight and turned to Tavelo. One by one, they all began to see.

"Those are the remains of a dock." She pointed.

"I see parts of a pier," Master Dakien added.

Tavelo spread his arms wide. "Before the great invasion our planet had two trade hubs. This one the enemy hit first and destroyed. The emperor sent out royal guards to minimize damage to the other. Since trade would be harmed if we stayed inoperable for too long, they decided to repair the one and leave the other to rebuild later."

"But that never happened," Master Strana seethed. "It was abandoned."

"Correct." Master Endaga's apprehension crept up. "With the coronation of the two emperors, the planet will regain dual power. Both docks are truly necessary. The architects have been looking into new structures."

"And the plan is what, exactly?" Master Bryhel's fingers clawed on the ledge.

She knows what I want.

Tavelo looked to his uncle.

"With ten major merchant clans, we will divide them in two. Five to run the East and the other five for the West." Tavelo felt the mood shift. Part elation; part sinister.

"And, how will this division of merchant houses be determined?" Master Boresso asked.

"That's obvious!" Master Dakien snapped.

"Whichever dock is closest to our clients' pathway

would reduce transport time," he continued.

Pridric stepped closer to Tavelo. They shared an unspoken thought as they saw gleams in the merchants eyes. Competition would start all over again.

❀ ❀ ❀

The Valkyrie removed herself from Chase's group the first chance she got when they entered the palace. She felt her role as Eterenia's personal guard ended after seeing the royal guards. Centuries of dedication despite her ability to live without ties. She chided her stupidity for getting bitten by the first vampire Queen.

As a being from the heavens sent to Earth as punishment, she had let down her guard, believing herself invincible. She spent the first twenty years on Earth drinking her sorrows away, her entire unit of soldiers along with her causing havoc.

The eighteenth century frowned upon the group of tall women in battle armor invading territories for the sole purpose of mayhem.

That fateful night on a dark English narrow street, a horde of vampires ambushed them. The Queen quite intrigued by them, tracked their movements across the lands. Her unit's excessive drunkenness caused their defeat.

Deep in thought, she almost dismissed the flash of pink color that crossed her vision. She slowed her steps and found the reason. Ahead, a soldier in full black battle gear with a peach colored robe over it stood angrily by a pillar.

Her hair, a magnificent mess of straw blonde, went everywhere while cascading down her back. A longsword lay sheathed in a holder on her right hip.

Not one to fear much of anything, she approached the slender beauty. The woman didn't acknowledge her presence, consumed by a rage she seemed to hardly contain.

Her red eyes bulging like fresh peeled fruit, the pupils mere dots.

"What has you so enraged, fair lady?" The Valkyrie stopped a few feet from her.

Startled, Princess Lenri glanced over at her, then resumed her fuming.

"A soldier had the audacity to offer his services to protect me during the coronation ceremony."

The Valkyrie sputtered. "That is insulting."

"I don't care for, nor have no need for, man." Her vehement tone sounded gloriously vicious.

The Valkyrie moved closer. "Nor do I."

This time, Princess Lenri turned to her with a softened expression. Still angry, yet endearing.

"Who are you?" Lenri demanded. "Who allowed you in this wing of the palace?"

The Valkyrie laughed, making Lenri frown.

"I was Eterenia Jaubro's personal guard on Earth." She made a bow. "My name is Anastasia."

"But you're not a human." Lenri cocked her head to one side.

"No. It is a long and shameful story."

"Then you will tell me this lurid tale of yours at a meal."

"That's quite forward of you," Anastasia gave her an opening gaze.

"Lenri. I am Manel's younger sister."

"Of course you are," Anastasia whispered, checking out her features.

"What was that?" Lenri wrapped her hand around the hilt of her longsword.

"Oh? If you wanted to play with me, all you had to do was ask." Anastasia tapped hers.

Lenri hesitated, her brow furrowing while she contemplate her next move.

"I do like to assess my potential companions with a thorough test of might."

"Then by all means." Anastasia took hold of her sword's hilt as well.

To her surprise, Lenri dropped her hand.

"I am hungry, so first we eat." She gave a tiny smile. "We must have energy if we are going to have a full bout."

She noted the undertone. Anastasia leered at her, and Lenri let her get an eyeful. She bowed to Lenri then stood. With a flourish of one arm, she held it out wide.

"Please, Princess, lead the way."

As the two walked down the corridor, Anastasia noticed the path. She had been briefed on where the nearest banquet hall lay, and that is not where they were headed.

This route led to the royals' personal chambers.

A full bout, huh? She grinned.

❀ ❀ ❀

The royal dining hall located between the two palaces had been stripped down to minimal decor since it rarely got used over the past few decades. Bare cream-colored walls combined with a long table that could seat twenty people covered in plain cloths made the room feel empty. Midafternoon sun light shone through the open block out curtains, casting lines across the interior.

Servants moved about in silence. Their feet made small shuffling sounds as they set up the main and side tables with off white dishes bearing no intricate design. The utensils made tiny clanks like chimes as they made contact. An uninspired setting.

Tavelo and Manel stood at the entrance, taking in the dull aesthetic. The servants finished their tasks and moved to stand against the walls. Manel tsked, walking towards the table. Tavelo rolled his eyes, and tilting his head back, let out a small sigh.

Behind them, Pridric frowned at the neutral flooring that did nothing for it. Dania pursed her lips so as not to say anything rude.

Eterenia simply nodded. She clearly had a plan already. Manel's siblings arrived. Lendor took one step into the room and grimaced.

"What fresh, dull dungeon is this?"

He glanced around the entire room.

Everyone turned to him, showing their displeasure at him calling out the obvious. He finally met their stares, though not deterred.

"They could've at least tried making it a bit more presentable. A few sheers, some royal banners. We were going to redecorate it regardless. Still."

He sat down at the table in a huff, continuing his scrutiny. Megen sat closest to the door his size blocking half of its view. Tervan came in followed by Adelia and Tamar. Tavelo saw Tervan sit across from Megen. *Why?* He prayed there would be no fighting. He looked over at Tamar who sat five chairs away from him.

"Are you finally going to speak to me?"

Tavelo cocked his head.

Tamar kept his head down, his face scrunched. He struggled with something, trying to figure it out. Tavelo waited patiently, as did the others, feeling the tension between them.

"I'm sorry," Tamar whispered. He gave a quick glance then returned his focus on the table.

"For what?" Tavelo asked, confused.

"I…" Tamar trembled. "For so long, I blamed you for everything that went wrong. The things I thought about you. How I despised you. It was wrong."

"Tamar," Tavelo leaned forward.

Eterenia stopped him.

"I felt so ashamed. Couldn't bear to look you in the eyes." Tears fell down Tamar's face. "What was I supposed to say after all the ugly things…"

Tervan gave him a pitiful stare, snorting softly.

Tavelo stood, forcing Eterenia to let go, and went over to him. He wrapped his arms around him and squeezed. Tamar resisted at first, trying to hide his tears, then slumped in his seat.

"I know," Tavelo said. "And you had every right to be angry. I neglected you and had the audacity to be surprised when you rebelled." Tavelo grabbed him by the chin and lifted his face so they could look into each other's eyes. "It is I who am sorry."

"How disgusting." Manel brought his feet up and rested them on the edge of his chair. He let his arms dangle over his knees. "Make him stop. It'll ruined our appetites."

"Manel," Tavelo glared up at him. "Behave." Manel gave a sheepish grin. "Let's have a meal without drama, shall we?"

"You're no fun, Tavelo."

Maxellia remained silent, sitting in the center on the right side. A wide metal band held back her hair, letting the rest go wild behind it. She had a look of angry defeat with arms crossed beneath her flowing robes. Lenri sat next to her as a safety measure.

Tavelo released Tamar. "Are you okay?" He whispered. Tamar nodded. He rose and went back to his seat at the end of the table across from Manel. Eterenia patted him on the thigh.

From the side doors came the food and drinks. Platters were carried out. The fare evenly distributed on the tables. Fruits and breads filled teh side tables while slices of cured meats, blood pudding, hearty grains and chilled breakfast ale with a lower alcohol content covered tthe main.

Manel snapped a finger. To everyone's surprise, Gallic appeared in the room, gathering fruits and a loaf of bread from the side table. He came to sit next to Manel and laid out the goods.

Tavelo glared at Manel.

"What?" Manel grinned, setting his feet down on the floor. "He likes catering to my every whim."

The others went the normal route, calling the servants to fetch what they wanted.

Boots stomping on marble, running at full speed,

echoed from the corridor and came to a stop at the entrance. Innego leaned against the door frame, catching his breath. He wore a body suit under the newly made East palace kefta.

"My apologies for being late." He stood straight. "I seemed to have overslept." His face flushed.

"In other words," Tervan turned to him. "You had a carnal feast until the early hours of day."

Innego gave him a dirty look before grabbing an empty seat on the left next to Tamar. He noticed the swollen eyes and raised his brow. Tamar simply nodded.

"Now, how does this dual coronation work?" Pridric asked. "The logistics sound murderous."

Manel shoved a large piece of meat in his mouth and began talking while chewing.

"Oh, it will indeed be a grand affair," he smacked. "The main atrium has not been used in over a millennium. It needs to be cleaned and decorated before the ceremony."

"Main atrium?" Tavelo turned. "Where is that?"

"Mmm." Manel guzzled ale to aid in swallowing his food. Some of it spilled over the edge, running down the sides of his mouth. "It's in the center of the two palaces, of course." He set his ale down and used the back of his hand to wipe the excess liquid away. "It's directly opposite this room on the other side."

Tavelo tapped a finger on his lips, thinking. Eterenia held a small red fruit up to his mouth and he took it. The juices moistened his lips, tinting them dark pink.

"We should take a look then after meal." He took a sip of ale. "Have you seen it already?"

"No. But, I can conclude it's condition isn't suitable, given how long it's been neglected."

And he was right.

Tavelo cursed inwardly as he stood with the rest of the group on the edge of a vast courtyard covered in decay, overgrown vegetation, and small creatures with nests in every visible crevice. Nearly a mile in size, it appeared to be more like a capital square than a large garden. The condition of the rectangular field resembled the aftermath of an apocalypse.

"Oh my stars," Dania breathed out in awe. "What a tragedy."

"What a mess!" Pridric blurted. They all looked back at him. With a disgusted expression on his face, he stepped down the broken stairs, careful of his footing. "We would need to work on this day and night non stop to get it up to par for the ceremony." He turned to face them. "We don't have much time."

Tavelo in turn, glanced over at Manel.

"Why didn't you tell us this sooner?"

"It's fine. The architects are devising a plan as we speak. Our house colors will be somewhat blended." Everyone waited for him to continue. He sniffed. "Our banners will be displayed strategically, and the backdrop will be glorious, I'm sure."

"That is unacceptable." Eterenia, Pridric, and Dania exclaimed in unison.

The three looked at each other then nodded in some unknown agreement. Tavelo tried not to laugh. He knew as soon as they left the decrepit outdoor atrium, one or all of them were marching into the royal architects' wing for a discussion.

"Just needs a little work," Manel muttered.

"I'm leaving." Megen turned away from the scene. He went back into the palace.

The younger siblings bowed slightly, each taking one of Maxellia's arms and steering her out.

Tavelo walked around the perimeter with his entourage. Tamar and Innego inspected the broken stone pavement. Dania poked at the various inedible vegetation. Pridric stood in the heart of the courtyard legs apart with arms crossed.

One hand cradled his chin.

Tavelo had enough.

He walked back to the palace stairs. Eterenia, Tervan, Innego, and Manel followed. Gallic stayed close by as usual. A stone crumbled beneath his feet, causing him to falter. He cursed, while regaining his footing.

Inside the palace, they walked the main corridor, engaging in small conversations. Loud voices filtered towards them from the adjacent hallway. Around the corner they came upon at least twenty guards from the De Luce coven facing Lariod.

The man standing ahead of them, Tavelo recognized as one of the army generals. His irises glowed bright red, his hand on the hilt of his sword.

"What is the meaning of this?" Eterenia yelled.

They paid her no mind, which infuriated Tavelo and her. This amused Tervan.

"Speak." Tervan commanded.

"This lowly ingrate says we're not worthy of becoming royal guards for your palace!"

"On what basis, may I ask?" He turned to Lariod.

"I bested his son to become a guardian for Adelia. And I have done so again during a sparring session this morning."

"And that is a problem, why?"

"This." Lariod produced a longsword. "It is far too heavy, causing the wielder to tire faster. There's also damage to the muscles, requiring longer healing time."

"That's because he's a disgrace!" The general spat. "To his name and our code. Warmon is not capable of fighting like the others."

"It makes you lazy." Lariod twirled the sword.

"They can easily cut through anything because of the weight!" The general retorted.

"Does this seem efficient to you?" Lariod handed the sword to Tervan.

He hefted it a few times and spun it. "Not in the least." He returned it to Lariod.

"Where did these come from?" Tavelo asked.

"A reissue after the last battle. Neither of you had authorized such a thing," Lariod answered.

He held the sword straight, tip pointed six inches from the marble floor. He let it go. The blade struck with a loud clink, embedding deep into it.

Cracks spiderwebbed around it.

Tavelo hissed.

"That proves our might!" The general continued to yell. "We can wield it with ease and destroy our enemies."

"Is that so?" Tervan stepped into the center before the general. "I always wanted to beat you to submission." He drew his longsword. "Let's see how well you do against mine."

"You're nothing but a petulant child spawned by that whore we were forced to call Queen."

Eterenia's eyes turned red and Tavelo managed to hold her back with Pridric's help. He felt on the verge of tearing the man to pieces himself. Tervan showed no emotion. His eyes remained a torrential blue. He swung his sword once, bringing the hilt behind his ear above the shoulder, the other arm extended.

No one spoke as the general launched towards him. In an instant, the two men became blurs of light and shadow. Sparks flew as their swords struck mid-air. The spectators moved further out in a semicircle to avoid getting struck. Minutes felt like an eternity as the fighting continued.

The motion suddenly stopped. The general went down on all fours, panting heavily, still keeping a grip on his sword. Blood seeped from dozens of slashes in his body suit. Tervan stood ten feet away, barely out of breath. He regained his stance, sword up.

"Come. You've only been at it a short time. Let's reach our full potential." Tervan's eyes glowed silver beyond rage. His calm demeanor only intensified it.

The general tried to stand and fell back on one knee. His arms shook, loosening the sword from his hands. He kept his fingers around the hilt, not willing to let go even though his muscles strained from excess fatigue.

"Get up." Tervan's tone, venomous. "No?"

Eterenia came towards them.

"I want these weapons removed from my army and the original ones reissued." She turned to the general's second in command who stood awe struck at his superior's defeat. "Is that understood?"

Wide eyed, he bowed his head.

"At least when they go back to their regular swords they will seem much lighter." Pridric glanced down at the sword embedded in the floor. "The one good thing this did was build muscle."

Tervan flash stepped to the general and kicked him in the abdomen from the side. The general's body went flying up into the giant pillar behind him.

"Stand down, Tervan!" Tavelo ordered.

Still enraged, Tervan turned away and happened to look up. Lurking in the shadows above on the upper promenade, Megen had his arms crossed as he stared down at him. He smirked before turning away.

Lariod pulled the sword out of the marble. Pridric gave him a curious look.

"And where is the general's son?"

Lariod didn't turn to him. "Resting."

"Hmm?" Pridric watched Lariod walk away from the scene.

Is that right?

Adelia half ran, half marched tdown the royal halls owards Lariod's personal chamber. Her flowy robes of various shades of magenta cascaded around her as each movement created a swift wind. Anger consumed her. *Well, maybe just a little put out.* She pressed her lips tight together.

A whimsical grin formed.

When she had awakened, no one was around. No mate, no children. No guardian. At the very least, Lariod should have come to get her up. Worthless! He probably went out sparring with the royal guards, as he chose to do often in the early hours of the day.

She rounded the last corner and came into dead silence. Of course. Everyone else had already gone about their tasks. Her footsteps suddenly seemed too loud. To lessen the sound, she slowed her pace, gently placing her feet as she walked.

At the doorway to Lariod's chamber she could sense someone inside. Huh. Taking a deep breath, she pushed the doors open with both hands and charged in. See saw a figure under the bed covers.

"Have you no shame for your derelict of duty?" She yelled. "I won't tolerate such laziness."

The figure slowly stirred, the multiple spreads unraveling until the top of their body emerged. Black hair in disarray fell across their shoulders. They rose from laying on their side to face her. Golden amber eyes, set in the pale face of Warmon, the general's son, greeted her.

Adelia stiffened a few feet away from the bed. She cocked her head to one side.

"I'm sorry. I didn't mean to wake you." She cleared her throat, regaining her haughty stance. "Where is Lariod?"

She noticed the thin vein lines running across his shaky arms trying to hold him up. He finally gave up the fight and laid back down.

"I'm not sure." His voice, full of pain, softer than she expected. "I think he went to see my father."

"Oh? Well, I'll find him eventually." She watched his eyes close. "Go back to sleep and rest."

Adelia turned around, a mischievous grin on her face, and walked out, shutting the door behind her.

❀ ❀ ❀

Soft grunts followed by a loud hiss emitted from the chamber ahead, making Caden slow his steps. Light shined onto the dark corridor from the open door on his right. He stopped in front of it, staying half in the shadows, and turned to find the reason.

Tervan sat on the bench at the foot of his bed wincing from the healer handling a wound on his left side. The deep gash already stopped bleeding from repair gel being applied. His cloak lay over his right shoulder, the rest of his upper body bare.

Their eyes met.

"Not at fast as you thought you were." Caden's gaze didn't waver.

"Is that criticism?" Tervan's expression changed to defensive.

"Not at all." Caden tilted his head.

They didn't move, not severing their connection. The way Tervan's face relaxed before turning away let Caden know he had acknowledged his feelings. Well aware they weren't the best people at showing their affection. Caden looked away.

The healer, finishing his work, gathered up his belongings, and left the room. He ignored Caden as he passed him. Tervan used his arms to pull himself onto the edge of the bed, scooting back so his head lay on the pillows. He exhaled, forcing the air from his lungs, his torso caving in to define his ab muscles.

Caden stepped into the room, closing the door behind him. Without a word, he slid next to Tervan and laid his head on his chest. He listened to the rhythm of Tervan's body.

This is better. He closed his eyes.

Dania stayed in the dark corridor cloaking her presence as she watched the scene unfold. She had come to check on Tervan for Eterenia. was. They really need to address their messy mother and son relationship. She felt a small amount of empathy for them.

This, though. She shook her head.

Oh Caden.

He now sat on the verge of having the worst taste in mates, followed closely by Manel. She didn't have any real hostile feelings towards Tervan. Just his personality left little to be desired. And Caden. Damaged, angry; far too sensitive.

Not one to ruin a mood, she decided to leave them undisturbed. On her way back to the royal corridor, she smiled. Eterenia would be shocked after reporting her findings.

A bit of palace gossip was good for morale.

Eterenia already sat relaxed in one of the plush seats in the smaller section of the nearly full tearoom. Gallic's mother sat next to her. On the other side were Tavelo, Pridric, and Manel. Right as Dania got ready to sit down on an empty chaise, Adelia bursted in, carrying a gust of wind with her.

"Good midday to you all." Her rigid tone grated. "Would have been even more lovely if someone had awakened me on time."

"Sit down, Adelia." Eterenia sipped her tea. They all felt, more than heard, her command. Dania plopped onto the chaise at the same time Adelia slid sideways into the nearest chair out of fear. "You're not some infant in need of pampering." She turned to Dania. "And what are you doing?"

"Well," Dania began. "Your tone sounded quite frightening." A servant came with more teacups, and bowed as they left. She picked up the carafe and filled her cup millimeters from the rim. "I saw something quite," she paused, taking a sip, "extraordinary. And disturbing."

"Oh?" Eterenia glanced at her. "I thought you were going to see about my son."

"Let him seethe," Tavelo interjected. "He only wants an outlet for his angst."

"He was wounded, my love." Eterenia glared.

"What?" Tavelo sat forward.

"I saw nothing of the sort." He frowned.

"Because you're not all that observant, Tavelo." Manel smirked. "I saw those strikes. He was lucky."

Tavelo went pale. "I didn't..."

Dania huffed.

"For your concern, I did go check on Tervan."

Eterenia's eyes narrowed. "And?"

"He was being comforted." The room went quiet.

"Well, that's ridiculous," Adelia scoffed. "No one in their right mind would want that idiot." She reached over to get a cup and stopped when Dania sipped her tea, eyes hooded over the edge. A glint in her eye made Adelia flinch. "Impossible."

They stared at Dania, tension forming in the air.

"Caden," she responded.

The sound of teacups clanked on saucers brought her gaze upwards to observe her audience. Eterenia had halted her cup midway. Adelia stared, stunned, still in the motion of tilting the carafe over hers.

"Well, that's just a confirmation for lack of taste."

Adelia finished pouring her tea and sat back in her chair.

Eterenia eyes went red. "Stop it."

"I don't think it's a lack of taste." Grasilda said. "Possibly bad judgement?"

"Our son is not some pariah!" Tavelo exclaimed. His expression became terse. "He lacks social grace, perhaps. And can be too blunt."

"This is not ideal." Eterenia's brow furrowed. "They will hurt each other in the long run."

"Oh don't be so pessimistic!" Dania set her cup in the saucer on her lap. "Is it not your wish for Tervan to find happiness?"

"Of course, it is!" Eterenia snapped.

"I think they are well suited for each other." Grasilda smiled.

A sinister look from Manel made them all pause.

"Does this mean we may still get a hybrid? Your Volshin blood and that of a Kataling?"

Tavelo turned his furious stare towards him.

"Manel. Stop pushing your father's sick agenda. There's no reason to keep being a slave to his whim."

Adelia cringed, hissing as she turned from them. Manel's eyes became gorged with blood. With it a face full of hurt and rage. Dania saw Tavelo regretting his words in an instant.

"I am not trying to harm you, Manel." Tavelo leaned over to him. "I want you to be your own guide. Not following someone else's map."

Manel eased back, his eyes reverting to normal. Dania felt everyone's relief.

"That dullard has no clue how to love anyone," Adelia blurted, breaking the mood.

"Adelia," Eterenia warned.

"And I found the general's son sleeping in that stupid guardian of mine's bed."

Tavelo, Eterenia, and Dania's brows shot up at that revelation.

"And here I was thinking he's out sparring." Adelia sipped her tea. "Guess he stuck his other sword elsewhere."

"Uhh, he did spar earlier." Pridric said. "There was an incident in the main corridor. Hence your brother's injury at the hands of the general."

Adelia sputtered, droplets of tea flew from her lips. "What did you say?"

"A small dispute over weapons and integration." Pridric frowned. "Stupidity at best."

"On that subject. Do we now have a situation on our hands regarding military might?" Tavelo asked.

"If your puny force can't fight on par with the royal guards, then we have no need for them." Manel sat up. "You can keep them for yourselves or send them to live outside the palace."

"Puny?" Pridric turned to him. "I recall us going head to head with the royal guards on Earth."

"We had to learn to fight because of how you pursued us," Eterenia added.

Manel waved their words off.

"Yes, I get it. How many times do you want me to apologize for that?"

Dania felt the hairs on her body bristle. *There's not enough in the universe for you to atone!* Tavelo let out a sigh and sat back in his chair. *What? She* glanced around the room. *No one is going to answer?* Eterenia continued sipping her tea.

"There's a saying on Earth." Pridric flopped his arms over the edges of his chaise. "May he who has not sinned cast the first stone."

The room went silent. Not one of them had the right to condemn anyone.

Lariod waited a few days before going into the quarters arranged for the coven soldiers. He had made the decision for Warmon to stay with him. The task at hand involved collecting his belongings from his assigned bunk. All the temporary chambers were located in the East palace. Emperor Tavelo didn't trust the royal guards on the West since he wasn't sure how many were on Maxellia's side.

He strolled along the corridors, turning at each corner with a slow pivot. No need to hurry. Regardless of what he encountered; the goal remained the same on arrival. Sparse traffic in the halls meant he only had to bow to a handful of royal constituents passing by. The silence comforted him. Each step he made deliberately softer to avoid his boots clomping on the hard floors.

At the entrance to the soldiers' chamber, he took a deep breath. Placing both hands on the door, he flung them open. The conversations inside faded as soldiers turned to him with disdain. He paid no heed and went directly to Warmon's belongings, still not fully unpacked.

And not by design.

Some of the clothes were spilled out onto the floor, tattered from multiple cuts. The large chest that housed his weapons and armor had been damaged from attempts to break its seal. None of the soldiers came near him. The general order it to compensate for his humiliation. Blaming his son for causing such a defeat. The soldiers were angry about it as well, but also had no choice but to obey.

He picked up any pieces of intact clothing and shoved them in a makeshift sack from one of the robes and tied it around his waist. The large black lacquered metal chest, six feet in length and three feet deep, had red and gold overlays that ran along its sides. They glinted in the muted sunlight peeking through an opening in the curtains.

He bent down and hefted the thing on his back, centering it before standing.

Without a word, he walked out of the chamber. Halfway down the corridor he heard the doors slam shut. A few people stared at him as he made his way back to his private chamber. He snickered, knowing it looked strange. His slicked back hair, curled up at his shoulders, started to feel warm. Too much sweat would render the hold useless.

He arrived at his chamber doors and used one foot to gently push the right side open. Locking it seemed silly since he knew what he had to bring back. He walked in and eased the chest down by the wardrobe on the far end, not making a sound. The sack he untied from his waist went into the bottom compartment of the wardrobe.

Taking a closer look at the seal, he realized he had been mistaken about its damage. Not to get in and sabotage the contents. No. To prevent Warmon from opening it. A message that the general no longer acknowledged him as a member of the coven army. Lariod's eyes went red. Using brute force, he struck the seam of the chest and cracked it open.

The hinges popped the top.

He rummaged inside until he found what he searched for. A nondescript black sword case with simple latches to hold it closed. Opening it revealed the longsword sheathed in shiny black leather, bound shut with red ribbon, adding to the hilt's elaborately designed.

Made especially for Warmon.

A magnificent piece of weaponry.

Lariod untied the ribbon, then drew the sword. He remembered fighting with it for the guardianship. Even then, something felt off about Warmon's stance. He twirled it, held it out straight, turned it sideways, inspecting the blade. *That's why!* He felt and saw the imbalance. The craftmanship left less to be desired.

Standing straight, he sheathed the sword and left, again not locking it. None of the coven soldiers would dare come to his chamber. They understood what that meant for them. He would not tolerate it.

He walked to the West side of the palace; the sword bouncing lightly in his hand as he kept his usual stride. No need for gentle steps. The halls were a bit more congested, and he had to do more head bows than he liked. Daylight flooded the garden on the other side of the glass enclosure, casting shadows onto the floor.

Royal guards occupied a war room used for investigating various weapons and strategies on the far wing next to the communications hub. The door sat open, and he counted at least ten guards inside. There were probably that many further in.

He casually entered, causing the first three guards halt what they were doing to glare at him. The first to address him was a large man twice his size in full battle gear.

Lariod kept his composure, steadying his breath.

"What brings you here?" The guard's voice almost boomed.

Lariod held out the sword.

"I want to know if this can be fixed."

The guard took hold of the hilt and dragged the blade out.

"It was made for a specific soldier," Lariod said.

The guard's lips thinned as he swiped the air then inspected the weapon.

"This was not forged here?"

"Earth craft," the other guard beside him spat out. "It's essentially trash."

"It's aesthetically pleasing. A truly Magnificent design," the large guard said.

"Beautiful doesn't win a battle." The guard on the other side of an inspection device looked over at it.

"How was this made?" The big guard frowned holding the blade straight.

"They have ancient forgers on Earth. They do so by melting metals at high heat."

"Really?" The sitting guard's eyes widened. "They use such primitive methods?"

The big guard handed the sword to the guard at the inspection device. Placed inside, it hovered in midair as its composition and measurements were being relayed on the holoscreen.

"The craftmanship is actually quite good." He pointed to the first part of the blade. "This is a minor flaw. We can repair in no time. It would mean deconstructing it."

"That's fine." Lariod moved to step back and saw them eyeing his own sword at his waist.

"Was that one forged on Earth as well?" The first inspector asked.

"Unlike that one, I was able to watch mine being made. It has no flaws."

The three guards gave him a dubious stare.

"We will inspect the other soldiers' weapons. If they are to assimilate with our forces, there can be no ill made tools for their positions." The inspector tapped an icon on the panel below the device. "I will start with this one."

The blade separated with ease from the hilt.

Humming to herself as she hastened down the hall, Adelia held the vial of translucent purple liquid tight in her left hand. Her red robes over a silver gown made her feel more regal. Her hair, in a messy fishtail braid, laid over one shoulder. People bowed to her and she relished it.

I was a Queen for a while.

She thought matter of fact.

In front of Lariod's door, she rapped on it lightly with her knuckles. Without waiting for a response, which she knew would not happen, she crept inside.

Warmon still lay fast asleep, buried under the covers. Moving to the right side of the bed, she leaned over him and saw the thin webs of bruised veins along the forearms and biceps. His eyelids, squinted shut with pain, fluttered from rapid eye movement beneath.

That's where I come in.

She smiled at her genius as she held up the vial. He opened his eyes and flinched from her. *Why do people do that?* She frowned, a second later resuming her smile.

"He's not here," Warmon whispered.

"Oh, I know. I came for you." That seemed to confuse him. "You need to get better." She removed the stopper from the vial. "This will help." She tilted the vial to his lips and slowly poured it in. He got it down in three swallows. When he struggled to sit up, she laid a hand on his shoulder, pushing him down. "Sleep. I need Lariod to stop worrying about you and get back to his duty."

His eyes closed as he fell back deep in slumber.

Footsteps approached, and she let out a sigh.

Lariod stopped at the foot of the bed.

"Is that the reason?" He unfastened the sash around his waist, cinching his cape and removed them both. "I believe he is my priority at the moment."

"I know that!" Adelia snapped. "If he means anything to you then I must care for him as well."

Lariod froze as he tossed his cape and sash on a nearby chair. She searched his face, trying to decipher the expression he had. Blank. Yet his eyes stared into some unknown place. His arms dropped to his side, and he turned to her.

"You're right. He does mean something to me." She had never heard such a soft tone come from Lariod. "Thank you."

Two Emperors

With the return of their family members and the protectors they sent along, the merchant clans had no choice in finding separate housing for them. They saw no feasible way to integrate everyone back into their homesteads. Tavelo sent Pridric to handle the logistics for each family. He was not amused. Pridric studied the map of the city looking for empty lots to build on. Not by any means amused.

The merchant heads were adamant about having minimal distance between them and their children, now adults. His own family demanded he return to finish his merchant training. He refused. Propping his forearms on the large oval table displaying the hologram of the map, he scanned the area. The tip of his long braid, lying over his right shoulder, brushed the surface.

On Earth, they stayed together out of necessity. This time, they had their own hordes to take care of. Even his newly formed clan needed a place to call home, forgoing the invitation to stay in the palace. He understood their sentiment.

How do we continue our independence in the shadow of our elders?

Pridric stood straight, easing his arms back until his hands held onto the edge. And there were the coven armies to deal with.

The doors of the war room opened. He twisted his upper body towards it, his gaze landing on Tavelo entering with his usual flair.

Arms wide, flinging the doors apart, he stood in the doorway wearing Endaga colors. The robes' hems swished along the floor and his hair hung loose. Pridric felt the corner of lips tug. No. Don't show adoration. He fought back the urge and gave him a disinterested stare.

"Have you yet to find a remedy to our problem?" Tavelo walked over to stand beside him. Pridric eyed him with contempt. "Don't look at me like that! I know how fast you can solve an issue. What's delaying your decision?"

"Staying close yet far away." Pridric attempted to lessen his tense tone.

Tavelo looked down at the map. He noticed the blue dots indicating empty land.

"They really don't want to let go."

"Among other things." Pridric drummed his fingers on the table's rim. "We also have something they do not."

"Hmm?" Tavelo glanced over at him.

"Our armies. I'm sure you recognize the issue."

"Which is why I have told our little group to meet here." Tavelo turned his head towards the doors still sitting open. "They're late."

"You always assume that," Tervan replied. He stepped out of the shadows from the other side of the room. "I was here before you gave that so called grand entrance."

Pridric snorted, covering his bottom lip with his left fingers. Tavelo's face went stern, making it even more comical.

Lariod, Warmon, and Eterenia arrived. Tesul, Adelia, and Armon were close behind. Eterenia saw the map and frowned as she moved closer to peer at the possible locations.

"Right on cue."

Tavelo linked his fingers together and rested them on the table ledge.

"We're discussing what to do with our armies."

"Are we not integrating with the royal guards?" Warmon asked.

"Only those who wish to," Pridric answered. "It would alleviate some of the housing issues." He turned to Tavelo. "Is there a dire need for this?"

Tavelo in turn addressed Tervan.

"What say you on the matter?"

"Truly?" Tervan folded his arms. "I have no intention of leaving my mother's life, or yours for that matter, in the hands of those incompetent royal asses."

Eterenia rolled her eyes, tilting her head upwards in exasperation. Tavelo pursed his lips.

"I agree with that assessment," Armon spoke. He nodded at Tesul. "I know you do."

"Then that means I'm stuck dealing with these two." Adelia gave a head tilt towards Lariod and Warmon. "Although I don't really need their lacking protection."

"Someone has to keep you in check," Tervan said snidely. "Princess."

Adelia's head snapped up, eyes glowing red as the two siblings met each other's stare. Tervan smirked, his eyes turning red. Pridric let out a loud sigh, disrupting their competition. Tavelo's shoulder's slumped slightly in defeat.

"Lets' see how many want to join the royal ranks. Then we'll have an accurate count for each family." Pridric pushed away from the table. "There isn't that many of us if you look at it realistically."

"Then those of us who tolerate each other can combine into one homestead." Tavelo said.

"And who would that be?" Adelia's brow raised.

"For instance," Pridric replied, pointing two fingers at Tavelo and Eterenia. "Their coven members in addition to Yutel's would make a decent sized one. Far smaller than our original ones, but a start."

"The whole family packed under one roof."

Armon's bottom lip went inward after he said it.

Tervan grimaced at the thought. Eterenia's face became thoughtful, causing Tervan to stare at her in fright. His eyes went wide.

"That would also give us the best stronghold with the biggest army." She nodded to herself. "Yes, we need to talk to Yutel and see if he agrees."

"Then that's all settled. "Tavelo winked at Pridric. "The rest is up to you."

"You're such an ass." Pridric shook his head.

"You love me." Tavelo walked to the doors.

The others stared at him in confusion. Right as he entered the corridor and turned out of sight, Pridric leaned on the table.

"I do," he whispered.

Eterenia glanced over at him, conveying that an explanation was in order. He simply averted his eyes, not wanting to do so at that moment. It's too long a story. Tervan tilted his head in amusement. Pridric had no doubt, the meddling soldier would find the reason in time.

❀ ❀ ❀

Servants rushed around the palace preparing for the coronation ceremony. Giant floral arrangements, bundles of fruit, and decorations in clutched hands sped past Tavelo and Manel as they strolled the main corridor. They wore keftas in their respective house colors. Everyone did short head bows to them along the way.

The halls filled with the sounds of boots striking the floors and hushed conversations combined at a high decibel.

"How many do you think will oppose my reign?" Manel suddenly blurted.

"A lot," Tavelo replied. "You made no allies over the centuries." He glanced at him. "But the masses

378

will come around. Some details about your plight have been circulating."

"My plight?" Manel's tone edged with venom. His lips pulled back, revealing gritted teeth.

"Calm down." Tavelo narrowed his eyes. "You understand what I mean."

"There's nothing wrong with me!"

Some of the people walking by gave wide eyed stares, slowing their procession to circumvent the two emperors. The mood shifted to unease. Manel clenched his fists at his side and closed his mouth. Tavelo kept his focus ahead, not daring to see the people's expressions.

"I didn't say that, Manel." Tavelo reached over and placed a hand on the small of his back. "You can't be this sensitive anymore." He leaned closer. "It shows weakness," he whispered.

Manel's posture straightened. His face softened. Unclenching his hands, he shook them out and let them hang normally. He exhaled slowly.

"I know. My world is consumed by those tiny creatures who are needy in every way."

Tavelo snorted.

"Welcome to the art of raising your spawn."

They came to the section overlooking the royal garden. The afternoon sun lit up the hallway. Not many people walked the trails, barely stopping to smell the flowers. A handful of trees were unburdened with a bulk of their offerings. Entire sections were nothing but greenery, absent of buds. Farther in servants surrounding Dania listened as she pointed to more trees needing plucked.

"She's having fun," Manel stated.

"Well, it keeps her busy."

"Hmm?" Manel cocked his head. "I thought she relished in the coddling of her doljas?"

Tavelo let out a laugh. "Even you should know we can only tolerate so much of that." He shook his head. "I love my children, doljas too, but they are exhausting." He nudged Manel. "Especially when they're brand new."

"Seriously." Tervan broke their casual chatter. "We're supposed to be going over the coronation plans on this little walk."

Tavelo and Manel pursed their lips at his rude interruption. They had simply forgotten Tervan and Gallic were walking not far behind them.

"They're lightening the mood," Gallic said. "This will not be easy."

The entourage looked out to the horizon and stopped for a moment to watch the ships from other planets landing. Dignitaries, trade commissioners, and contractors were arriving since the week before to take advantage of their invite to witness a new era of Cellaxa.

"Those greedy parasites won't waste any time bargaining once the ceremony is over," Manel said.

"That's a given." Tervan nodded at one ship. "There's our competition from the next system over."

Manel tsked, turning away from the view. Tavelo's stare became hooded. He too, looked off.

"We need to establish our position once more at the top of the trade guild." Tavelo resumed walking with Manel, Tervan and Gallic following more closely. "This is part your doing, Manel."

"And I am going to fix it." Manel looked back and saw the frown on Tervan's face. He let out a loud sigh. "Fine. The coronation should only last an hour once started."

"Security?" Tervan asked.

"Palace guards will maintain the perimeter. Our personal guards will form a bubble around us." Manel's head tilted upward. "There will be Volshins in the sky so no one would be able to get near us."

"There's always a route for the tenacious," Tervan huffed.

"And they would be stupid to try considering how much might we have," Tavelo added.

"How does it end?" Gallic asked. "Do we form a procession back into the palace or are we going to walk down into the garden to mingle with the guests?"

Manel smiled, scaring Tavelo and Gallic. Tervan seemed interested.

"Oh, you'll see." Manel's devilish grin spread. He tilted his head towards Tavelo. "You'll like it."

"By the look on your face, I absolutely will not."

❀ ❀ ❀

From the top tier of the palace overlooking the center courtyard Pridric and the Trade Commissioner watched the merchant clans mingle with the off-world dignitaries. A sea of color and texture moving along the trails that formed a maze. Servants stepped carefully, not allowing their trays to get jostled. Spilling anything on an honored guest meant strict reprimand. The sun rose high on the horizon with a few hours left before setting.

The two banners, positioned on either side of the main platform. flew each emperor's colors, swaying in the gentle breeze that came off the ocean. In the center, as instructed, a circular emblem combined the two crests like Yin and Yang. Plush, dark carpeting laid beneath two thrones built for the occasion and carted out to display.

Volshins patrolled the sky while Katalings worked as gatekeepers at every palace entrance. Pridric approved. He had corralled, cornered, and cursed many in the royal house to get what he needed for the event with Dania as his support, ruling with an iron fist.

"This is most elaborate," Commissioner Polp said.

"As it should be." Pridric leaned over the ledge, extending his forearms so his hands dangled. "The coronation of two emperors, a sight not seen for nearly two millennia, is historic."

"Yes. That is all fine and good. My concern is how they will keep all of them in check." Commissioner

Polp pointed at a cluster of merchants surrounded by off worlders already negotiating. More exactly like it formed. "I fear some rules are on the verge of being broken before we even start opening the second port."

The only merchant clans not engaging were the Endagas and Dakiens. Whenever a group of traders approached them, a proxy intervened to display the digital business cards for scanning. They were then instructed to make an appointment as would usually be the case.

Pridric zeroed in on his own clan. His brother looked comfortable in his element, being charming, conveying authority. Even when their parents were alive, he always seemed to dominate the situation. To his surprise, his brother looked up and met his gaze. A sinister grin formed. Pridric reared back from the ledge, startled by the fear that look invoked in him.

"Is everything alright?" The Trade Commissioner asked, concerned by his movement.

"Ahh," Pridric managed to say "Yes, of course. I need to check on the rest of the preparations." He turned away. "Please excuse me." He left Commissioner Polp alone on the balcony. His body trembled.

He took deep breaths as he walked to calm his nerves. He hated the way his family made him feel. Their visceral reaction to his every move bordered on excessive. Nothing he did deemed satisfactory in their eyes. Pridric clutched the front of his robe, a turquoise blue with silver detail embroidered down the front and along the sleeve cuffs. Endaga colors.

As he neared the staging chamber where Tavelo and Manel would be, he could hear raised voices. By the sound of it, there were too many people in that room. He walked up to the entrance and his head tilted back in awe at the scene.

Tervan stared down Megen. Gallic shielded Manel from Maxellia while the two younger siblings held her back. Eterenia blocked Tavelo from interfering. The Valkyrie and Gallic's cousins had their hands on the hilt of their swords ready to draw.

"Enough!" Pridric walked into the middle of the fray. "Everyone except the emperors, leave."

They all stared at him in disbelief. When none of them moved, his eyes burned silver. The Valkyrie wrenched Lenri away from her sister and fled the room. One by one they reluctantly left, Tervan not taking a step towards the door until Megen did first. The behemoth smirked at him as he glanced back.

Alone with Tavelo and Manel, he raised a hand to stop them from explaining. His eyes reverted to normal and he crossed his arms.

"It's already a madhouse out there. The royal magistrate will follow the two of you out to the main platform and give some historical context. Then you will be introduced. Make your speeches short."

"And then we show our true might," Manel added.

Pridric gave a confused look. He turned to Tavelo who shrugged.

"What does that even mean?" Pridric's eyes went wide with fear. "I hope you're not suggesting to attack the crowd out of some sick bloodletting pleasure?"

Manel's eyes narrowed into slits. "No." He replied in a venomous tone. Pridric stepped back. "It's nothing to be concerned about." This time, his voice softened, almost angelic. The hairs on Pridric's arm prickled.

"It better not be." Tavelo stared at him.

"I told you, you'd like it." Manel looked to Pridric. "My sister wants to contest my coronation and get the people to vote in her favor."

Pridric inwardly sighed in defeat. He didn't want to know what the fight was about. Now that he knew, it didn't surprise him.

"So, she wants to rule instead?" Pridric asked.

"Oh, no." Manel snorted. "She wants them to agree with her and appoint someone else."

"Megen?" Pridric yelled.

Him being the only other option.

"He refused. Angrily so."

Manel walked over to the long table covered in fruits, meats, and drinks set against the wall. He rummaged through the options and selected a small yellow fruit. Biting into it, he talked while chewing.

"The last thing he ever wants to be is emperor. Our father cured him of his desire to succeed."

"Just," Pridric waved his hand outwards. "Be ready when the escorts arrive."

Pridric left the room. Gallic and Tervan stood dutifully on each side of the entrance. He gave them a nod and proceeded to his own chamber to make sure Dania was ready as well.

Manel got within inches of Tavelo. They stared into each other's eyes for what seemed like minutes.

"Take them off," Manel ordered.

Tavelo angled his head to the right. "What?"

"Your clothes. Take them off." Manel didn't move.

"One, I have no desire to engage with you in that way. And two, we don't have time for that either."

Manel's eyes turned red.

"That's not what I want."

"Then…"

"Do as I ask."

Tavelo, in no mood to argue, stripped, tossing his clothes on the empty chaise behind him. Stark naked, he gave Manel an accusatory stare.

"Now put your kefta and boots back on."

Tavelo frowned, still not understanding what his plan entailed. As he grabbed his robe, he finally noticed Manel was wearing only his.

Seeing his expression, Manel grinned.

A knock on the door signaled the escorts arrival. Manel flung the door open to a group of armed guards, each wearing the combined crest of the two emperors. Tavelo joined him and the two were surrounded in a bubble of security. Gallic and Tervan took up the rear of the procession as they moved down the corridor.

With each step closer, they could hear the sounds and voices coming from the courtyard. Their families were far ahead, stepping down the first shallow steps to the main platform. They dispersed to their designated sides. The escorts moved away to form two single lines beside the emperors.

Tavelo and Manel inhaled sharply in unison at the sight before them. The courtyard overflowed with people waiting to see the show. Tervan and Gallic took their positions by the banners. Maxellia appeared to be chomping at the bit to say something. Lendor gave her a stern look while shaking his head.

The royal magistrate appeared, standing between the two thrones. Manel and Tavelo had yet to sit in them awaiting the coronation to begin. A portly man, the magistrate cleared his throat loudly, the sound traveling from his earbuds and delivered through the audio system, getting everyone's attention.

The live planetary feed displayed high above the courtyard and across the planet. Its holographic features shimmied every now and again the farther away they were. Tavelo and Manel changed their minds and decided to sit for the Coronation Speech.

The magistrate raised his hands out, palms up.

"In the beginning we were an uncivilized horde of creatures ruled by bloodlust and destruction. Not caring about the chaos spreading across our planet by our own hands. The only entertainment was in killing each other for sport, dominance, and greed. To stop our fate towards extinction, the ancient ones already the dominant species, rose to power and wrangled the population in line."

"Resistance was met with swift punishment. Those who submitted were given the choice to find their craft, hone a skill. The trade organization was created to bring wealth and contentment. Our people thrived."

"One to rule the East and one to rule the West, they encourage us to find our paths to redemption.

Trade with other planets gave us a new sense of pride. We built the palace as a symbol to show unity." The magistrate's expression grew dark.

"Alas, when an enemy attacked our planet, that broken unity. Invaded by traders who only saw a planet with treasures to steal. In our pursuit to rebuild, we lost our sense of selves. Now, over two millennia later, we have regained the missing pieces in our path to glory."

"Glory?" Maxellia shrieked. She stepped forward faster than Lendor could catch her. "Do you want a monster who terrorized us for centuries to ascend the throne once more?" She pointed at Manel. "A tyrant with no regard for the bloodshed he has caused?"

There were hushed voices in the crowd. Angry faces turned towards Manel. He simply glanced over at his sister with disinterest.

"Denounce him so that we may find someone worthy to rule our Kataling bloodline!"

"And who would that be, my dear sister?" Manel ignored her and address the crowd. "Have I been a less than desirable ruler? Of course. Look who my father was. You may not know of his treachery, but the royal advisors and his children do. All I can give you is my word." Red eyed, he bowed at the waist in a ninety degree angle, never wavering his stare. "I will make Callaxa a force to be reckoned."

When he stood, silence engulfed the crowd. The atmosphere changed to pride. Maxellia's face scrunched up in horror as she realized she had lost. Tavelo gave her a look of pity. Lendor dragged her back in formation next to him on the platform.

"Are there any who disagree with the coronation of Emperor Manel?" The Magistrate waited for any response. "Then let the coronation begin."

A West royal guard came out from the palace carrying a large black cushion with two crowns set upon it. One silver with oval shaped blue gems an inch apart along its circumference.

The other gold with red gems of equal design. He made his way down the steps to the magistrate and stood before him.

"To rule the East with the ancient blood of the Volshin, I give you Emperor Tavelo of the Endaga clan." He plucked the silver crown from the cushion and held it over Tavelo's head. "With this, I crown thee, East Emperor of Callaxa." He placed it on Tavelo who then stood.

The magistrate went over to Manel.

"To rule the West with the ancient blood of the Kataling, I give you Emperor Manel of the Mallen royal house." He turned to retrieve the gold crown and held it above Manel. "With this, I crown thee West Emperor of Callaxa." Manel stood once it was placed on his head.

They walked to the edge of the platform, moving to stand twenty feet apart. The crowd cheered, and dignitaries clapped loudly. Manel turned to Tavelo.

"Let it be known. Disrespect to Cellaxa will be met with the might of its emperors and the people who love our world. If you become our enemy, here lies your fate."

He nodded to Tavelo who understood. Together they whipped off their robes, baring all for everyone to see. Gasps erupted, though short-lived. Removing their crowns, the two morphed into their full ancient forms. Tavelo's height rose to the top of the palace while Manel's bulk cracked the platform. A thin line ran along its length, yet it held.

Their boots became leather strips of confetti that dusted the front row of spectators.

They let out high-pitched shrieks that made the crowd stare up at them in stunned submission. Tavelo raised his long neck proudly to the sky. Manel shook his head from side to side, huffing. Steaming snot sprayed out onto the guests in the front of the platform.

No one spoke.

The second shriek came from Tavelo as he batted his wings once, causing a force of wind so great it bent the trees and knocked the already slime covered guests ten feet back.

Further back in the crowd, Master Strana watched with eyes burning silver. He held a drink halfway to his lips, not wanting to indulge in the festivities any longer. Master Boresso stepped up to him and placed a hand on his shoulder.

"Looks like the end of a tumultuous era." Master Boresso smiled.

Master Strana tossed the remainder of his drink in the nearby bushes then moved away.

"The end?" Master Strana bared his teeth.

A gruesome expression spread across his face. Master Boresso was intrigued.

"This is only the beginning."

TO BE CONTINUED…

ACKNOWLEDGEMENTS

Thank you for continuing to read the Blood Saga series. I hope you are enjoying it as much as I did writing it. Alien blood suckers are fun, sexy, and not talked about much. This is my due diligence to spread the word. The last installment of the series, Blood Devotion, is coming soon.

Big thanks to:

NIWA: The Northwest Independent Authors Association for letting wrters be part of a great community.

NaNoWriMo (Narional Novel Writing Month.

For supplying an awesome platform that drives writers foward.

PNWA (Pacific Northwest Writers Association

Craig Martelle and 20BooksTo50K

For all the tragic souls who volunteered to beta read my first vampire novel and gave me uncensored feedback. My gratitude is infinite.

I cherish you all.

ALSO BY MAQUEL A. JACOB

THE CORE TRILOGY
CORE OF CONFLICTION
SEEDS OF CONVICION
BONDS OF CONTRITION

CURVE OF HUMANITY
ORIGINS
SHADOWMEN OBJECTIVE
PURGE SEQUENCE
CRIPPLED EARTH
AFTERMATH
HOMECOMING

WELCOME DESPAIR
A COLLECTION OF SHORT STORIES

THE BLOOD SAGA
BLOOD DOCTRINE
BLOOD DOMINION

BLOOD INCEPTION
(*A BLOOD NOVELLA*)

*****COMING SOON*****

BLOOD DEVOTION
THE CORE SERIES TRILOGY 2

ABOUT THE AUTHOR

Hi there!

I'm Maquel A. Jacob. I've had a passion for the written word since the age of seven, reading everything I could get my grubby little hands on, which included encyclopedias and the thesaurus. At twelve, I had my first encounter with a Stephen King novel and got hooked. They inspired me to write my own brand of fiction, combining multiple genres to keep things interesting.

I am a HUGE Anime fan, love a great bottle of wine and rock out to heavy metal music. Green and lush Oregon is where I currently reside, spinning imaginary worlds in my head and daydreaming.

For updates, FREE short stories, Newsletters

...and more

Visit: www.maquelajacob.com
Like Maquel A. Jacob on Facebook
Follow on Twitter @MaquelAJ1

Also find me on Goodreads